I0670722

RESURRECTION X

DANE HATCHELL

SEVERED PRESS
HOBART TASMANIA

RESURRECTION X

Copyright © 2015 Dane Hatchell
Copyright © 2015 by Severed Press

WWW.SEVEREDPRESS.COM

ISBN: 978-1-925342-19-2

Resurrection X is my first novel and is dedicated to Robert Crais, 2006 recipient of the Ross Macdonald Literary Award, who is known for his great detective fiction. I met bob some 40 years ago in our home town, and his success inspired me over the years to never give up my dream to write.

A special mention is given to Frank Herbert for creating the wonderful universe

of Dune. A special homage is given to Mr. Herbert in the epilogue. Imitation is the sincerest form of flattery.

A big thank you goes out to Gary Lucas at Severed Press and the fantastic opportunities he brings to writers and readers who delight in the things of darkness.

PROLOGUE

The Dark Times: The year 2020

Platoon Forward Observer Steve Rogan scanned the streets below from atop the roof of the Broadmoor First Baptist church. Once-dead bodies reanimated to life filled his Omega Class range finder in every direction. He knew things weren't going well for the good guys but had never seen it this bad.

He let the range finder drop to his chest, dangling by the strap, and wiped a crusty accumulation of dirt and tobacco spit from the corner of his mouth. The noonday sun baked the back of his gritty neck, and a fly had nothing better to do than make high speed passes by his left ear. The military had been so close early in the war to put an end to the alien menace. Now, Vegas odds were against a victory for the Living. *All because of some stupid twist of fate.*

His mind drifted to the early reports in the news nearly two years before. A group of relatively small asteroids had entered the solar system, and the projected path put them directly in Earth's orbit. Fortunately, their arrival proceeded the Earth by a few weeks. What had been ignored was the massive trail of dust following the pack of rocky missiles. The Earth hit that dead center. The debris was dismissed as *harmless space dust*, destined to cloud the skies for a few days until it settled. The yellowish rains that fell afterward did cause some alarm, but scientists agreed the alien microbes in the dust were benign. The microbes resembled Earth viruses and were not considered a true life form, as they did not self-replicate.

Being alien with incompatible DNA, the virus was unable to infect any living creature on the Earth, much to everyone's relief. However, no one suspected the microbes would work their way into the ecosystem and mutate. No one suspected the alien virus would rekindle the fires of life in the dead, or any of the other horrible effects it would have on mankind.

Rogan returned the range finder to his eyes.

"What're you looking for? The cavalry? They ain't coming," Andy Wells said as he sat cross-legged on the flat, concrete roof near Rogan. His tattered boots stained with human gore didn't have much rubber left on the tread. One of the two MREs warming on galvanized flashing disappeared into his hand, and he tore open a corner with his teeth. A portion of noodles and red sauce crowned through the hole before he squeezed some into his mouth.

Rogan continued his watch, ignoring his platoon mate much like the annoying insect dive-bombing his ear. "We almost had these damn things beat. The virus spreads so rapidly now their numbers have been growing exponentially."

"*Ex-poh-nen-shell-lee.*" Wells had lengthened the syllables into a near sentence. "That's a mighty high-dollar word for a high school grad-u-ate. You sure you ain't had no college?" Wells' tongue chased a dangling noodle from the food pouch.

"Andy, is your main goal in life to—hey, what's that?" A group of the walking dead Rogan had been following jacked up the pace of their lumbering gait. He panned the range finder and discovered why.

"Oh my God," Rogan said in a whisper.

"What?" Wells tore the pouch and lapped the sweet sauce clinging inside.

A group of five—a family more than likely—consisting of a man, a woman, three children, and a dog, ran in desperation up the street a couple of blocks away from the church. The filthy clothes on the family resembled the rags worn by the undead in pursuit. The man clutched a toddler tightly to his chest with one arm and pushed his wife to run faster with the other. He kept turning and barking something to the two other children, a boy and a girl— both who couldn't be over ten years in age. Rogan watched the fright in the father's face and realized how he'd become numb to this repeating scene.

The little girl tripped in her frenzied flight, landing on her elbows and knees. Skin peeled back exposing red-wet flesh and sending the rich scent of blood into the winds.

The dog, a cocker spaniel, dashed back to her side. The poor thing, it yipped and danced around, as if beckoning her to rise.

2

Seeing this, the man nearly threw the toddler into the woman's arms and rushed back to the girl's aid.

At this time, an athletically built male zombie with a blank stare, and a huge chunk missing from its neck, reached out to grab the girl as she struggled to lift herself off the street.

Before the zombie's gore encrusted fingers found the girl's foot, the dog sprang into the air and chomped down onto its hand. The cocker spaniel attacked like a pint-sized wolf and viciously shook its head until the hand tore free of the wrist. The dog rolled to the ground clutching the undead prize in its jaws.

The man reached the scene and put the full force of his heel into the nose of the ravenous zombie. Its head snapped off and rolled directly in front of the murderous horde only a few yards away.

"I said, 'what?' " Wells followed with a burp.

The zombies covered the man like a swarm of fire ants. He disappeared into the crowd.

The girl was next to go, caught up in the wave of zombies that headed straight for the boy, the woman, and the toddler she held.

"Nothing," Rogan said. The walls he had built hiding his emotions over the months began to crack. No, they had cracked a long time ago, but he refused to acknowledge his weakness. He felt scared for the family now. And if he didn't get his shit back together, soon would start feeling scared for himself.

The woman and the boy screeched to a halt as another group of walking dead appeared in front of them. Trapped, with nowhere to run, the woman dropped to her knees, and angrily shook a fist toward the sky. She bent over and covered the toddler with her body.

The zombies overwhelmed the fragile humans in a flood of gnashing teeth and flashing nails. Mercifully, the rooftop was too far away for the screams to reach.

"Come on, really, what do you see?" Wells said, pulling at the cuff of Rogan's pants.

"I said nothing you ignorant fuck! Now fuck the fuck off!" Rogan tore the range finder from his eyes and glared at Wells. His mouth widened showing teeth. The edges of his lips quivered.

Wells looked up into the face of his friend, a brother in his platoon, and winced as if he expected to be hit. He went to speak, perhaps to ask for forgiveness, but lowered his head instead and stared at the roof.

Rogan broke his laser stare and turned his attention back toward the skirmish, raising the range finder to his eyes. *Gone, all gone.* As if it never happened. And that's how he'd managed to keep it together over the months—just forget that it happened—a luxury his mind would no longer afford.

Some dark splotches stained the street, but even that could have been there before. The streets had been painted with blood and human remains for a long time. Would it ever end?

The radio microphone squawked on Wells' collar. "Second Platoon, Wells, are you still with us?"

Wells cleared his throat. "Yeah, we's still with ya. Not sure for how much longer though. Thems flesh eaters got us surrounded so thick the wind won't blow between 'em."

"Listen up, there's a new development in the war. Bombers are in the air and heading toward your area. Their ordinance is a modified version of an aerosol bomb that will disperse Z-gas. Z-gas is a biological agent heavier than air. Each bomb released will disperse a vaccine covering an area several square miles wide. This gas is not harmful, repeat, not harmful to the Living. It only affects those dead bastards carrying the alien virus."

Wells smiled at Rogan, giving him a thumb-up. Keying the switch on his microphone, he said, "What's this here gas gonna do? Make their heads explode or something? That's the only way to kill a zombie—blow its head off."

"That's a negative. The gas won't kill them, but it will make them docile—they won't attack anymore. There will be further orders once the gassing is complete. Do not engage any of the undead until told to do so. Hold your position. Expect another call in twenty-four to thirty-six hours. Clear?"

"Oh, we's clear, with fingers and toes crossed. Wells, Second Platoon, out." He rose to his feet and wiped his hands on his pants. "What do you make of that, *amigo*?"

Rogan wasn't sure what result this new assault would bring. At least it offered a hope he didn't have five minutes before.

A hope not offered to that poor family of five.

CHAPTER 1

Modern times: Dallas, Texas, the year 2025

"If I had known you were going to be so annoyed at the restaurant, I would have ordered pizza to the cabin," Bob Sanders said to his girlfriend, Lisa Goudard, as the couple sat at Cafe D'Esprit while browsing the drink menu. "This was supposed to be a special night for us, to celebrate our one year anniversary."

"Those two over there are ruining the night," Lisa said, nodding her head to the side. "Disgusting, if you ask me."

Bob casually twisted his gaze toward the couple. "They aren't bothering anyone. They're just eating. This *is* a restaurant."

"Their kind shouldn't be allowed in here. Look at them. One of them has sauerkraut hanging off his chin." Lisa raised her upper lip and scowled. "They're troublemakers—nothing but equal right activists trying to stir things up. Some left wing organization put them up to this. You know most Sub Zs can't even think for themselves."

Two members of the Non-Dead sat in a dark corner near the kitchen door. The chairs pushed so close one side of the patrons' arms touched. Each wore the standard City Maintenance attire of dark blue, long-sleeved jumpsuit, and Department of Sanitation cap. The shadows hid the level of decay of their leathery faces.

"I'm sure eating at a public establishment makes them feel more," Bob paused to choose the correct word, "human. Besides, it's the law, and the restaurant can't afford to have the Feds bringing a discrimination suit against them."

Lisa dropped the drink menu and put her hands on the table. "But the Non-Dead don't even need to eat solid food like we do. The alien virus infesting their body feeds off that skin cream they grease up with." Lisa shuddered. "I can't imagine what it's like to be infected."

"No, Sub Zs don't need to eat, but sauerkraut helps preserve internal organs. It adds months, if not years, to the amount of time they remain useful for service."

"You liberals are insufferable with excuses." Lisa closed her eyes and brushed off the air between them with the flick of her wrist. "They're nothing but zombie trash."

Bob grimaced. "Not so loud with the Z-word. The waitress will hear you."

Lisa glanced toward clanking dishes. "You're worried about the waitress over there? From the looks of her she's getting close to the end of her usefulness. She'd be better off concentrating on her job and ignoring what the Living are saying about her."

"Speaking of a waitress," Bob poked up his head and searched around the room, "where's ours? I need a drink."

"She's probably in the bathroom, putting her face on. Get it? Literally putting her face on—because it got eaten off!" Lisa giggled.

Bob took a deep breath and huffed. "Honey, you have to face the fact the Non-Dead are here to stay."

Lisa's lips tightened like she was about to explode.

Picking up the beverage menu, Bob said, "You'll loosen up a bit once we have a drink or two. What'll it be? White wine? How about some champagne? I'm pulling out all the stops tonight."

"You don't like my humor because you don't understand it."

"Please, can we just move on? I don't think jokes like that are appropriate. Not in this day and age, and certainly not in a public place. Would you prefer a cocktail from the specialty menu? How about an Appletini or a Cosmopolitan?"

Lisa crossed her arms. "Champagne. Make it two bottles if you want me to loosen up."

The warm hum of background conversation died as a woman at a table near them let out a shriek. She sprang from the chair and tossed her napkin to the floor. "I need to see the manager. Now!" Seething, she mumbled something through clenched teeth.

"What the hell is going on over there?" Bob said, hoping to turn the tide of tonight's events.

"Her soup was probably cold or something. I've noticed she frowns at everything her date says to her. She even sent back the first bottle of wine, turning up her nose after the first sip. Some people are impossible."

Bob raised a finger and went to speak. Then, deflated like a punctured tire. He cleared his throat. "Yes, some people *are* impossible." The water glass went to his lips before he incriminated himself.

The restaurant manager briskly walked behind Lisa, approaching the upset customer.

"My good ma'am, I am so sorry there was a slight problem with the soup. Café D'Esprit prides itself in its five star rating. I assure you, that rating could not have been achieved without the highest level of cleanliness in our kitchen. I greatly apologize for the fly you have found in your soup. The vile creature must have flown in from outside as our distinguished diners enter and leave."

The woman slowly shook her head.

The manager bowed, his eyebrows raised, and palms open in front of his chest. His smile pleaded for a reprieve.

She leaned forward with hands firmly on hips. "I didn't find a fly in my soup. I found an *eye* in my soup!"

Two tables over a large man dressed in a tuxedo quickly brought his napkin to his mouth. He gagged and dry heaved until his face turned a deep shade of red.

A young woman with long blonde hair one table away erupted a flow of ratatouille and chardonnay over the ivory white tablecloth. Vomit shot out her mouth and nose with the force of a fire hose. Her date twisted his ankle and fell as he leaped to safety from his chair in his efforts to avoid the spewing emesis.

Lisa smirked victoriously, nodding her head.

Bob cradled his face in his hands.

CHAPTER 2

Two hours later, a 2025 North American Motor's Evergreen Sedan skirted the piney woods, headed toward Dallas.

"Of course the Non-Dead don't deserve the right to vote." Lisa glanced at Bob momentarily, and then returned her eyes to the road. "They don't have to pay taxes, or buy food. They live in free housing and get free health care. All their needs are provided."

"But the Non-Dead do work, right? Their pay is only a fraction of minimum wage. If they don't work, well, you know what happens to those who aren't capable of working any longer. *In-cin-er-ation*," Bob said, his eyes glued on the dark road ahead while he drove.

"Yes, the Non-Dead work. They have to work. Our way of life, as fucked up as it is now, would return to the 1800s if we didn't have them. Losing half the people on the planet during The Dark Times makes every Living human a priceless commodity.

"I like electricity. I like cars, new clothes, shoes, makeup, and perfume. If the zombies, or Undead, or the Non-Dead, or whatever PC term they come up with next...wait, tell me why they picked Non-Dead again?"

"Non-Living was rejected because it contained the word *living*. They were given the status of Non-Dead to indicate that they are technically *dead*," Bob said.

"How do you even remember all of this crap? Anyway, if the Non-Dead are being kept alive, I mean functioning, or whatever the hell they are, by us, then, they owe their existence to us. They are nothing more than machines. You wouldn't give a tractor the right to vote, would you?" Lisa grabbed her Louis Vuitton handbag from the floorboard and rummaged through it, coming up with a tube of lip balm.

Bob slowed the car as the road rose ahead and wound to the east. "I understand your point. Put things in perspective to be fair. You don't have to leave your comfortable home in the city and live out in the country where the food is grown because the Non-Dead are there to work in our place. We treat them no better than beasts of burden to show our thanks.

"The Non-Dead repair the roads and pick up the trash. Most of the service industry is filled with the Non-Dead labor force. That frees up the Living from menial tasks to pursue more intellectual endeavors. You have noticed that some of the movie theaters have reopened, haven't you?"

Lisa chuckled. "Yeah, where you can watch a rerun or a new movie made on a cellphone and home computer."

"Hey, Hollywood is just beginning to turn out a product. The new movies focus on content and dialogue, emphasizing the story. You should appreciate that over the flash and special effects of the Hollywood of old.

"Lisa, you just have to become more progressive or you'll be left behind as the world moves on without you.

"The Non-Dead are being granted more opportunities in the workforce in the northern states. Zombie Brew Company is one of the first to make full compliance with the EEOC's amendment to the Americans with Disabilities Act. That was a pretty bold move by Gill Gates, the billionaire. He put his money where his mouth is. The new company follows the right to work initiative integrating the Non-Dead to share equal duties alongside the Living. He didn't do that just to piss off the Conservatives. He wanted to avoid dealing with the blood-sucking Living Union, too. You should appreciate that.

"Plus, by naming it *Zombie*, he's trying to defuse the power of the word's negativity. You remember how *bad* came to mean something *good*? He's going to do a similar thing with *zombie* and turn around the attitudes where the Non-Dead will be accepted as equals."

Lisa shook her head. "The Non-Dead already have enough rights and benefits. There's no need to let them vote or get an equal rights amendment. Most of them are so far gone in the head they wouldn't understand if it passed anyway."

"You're lumping the Sub Zs in with the Sub Ys. Why do you Conservatives insist on doing this? There would be a qualification test for the Sub Zs to prove competency. Sub Ys are mentally no different than you and me. You're painting a far worse picture than you need to." Bob breathed a sigh of relief as the curvy rural road straightened. Soon he would be merging onto the highway. He and Lisa had enjoyed a nice weekend together, a quiet intimate time in a rented cabin by the lake. It wasn't until the two had dinner at Cafe D'Esprit that the world's problems once again became a barrier between them.

Lisa applied more lip balm and returned the tube to her bag. A trail of billboards pointed the way to the city. Most were old and in disrepair. Only a few had working lights.

One billboard shone brightly in the distance. The smiling face of Reverend Will Hatfield, pastor of Streets of Gold Church, welcomed those traveling the highway to come and worship with him.

The Church had a long history of staunch right-wing conservative policies, having fought *Godless liberal heathens* on many fronts. First, it was racial equality. Then abortion, then gay marriage, and now the fight was against the granting of equal rights to the Non-Dead. The Streets of Gold Church thus openly supported political candidates who sought to prevent the Non-Dead from acquiring any additional rights.

More cars crowded the highway as the lights of the city grew larger. Bob turned up the volume on the radio to mask the silence.

Lisa picked at a loose cuticle on her thumb, her thoughts seemingly a million miles away.

The steering wheel started to pull ever so slightly toward the curb. Bob wondered if it was the angle of the road, a tire, or his imagination. A mild vibration in the steering wheel swelled the farther he drove.

"Lisa, the car feels like it's pulling to the right. Do you hear anything unusual?"

"I hear a thumping noise. I thought it was from the tires running over the grooves in the road."

"Well, it might be, but I think I can feel the pull getting worse. I'm going to turn in at that convenience store and check it out." Bob lifted the turn signal lever, engaging the switch.

The tires bumped against the curb leading to the parking lot. Lisa's head bounced in response. The car passed by the gas pumps and stopped near the side of the building away from the entrance. Bob turned off the engine and got out.

Lisa lowered her window when he came around her side. "See anything?" She fanned the air and looked back at the fuel pumps.

"The front passenger tire is sitting a little low," he said, giving it a few short kicks. "Open the glove box and get out the air gauge."

Lisa opened the compartment and immediately fought to suppress the compressed paraphernalia as it spilled out the sides to the floor. "Why do you have so much crap in here? How do you expect me to find the tire gauge?"

"It's not crap if you need it one day," Bob said.

"It's crap. I know what crap is, and this is crap." Lisa slowly let the glove box door down and dug through the contents. "Here's a half-eaten granola bar."

"And if we were stranded in a blizzard, and that's all we had to eat for a week, it would be worth a million dollars to us."

"That's a *huge* load of cr—wait. I found it."

Bob sheepishly smiled as she handed him the gauge, knowing she was right, but refused to admit it. He bent over and removed the valve cap, positioning his body to use the faint light overhead to read the gauge. "It's over ten pounds low. I guess I picked up a nail or something. I'm going to have to change it."

"Maybe you should move the car first. You parked right in front of the dumpster. The sign says 'No Parking.' "

"It's only going to take me about fifteen minutes. I don't think a garbage truck will be coming tonight to dump it anyway. You need to get out because the jack goes right under where you're sitting. Go inside and get us something to drink. I'll try to hurry."

Lisa lowered the visor, examining her makeup in the mirror after brushing her hair away from her left eye. She opened the door and planted both feet firmly on the ground before standing. She straightened her skirt and placed her bag over her shoulder before walking toward the door.

Even getting out of the car is a big production for her, Bob thought. The trunk popped open with the push of the remote. The spare tire compartment and tools hid under the false floor, which he lifted. *This shouldn't take long. Let's see, righty tighty, lefty loosey*. He unscrewed the tire clamp until a foreboding chill prickled hairs on the back of his neck.

Nothing was there when he darted his head around. The only area partially hidden from sight was at the far end of the dumpster. He was about to lift the tire from the wheel well when something rustled nearby. *What was that?*

If someone wanted to rob him, or worse, he had better find out before Lisa returned. He scanned the area by the dumpster, with the emergency flashlight in one hand, and a tire tool in the other.

Bob wasn't spoiling for a fight but didn't want to appear to be an easy target. As he moved closer to the dumpster, he glanced over and saw an older gentleman wearing an ancient Dallas Cowboys football cap, watching from the gas pumps. Bob nodded, and the old man nodded back.

I guess he's wondering what in the hell's wrong with me. Bob turned his attention back to the dark corner, aiming the flashlight. The light beam blinked out. *Greaaat*, he thought. He took the tire tool and tapped it . . . nothing . . . *tap tap* . . . nothing . . . *tap tap* . . . flicker. Bob pointed the lens toward his eyes . . . nothing . . . *tap tap* . . . *light*! The beam returned to shine directly in his eyes.

He redirected the light to the target, but the sudden burst left him seeing nothing but a bright yellow orb. The tire tool firmly in hand remained poised ready for action until normal vision returned. Fortunately, nothing waited to attack.

Bob looked back at the old man, who still watched as intently as before. So, he gave him another nod. The man nodded back, giving him a half smile as the nozzle handle went limp when the pump shut off.

Bob made three steps toward the car before the smaller of the two doors on the dumpster clashed open. A ravenous Non-Dead ran out and attacked.

A primal scream electrified the air. There was no way to tell if it came from Bob or the zombie that attacked him. It didn't matter. Everyone at the pumps frantically scurried into their vehicles. The old man pulled out his cell phone and pushed 616 on the keypad— Zombie Emergency Hotline.

Bob raised his left arm in defense. Teeth sank deeply into his forearm. The tire tool fell from his hand, clanging loudly as it hit ground. A sickly crunch followed as the jaws of the walking dead crushed bone. Gnashing teeth gouged out tendons, muscle, and ligaments.

Bob struggled to roll off his back. He beat the monster with the flashlight and cried for help. Blood pooled around his sides outlining his body. His bowels loosened soiling his pants.

A dull ringing started in his head and grew louder. The flashlight dropped from his useless grasp. Bob's vision clouded from his peripheral. The ringing turned into silence as the jaws of death gripped his neck, swelling the pressure on his brain like a balloon about to burst. Blood pumped from a torn jugular draining life's essence from his body.

Paying a visit to the bathroom was tops on Lisa's list. The drinks could wait. She was no fan of public restrooms but couldn't hold it any longer. Taking a few minutes to pee, a few minutes to adjust her clothing, and a few minutes to check her makeup, seemed like enough time for Bob to change the tire.

When she left the bathroom, the sales clerk—some greasy young man who ogled her when she walked in—had left his station. In fact, no one else was in the store. The office door that had been open when she entered was now shut.

Lisa peered through the Plexiglas store front toward the car. The tire hadn't been changed. Bob was nowhere to be seen. She hurried to the door, the deadbolt had been latched shut.

She turned latch mechanism, burst through the door, and shouted, "Bob! Bob! Where are you?" She ran past the rear of the car and saw a figure straddling another on the parking lot.

An old man in his car by the gas pumps laid on the horn, waving frantically as if trying to shoo her away.

She yelled Bob's name again and ran toward the scuffle. Bob was on bottom, in the heat of attack. "Get off! Get off!"

Bob wailed in agony as the zombie devoured him with the zeal of a starving animal. Lisa grabbed her purse by the straps and repeatedly slammed it against the assailant.

"Get off, motherfucker! Help! Someone help!" A cell phone, a tube of lipstick, and tissue flew out the purse, spilling onto the parking lot.

The zombie turned its head with the speed of a striking rattlesnake and snapped, leaving teeth marks in Lisa's right forearm. She screamed and stumbled backward, crashing into the rear of the car before landing hard on her side. The bite burned like it was on fire.

A siren wailed in the distance, growing louder by the second. A black van with Z.M.A.T. printed in large white letters, and an ambulance following close behind, roared into the parking lot. Every door of the van flew open, and eight armed men in black poured out. Zombie Medical And Tactical, a non-politically-correct name surviving the infancy of the outbreak, had arrived.

A burly combatant with 'Lt. Banes' neatly sewn above his right breast gave the orders. "Get into position and wait for my call." The men hurriedly formed a circle around the zombie. "That's a well preserved specimen. Be careful with it. Go! Go! Go!"

Ballistic cannons shot nets draping the zombie from four different directions. The monster twisted to free itself from the web-like cage.

"All right, take it down!"

One team member hit the zombie behind the knees with a telescoping aluminum pole, sending it to the ground.

"Juice it!" Banes ordered.

Another member sprayed the writhing undead in liquid shrink. The nets slowly contracted, becoming tighter and tighter until the zombie could barely move more than a finger.

"Medical! The area's secure!" The lieutenant stretched and pulled out a cigarette from his front pocket. The local police were on the scene with the jail bus. He watched his team load the zombie aboard the bus and check the area for any more strays.

"I wonder how this one got here," one of the men said to Banes, as he closed the door to the bus.

"Good question. This is only our seconded call this year. It's usually the campers and hikers that find rogue zombies," Banes said.

Lisa shivered as she lay on the hard asphalt, unresponsive, but with eyes frozen open.

Two paramedics pushed a collapsible stretcher to her side. Paramedic one dropped to a knee, produced a large flashlight, and turned it on. After a quick examination, he said, "She's clean, Johnson, except for the arm."

Johnson focused a smaller flashlight emitting a pale greenish beam on the bite. The teeth marks glowed. "There it is in all of its glory. Cole, start the treatment."

Cole retrieved a foil pack from the medical kit, tore off the corner with his teeth, and removed a contraption resembling a sponge with a handle. He put it directly on the bite mark and pushed. It made a slight *click,* and liquid oozed through the sponge onto her skin. The sponge went into a waste bag.

The two lifted Lisa onto the stretcher and wheeled her to the ambulance. Once inside, three taps to the back window had the vehicle moving and on the road.

Cole took a sample of her blood while the other readied an IV. A few drops of blood added into a graduated cylinder containing a clear liquid remained clear after a gentle shaking. "We have confirmation the infection is still in the early stage. She's a legal candidate for RY."

Johnson removed a vial marked 'RY' from an ice chest big enough to hold two six-packs of drinks and prepared a syringe. He put the IV into the uninjured arm and slowly injected the syringe filled with the medicine.

Lisa's head flopped to the side, he brushed the hair away from her face. "This is a crying shame. Looks like we lost a pretty one. I would have so *hit* this, but not now."

"Hey, quiet. She might still be able to hear you. Stop thinking with your dick," Cole said.

Lisa opened her eyes. A teardrop snaked down her cheek.

"Now-now, don't be afraid," Johnson said, gently patting her hand. "We got you in time. You're going to be just fine."

The arm with the IV started to shake, and then the rest of Lisa's body began to twitch.

"We're going to have to put you to sleep now. You'll learn more when you wake up."

Another syringe went into the IV.
Lisa's eyes fluttered closed.

CHAPTER 3

The sky above was the brightest blue Lisa had ever seen. A wisp of a single cloud rolled through the winds like a tumbling wave. She wished it had a hand she could take and dance alongside.

Birds adorned the branches of towering pine trees, singing a multitude of songs of life's delight. A family of ducks led by the mother waddled past and into the calm waters of the crystal clear lake. She heard the splish-splish-splish of each duckling as its bottom hit the water.

"It's good to be alive, isn't it?" A soothing voice said.

"Yes." Lisa felt the warm breeze against her cheeks, ferrying the spicy-sweet scent of gardenias past her nose. "It is so good to be alive." She turned around. "Oh, Bob, it's you."

Bob wore his best black suit and his signature purple tie. Lisa never understood his obsession with the color purple. He bent over and snapped a single emerald rose from a medium-sized bush and brought it over to her.

"For you, my dear. It matches your eyes and the envy all other men have for me when they see us together."

"Aw, that's nice for you to say." Lisa reached out and wrapped her arms around him.

"I am your knight in shining armor," he whispered in her ear.

"I know, I know." Lisa smiled, feeling so happy that she thought she was going to burst.

Something felt wet under her hand on Bob's back. She pulled it away and found it smeared with deep-red blood.

"Bob, are you hurt?"

He said nothing. Lisa felt her insides plunge as if riding down on a fast elevator.

Then, she remembered. The convenience store—the parking lot—the attack of the Non-Dead. The blood . . . the blood.

Bob dissolved into empty air.

Lisa reached out into the vacant space with no lifeline to hold onto. The world of beauty threatened to kill her with loneliness.

*

"Miss Goudard, are you awake?" the nurse asked as Lisa's eyes fluttered open.

Lisa heard the voice of a woman, but couldn't comprehend a word of it. Her mind a swirl of discordant thoughts. Some still trying to hold on to parts of the dream, others forcing her back to reality.

A weave of shadows draped across the room, and the ceiling loomed above as a closed lid of a funeral casket. The only glow of light came from a floor lamp shoved in the corner of the windowless room. The air felt cold and stung the back of Lisa's throat as she took a deep breath. A soft electronic beep chirped in slow rhythm, confusing her further.

A warm hand touched Lisa's arm. "Miss Goudard? I'm Jennifer, your nurse. How are you feeling?"

Lisa propped herself on her elbows and gazed around the sterile room. Drab whites and beige smothered any chance of hope. Her left shoulder itched, and when she went to scratch, her nails scraped against a large adhesive patch.

"Careful, that's your ATP patch," the nurse said, pushing a red button on the intercom hanging on the wall.

"ATP patch? Did I get cut or something?"

"No, nothing like that. The ATP patch is how you're getting nutrition. You were in a coma. At least we didn't have to use a feeding tube."

"I was in a coma?"

"A chemically induced coma," the nurse said.

"Why am I here?" Lisa closed her eyes. "My God! Bob! I remember!" She ripped the sheet away from her legs and sat sideways on the bed. The room rocked over a twenty foot wave. She jutted both hands to her side to steady herself from keeling over.

The nurse placed her hands on Lisa's shoulders. "Just a minute, hon. It's too soon for you get up."

Lisa lowered her head to keep from passing out. The flimsy hospital gown covered only to her upper thighs, exposing the full length of her legs. A few days of hair growth told her how long it had been since she last shaved. Both legs were ghastly pale, as if they had never been exposed to sunlight, and worse. She looked at her palms, and then turned her hands around, feeling as if she were wearing someone else's skin. Her ruby red nails were a startling contrast to her lifeless looking skin. "Oh my God, this can't be happening to me."

The door opened, flooding the room with bright fluorescent light from the hall. A thin woman wearing matching pants and jacket entered, softly closing the door behind.

"You can go now," she said to the nurse, as she moved to the front the bed. "Hi, Lisa, my name is Anne Watson. I'm a social worker for the hospital. My job is to help transition trauma victims back into normal life." She extended her right hand.

Lisa reached and took her hand; again, it felt strangely warm. "Please tell me what's going on. I know something bad has happened to my boyfriend, Robert Sanders. He's . . . he's dead isn't he?"

Anne gently squeezed Lisa's hand. "I'm afraid so, dear. He was attacked by one of the untreated infected. Mr. Sanders suffered physical trauma beyond what the RY treatment could do to save him."

Tears welled in Lisa's eyes and slid down her cheeks. She wiped them away with her free hand, seeing the bite mark on her forearm. "It bit me too."

"Yes it did. The entry point of the alien virus won't ever heal. Fortunately, the medics gave you the treatment in time. Don't worry, there are plenty of beauty aids available to help hide imperfections on the Non-Dead."

Lisa frowned. "Non-Dead? I thought you said the medics got to me in time?"

"In time to keep you from a physical death. They were able to give you the Resurrection Y medicine. Had they not arrived in time, and you had died from the infection, Resurrection Z would have been used. That is, if you were registered with the state as a willing donor. You are a Sub class Y Non-Dead now," Anne said.

"But I didn't die and turn into a Sub Z. I'm still me, not some stupid lobotomized human. How can I be stripped of my status as a Living citizen of the United States? So what if I'm infected with an alien virus? Other people have AIDS. It's a virus, it kills, but their citizenship isn't affected." Lisa's voice had become stronger.

"It's for national security, primarily. At least, that's what the laws are based on. You must appreciate that your physiology excludes you from being equal to the Living. You can no longer donate blood or organs. You're not able to give birth. Your body has changed in more ways than you can see on the outside. Politicians have set a standard of laws to separate the Living from the Non-Dead. The Living have rights that need to be protected too, you know."

Lisa slapped the top of her bed. "But I didn't choose to become a Sub Y like some others. I didn't have a choice."

"That was a onetime special act of congress for people suffering paralysis. America needed to quickly build the work force. But there are others such as you who received treatment after becoming infected with the virus. The laws apply to all treated with the RY drug the same. I'm sorry."

"But why should laws apply differently to Sub Ys? Sub Zs are so far gone that most are nothing more than simple-minded work machines. There is nothing the Living can do that the Y class can't. The only difference between a Living and a RY is the presence of the virus." Lisa realized she just had used one of Bob's arguments he had used against her. She bit her lower lip.

"Hell, I'll be back at my job tomorrow—behind my desk—like I never left. Don't tell me I'm a member of the Non-Dead." Lisa snatched her hand back.

Anne looked to the floor. "I'm sorry dear. You will no longer be able to continue your job as a state health inspector. The National Union of the Living won't allow it."

"What year is this? What am I? Nothing but a fucking slave? This country went to war over slavery. It was wrong back then. It's wrong now."

"The stark reality of your situation is that you carry the virus. You are now a member of the Non-Dead. Lisa, try to overcome your fear. The country still needs you. You can still contribute to society and in turn lead a rewarding life."

Lisa put her fingers to her lips. "I've lost Bob. I'm losing my job. I'm not even considered equal to other humans now." She raised her eyes to meet Anne's. "Put down the pompoms, and go fuck yourself."

Anne shook her head. "I understand how you feel. You are not alone. Time will heal you. You'll learn to adjust and find your way back into society. It won't take you long. You're just going through the initial shock. Trust me. I've seen others as upset as you. Today, they live content, fulfilled lives."

Lisa glanced down at her pale feet. The ruby red polish made her toes look even deader.

CHAPTER 4

"It's about time you got here. I'm dying to see what my face looks like. There's not one mirror in this whole damn room, and I was told that you would be bringing one with you," Lisa said. She still wore the flimsy hospital gown, feeling the air on her bare bottom as she sat on the bed to greet the visitor.

A large woman shaped like a bowling pin, dressed in a mustard-yellow pantsuit, and wearing shoes where her toes stuck past the footbed, closed the door and entered the room.

"Good afternoon. My name is LaQuisha Johnson. I'm here as a representative of Avan Products, Incorporated. The hospital allows us, with your permission of course, to introduce you to our line of beauty products which will help your appearance as you reenter the workforce and start your new life. As an appreciation for your time, I will also give you a free week's supply of your first month's purchase."

Not the first time you've made this pitch, I bet, Lisa thought, and rolled her eyes.

"Miss Lisa, here is a free catalogue from Avan." LaQuisha removed a thin magazine-sized catalogue from a tall brown tote bag. "Our catalogue includes wigs, prosthetics, and makeup specifically designed for the Non-Dead. Avan provides you with all the necessary image enhancement products to give you the self-confidence to intermingle with the Living without feeling out of place."

Lisa took the catalogue and flipped through the pages. "Ooo, look, I can get a new arm, or maybe a new leg. Hey, this arm even has a hand with a *bionic grip*. That could come in handy if I wanted to strangle annoying people who wanted to take advantage me because of my misfortune."

LaQuisha frowned, forcing her brows almost halfway down her eyes. "Our prosthetics are made from a combination of modern latex and polymers molded around a carbon-graphite skeletal structure. In a process that does not create any greenhouse gases to further contribute to climate change—"

"Okay LaQuisha, I get it. You're here to help me with the latest-greatest cosmetic achievements of man. Cut the sales crap, and give me a mirror. I bet I look a sight."

LaQuisha stopped cold as if losing place in her thoughts and pulled a hand mirror from her bag. She passed the mirror to Lisa.

Lisa's eyes went wide when she saw her reflection for the first time since crossing over to the Non-Dead. It was worse than she had imagined. Even worse than the time she spent four hours throwing up in the toilet after a *fun* night of drinking.

She repositioned herself on the bed to see herself in better light, brushed her hair aside, and gently pushed her cheeks.

LaQuisha started, "The virus your body contains has affected the melanocytes in your skin, which are responsible for melanin production, which determines skin color. This has led to your condition which is similar to albinism."

"I know. I read the pamphlet, 'Now that you are a member of the Non-Dead.' You don't need to give me a science lesson." Lisa pointed to a stack of booklets on the nightstand.

LaQuisha picked back up, "Avan has a line of ATP cream with fifty-three realistic skin tone shades we call Skintastic for you to choose from."

"I don't have to use the cream. I'm well-preserved enough that I don't have to cover my whole body with the cellular food like most Sub Z Non-Deads. I'm Sub Y. My heart still beats, even though it's only about twenty times a minute. I can get my cellular nutrition through, what was that name again . . ." Lisa thought for a moment, "Adenosine triphosphate, from the patch. My blood still flows fast enough to carry the nutrients throughout my body."

"Well, Miss Lisa, we have the body makeup available without the ATP, also in the same fifty-three Skintastic shades. I'm sure you'll want to return to your natural skin tone, unless you plan on going Full-Zombie."

Despite being politically conservative, Lisa had always considered the Full-Zombie lifestyle to be a mockery of the Sub Zs. A small group of Sub Ys had started the movement by no longer concealing their hideous wounds or coloring their pale lifeless skin, to show unity with their abused brethren.

The Full-Zombie movement hadn't gained any real momentum until members of the Living joined in. They dressed themselves to look Non-Dead, covering their exposed flesh with white makeup, and drawing dark circles around their eyes. Some even applied fake scars and engineered ghastly, imitation wounds and wore this façade in daily life. It was a totally *in your face* public statement supporting equal rights for the Non-Dead.

"No, no Full-Zombie for me. I've spent the last few years keeping fit and presenting myself as best I can. I like to say that if I die the prettiest corpse, I win. I'm not about to march around looking like a decaying albino from a George Romero movie."

"Then as a representative of Avan, it is my professional opinion that you should choose from our ATP Skintastic collection. Your skin can return to the warm tone that says, 'Hey world, I'm alive.' The patch will only serve to call attention to your Non-Dead status."

Lisa relaxed her body and smiled. "You know, LaQuisha, you're right. I'm sorry if I've been rude. I've been through a lot. What would you like to show me?"

LaQuisha removed a floral-patterned plastic box from her bag, placed it on the bed, and opened it. Vials of makeup graduated in shade from darker to lighter, each with an exotic name for the color, filled the compartments in the box.

"For a Caucasian of European descent such as yourself, I recommend you choose from numbers sixteen through thirty-two." LaQuisha slowly trailed her index finger along the colors.

Lisa selected two of the vials and held them up one at a time to her face as she studied the mirror, and then removed two more from the box and did the same. "I think it's between Soft Honey and Natural Tan."

She removed the caps from each vial and used her finger to apply the two creams to opposite cheeks. The mirror went up to either side of her face, moving back and forth as she decided. "I have all the sex appeal of a mannequin."

LaQuisha giggled. "Oh no, Miss Lisa, not with a body like yours. The cream will serve as a color foundation. You'll still have to apply blush, eyeliner, and lipstick to look more like your natural self. We have a line of products that are compatible with our Skintastic ATP cream lineup. You know, Miss Lisa, your eyes are a beautiful shade of green. As an RY recipient you've retained your natural eye color. If you had become a Sub Z, you'd have to wear colored contacts."

"Like I would even care what my eye color was if I was a Sub Z."

"You'd be surprised how much owners, I mean employers, spend to make their Sub Zs more presentable."

"I think I'm going with Natural Tan." Lisa continued the comparison. "My, Avan tries every way possible to make a buck." She gave the mirror one last glance. "You did say that my first week is free if I buy a month's supply, right?"

"That's correct, Miss Lisa."

"I bet this stuff isn't cheap."

"Avan prides itself on being competitive in the market while offering superior quality. The ingredients are all natural. The pigments are extracts from organically grown fruits and vegetables. All of our Skintastic products have a soothing effect on the skin, with refreshing properties, and leave the skin feeling soft and smooth. It also contains rosehips, a powerful antioxidant against free radicals. That will help in the prevention of wrinkles, aging of the skin, and sun damage."

"Wow, now I'm more afraid of how much this stuff costs."

CHAPTER 5

The room's warm lighting paired with a mystic hue of green coloring the walls. Barely audible, the gentle song of a lazy rainforest drifted in the air from concealed speakers. Dark mahogany bookshelves lined one of the four walls, filled with massive volumes of hardbound books erect in perfect attention.

Lyn Atkins, staff psychologist from the Department of State Health Services, sat at one end of an ash rectangular table. She nestled in her Windsor back chair and scribbled notes on a yellow pad. Two personnel folders lay within easy reach.

Dotting her period with enough force for the other two in the room to hear, she pulled her glasses to the end of her nose and eyed Lisa Goudard sitting to the right, and then Byron Poundstone sitting to the left. The laser etched Z Class ID number on Byron's forehead a modern improvement over tattoos used in Hitler's concentration camps.

Lisa shook in her chair, holding back fiery rage. The monster who had killed her fiancé and forced her into the class of Non-Dead sat across the table. Dr. Atkins had briefed her in a previous session what emotions to expect and how to control them. Now, face to face with him in the same room, controlling her feelings was more difficult than she had anticipated. Byron appeared much younger than the zombie who ruined her life.

The sub Z class Non-Dead held the blank countenance of his kind on his face. The madness induced by the virus no longer controlled him. His daily ATP application didn't contain any of the costly skin color pigmentation, leaving his skin sickly pale, and dark circles surrounding his eyes. The irises, no longer having color, were pale gray, reflecting the light emanating from his soul.

Byron looked nothing like the creature that had attacked her though, seemingly now as harmful as a five-year-old chasing after butterflies.

Lisa let out a sigh and then breathed in deeply. A wave of nausea surged from her stomach to her head.

Lyn watched the two instead of writing more notes. No doubt the session had already begun, and observing Lisa's reaction was all part of the therapy. Lisa's fuse had been lit the moment she saw Bob's killer, there was no hiding that in her body language. Therapy was just a game. Lyn would be the judge. Lisa didn't know if she wanted to win, she only wanted her life back to normal. She reached for a tissue in her purse and gently wiped her nose before the clear liquid ran down her lip.

"Lisa," Lyn began, "you know why you're here. Let me be upfront with you. I can't roll back time, and I can't perform miracles."

Lisa turned her gaze to Lyn, her expression devoid of hope.

"What I can do, is what I have done for many others over the last several years. I will give you tools you can use to integrate back into society—to lead a fulfilling life."

Lyn removed her glasses and laid them on the table. "Across from you is the man who has brought you all the heartache that you have gone through over the last week. He is no longer a memory—a ghost of the past—a boogeyman to fear. He's real, sitting in front of you. But what he is today is not what he was when he attacked you.

"Yes, he is responsible, but there were circumstances beyond his control that led him to do what he did. We're not here to discuss Byron's condition. We're here for you to face Byron and for you to tell him how you feel."

The door to the room squeaked open. An attractive man in his middle thirties entered, dressed in a fine tailored black suit. "Sorry I'm late. The receptionist said it would be all right to come in. Forgive me for interrupting."

Lyn smiled and rose from her chair, greeting the man, with a gentle handshake. "Mr. Poundstone, I'm so glad you could make it. Please have a seat at the end of the table. We've just started. I wanted you here so Byron might feel more comfortable."

Lisa found herself staring at the man. She had seen him somewhere before.

"Lisa Goudard, this is Representative Rick Poundstone. Rick is Byron's older brother and is here for his support. He has also told me he would like to express his condolences to you."

Rick turned toward Lisa and hesitated as if lost for words. "Miss Goudard, I don't know how to begin to tell you how much I regret what has happened to you and your loved one." He went to say more, but the words seemed to stick in his throat. The silence that followed iced the room.

Lisa overtly swallowed and nodded her head, choking back the tears.

"Let's continue." Lyn stepped back to the chair and sat. "Lisa, it is time for you to express your feelings to Byron. Tell him everything you need to about what he did. Tell him exactly how you feel. Don't hold anything back. If Byron has any hope of forgiveness it will only come if you open up and let it all out."

Lisa slammed her open palms to the table.

Byron jumped in his chair and darted his head her way.

"Forgiveness? This man destroys my life and you want me to forgive him? Has the world gone fucking mad?" Lisa jumped to her feet and knocked the chair backward. "I'm buying sodas. Bob's changing a tire. This maniac jumps out the darkness and attacks him. Hell, attack is too kind a word. This animal eats him!" She pointed her finger and shook it. "He tore the flesh off bone of a living person—with his bare teeth. He ate Bob alive!

"All the while Bob pleaded and cried and yelled for mercy. But there was none. Second after second ticked by as he chewed chunks of meat off the man I loved. I could hear this monster swallowing and smacking his lips! He ate so much of Bob he couldn't even come back to exist as I am, a fucking Sub Y." Lisa lowered her head. "At least we would have had each other . . . ."

Shaking off her remorse, she slammed her palms to the table again. Everyone in the room jumped.

"No. Bob's gone. I'm alone. You took my life from me. And what's left of it, I really don't know what the fuck to expect. Everything has changed. Everything is different. I feel like I'm a foreigner in my own country."

Lisa paused and leaned on the table.

The gentle voice of a regretful child spoke, "I'm sorry. I didn't mean to hurt you." Byron reached across the table and gently touched Lisa's hand. "Don't be mad at me. I don't even remember."

Lisa snatched her hand away and collapsed in her chair, wailing uncontrollably at the top of her lungs.

Rick rose and reached out a hand toward her. He pulled it back as if sensing she would not welcome his comfort.

Lyn went to Rick's side and whispered in his ear. "Don't worry. This is a good sign. She's letting go. Why don't you take Byron outside? His custodian is waiting and will take him back to the Institution."

"What about Miss Goudard?"

"She's in the early stages of her rehabilitation. The state will be with her every step and will help any way possible. These are matters for us to deal with. You need to get back to your life and concern yourself with the People's business."

Rick acted as if he wanted to say more, but the only door available was the one leading out the room. Taking a business card from his pocket, he wrote his cell phone number and a note that said, 'Call me for any reason, even if you only need someone to listen,' and slid it toward Lisa. He took Byron by the hand and left the room, closing the door leaving Lisa and Lyn alone.

"Why is it so important for me to forgive that son-of-a-bitch? I'm not the one at fault here. It shouldn't be about me. He's the one that did wrong. Screw his feelings. He should feel like he's hated for what he did." Lisa added another used tissue to the growing pile on the table.

Lyn warmly smiled. "Forgiving Byron isn't for his sake, it's for yours. The block in your life's road can only be removed if you forgive him for what he did. If you don't, you'll just keep bumping into that block again and again. The life you live will be miserable. You'll never be able to break the chains of the past."

Lisa listened and let the words sink into her subconscious. She realized the only way to get to the end of the road was to take the first step. There *was* a block preventing her from moving forward in life. She had to find a way past it.

CHAPTER 6

When the hospital doors automatically closed behind Lisa, a gray, overcast sky welcomed her to a new world. A world stripped of all illusions, as if the vibrancy in life had faded. It had become a cold, savage place where existence came at the expense of others. Eat or be eaten. Lisa no longer felt like the hunter. She was vulnerable prey.

Cigar smoke assaulted her first breath of outside air. It came from a short, pudgy man standing by the door who looked at a folded sheet of newspaper. His greased-back hair framed a pitted and scarred face. The bulbous nose crooked and red on the tip. His gaze drifted up, back to the paper, then back up again. She quickly walked away.

With little cash in her purse and her car at her apartment, waiting out front for the city bus was the only option. The bus route would bring her to within two blocks of home.

Lisa had no desire to be in close contact with others. She especially wanted to avoid any of the Non-Dead for a while. She wasn't like them and didn't want to be thought of as one in the eyes of the Living. Just seeing a crew of Sub Zs cleaning the parking lot turned her stomach.

A grim realization came to her. If she did take the bus, she would have to sit in the back with the rest of the Non-Dead. This had been another law passed to appease the Living, forced into sharing Reconstruction resources with the Non-Dead.

With her purse hanging from her shoulder and a tote bag in each hand, Lisa was lost in her thoughts until she heard footsteps approaching. She quickened her pace, only to hear it matched by her pursuer.

It was broad daylight; there were people about on the sidewalks and driving on the highway. Lisa knew she had no reason to run and would make a scene if necessary. She was about to turn around and confront whoever was following her, when he spoke.

"Miss Goudard?"

Lisa stopped and slowly turned around. "Do I know you?" It was the seedy character with the newspaper.

The man took a long draw off his cigar and spit out a little piece of tobacco. "No, we have not met."

"Then how do you know my name?"

"I read in the paper about what happened to you and your boyfriend."

"Good for you. When I first saw you, I wouldn't have guessed you were intelligent enough to read." Even though Lisa wore flat shoes, at five feet seven inches she towered above him.

The man frowned but maintained his composure. "I'm sorry for your loss."

"Okay, you're sorry for my loss. Boo-hoo, thank you, and goodbye." Lisa turned and walked away.

The soles of his shoes slapped the concrete in chase. Lisa had to come to an abrupt halt as he darted in front and blocked her path.

"If you would hold your horses for a sec, I'd like to make a little business proposition."

"I've got a job as a state health inspector. Now piss off before I yell rape."

The man raised his hands in the air and lowered his head. "Miss Goudard, forgive my lack of professionalism. My name is Normie Cantrell. I'm in the entertainment business."

Lisa took in a breath of air and exhaled loudly. "Oh, I get it. You want to make a buck off my tragic story—how I lost my boyfriend and became a member of the Non-Dead. I bet you want to start a blog about my daily life, and want me to Twitter every time I blow my nose, or go to the bathroom. I can see it now, *For only forty-nine ninety-five a month you can watch Lisa on her live webcam as she sits on her couch and picks at her toenails.*"

Normie hesitated. "Ya know, I never thought about that angle before. But it does sound like an idea we could incorporate, to expand your appeal to the national level."

"Mr. Cantrell, the answer is no. No thank you. Please move or I yell."

Normie narrowed his eyes. His lips formed an evil grin. "You're wrong lady. You ain't got no job no more. You are about to go back to a world that ain't holding your place in line."

Lisa's shoulders rose and her back stiffened. "I'm sorry, I can't understand what you're saying. I don't speak asshole."

Normie shook his head and rolled his eyes. "You're going to find the only jobs out there for you don't pay diddly squat. Oh sure, you'll find work. Like wiping asses and changing diapers on old people at the hospital. Waiting tables while the diners ignore you like you're nothing more than a piece of furniture. How's about cleaning? You good at pushing a broom and slinging a mop? That, Young Miss, is what your new world will be like. That is, unless you come work for me."

There was no denying her future was uncertain. Cantrell's words rubbed her nose in the muck of her new reality. "You said you were in the entertainment business. What is it you do?"

His mouth widened and tobacco stained teeth showed ready for the first bite. "From the moment I saw your picture in the paper, I knew we could start a partnership that would make a ton of cash. I've been in business for a long time. Baby, let me tell you, you are going to be the hottest thing this city has ever seen."

"Don't *baby* me. Spit it out."

Normie reached in his front coat pocket pulling out a business card and presented it to her.

She read it aloud, "Dancing Bare, Gentleman's Club. Normie Cantrell, *slime bucket*, owner."

Normie frowned. "Hey, I'm a legitimate businessman. I pay taxes."

"I think the picture of the dancing bear with the top hat and cane is cute. Why don't you buy a bear costume, and then you can get up on stage and shake your ass. My ass is going home." Lisa handed him the card.

"You don't have to say yes today. Think about it. Sleep on it. I'm in the book—call me."

Lisa strained a big smile on her face while tilting her head. "Ah, Normie, you big lug . . . Eat shit and die!" With that, Lisa pointed her head forward and sped off, daring him to stop her.

As she brushed past him, he slipped his card into the side pocket of her purse. Planting a seed for the future.

CHAPTER 7

The midnight blue 2024 North American Motors Elite Sedan passed through the wrought iron double gates as they opened on command of the estate owner, Joel Spencer. The forty-five year old Living Party nominee for U.S. Congress returned home from a campaign luncheon, where the good people of the state parted with hard-earned cash in hopes of sending him to Washington. The rubber chicken lunch had added over ten thousand dollars to his war chest. This solidified him as a serious candidate for the House Republican nomination, challenging his long-time friend and incumbent Republican representative, Rick Poundstone.

A political storm brewed across varying demographics setting the country at odds for one of the biggest showdowns since slavery. The Democrats currently pushed legislation to allow the Non-Dead to become full union members in the work force, receiving equal benefits as the Living. The Republican Party sought to prevent equality to maximize profits for business. Unfortunately for the party, the Living Party rose as a splinter group and threatened to divide the membership. The Living Party promoted an agenda in favor of eliminating the Non-Dead from the workforce and instigating a mandatory national birth program. The goal was to replace the Non-Dead with new members of the Living.

The federal government controlled the number of newly dead resurrected with the Resurrection Z treatment. Of course, the state paid a one-time cash benefit to the family as a *gesture* of gratitude. The state would recover its investment hundreds of times over during the service time of the newly resurrected Sub Z.

The Resurrection Y drug was a derivative from a mutated strain of Resurrection Z virus. RY's purpose was to counter the original alien virus if given before the victim died of a recent infection. Or, it could be used to heal those with a debilitating disease or injury. Even those dying of cancer could be saved by the application of RY.

Preventing death outside of the alien virus infection using RY was ruled to be illegal in the United States and most of the world. The fear was RY would be used as an immortality drug, changing the future of humanity forever, and ultimately leading man to extinction.

Spencer knew the Living party was gaining momentum. Still, he would have to fight with every dirty trick available if he were to upset the incumbent.

He parked the car in his triple-wide garage and exited with briefcase in hand. Mack Teller, the property caretaker, trimmed branches on the Indian Hawthorns nearby. Mack also provided political cover for Spencer, for he was a member of the Non-Dead, Sub Y.

Mack had spent twenty years of his life in a wheelchair after crashing his bike into a car, right before entering his teens. A one-time program sanctioned by both the government and the Catholic Church made the RY treatment available for paraplegics under fifty years of age.

Mack gave up the status of being a member of the Living for full use of his limbs. His mind and personality remained unaffected, as his treatment allowed him the transition without dying first. The RY treatment of the modified alien virus worked inside his body repairing the neural network, allowing his body to function as nature intended.

After physical rehabilitation, Mack's legs returned to normal without any restrictions. Spencer hired him to maintain the ten-acre estate, paying him a pittance, and giving him a place to live on the property. Spencer never passed up a chance to use Mack as a badge of honor, proudly proclaiming himself to be a man beyond prejudice.

The clippers snipped an errant branch. It fell to the ground. Joel Spencer came into Mack's view as he bent over to pick it up. "Hello, Mr. Spencer, back from your luncheon, I see."

Spencer was fond of Mack, viewing him in his heart as a prized possession. "Yes. It was a very important event. Nothing you should concern yourself with though."

Mack made two more chops with the clippers, and then stepped back, eying the symmetry of the hedge. "I understand. I have duties around here that I should be more concerned with."

"Yes you do, like checking the air in the tires on the Harley. Go ahead and change the oil while you're at it, and give it a good cleaning."

"Mighty fine, sir. I'm happy to do it."

"And take your time when polishing the chrome. It was all smeared the last time."

"Yes, sir. I will."

"What's the matter with the rock pond? On my morning walk I noticed it was dark. Is there a problem with the filter?"

Mack let the clippers down to his side. "No, sir. No problem. I accidentally added half a cup too much dye after I cleaned it. It'll look normal again in a few days when the level drops enough for me to add some more water."

"The grass west of the house is scalped. What happened?"

"Well, sir, one of the blades on the finish mower got off balance. It chopped up the grass a bit before I realized it. Got a few pieces of sod coming in tomorrow. I'll have it good as new in no time."

Spencer glanced down at his watch, then at Mack. "Sounds to me like you need to pay more attention when you're working. What's got you so distracted?"

"Nothing. I'm going through a little bit of bad luck, that's all."

"Just keep your head in the game." Spencer pointed to his head. "I don't believe in bad luck. We make our own luck." He turned away from Mack and headed for the door.

"Don't you worry about a thing, Mr. Spencer. I'll make sure to keep my head in the game and lick it to completion."

Spencer almost stopped to ask what Mack meant by that last remark, but figured he had wasted enough time making his point. If Mack started to get unruly, he might have to find a replacement. He didn't want to do that, though. Mack had proven his loyalty unlike anyone else, Living or not, but he wasn't going to put up with an uppity employee. He would simply find another Sub Y willing to work for the crumbs off his table.

CHAPTER 8

The parking lot was nearly full, and Lisa found herself at the very back by the security fence. State employees clocked in at 7 a.m. She had never come in to work this late before.

It was Wednesday, the day after she checked out of the hospital. Only a little more than a week had passed since she lost Bob and her full U.S. citizenship. A week she had spent alone except for the doctors, nurses, and other caregivers who helped her adjust to this new life. No one had called from the office or even sent a get-well card. She had no real friends in life who would be concerned enough to check in on her. Of course, Bob's liberal friends hadn't called. None of them had any love for his conservative girlfriend to begin with.

She had considered joining a support group but didn't think the time was right to face a room full of whiny misfits. If God, or fate, had chosen her to bear this affliction, she was going to have to prove to the world of the Living she was not inferior. Her resolve had her determined to be more than just an equal, and she vowed to prove she was superior.

The visor's mirror showed her dark brown hair hadn't frizzed from the morning's humidity. Another application of Toast of the Town on her lips had them plump and sexy as ever.

On the outside she was a well-disciplined activist ready to take on the world. The challenge was to keep it together on the inside.

Tears welled in her eyes and formed large drops before dripping down her cheeks. She patted her face dry with a tissue, being careful not to smear any makeup. "I keep telling myself to be strong, Bob . . . it's just so hard to go on . . . ."

Death had been a common occurrence over the two years of The Dark Times. Everyone had lost family members or close friends. Lisa had lost her mother and father, her younger sister, and older brother. It was through those tragic events she had learned how to ignore the void left behind by a loved one's sudden, violent death. It was a survival mechanism. Those who were distracted by mourning the dead were usually the next to die.

Losing Bob had cut deeply, penetrating through the walls of all of her defenses, and churning her insides to mush.

Lisa made a few touchups to her makeup. *It's me against the world.*

The mechanical clank of the four door locks cemented the moment in time as she closed the door. *I'm locked into my fate too.*

The weak *click* of her four-inch heels against the parking lot's surface echoed her shattered confidence—not befitting a determined woman. She quickened her pace, and lengthened her stride, until the shoes hitting the pavement drummed out a familiar rhythm.

As Lisa climbed the steps of the State Building, she passed a young man dressed in a business suit. He stopped to watch her backside, his eyes following the sway of her hips. *Life is not entirely different from before, after all*, she thought as she glanced back.

Lisa entered the building, ignoring the guard as he sat behind his desk reading the morning paper. She walked up to the turnstile and placed the ID badge in front of the card scan. The light on the turnstile blinked red. A raspy alarm buzzed on the guard's desk. Lisa futilely pushed with both hands on the turnstile bar.

"Excuse me, miss?" the guard had abandoned his post and approached her. "May I see your identification badge, please?"

Lisa feigned surprise. "You know me. We've both worked here for years. My name is Lisa Goudard. I work for the Department of Health. The card is old and probably worn out. Would you please let me through?"

"Yes ma'am. You do have a familiar face, but I still need to see your identification badge."

The guard pried the badge from her fingers and went back to his desk. He tapped his computer screen and entered a few lines of data on the keyboard. A number came up. He picked up the phone and made a brief call.

"Well, are you going to issue me a new badge, or what?"

"No, ma'am." The guard cleared his throat. "Your supervisor will be down to speak to you shortly."

She opened her mouth to protest but knew it would be a waste of time. The system was cutting her off. The fantasy of striking some kind of deal with her Department Head or the State's Attorney General evaporated in the harsh light of reality.

A few minutes passed while she paced the lobby.

"Lisa, we've been waiting for you," a voice said, harboring subtle agitation.

She turned around. Adrian P. Waller, her immediate supervisor, stood alongside Penny, Delayna, and Stacy, her officemates.

Lisa was surprised how much comfort seeing a familiar face brought.

Adrian adjusted his grip around a cardboard box and tilted his head back, peering down his nose. Penny had raised her eyebrows into high, penciled arches. Her traditional fake smile showed enough teeth to use in a toothpaste commercial. Delayna smirked victoriously, as if she'd just stolen Dorothy's ruby slippers right off her feet. And last of all, Stacy, her gaze glued to the floor.

Penny was the first to break the silence. "Lisa, you look so . . . natural."

You people know me and now act like I'm a leper or something. Her hopeful smile vanished. "Natural, huh? Isn't that what you say about a corpse made up for burial?"

Penny blushed, her smile quivered at the corners of her mouth. "No, no, no, dear. That's not what I meant. You still look like your old self, in fact even better. You have such a pretty tan."

"You can come closer than ten feet to me. I'm not going to bite you." Lisa crossed her arms and shifted her weight to her left foot. *If we're going to dance, you're going to have to make the next move.*

Penny maintained her smile, Delayna shook her head in disgust, and Stacy continued to stare holes in the floor.

Adrian finally broke the tension. "We're glad to see you up and about. Such a tragic thing to happen to someone so young and vibrant. Isn't it amazing, though, what modern science can do? You should consider yourself lucky. You've been given a second chance. Why, if I didn't know any better and passed you on the street, I'd think that you're as human as the rest of us."

Lisa rolled her eyes. "So, I'm not human now?"

"Wait, wait. Don't twist my words. You know what I mean. You're different because of your . . . condition."

Lisa put her index finger to her head. "Hmmm, my condition . . . my heart still beats. I still breathe. I have two legs and two arms. I walk, talk, feel pain, and need love. I still need food, clothing, and shelter. I can even fart. And let me tell you, my farts smell better than the stink you're putting on me.

"I can do anything any of you can—anything I could do before. Tell me again how I'm so different?"

The green-eyed monster of jealousy finally raised its unholy head as Delayna jumped in. "Oh, Lisa, you're still the self-centered bitch you were before. Always so confident, getting what you wanted by running over whoever got in your way.

"Well, it's time for you to wake up and smell the sauerkraut. Those days are gone. You're not like *us* anymore. You're one of them. You don't need to eat like we do. Your heart doesn't beat like ours. You can't have children like normal women. Your day is over, sister. It's time for you to get in the back of the line."

Lisa bowed her back. "Delayna, you really are a piece of work. I've always treated you and everyone here with the utmost respect. I know I'm opinionated, but I've always been fair. I have a strong personality, and I've tried to push my way to the top. But the real reason you've never liked me is because you can't stand all the attention men give me. I admit I dress in a way to be noticed. But I've never tried to lure any man away from you—or anyone else, for that matter. I've never needed to. I've got news for you," she stabbed her finger in Delayna's direction, "and the rest of you. I'm not going to get in the back of the line. I'm the same person I was, and nothing about me, the real me, has changed. Get used to it."

"Bob," Stacy spoke softly. "I'm sorry about Bob."

Lisa's face flushed, and tears ran like a dripping faucet.

"We're all sorry about Bob," Penny said, sounding more believable this time. "For you to have to deal with his death and your change, too, well, it's too much. I don't know how you're holding up."

"Thanks." Lisa wiped the tears away and licked her lips. "I try to turn those emotions off. But I miss him. I really miss him."

"Any word when the government is going to release his body? I'm sure you'll want to have a memorial," Adrian said, his knuckles white from clutching the box.

"Nothing yet. I don't know if I'm going to have a memorial. Bob didn't have any family left. His friends haven't called me either," Lisa paused and wiped her nose with a tissue. "We spoke once about how we wanted our bodies handled when we died. He told me he wanted to be cremated. Heck, that's probably how the government will return him to me—a pile of ashes in a metal container." She looked back at Adrian. "It's like I'm dead too. It's like I'm dead and walking through life where I don't matter anymore."

"You are dead to humanity," Delayna said.

The blow lit the fuse. "Fuck you." Lisa burst like a bomb. "Fuck all you condescending bastards."

"Lisa, that's no way to act. Put yourself in our position," Adrian said.

"No, you put yourself in my position. You arrogant assholes can't see an inch beyond your own prejudice. Fuck off, all of you."

Penny still smiled like an ice queen. Delayna threw her hands in the air and walked off. Stacy had never taken her gaze from the floor.

"This has gone on long enough," Adrian said, stepping to within a few feet of Lisa. "Here, let me carry your belongings to the car for you."

"If I'm not good enough for the job, then there is nothing in that box worth taking home with me."

Adrian balanced the box on one knee and fished out a golden obelisk-shaped award Lisa had won for State Heath inspector of the year. "At least take this as a keepsake."

"I'll take it if you give me some of your favorite lubricant to go along with it," Lisa cheerfully said.

"My favorite lubricant? Why?"

"Because if you don't get that thing out of my face I'm going to shove it up your ass."

CHAPTER 9

Reverend Will Hatfield slowly paced behind the podium, admiring the hundreds of people gathering on the warm Saturday afternoon at the rally held in the courthouse parking lot.

Several members of his church scurried about, running wire to speakers, and extension cords to generators. His loyal flock followed him with fervent devotion, and granted him the authority to explain the reality beyond news headlines, and how that reality affected God's plan. Hatfield was the perfect shepherd to guide his sheep in today's sinful world.

Hatfield heralded that the integration of Non-Dead into society would eventually lead to the downfall of humanity. As God told Lot to leave Sodom before its destruction, He told the Reverend that humanity should separate from the Non-Dead. The Non-Dead must return into the ground from whence they came.

The police had forced the group of *zombie-lovers* to a dedicated area near the main highway. Protesters had to be kept far enough away so flying projectiles from radicals couldn't reach the stage.

A technician placed a microphone on the podium and connected a cable to the bottom.

"The heathens have crawled out of the hole," Hatfield said, wearing a smirk as he gazed toward the protesters. "About double the normal crowd. Must be about forty of them out there."

The technician glanced over his shoulder. "Good. More to hear your message, Reverend."

This group had arrived well-prepared. Each held a hand-painted sign and dressed in Full-Zombie attire. Most protesters were Livings. The rally's permit limited the number of Non-Dead participants to no more than five.

"Those poor Non-Dead devils don't even understand what they're here protesting," Hatfield said.

"Pitiful, ain't it?" the technician said before leaving the stage.

Black clouds which had rolled in earlier that morning started to dissipate, giving way to sunshine outlining a graying cloud above. Its rays squeezed through, painting a portion of the sky with the individual beams touching down in the distance. It was as if the finger of God had pierced the darkness, showing that God is light, and there is no darkness in Him at all.

Hatfield's microphone came alive, the feedback echoed over the parking lot. The sound engineer made a few adjustments on the mixing board, and then gave the Reverend a hand sign for him to *go*.

He stepped up and posed in front of the podium, resting a hand to each side. The crowd's murmur subsided.

When all eyes were on him, he began his speech. "Greetings, my friends and my neighbors. Greetings to all the good people in Dallas, to all those from the state of Texas, and to those who are visitors from across our blessed land. I welcome you, the Streets of Gold Church welcomes you, and the Party of the Living welcomes you."

Hatfield paused and extended his hand toward the protesters in the rear. The motley little band had remained silent during his opening but had continued to wave their signs high in the air. "To the brethren in the back. It is my desire to offer you my hand in a gesture of peace. That you may come to learn the great plan my church and the Living Party share. A plan designed to ensure the survival of humanity. A plan that puts mankind back on the track which God originally intended. That we should be fruitful and multiply, and once again provide for ourselves—without the need to disturb the peace of our dearly departed.

"Paul writes in Second Timothy, 'The Lord's servant must not be quarrelsome, but must be kind to everyone, able to teach, not resentful. Opponents must be gently instructed, in the hope that God will grant them repentance leading them to a knowledge of the truth, and that they will come to their senses and escape from the trap of the Devil, who has taken them captive to do his will.' "

Random shouts of *Amen!* ejected from the crowd.

A few TV cameras in the audience panned to Hatfield, and then to the protesters.

He continued, "My friends, if we are sure of nothing else, we are certain of one thing. The Devil is a liar and a deceiver. Thus he was in the beginning, and thus he shall ever be. He is a false prophet, a charlatan, an imitator of the goodness of God, with hollow and inferior gifts.

"The celestial storm that rained the accursed virus upon the pure lands of the Earth was spawned of the Devil himself. It was an attempt to spoil the most beautiful promise God has ever given to man.

"First Corinthians chapter fifteen tells us with the hope that is in Christ, one day God shall raise the dead in the like manner. Our body is sown in corruption. It is raised in incorruption.

"Are the dead who are raised by the hand of man, using the tools of the Devil, incorruptible?"

"No!" Hatfield's followers shouted in unison.

Hatfield waited for the echo to fade, and then continued reading from the Scriptures. "It is sown in dishonor. It is raised in glory. It is sown in weakness. It is raised in power.

"Are the Non-Dead raised in glory? Are the Non-Dead raised in power?"

"No!"

He continued reading. "It is sown a natural body. It is raised a spiritual body."

Reverend Hatfield removed the microphone from the stand and stepped away from the podium. He changed the cadence of his swelling rant to a rapid, monotone chant. "There is a natural body, and there is a spiritual body, brothers and sisters. Do not be deceived." He let the word *deceived* twist in his mouth and end on a high note.

He began the rapid chant again, "The Non-Dead are still bound in a natural *body-ah*. A body of *weakness-ah*. *Sooown* in *dishonor-ah*. And raised by man in *dishonor-ah*. Leading humanity down a road of *destruction-ah*. Like the Pied Piper leading humanity to the jaws of *extinction-ah*." Hatfield then pressed his mouth against the microphone, and screamed, "Be ye not deceived!" His words reverberate over the crowd.

Then in a gentle instructing voice, he said, "God is not mocked."

Hatfield stepped back to the podium and raised his eyes and hands toward the heavens above. The crowd responded with applause peppered with hoots, hollers, and shouts of praises that surely God Himself could hear as He sat on His eternal throne.

The ovation continued for several minutes before the Reverend waved his arms to the faithful. "It is time for me to introduce our guest, a man of faith who I have known for many years. My friends, I am confident enough in this man to say God knows him too. I give you the challenger to the status quo of the Republican Party, the nominee of the Living Party, the next representative of the thirty second District to Washington, D.C., Joel Spencer."

Now worked into a frenzy, the crowd again roared their approval at nearly deafening levels.

Spencer took his stand behind the podium after giving Hatfield a long, exaggerated handshake. Raising his hands to quiet the crowd only produced more adoration.

As he gazed over the crowd he focused on the group of protesters in the back. His jaw tightened, and then his mouth opened in surprise. After the unusual pause, a smile sprang to his face, his attention then turned back on the audience.

"Please, please, you are too kind." The applause hushed as he continued to motion for quiet. One last rebel yell cut through the air before he began to speak.

"My thanks to the good Reverend for his inspiring introduction. My thanks to all the people who are here in support of the principles I stand for. And to those who wish to learn about my plans to take Texas—and America—forward, to ensure a safe, productive future."

He waited for the obligatory claps to stop. "My message is not one of hate. It is one of hope and of compassion. Let us not in haste stray from the path God has intended man to follow. Let us not sacrifice our children's future, or their children's future, so we might have more worldly things to enjoy today.

"The Book of Proverbs says, 'Riches profit not in the day of wrath: but righteousness delivereth from death.' Paul says, 'We look not at the things which are seen, but at the things which are not seen: for the things which are seen are temporal; but the things which are not seen are eternal.'

"To my supporters, and to those who oppose me, my proposal is very simple. It is a proposal which brings dignity to our loved ones who have passed away and have been blasphemously brought back to life. My plan will return the Living to their rightful place on Earth—their place as the sole caretaker of it as God intended."

Spencer detached the microphone from the podium and stepped closer to the crowd. "We need to enact into law a policy that will encourage married couples to make procreation a priority, in order to save us from extinction.

"You'd think it would be easy to encourage couples to spend extra time in the bedroom, wouldn't you?" The audience laughed right on cue. Spencer smiled and nodded his head.

"I understand the fear many feel. I understand the uncertainty in your hearts about what the future might hold. But the sure and certain danger that faces us is far worse than any uncertainty about the future. We know if we don't begin reproducing at a much higher rate the human race will no longer be able to sustain itself as a species on this planet.

"I will sponsor a bill that will require married couples of childbearing age to reproduce, barring any medical complications, of course. Also, the bill mandates a reduction in the number of dead who will be raised using the RZ virus, until the new generation of Living can take over the duties the Non-Dead now perform.

"But what of the Non-Dead that remain once our country's population is replenished? The bill provides for them also. They will be allowed to perform their duties until natural degradation, or some debilitating accident, prevents them from further service. We will honor the Non-Dead who helped us through our great time of need.

"But we must ensure humanity's future. I believe this is a plan that will work—with your help. It must work, or mankind may not exist to see the next century."

Spencer briefly stopped again as his gaze froze on the protestors.

"In the Book of Ecclesiastes, Solomon tells us, 'The living know that they shall die: but the dead know not anything—' "

"I know in the last several months your wife has been photographed with a black eye or two. Why do you beat your wife, Mr. Spencer?" a woman shouted from directly in front of the stage, close to Spencer. His microphone picked up the accusation and amplified it across the area. A camera operator from News Crew 2 shoved a camera her way.

"That's a damn lie!" Spencer shouted, disrupting the crowd. He grimaced and bit his lip.

The woman held up a handful of newspapers. *"The Libertarian Weekly* published photos on three different occasions over the last year and a half. In an interview, Spencer's wife claimed she tripped and fell. Are you tripping your wife, Mr. Spencer? Is she falling on your fists?" Other news teams filming the event pushed closer to her. She held one of the newspapers out in front, allowing the cameras to focus on an alleged photo.

"Where did you get that, miss?" A reporter who wore a blue sports jacket—and a dome of hair plastered with so much hairspray a hurricane couldn't have blown a strand out of place—thrust a microphone near the woman's mouth.

Spencer froze, his chin hanging down to his chest. The crowd began to buzz.

"The photographs have been available for months. It's your fault—the mainstream media. You are guilty of protecting politicians. Not one major market would touch those photos. Thank God *The Libertarian Weekly* had the balls to publish the truth," her voice rang loud and clear, as cameras flashed, and videos rolled.

The reporter in the blue jacket came to her side and faced the camera, then spoke into his microphone, "And your name is?"

"Lisa Goudard. My name is Lisa Goudard."

Spencer shook his head and formed a reassuring smile. "You know, it's easy in today's world to create a news story. All you need is a photograph and a computer. You, me, anyone can create a picture to show anything they want."

Spencer hurried to the opposite side of the stage, away from the woman. All heads followed. "Don't be so easily fooled, my friends. My lovely wife and I have been happily married for twenty-five years. To accuse me of such a vile act is not only an insult to me, but even more so to her. To believe my wife would think so little of herself as to stay with a man who physically abused her . . . " He pointed his finger at Lisa. "Let me tell you one thing, miss, I am a public figure, and I am occasionally subject to false accusations. But you have no right to insult my wife like that! How dare you!"

"You tell her," a voice yelled from the crowd.

His back arched, and his chest swelled. "You have been deceived young woman. You have been deceived by the Devil himself. The Devil is the father of all lies. Seek God and the truth, for the truth will set you free."

The crowd cheered in support. Spencer gave a nod, and two men with security T-shirts under jackets bailed from the end of the stage. Both bullied their way to the woman. One grabbed Lisa from the side.

"Let's go, miss. You can watch from the back with the rest of the protesters," the tall, middle-aged security officer said. Dark glasses hid his eyes.

When he grabbed her right bicep, she jerked her arm away. "Don't touch me! Get your hands off me!"

The Security Officer quickly pulled his open hand near his face and stared in obvious revulsion. Body makeup covered his palm. "Hey, she feels cold! She's one of them. She's a zombie," he shouted.

"What luck," Spencer whispered. He lowered his gaze to the stage floor while shaking his head, looking like a wounded soul.

Lisa stumbled backward toward the reporters, with only the two men from church security between her and some of the more agitated members of the crowd.

A fountain drink in a large plastic cup sailed through the air and crashed onto the side of Lisa's head, drenching her face and chest in sticky, sweet cola.

"Brothers, sisters, please calm down. Let the poor misguided woman go. Pray for her. Pray that she learns the error of her ways," Spencer said. The crowd quieted. "My unfortunate woman, your confusion is due to your affliction. I understand, and I forgive you."

"I'll debate you anytime, anywhere. You are not my superior," Lisa yelled.

"Pride goeth before the fall," Spencer spoke softly. "You have already broken one of the Ten Commandments bearing false witness against me. Go, and ask forgiveness of God, as I have forgiven you. Gentlemen, please escort the lady away."

The two men grabbed onto Lisa's arms and forced their way through the crowd. She kept her head low while barraged by curses from the *holy people* of the church. Some showed their disdain by spitting in her path.

An old woman tossed a drink onto Lisa's chest, and then another half-full cup sloshed out of the crowd as she walked by. Her white blouse turned transparent from the drinks and clung tightly to her skin. Her hourglass figure, which had been tastefully presented in her outfit, was now displayed as if she were parading in a wet T-shirt contest.

"Wow, look at the tits on that thing," an old man said.

"Hey, baby. You want to go for a ride?" another heckled.

The women acted none too impressed with the attention from the men, and berated her with calls of *bitch, slut*, and *whore.*

What started as a poke in the giant's eye had twisted into an unruly scene, where Lisa's safety, if not her very life, was in jeopardy. Weeks of anger and frustration had clouded her judgment. Instead of winning hearts and minds for her cause, she had the tables turned, and found herself the pariah. *How could I have been so stupid?*

A hand reached from behind, between her and the church escort, and ripped her blouse from the right side of her chest. A finger caught a bra cup and pulled it down under her breast.

"Look at that nipple. It's gray!" a voice called out.

Lisa hunched over and snapped the cup back into place. Her heart pounded as bodies fell in line to block her path.

The excited crowd snatched one of the security officers from her side. He yelled to be released, and then cried out in pain as he was shoved facedown to the pavement.

His companion leaped to his aid and yanked out a gold plated Colt .45 from the shoulder holster hidden beneath his jacket. Before he could say a word, a stainless steel insulated bottle crashed into the back of his head, knocking him cold. His pistol bounced on the concrete parking lot.

Lisa shook uncontrollably as the angry faces surrounding her twisted in wicked glee.

A balding man wearing a white collarless shirt and black blazer pointed an accusatory finger. "And I saw the dead, great and small, standing before the throne, and books were opened. Another book was opened, which is the book of life. The dead were judged according to what they had done as recorded in the books. Anyone whose name was not found written in the book of life was thrown into the lake of fire!"

"Wait! No! Please! Let me go!" Lisa cried.

A woman grabbed her by the hair and pulled her to the ground. "You need to learn your place, you Jezebel!"

"You should stay with your own kind!"

"Undead trash! Go home!"

Lisa jerked her right hand up from the pavement when someone stepped on her little finger. The crowd gathered closer. The wall of death tightened its grip.

"Please! Just let me go. I didn't ask to be infected. It wasn't my fault. I just want my rights back."

"If your hand or your foot causes you to sin, cut it off, and throw it away. It is better for you to enter life maimed or crippled than to have two hands or two feet and be thrown into eternal fire." The balding man stopped by her side, reached in his front pocket, and opened a lock blade knife.

Someone gasped, and exclaimed, "He's got a knife!"

The crowd backed away.

"Troy! What in God's name are you doing!" a woman's voice called.

He dropped to his knees and held the blade up to her face. "You lust for a life you no longer have. If thy right eye offend thee, pluck it out! It is better for you to lose one part of your body than for your whole body to be thrown into Hell."

Lisa threw her hands in front of her face, and cried a shrill, "No!"

A policeman finally pushed his way to the heart of the fray as the man raised his knife. The officer tackled the man, grabbed the wrist that held the knife, and smashed the hand to the ground. Two other police officers joined in, subduing the man, and cuffing his hands behind his back.

Lisa pulled herself to her feet, arms raised to deflect the next blow. The officer who disarmed the attacker put his arm around her waist and forced an open path to safety.

CHAPTER 10

Margaret Spencer laid a lavender colored sheet over the breakfast table in her kitchen. Next, fresh cut flowers, in a wicker basket she and Joel haggled over on their first trip to Jamaica sixteen years before, went on top. She made a detour to the refrigerator and poured herself a glass of white wine before continuing her task. *It's five o'clock in New York*, she rationalized.

After a sip of wine, Margaret removed a vase from the bottom of a cabinet. Six pink roses went into the vase, then clippings of leatherleaf fern followed in the arrangement. Stems of purple foxglove with bell-shaped flowers hanging low went in among the roses. As a final touch, she added sprigs of baby's breath to give the bouquet a rich, full appearance.

Margaret stepped back, admiring her work of art. Such a simple thing, but it brought her joy. Simple pleasures carried her through the mire of what her life had become.

She drank more wine, feeling the warmth spread, and considered where to put the last rose. Was there a place for this odd-flower-out bloom? She too felt out of place in the world.

Another taste of wine eased the pain for a moment. Then Margaret's thoughts strayed to Rebecca, her only child. The only child she would ever bear. Because she couldn't give him a son—or that was his excuse anyway—Joel had found someone else in a nearby town who could. Ironically, the affair came to light just before The Dark Times hit. Joel had already left to start a life with his new family. She and Rebecca survived during the two years of the zombie war with the aid of church members. Joel tragically lost that woman and his son, and reunited with Margaret and Rebecca not long after the Z gas tamed the undead. Margaret forgave him, being basically weak, even blaming herself for his affair. She regretted ever letting him back into her life.

Rebecca was well on her way to independence, at the age of twenty-one, and in her second year of college. It had been hard watching her grow up and move from home. Margaret understood though, as bitter sweet as it was.

Rebecca's had a rebellious streak from birth. Margaret chuckled. *She sure was a pain in the ass to deal with while growing up. I'm just glad she didn't let Joel screw up her head like he did mine.*

If only I could live my life over again. I would be just like Rebecca. I guess it's all part of your glorious plan for me, God. I may not understand it, but I accept it. Like the hymn says, 'It is well with my soul.'

The door from the garage opened, and the sharp *slap* of books hitting tiles in the rear foyer announced her husband's arrival.

Joel Spencer entered the kitchen pulling his tie loose from around his collar. He was clearly surprised to see Margaret in the kitchen, a glass of wine in one hand, and a single rose in the other.

"I didn't think you'd be home. Aren't you supposed to have a treatment today?" he said, sounding disappointed.

"Good afternoon to you, too."

"Don't start with me Margaret."

"The treatments make me sick. I didn't want to feel ill today. I wanted to enjoy the garden. The morning was so pretty. I couldn't bring myself to go."

"You're gambling with my future." Joel opened a top cabinet and pulled out a bottle of Jack Daniel's and a tumbler. He poured two fingers of whiskey in the tumbler and threw back a mouthful. "You're drinking wine and playing with flowers like you don't have a care in the world. If your health turns for the worse before the election is over, you could destroy my chances of winning."

"Joel, you know how to say the sweetest things." Margaret drank her wine and rolled the rose under her nose.

"Don't get smart with me, woman. I've had a difficult day. I shouldn't have to remind you to keep your part of the deal. I kept mine when I signed the papers giving Rebecca half of everything we own when you die. Your job is to remain my wife until the election is over. If you die before, or word gets out about the cancer, the deal's off."

Margaret stiffened her back. "The treatment for the melanoma is to put money in Doctor's pockets. Luxury cars and mistresses are expensive. I've done enough reading on the subject to know the treatments don't add much to the quality of life. Stop worrying. I've got two years easily to live—even if I stopped taking treatments. If you get the nomination the election will be over long, long before that."

"Oh, I'll get the nomination all right. The campaign is peaking against Poundstone, and the polls project me to be ahead by ten points for the primary." Joel finished his whiskey and set the glass in the sink.

He put one hand on his hip and pointed at Margaret with the other. "Do you know what your daughter did today?"

"She's your daughter too."

"Can it. Do you know what Rebecca did?"

"It's Saturday. She probably woke up in her dorm at noon and is planning what to do with her friends tonight."

"She was at the rally."

Margaret turned her back to Joel. "Oh really, did she sit with you on the stage?" Her body tensed.

Joel took two steps closer. "You knew she would be there, didn't you?"

Margaret closed her eyes and tightened her jaw. "No, I didn't know she was going to be at the rally today."

Joel stepped closer. "Maybe not. But you do know she's involved in that Full-Zombie movement, don't you?"

"How could you tell? Full-Zombies wear makeup."

"Her hair. Her body shape. And, the guy next to her, that Ben guy, was there. There's no doubt it was Rebecca."

Margaret brought the wine glass to her lips and stopped. She turned to face him. "Yes. I know she's involved in the moment. It's her life. She can do whatever she wants."

Joel's face turned crimson, his upper lip lifted revealing clenched teeth. "I ought to make you pay for this."

"If you lay one finger on me I'm calling the police. I don't care if that breaks the deal. I'll see you fall before I let you hurt me one more time."

Joel balled up his right hand and reared it back.

"If you hit me you better kill me. So help me God if you let me live I will bring you down." Margaret hoped her threat sounded believable. She wasn't used to taking up for herself.

Joel spun around and opened the refrigerator, removing a bottle of water. "I have a strategy meeting tonight, won't be back until late. Don't wait up." He never turned around and left the kitchen through the living room, picked up two folders off his desk, and then headed out the rear door.

As he put his hand on the car's door handle, his head turned to his Harley-Davidson Night Rod Special in the back of the garage. A cruel smile curved his lips. He strode to the passenger's side and removed his gold plated Colt .45 and holster from the glove compartment.

After threading the holster on his belt, Spencer opened a garage cabinet, and put on his black leather jacket and helmet. He brought the beast to life, and gave it the throttle, nearly scraping the bottom of the garage door with his helmet as it lifted. Mack was busy mulching the flowerbed by the side of the house as he approached.

Spencer raised his visor, pulling alongside. "There's a light burned out on the chandelier in the living room. See it gets replaced."

Mack rose from his knees and brushed the dirt from his hands. "Yes, sir, Mr. Spencer. I'll take care of that right away." He turned his gaze toward the kitchen window. Margaret stared back.

Spencer left Mack in a haze of exhaust fumes and the thunder of a near wide open throttle.

Margaret purged all the poisonous thoughts of Joel from her mind. She didn't want the torments of her life's history playing over and over again.

When Margaret topped off her wine glass, a container of Creole cream cheese alongside a few pieces of fruit reminded her she hadn't anything to eat since breakfast. She retrieved the cream cheese, a jar of pepper jelly, and an apple and pear, then placed them on the counter.

After unwrapping the cream cheese, she prepared the fruit and opened a box of whole-wheat crackers, arranging a handful in the middle of a silver serving plate, laying out the slices of fruit in a circle around the crackers. Margaret placed the plate on the table after she carried the flowers into the living room. She admired the presentation while she opened the pepper jelly and felt silly for thinking she should photograph it.

A knock at the back door had her delay her late lunch. It was Mack, with his face pressed against the glass. He held a ladder in one hand.

She went over and opened the door. "Mack, I was about to eat a little snack. Would you care to join me?"

Mack smiled. "Well ma'am, Mr. Spencer thought it best I come and change the light on that fixture right there." He nodded toward the chandelier.

"We don't like disappointing Mr. Spencer, do we?" Margaret teased.

"No, ma'am. It won't take me long to get up and do it."

"It never does, does it?" Margaret laughed. "Come in. I have something to show you." Margaret headed for the kitchen.

Mack opened the ladder and set it upright in the middle of the floor, then followed her to the kitchen.

"Ta-da! This is pretty enough to be in *Good Housekeeping*, isn't it?" She presented the platter to him with a show of spreading hands.

"Seems to me like that wine has gone straight to your head. Who gets excited over a plate of fruit and crackers?"

"Party pooper," she said, sticking out her bottom lip. "Won't you join me for a bite?"

"I don't think I can take the time. Mr. Spencer wants that light changed before he gets back."

"Don't worry about him. He won't be back until past midnight."

"Well then, I don't see how it would hurt anything," Mack said, removing his straw hat.

"Goody! Now, what will it be? Cream cheese or pepper jelly?" Margaret held a butter knife in her hand.

"I think I would like me some of that cream cheese." Mack moistened his lips with the tip of his tongue.

Margaret unbuttoned her blouse and unhooked her bra in the front. She then scooped a layer of cream cheese with the knife and spread it over her left nipple.

Mack moved closer and gently gave her a deep kiss. He moved his hand up to her left breast, cradling it as he moved his lips and tongue down her chest, and licked the cream cheese from her soft, pink nipple. It firmed from each stroke of his tongue.

Margaret softly moaned, knowing it would arouse Mack even more. They were both cripples, one way and another, emotional or physical, before they'd found each other.

Mack pushed the plate aside, laying Margaret gently on the table, and removed her pants and panties. He lifted her thighs and spread them. Teasingly, he said, "Mr. Spencer told me earlier to keep my head in the game when I did a job. I promised him I would and that I'd lick it to completion. I aim to keep that promise."

CHAPTER 11

The Reverend Will Hatfield relaxed on a green leather recliner, his feet lifted even with his heart and a Bible open on his lap, but he was no longer reading. His mind was lost in meditation, above the trials and temptations of the world.

*

One year Earlier

"Take a seat, Scott." Reverend Hatfield gestured toward a chair for retired Captain Scott Fenton and closed the door to his office. "I appreciate you making time for me this afternoon. I understand you have a sitter stay with your wife while you're away. How's she doing?"

"Mary Ann's having a good day. Thank you for asking," Scott said. The seat cushion burped air as he sat.

"How long did you say she's had MS?

"It started nearly ten years ago. It wasn't all that bad at first. Her only symptoms were annoying twitches in her face. She wasn't wheelchair bound until two years ago."

Hatfield took a seat behind his desk and adjusted his pants. "I don't mean to keep you from Mary Ann any longer than necessary. I know it's only been a week since you moved to Dallas and joined the church, but I have something I feel is very important to share with you." Hatfield leaned forward. "I know you are a trustworthy man. You were a captain in the Army Medical Corps. You have professed your faith in God to me. I believe you. Now, what I am about to present to you must remain between us. Do I have your word on that?"

Scott raised his eyebrows. "I can sense something's weighing mightily on your soul. There's only me, you, and the Lord to hear. It will go no further than that."

"Thank you." Hatfield repositioned himself in the chair. "The Scriptures state God has predestined us according to His purpose. I have always believed that, but I didn't truly understand what the saying meant until I met you."

"Me?"

"Yes, you. Allow me to elaborate. There are many Scriptures in the Bible that are troubling. Tidbits of literalness and sprinklings of metaphors that have allowed multiple interpretations— sometimes even from a single passage. The Church over the centuries has split into denominations because of the confusion. Only the Spirit knows the true meaning, the true intention of God's word.

"The Spirit spoke to me directly after our first visit. You told me how you were part of the team that developed the Z-gas and went on to create RZ and RY. I thought it was an interesting testimony at the time, but that information turned out to be the key that unlocked the mystery."

"I'm not following you, Reverend."

"Later that night during my private communion with the Lord, I read a passage from First Corinthians. 'The last enemy that shall be destroyed is death.' That led me to think of a passage from Revelation. 'And God shall wipe away all tears from their eyes; and there shall be no more death.' The Spirit entered me and dropped the scales from my eyes. Death was introduced when the Devil deceived Adam and Eve to eat the forbidden fruit. God countered by sending His son to bring the promise of eternal life. The Devil has sent the virus to mock the promise of God by raising the dead in corruption. Scott, you must turn the spear of the Devil into the sword of God."

"How do you figure?"

"The alien virus contains the genetic code for immortality. Before God can establish a New Kingdom on Earth, the last enemy, death, has to be defeated. In the Devil's feeble attempt to destroy mankind, he has provided the seed for everlasting life. God has sent you to work with me to usher in the New Millennium. You will engineer a strain of the virus that will affect the regenerating properties of the body without the curse of the transformation." Hatfield reached out and touched the back of Scott's hand as it rested on his knee.

The Spirit swelled inside Scott. The pieces of his life came together and formed the grand picture. His education in Bio-engineering, his service in the military, his wife's multiple sclerosis, and the timing of his relocation to his hometown. All of his life was perfectly orchestrated to put him in precise time and space with the Reverend's vision. *This can't be by chance. It must be predestined!*

*

A noise in the background pulled the Reverend from his rest in the spirit, back into the physical world of his home office. He wasn't aware how long the phone rang before he answered.

"Hello."

"Brother Hatfield?"

"Yes."

"If you have the time, I would like to get an update on the situation."

"I was resting, listening to the Lord. But I know He wouldn't mind a brief interruption to progress His mission. First, tell me, Scott, how are things on your end?"

"About as well as expected without having a live subject for testing. There isn't much blood to work with. What we have on hand, because of the age, makes me question the reliability of the results."

"I see." The Reverend paused. "It's truly a shame our first subject escaped. The Devil is working hard against our plans."

"Well, he wasn't ideal for the research anyway. It would have been preferable if he had lived at the clinic. I understand we couldn't have done that without someone, like his brother, asking too many questions. I was making progress with his blood, though." Scott hesitated, and cleared his throat. "Brother Hatfield, I still have strong regrets about what happened to Byron. It's my fault, and I can't seem to shake the guilt."

"I understand. But who are we to question the Lord's will? Byron signed up for the mission believing in the vision as strongly as we do, at least what he understood of it. I'm more concerned about which memories will resurface, and who he could unintentionally expose them to. He might very well become a thorn in our side."

"I don't think you need to worry about that. Byron's memories were erased when he died during gene therapy. The alien virus strain we tested on him revived him as an ignorant, savage, monster. The Z treatment makes him submissive but doesn't bring any of those memories back.

"It was a direct attack by Satan himself, no doubt. Our gene therapy had kept the virus dormant in his body for over two weeks. He was showing initial signs the altered genes we introduced into his system had started to fuse with the targeted DNA in the alien virus. Everything appeared to be going as planned. I'm convinced I'm on the right path. We desperately need a new volunteer to further the research."

"Scott, I have full faith and trust in you. You know that. My offer still stands. I'm willing to put my life in your hands and my faith in the Lord. When you are convinced you have the right formula, I will be the first to test it. If the Spirit is true, then we will succeed."

Scott nervously chuckled. "I trust in the Lord a whole lot more than I trust in myself. I need more data, so I can determine what went wrong with Byron, and how to avoid it next time. I don't want to do anything prematurely. When I administer the treatment to you, I must be nearly one hundred percent positive it will work. When I give my wife the treatment, I must know it will cure her."

"I believe your hesitation is the Spirit guiding us in this matter. As always, I have to worry about my human spirit getting in the way."

"Your humility continues to strengthen my faith that God is pleased and wants our work to continue. Have you approached anyone else who might be willing to volunteer?"

"I've opened a door or two with only a handful of my most trusted members of the flock. So far, no one has taken the first step forward."

"How about Byron? Can you pull some strings and get him a work assignment at the Church?" Scott asked.

"I'm working some of the channels for Byron. He still has a way to go before they'll allow him to work in the private sector.

He'll be on the road crew until he's proved he's developed enough social skills to associate with the Living unsupervised.

"If we get him assigned to the Church, he still would have to live at the State compound. He'd get regular medical check-ups. If your needle marks are discovered by a medical technician, there will be an investigation. We'd have to be very careful," Hatfield said.

"What about Byron's victim? Are you having any luck with her?"

"As for that Goudard woman, I'm approaching her from different angles. Nothing has produced any fruit yet, but I am hopeful." The tone in Hatfield's voice changed as he remembered her antics at the rally earlier that day. He was shocked to see her attend, and even more so at her uncouth outburst. She was a self-made activist. He was confident today wouldn't be an isolated event. More trouble was sure to come. The Devil had no need for rest.

CHAPTER 12

The NAAND office was located in a strip mall not far from the courthouse. Previously, it had housed a branch of Payless Shoes. The discolored block letters of the store's name still shadowed the façade. The building was situated near the center of the city and was equipped with full utilities.

Even though local, state, and to some extent international commerce carried on, limited resources forced the majority of people to abandon rural life. It was far more practical to supply the electrical, water, and sanitation needs for a million people in a concentrated area than if they were sprawled over the countryside.

A paper sign taped to the front window announced, 'Nation Association for the Advancement of Non-Dead.' The large letters had been hand painted in blue and red. Another smaller sign underneath stated, 'Volunteers Welcome.'

Inside the mostly vacant office, Rebecca Spencer sat on a metal foldout chair behind a three by ten plastic table. She and a classmate from college commanded two of the four available phones, to solicit contributions, and to answer questions for those curious about the movement. In the back, additional tables and chairs waited in reserve for the monthly meeting. A few empty shelves lined the walls, covered in a layer of white dust.

"Good afternoon, ma'am. My name is Rebecca, and I would like to take a few minutes of your time to speak to you about a national letter that the N-double-A-N-D is sending to Congress. We aren't asking for contributions, only for your signature and support." An electronic crackle carried over the phone. "Hello? Ma'am?" The call terminated, leaving dead silence.

"Okay, I don't know if she hung up, or if we were disconnected," Rebecca said to Katy as she waited for someone to answer her call.

Katy rolled her eyes, stuck her tongue through a large wad of gum in her mouth, and blew a small bubble. Giving up on the call, she put down the phone, and bit the bubble. *Pop.* "I'm really not in the mood for this today. I got calculus and biology assignments. I got my period, and I'm horny as hell."

Rebecca squinted her eyes and faked a smile. *How quaint. That was way too much information.* She liked Katy as she did most of the other volunteers. But as in society, there were various classes of people in the movement. Unfortunately, in her Chapter, the membership had more interest in the social aspects of the meetings than the cause. Couples hooking up after a meeting were more common than not. Some partied afterward into the wee hours of the morning. Having been raised in a conservative home, she had never been associated with such a promiscuous group of people.

The door opened, letting the roar of the highway in, as well as the young man who had attended the rally at the courthouse with her. His faded jeans and baggy shirt didn't call any special attention in his support for the movement. Full-Zombie attire was better suited for demonstrations. Both wanted to keep any controversy surrounding the movement apart from their academic standings in college. Plus, Rebecca still had to retain as much anonymity as possible to protect her father before the election. This was a promise she had made to her mother. A promise she would keep until that time, but not after.

"Hi," Ben O'Brian said, tightly holding a DVD case as he slipped his backpack from his shoulders, and tossed it to the floor.

"Hey yourself," Rebecca said.

Katy gave Ben a big smile, showing her bleached white teeth while chewing gum, but said nothing.

"Is that what I think it is?" Rebecca said.

"Yep, Jerry came through for us. It's all here, the raw footage from the rally filmed by Channel Two."

"Have you seen it? Did you get her name?"

"No, Jer was scared we'd get caught. He left it on a desk, and I picked it up when no one was watching. I couldn't take the chance of getting caught, so I went in the bathroom, and shoved it in my pants. I didn't get searched by the guard on my way out, but he did go through my backpack. Good thing he didn't frisk me."

"Your pants? *Eww*. I hope you wiped it off," Rebecca said, scrunching her nose.

Ben frowned. "I'm wearing underwear. I certainly hope you're kidding." He stared at the floor. "You know the only time you act like you want me around is when we're doing activist stuff. When we met last year you wouldn't even give me the time of day until I agreed to come to a N-double-A-N-D meeting."

"What are you talking about? We spend tons of time together—studying and hanging out. We've become very close friends."

"Yes we have. And I love being your friend. But I would like to squeeze some old fashion lust out of you from time to time."

"Ben, not here, not now. We've gone over this before. My life's too complicated for me to get involved in a relationship. College, and," she caught herself before the words came out, and darted her gaze toward Katy, "and you know—other stuff. Just give it some time. We'll see." Rebecca rose from her chair. The metal legs scraped across the tile floor as they slid backward.

Ben tightened his lips, small dimples pitted his chin. "Put the DVD in the computer and let's watch it."

Rebecca snatched the case from Ben's hand as he opened his arms to give her a hug. She headed straight for the computer.

He shook his head, and after hesitating a few seconds, followed.

She moved the mouse to unlock the screen and inserted the DVD into the player. The picture came to life with reporter Bill Percel, all decked out in his blue suit and perfect hair, adjusting his tie, and readying to speak into his microphone.

"This could take a while." She hit the fast forward icon on the screen, advancing the images. "Remember, it happened right after Spencer started to speak." The images sped by: the guitar player who warmed up the crowd as they gathered, Reverend Hatfield's introduction, and then Joel Spencer. Rebecca pushed play and waited until the camera shifted from Spencer on the stage to a woman down in front. "There she is. Turn up the volume."

Ben turned on the tiny portable speakers. The two listened as the woman hurled her accusation at Rebecca's father and his indignant rebuttal.

Percel then asked, "And your name is?"

To which the woman replied, "Lisa Goudard. My name is Lisa Goudard."

"Lisa Goudard. She's so beautiful," Rebecca said, eyes intently focused on the only woman she had known to stand up to her father. She pushed the pause icon, freezing the picture.

"Rebecca, what are you doing?" Ben said.

Lisa Goudard is a woman brave enough to call my father down if front of hundreds of supporters. I wish I could do that. Mom didn't tell me about the photos. Her story about getting a little banged up playing volleyball at the gym could have been a cover up. What else is she keeping from me? What else has he done to her?

"Rebecca?"

"What?"

"Okay, you have her name. What are you going to do now? One Sub Y shows her ass at a rally. Big deal. She was hauled off in shame. What good is she to us?" Jealously tainted Ben's tone. "None of the news agencies reported on her outburst. The people at the rally are the only ones who know it happened. All of them are Spencer supporters. She didn't change anybody's mind there. It's as if the event never happened. Bringing her into our Chapter won't be any different than anyone else walking in off the street."

Rebecca grabbed a nearby chair and sat as she closed the media player window and connected to the internet. Her fingers danced on the keyboard, typing in Lisa Goudard's name on a search engine, and clicked on a link from *Dallas News*. She read the tragic story. The attack, the death of Robert Sanders, and the injury Lisa received from the Non-Dead. The story ended by reporting Lisa Goudard was expected to have a full recovery.

Rebecca closed the tab and scrolled down the search engine choices until she found Lisa's address and telephone number. Without moving her eyes from the screen, she reached up to Ben, with an open hand. "Pen, paper."

Ben's expression tightened in anger as he opened his mouth to speak. After a moment of hesitation, he went back to the desk, and retrieved the two items.

Katy batted her eyes and showed her teeth and gum chewing abilities but still said nothing.

He handed Rebecca the pen and pad. She took it with a glance and offered no words of gratitude. The printer next to the computer came to life and rolled out a single page.

Ben's cell phone buzzed. He opened it to the incoming text message. It read, *What's she up to?*

He messaged back, 'At the office. She has the name of that woman from the rally.'

Waste of time. Don't worry about it. Working toward shutting that woman up.

'*OK.*'

You're doing the right thing by helping me keep tabs on Rebecca. I only wish I'd had known about this sooner. I'm going to send you a check to compensate for your time. Play your cards right and I'll have a place for you in Washington when you graduate. Keep me informed.

'*OK,* bye.'

Ben closed his phone and clipped it to his belt.

"Who was the text from?" Rebecca asked.

"Uh, a guy from calculus. It was nothing important. Hey, how would you like to grab some dinner later?"

"Not tonight. I've got some other things I need to take care of."

"What could be more important than spending time with me?"

"Do you always wear your feelings on your shoulders? It's not that I don't want to spend time with you. I've got some personal things to do. We'll have lunch together at school tomorrow, my treat. Okay?"

"Okay," Ben said abruptly.

Rebecca expected a greater protest and was relieved when he gave in so quickly.

CHAPTER 13

The electronic glow of the television and the setting sun peeking around the edges of the drawn curtains lit the room. Lisa hid under a thin blanket, curled up on her maroon microfiber couch, staring at the television, oblivious to what was on the screen.

Her eruption at the rally had been nothing short of disastrous. When she relived the memories of the walk through the crowd, she plunged into a bottomless pit of despair. Her soul felt torn apart by the talons of fear and the shame of utter humiliation. *What in the hell was I thinking?*

Lisa's identity had stayed out of the news, which proved to be a blessing in disguise, though her anonymity did nothing to advance her cause.

She could see firsthand how the media worked in unison to steer the political attitudes of the masses. Only one of the two local nightly news programs carried the story of the rally. The only reference to the NAAND protesters was a five-second clip at the end of the segment. A still-shot of five protesters with the writing on their signs blurred followed with the closing words, *A few members of the opposition protested.* Both reports ended with the exact same clip. The media were getting their marching orders from a single source.

Lisa supposed the media had always operated that way. The rich and powerful moguls teamed up with politicians to manipulate social agendas, with partial truths and intentional omissions, presenting stories with just enough credibility to influence the masses to do their ultimate bidding.

The ATP patch on her shoulder itched terribly. There was no need to wear the expensive skin toned ATP makeup while sulking at home. She obtained a free supply of patches from a nearby Non-Dead rehabilitation center. Money was tight now that her paycheck from the state was a relic of the past.

The financial system around the world had frozen soon after the dead reanimated. Anarchy ruled the land. What couldn't be acquired by barter was taken by force. Fortunately, the military stayed intact, and was able to maintain some semblance of order. Moreover, through the incredible leadership of four-star General Frank Herbert, the military eventually stopped the onslaught of zombies. Holding on nearly to the breaking point, buying enough time for the Z-gas to be developed, and finally bringing the outbreak under control.

The financial market eventually returned to order after a slow start. Once goods became readily available, Lisa bought whatever she could afford that caught her fancy. Life without new things had been a life without hope. Her addiction to the newest fashions and the finer things money could buy was born from the sacrifices made during The Dark Times. With the future so uncertain, she adopted a *live for today* attitude. If it all came crashing down again through another outbreak, she would have no regrets. If the world came to an end tomorrow she would meet it with wine on her breath, chocolate on her fingers, and dressed in the latest fashions.

Her eyes focused on the television as a familiar face came into view. Former Vice President Joe Biden appeared on a small stage next to a member of the Non-Dead. Biden looked so old she first thought he was a Sub Z, withered from the loss of skin elasticity. She turned up the volume to hear him speak.

"Ladies and gentleman, it is with great honor that I have the privilege to introduce my choice, the next Senator of the great state of Delaware, Martin J. Allen." Tremendous applause rose from the background.

"I mean, you got the first mainstream Non-Dead running for office who is articulate and bright and clean and never tasted human flesh." He paused. "I mean, that's a storybook, man. He has a desire to represent his state and serve his country. An ex-president of Electrical Union one-o-two, this man knows how to get the job done. Remember him as your write-in candidate on October fifth."

Someone *booed* in the background.

Biden's face contorted as if he smelled something bad, and he shook his finger toward the camera. "Hey, Sub Ys are people too."

More applause rose in the background. He continued. "Send a good man to Washington, a loving, caring member of the Non-Dead. It would be one big fucking deal."

An electronic beep blocked out the word *fucking*, but Lisa read his lips, and knew well of his reputation. This was national news, and it contrasted greatly to her local news. The liberal northeast appeared to be more progressive in the Non-Dead zeitgeist.

Perhaps the answer to all her problems lay in starting a new life in a state with more liberal laws for the Non-Dead. But where would she go? What would she do? Some glorified manual labor job?

The phone rang shattering thoughts of a new life. She picked it up; the caller ID listed a number, but no name.

"Hello," she answered, hesitantly.

"Am I speaking to Miss Goudard? Lisa Goudard?"

"Yes, and you are?"

"My name is Ted. I represent Hennington Biomedical Research Center."

"Never heard of it."

"Yes, well, it's a private research lab. We've been in operation only for the last year." Ted stopped and cleared his throat. "Because of your current condition, our medical team would like to study your digestive system, and your ATP absorption abilities. Sub Ys are unique in that they can still absorb nutrition from the stomach, although the virus in the body is more efficiently fueled by the ATP."

"Gee, you sure do know a lot of my personal history. I don't remember signing any papers releasing my medical records to you. I don't post personal information on the internet. How do you know of my, 'condition?' "

"Medical Records for the Non-Dead are not protected by the privacy act. It's a carryover from the days when the virus was rampant and no way to prevent it. All stops were removed to expedite the sharing of information in the quest to discover a vaccine. Our findings lead us to believe that you would be an excellent candidate for a twelve-month program our research team is ready to implement."

"What kind of research?"

"Our team believes if we can find ways for the Living to use ATP as a nutrition supplement, hunger around the world could be cured."

"Sounds noble, but what's the other part?"

"The other part? What do you mean?"

"The part where you guys make a shit-load of money after sticking me with a needle a thousand times a day."

"ATP is the basic nutrient that fuels the cells in the human body. There is no excessive weight gain associated with its production and absorption. The cells absorb only what's needed to carry out natural functions. The fat cells in the body cease the need to store energy for reserve, so they'll shrink. Thus, we hope our findings will lead to a product to aid in weight reduction in the developed countries."

"Got it. Get rich off fat people trying to lose weight. That sounds like a pretty good scam. It's been working for years."

"So, you're interested in joining us then?"

"Details?"

"My, you are quick to the point."

"I shave with Occam's razor."

The silence that followed meant her last comment flew right over Ted's head.

"You'll live at the Dallas facility for the entire twelve months. All your basic needs and limited luxuries are included. A monthly deposit of five thousand dollars will be made in your account for your participation."

Five thousand a month was more than she had been earning as a health inspector for the state. The proposition sounded too good to be true.

"All you need to do is get your personal affairs in order. We'll send a van from the Center to pick you up when you're ready, preferably by the end of this week. You won't be allowed to leave the facility once you're admitted. Your environment must be totally controlled. You can sign the paperwork when you arrive."

"I'll have to think about it. What's the phone number so I can reach you again if I have any more questions?"

"Miss Goudard, we have signed five other test subjects, and the team was hoping to start immediately. I'm sure you're aware how competitive the pharmaceutical business is. We need only one more person to begin the process. Is there a problem with the compensation? I am prepared to make you an offer of seven thousand dollars a month to help you with your decision."

Lisa's suspicions strengthened by the exorbitant offer. "Nah, I was thinking more like ten thousand."

"Miss Goudard! Seven thousand dollars is more than the other participants receive. This is a business risk on our part, and there's no guarantee we will recoup any of our investment."

"That's my final. Take it or leave it."

A few seconds passed. "Very well, in the interest of the success of this project, we will agree to your terms. Can you be ready for departure in front of your apartment building, say, tomorrow afternoon at five p.m.?"

"I don't think so, Ted."

"Excuse me?"

"Okay, buddy, I don't know who you are or what you really want, but this story stinks to high heaven. What's this really all about?"

The phone went dead in her ear. She scrolled through the previous calls on her phone and pushed redial. A recorded voice answered, stating that number was disconnected, and no longer in service.

Her convoluted life became more confusing. Perhaps her outburst at the rally hadn't gone as unnoticed as she had believed. Perhaps supporters of Spencer's or Hatfield's church were trying to pull a fast one and get her out of the way. That would make sense. *A van picks me up in front of my apartment, takes me for a ride, and I'm never seen or heard from again.* Lisa wasn't one to entertain conspiracies, but felt she was becoming the focus of one.

A knock on the door startled her to her feet. The cold touch of fear crept up her spine. The knock came again, soft, and unthreatening.

Calming herself, she walked slowly to the door, hoping the unwanted visitor would go away. The knocking continued. Lisa peered through the tiny peephole of her apartment door and saw a young woman who looked to be in her early twenties.

She unlatched the deadbolt and opened the door until the safety chain fully extended—determined to take control of her life and not hide in fear of others.

"It's late. Who are you, and why are you here?"

"Hi, Miss Goudard. I represent the N double A-N-D—"

Lisa shook her head. "I gave at the office. Isn't there a law that prevents door-to-door solicitations?" She was about to slam the door shut, then hesitated. "How do you know my name?"

Rebecca Spencer closed one eye and winced like a blow might come her way. "I was at the rally on Saturday. I was with the protest group in the back. We heard what you said. That took a lot of guts."

Lisa was aware of the NAAND and had information on the organization in a pile of papers that had been shoved at her when she left the hospital. She had intentionally avoided any of the support groups, thinking she could make a case for herself with the Living on her own. That strategy had failed miserably. Lisa closed the door, removed the chain, and let Rebecca in.

"Forgive me, I look a sight without makeup," Lisa said, realizing she was barefoot, wearing pajamas and a robe, and no skin tone coloring.

"Oh, don't worry about that. It's late, and I did show up here uninvited." Rebecca looked relieved and then her lips formed a grin.

"What?" Lisa asked, noticing the smile.

"You sure looked a lot different at the rally."

"You mean a lot better. Gee thanks." Lisa found herself immediately liking this girl. At least she seemed honest.

"My name is Rebecca, and I have taken it upon myself to invite you to join the movement to fight for equal representation of the Non-Dead. I'm not trying to shake you down for money. The organization is seeking active participants. We feel the most effective way for change is through dedication. We hope to win the attention of others by being brave enough to take a stance and to encourage others to do the same. To move forward and do what is right for the Non-Dead."

"Yeah. I think I read most of that verbatim in a handout."

"Sorry. I memorized the lines. We're taught to do that. How about this? Our Chapter has over a hundred members. We meet on a regular basis and discuss strategies how we can promote equal rights for the Non-Dead. Would you like to check out a meeting and see if our organization is right for you? We serve refreshments."

Lisa thought for a moment. "I was going to say no—but then you said *refreshments*." She smiled for the first time since meeting her new guest. "I'll be happy to attend a meeting and see if it's something I want to be a part of. I'm not making much traction on my own. What have I got to lose?" Lisa crossed her arms. "One thing though, I'm not going out in public looking like I do now. No Full-Zombie for this girl."

"No problem. Full-Zombie is one way we try to get in the face of the opposition. I was in Full-Zombie at the rally. But I didn't look anything like you do. You still are so pretty in your natural state. I looked like I was dressed up for a costume party."

"If I could blush, I would. You sure are a good salesperson."

"Oh, it's not like that at all," Rebecca said.

"I'm teasing. Say, Rebecca, you look vaguely familiar. What's your last name?"

"Uh . . . Miller."

"That doesn't ring a bell. Something about your face . . . you were younger. Your hair was brunet, not blonde."

"Miller is my mother's maiden name. I go by Rebecca Miller at the N double A-N-D. My real name is Spencer."

Lisa frowned. "Spencer? As in Joel Spencer, slime bucket politician? Daughter of Margaret and Joel Spencer?"

"Yes. He's my Dad," Rebecca softly said.

Lisa threw her hands in the air. "I should have known! I recognized you from the files at the library. When I'm not job-hunting, I look for dirt on politicians.

"First the phone call. Then you come knocking on my door. What is it that you people want from me?"

"I don't know about a phone call. Yes, I am Joel Spencer's daughter, but I'm not here because of him. He and I couldn't be further apart politically. He'd kill me if he knew I was part of the movement."

"Really, your own father would kill you?"

"No, you know what I mean. I can't stand that arrogant bastard and everything that he stands for. The Living party, Reverend Hatfield's church, I was raised in that conservative philosophy. But now they represent everything I don't want to be."

"You expect me to believe you?"

Rebecca stiffened. "I can't help what you believe. I came to you because we need you, and I thought you might need us. Thinking that maybe we could help each other. I told you my real name. I can't help who my father is. So, I hope to see you in a few days at our next meeting. Here's a flier with all the information." Rebecca handed Lisa a folded pink piece of paper and turned for the door. "I didn't mean to upset you. I apologize for that. I hope you'll be there. I would like nothing better than to introduce you to the others."

Rebecca walked out of the door with Lisa still holding the flier.

Lisa locked the deadbolt and attached the chain as her only response. She let her robe drop to the floor as she headed to the bathroom and undressed once inside. She stepped into the shower, turned on the water, and let the water warm before flipping the handle. The soothing waters showered from above. Tears flowed uncontrollably. She hoped the water shooting from the showerhead was loud enough to drown her cries so her neighbors wouldn't hear.

CHAPTER 14

The sun pushed against the darkness with a soft orange glow as it crowned above the horizon. Andy Wells wiped the sleep from his eyes while slowing the big yellow school bus and turned in to the North Dallas Non-Dead Institution. Once a correctional facility for wayward youths, it primarily served as a home for Sub Z class Non-Dead. Its secondary function was to supply the manual labor force for county and state jobs.

Andy parked the bus in the usual spot, and fought back a wave of nausea when the stale air of the Institution hit his nostrils, just as he entered through the main door.

Jack Higgins was the guard on duty. "Mornin', Andy. Back for another fun-filled day crackin' the whip?"

"You know it, Jack. Gotta keep them slaves in line," Andy said, stopping to stretch and yawn.

"*Massa* Wells has a nice southern charm about it," Jack chuckled.

Andy raised his hands in the air. "I'm a bigger man than that. We's keep it simple. Theys just call me Andy, those that can talk, that is."

"I just thought it was funny and all. Say, are you feelin' okay? You're lookin' pale."

"Huh? Ah, stomach's been giving me some fits lately. Been having problems since I left the Army. I might have an ulcer or sumpthin'," Andy said, remembering the six shots of whiskey and four beers from the previous night.

"You should go see the nurse. She's a really cute Chinese girl. Tits are kinda small, but she's got some nice lookin', dick-suckin' lips."

Andy giggled. "Well, I'll think about it. I'll be better after I drop my first deuce of the day. Let me get going. See you, Jack."

"Take care, Andy."

Andy headed down the hall past numerous displays of awards and photographs. Phil Smith, otherwise known as Z439810, was the recipient of the Laborer of the Month award.

The bulletin board had a large calendar with special dates highlighted in yellow, along with various items for sale next to it. Hunting season was coming soon, and men were getting rid of last year's equipment to have an excuse to buy something new.

Joshua Hatfield's annoying face was also there to greet Andy as it did every morning, on an 11" x 17" poster, listing Wednesday night at 7 p.m. as the time for worship service. Joshua was Reverend Will Hatfield's nephew. The laws permitted ministries the privilege to visit once a week to spread the Good News.

Joshua's thick, sandy blond hair and plastic million-dollar smile agitated Andy every time he passed the poster. He figured Joshua to be in his early thirties and bet he had never put in a hard day's work in his life. The Streets of Gold Church was paying him to dress in thousand-dollar suits and run his yap in front of a bunch of Non-Deads that didn't know any better if he were talking about God or the man in the moon.

I bet that boy gets all them old widders at the church to leave their fortunes to him when they die, after he charms the gray out of their hair, he thought.

The scripture at the bottom of the poster chapped his ass too: 'Blessed are the peacemakers, for they will be called the sons of God.' Andy felt himself to be a peacemaker. The Army trained every recruit to be one. You brought peace by killing the enemy. He didn't think himself worthy enough to be considered a son of God.

He pushed Joshua out of his head and continued down the empty halls. Morning wakeup for the *guests* of the Institution was still twenty minutes away. Andy needed a shot of caffeine in the worst way to help clear the haze from his head.

The Warden, Samuel Cain, scribbled notes on his daily work list when Andy entered the break room. He put a check by Andy's name on the schedule and went back to adjusting the assignments.

The other five crew bosses were in various stages of their morning ritual—reading the paper, eating cereal, and shooting the bull around the coffee pot.

"Hey, fellers, got any fresh coffee?" Andy asked.

The party of three opened their ranks and allowed Andy to join the discussion.

"Sure, man, come get you some," Larry said, as he stepped out of the way.

Jim picked up his story from where he left off, "Like I was saying, my brother-in-law comes to see me on the jobsite to collect on a bet. I took Yarshinka over Cummings in the tennis match—"

"I hate that we have to resort to bet on prissy-ass tennis matches. Give me the good old days where we could bet on football and horse racing," Greg interrupted.

"Yeah, like I was saying, my brother-in-law came to collect his hundred bucks while we were repaving Camelot Subdivision. Now, he's an EMT, and he always has some story about car crashes and scraping bodies off the side of the road, and hauling them to the hospital. He brags he has seen so much blood and guts that he has an iron system, and nothing can gross him out.

"So, I got to thinking, and when he came by, I asked him if he wanted to go double or nothing on a bet. Well, that man would bet on tails if you gave him two to one odds on a double-headed quarter. I bet him I could make him toss his cookies in less than a minute, double or nothing.

"He laughed in my face, and asked me if I was *stupid or something*. But he said he was willing to take more of my money, and we shook on it.

"Ol' Nine-nine-six was shoveling up some asphalt that had leaked down into a ditch. I told him to go over in the yard and scoop up a pile of dog shit I spotted. Now, Nine-nine-six is about as bad as it gets on the intelligence level. Heck, he's borderline incineration from month to month. Anyways, that dog shit was real fresh. Kinda had a green tint to it. I had Nine-nine-six scoop it up and bring it over by us.

"My brother-in-law says, 'Dog shit? That's supposed to make me hurl?' And then laughs his ass off.

"I said, 'Start your watch,' and told Nine-nine-six to eat it.

"He grabbed a handful of that steaming pile of shit—some of it oozed between his fingers—and shoved it in his mouth.

"Well, ol' iron system brother-in-law starts dry heaving and loses the color in his face. He was fighting back from puking like a mo-fo. After about thirty seconds though, he started pulling it back together.

"I didn't have much time left. So I told Nine-nine-six to smile. Well, he opened his mouth wider than a horse licking peanut butter off its gums. Except Nine-nine-six showed a mouth of rotting teeth with dog shit smeared all over them.

"I had to jump back so brother-in-law wouldn't up-chuck on my boots!"

Jim's audience of three roared in laughter.

"I guess you could say it was his shit eatin' grin that won yer bet," Andy said.

The men gregariously howled once again.

"Gentleman," Cain said. "Excuse me, gentleman. It's getting to be about that time."

The four men left their moment of mirth and joined the other two crew bosses over by Cain.

"Sherman and Edwards, back to Highway seventy-three extension. Calloway and Hooper, pot holes on Airline Boulevard. Fillmore and Wells, back to Interstate six ten.

"Okay, men, let's get 'em up and move 'em out," Cain said.

As Andy walked past, Cain placed a hand on his shoulder. "Andy, you'll have a new addition to your crew today, to replace," he flipped through his papers until he found the number, "Z-five-six-nine-three-four-two."

"Yeah, ol' George. I sure do miss George. He reminded me of George Burns. That's why I called him George. If you stuck a cigar in his mouth, he looked just like him. I giggled every time I thought about it," Andy said.

"Okay, moving along. You'll have a very special member of the Non-Dead added to your crew. He's the brother of Rick Poundstone, as in Congressman Rick Poundstone."

"Congressman? Whoa," Andy said.

"His name is Byron. He has completed his basic training and is ready for the workforce. I'm not telling you to treat him special. But I think it would be in your, and our, best interest to make sure he doesn't get hurt. We wouldn't want the Congressman to crawl up in our business over here."

"I hear what you're saying. Orders received loud and clear, sir," Andy said, giving a salute.

"Knock it off, Andy. This one finished his training in record time. Keep him busy. They tell me he starts walking in circles if you don't give him enough work to do."

"Don't you worry none. I'll keep him busier than a one-legged man in a butt kickin' contest," Andy said, and then walked away.

*

Andy was two steps from the barrack's door when morning reveille blasted over the intercom. Each day, promptly at 7 a.m., music woke the Non-Dead from their nightly slumber.

He entered the 20'x40' room and turned on the overhead lights. "Good morning, Ladies and Gentlemen. Time to rise and shine— yer on the government's dime. Work a little, work a lot, it all pays the same." He began each morning with the same wakeup call, despite the fact there were no women at that Institution. The music too, was always the same, "Another Day" by the *Beatles*. Andy didn't like the song. Andy didn't like the *Beatles*. The Non-Dead performed best sticking to a routine.

Ten cots lined one side of the room and directly opposite mirrored another ten. The rest of the room was devoid of furniture.

The Non-Dead promptly rolled out of bed in all their naked glory and began removing the linens from their individual cots. Sub Z's shed bits of dead skin during their sleep time, more so than members of the Living. Each would be responsible for making their bed before lights out at the end of the day.

Andy led his crew out the barracks over to the laundry room where each deposited the linens in a large bin. Then, they continued down the hall to the showers.

Once arriving, Andy turned the power on what was essentially a moving sidewalk. It ran the length of the room, between rows of showerheads to either side in the front, and past a series of blowers to the rear. In the morning, a mixture of ATP bathed the Non-Dead for the daily supply of life-giving nutrients. After a long day of work, the showers switched to a mixture of soap and water to scrub them clean.

Andy took a step onto the conveyer and rode it to the end where he pushed another button. "Okay, soup's on! *Fallllllll* in!"

A green light flashed once by the shower's entrance. The first Non-Dead stepped on the rubber mat, bringing him through an atomized spray of ATP solution. The green light flashed again, and the next followed. The sequence continued until each member had received a fine coating of ATP, followed by the gentle flow of warm air from the blowers.

Next Andy led them to the dressing room. Each donned the traditional dark-blue jumpsuit of the Sub Z labor force. Every front pocket contained a daily ration of rawhide sticks. Chewing, or gumming (depending on the health of the teeth), rawhide helped the Non-Dead keep their focus throughout the workday.

Andy waited outside by the bus with the checklist in hand. As each of his crew filed in, a mark went by his number, along with a welcoming by the nickname Andy had given him. "Let's keep the line moving. Tater Tot, pick it up, boy, and get in. Booger, Chester, Brad Pitt, Abdul, Pie Face, Snake Eyes, Slim Jim, Butterbean, T-bone . . . ."

Byron Poundstone stepped up next in line. "Hold on a minute there, newbie. Hmmm, Byron . . . Byrooone . . . By-ron-i . . . Byroni . . . Byroni macaroni . . . ." None of the names he conjured grabbed his fancy.

Andy then toyed with Byron's assigned ID number, Z222360. "Two two . . . Tu Tu . . . Too Tee . . . Tooty. Hey, I kinda like Tooty. From now on, big guy, when I call Tooty, that's you. You come a-running when I call for you."

"Okay," Byron said, and entered the bus.

With all the crew present and accounted for, Andy climbed onto the bus, and took the driver' seat. In the first seat on the opposite side, Byron sat and stared out the window.

Andy shook his head and threw his hands in the air. "For the love of—what the heck are you doing in the front, boy? Didn't they teach you in basic when you enter the bus you go to the next empty seat in the rear and sit yer ass down? I know they didn't teach you to take the first seat you come to. I thought they told me you's a smart one?"

"They let me sit in front sometimes when they took me places. I like to look out the front window," Byron said.

"Well, that ain't the way we do it here. And it ain't the way I run the show." Andy cranked the engine. Radio station 107 KREA filled the cab with a classic country hit. "Tell you what. You're new, and we's running late. Enjoy the view, 'cause yer ass will be in the back where it belongs for the ride home."

Byron turned his head away from Andy, searching outside the window like he was looking to see something familiar.

As Andy drove out the Institution and down the highway, he noticed Byron tapping his foot to the beat of the song—something he had never seen a Sub Z do before.

CHAPTER 15

The rider pressed his chest against the gas tank of his motorcycle as he leaned into the curve. He traveled in excess of eighty miles an hour. Such speed would have been foolish if he had never traveled the route before. He knew the road so well he joked to himself that he could probably ride it with his eyes closed.

The cloak of night shrouded his escape from the pressures of daily life. The hunger for freedom had grown into a ravenous monster ready to devour any obstacle that dared to step in his way.

The weight of his responsibilities muddled his mind and pulled at his body, till sometimes he felt the urge to climb on his motorcycle, and ride without a destination in mind. He would keep riding and not stop until he was sure his life was too far away to ever catch up with him again.

He would never realize that dream. His purpose in life was too great for him to act so selfishly. His obligations were to God Himself. Though his spirit was willing, he was only a mortal man, and found that his flesh was weak. Tonight, he would reward himself for his self-denials. He needed inner release to give himself a boost of power that would be enough to tide him over the next week.

The time was close to midnight. The highway was a black void cutting through trees that stood on either side as dark sentinels guarding the road. Garland was a small town, one of the farthest from Dallas that still had electrical service. The available power fueled the cheap hotels, convenience stores, and bars. The area had evolved into a refuge for biker gangs, illegal aliens, or any drifter sort.

Garland operated under the law of the Old West: Every man armed, and every man knew pulling a gun to start trouble would aim several more guns back at him. The strategy proved successful, drawing the reprobates of society to Garland like flies to dead meat.

The State Police laid a heavy hand outside the town limits to ensure its disease didn't spread. The residents understood to keep to themselves or risked rule by the boot of the law.

The glow from the business district in the distance grew larger. The handmade sign, 'Welcome to Devil's Bone,' placed in front of the Garland welcoming sign, was nothing more than a blur as his engine screamed past. The rider let off the throttle to slow from his speed of one hundred ten miles an hour as his first stop sped into view.

The engine whined down in pitch as the rider steered into a dimly lit fuel and food store named Hit the Spot. He came to a stop in front of the bagged ice freezer, killed the engine, and flexed the stress from the long ride out of his arms and hands.

The smell of gas fumes, spoiled milk, and puke from the dumpster on the side of the building permeated the air as he lifted his visor. The gold plated Colt .45 rested in its pancake holster in the small of his back, ready for action.

The rider dismounted and walked toward the front door. Two underage boys sipping from twenty-four-ounce beers gave him a wary stare as he ambled by, still wearing his metallic red full-face helmet.

A blackish-red cockroach with its antenna curiously searching the surroundings perched on the door handle. The rider carefully maneuvered his right hand over by its front legs. After checking out the leather-clad bridge, the roach crawled onto the back of a finger.

The two teens curiously looked at one another. One wrinkled his nose.

The roach climbed across the hand, over each knuckle, until it rounded the little finger. The rider turned his palm upward and held the roach toward the teens. "What do you think I should name it?"

The teen who had wrinkled his nose, said, "Why?"

"I like to name my pets. Do you think it's a boy or a girl?"

"I don't know. How can you tell?"

Pinching the roach gently between his thumb and forefinger, he lifted his helmet with his other hand, brought the roach up to his lips, and kissed it. "It's a girl." The rider stepped forward and shoved the roach toward the teen's face. "Your turn. She likes you."

Beer sloshed over his T-shirt as he jumped in retreat. "You crazy? Get that thing away."

"How about you two pricks get the fuck out of here before I make you eat it?"

The two left in a slow trot down the oil and antifreeze stained parking lot, past a dim streetlight—occasionally glancing back along the way—until they were out of sight.

The rider reached in his pocket, pulled out a clear plastic container, and held it to the light. The roach trapped inside was dead. "Well, my new friend, looks like the previous tenant has seen better days."

He opened the lid and emptied the dead insect to the ground, carefully scooped the live roach in the mouth of the container, and resealed the lid. "Welcome to your new home."

A small Hispanic man worked behind the counter. His hand plunged underneath the counter as the rider entered the store.

A typical response, as people had a tendency to become unnerved when he didn't remove his helmet.

He ignored the clerk and headed for the liquor shelf.

His fingers traced a row of bottles until it stopped on a half-pint of Jack Daniel's. A weathered old man in an Army jacket heated food in a microwave and glowered at him when he picked up the whiskey.

The rider moved back to the store's front and put the bottle on the counter. "This is it for me."

The clerk's hand remained hidden. He narrowed his stare as if waiting for a reason to pull out his weapon and start blasting.

The rider slowly moved his right hand to the front of his jacket and unzipped a pocket, pulling out a twenty-dollar bill. After he placed the money down, he picked up the whiskey. "Keep the change."

The awful smell hit his nostrils again as he exited the store. The parking lot was empty. He opened the bottle, with his back to the door, and lifted his helmet high enough to put it to his lips, poured it down, and felt its fire hit the back of his throat.

The aromatic-sweet, caramel color liquid instantly quenched his craving for alcohol. It had been a few days since his last drink. The bite of the spirits followed down to his stomach and back up his nose as he gulped the bitter medicine.

He gasped for air as he yanked the empty bottle from his lips, letting the helmet drop around his face again. The rider felt the warmth of the alcohol rise within, bringing more distance from the tribulations of life.

A trash can with an ashtray on top filled with smashed cigarette butts gave him a craving for a smoke, when he tossed the bottle into the opening on the side. Smoking would be too burdensome a task while trying to keep his identity hidden.

The rider reached in the ashtray and picked out a half-smoked cigarette. Lifting it to his nose, he breathed in long and deep. He called upon all his willpower not to lift his helmet and light it. The cigarette dropped back into the ashtray. A puff of gray dust rose when it hit.

The wanton lust to debase himself was nearly overwhelming. He fought the urge to get on his knees and lick the ashes. To taste their bitterness on his tongue. To breathe it into his lungs.

The rider broke the spell of his temptation and focused on the night's mission.

He mounted his cycle and kicked the engine to life. His next destination was only a short distance down the road.

*

The rider pulled to the rear of the building where overhead the strip club's sign shined brightly in white neon outlined in red. A neon blue chubby bear, wearing only a necktie, *moved* his legs in a dance while lifting the top of his hat. The Dancing Bare was the most popular club in Devil's Bone.

The rider parked between a shiny new North American Motors luxury SUV and a dilapidated white Toyota Matrix made before The Dark Times. Muffled sounds of high-energy music from the 1980s emanated from the building as he trekked toward it.

He removed his gloves and entered using one of numerous keys from a ring attached to his belt. The volume of the music increased as he walked down the narrow hallway, past a number of closed doors, and finally to a plush office filled with large dark wooden furniture.

A topless, small-breasted girl barely over legal age—if that old—ran past him. He lowered his hand down to his crotch and bumped into her with the front of his body as she wrestled to unhook an earring.

"Hey," the rider said.

She turned to him and exhaled an exaggerated huff.

"Tell Normie that Rex is here to see him."

She rolled her eyes and moved to the side. Rex stepped into the office and raised the back of his hand to smell her musk.

*

Normie Cantrell sat on a stool with his back to the bar watching his talent perform on stage. A Churchill-sized cigar stuck in one side of his mouth while he blew smoke out the other. Two younger men on either side towered over him, arms folded—ready to stop any trouble before it began.

The young girl made her way past two tables of men with gazes glued to her. Normie was as still as a statue, clutching the lapels of his sports jacket when she went to his side, and whispered in his ear. The girl then left the same way she came. Normie slid off his stool, adjusted his collar, and headed for his office.

*

Rex leaned back in Normie's chair behind his desk. His feet crossed and propped on the edge. The roach crawled hopelessly against the side of the container a few inches away.

"I see you've made yourself at home," Normie said as he walked in.

Rex still wore the helmet. "Su casa es mi casa."

"Do you always have to bring a damn bug with you? Do you know what kind of germs those things carry? I pay good money to keep those things out of here."

"I picked up Suzie on my way up. She's the perfect companion. Never complains how much I drink or what time I come home."

Normie went to speak, and then stopped. He took a puff from the cigar, and spoke, "You ready for a drink? JD?"

"Yes, and yes."

"Ice?"

"No, just a straw."

"You know you can take that silly helmet off in here. There ain't no cameras. *Jeez*, I get the feeling you don't trust me." Normie poured a tumbler full of whiskey nearly to the brim, inserted a straw, and placed it on the desk in front of Rex's boots.

"Trust has nothing to do with it. Self-preservation, on the other hand, is a much stronger motivator. I can't go down without you going down. I know you love yourself too much to risk that," Rex said, dropping his feet to the floor, and sitting upright.

Normie poured himself a drink and took a belt. "I always know what day of the week it is when you come to visit. Why so often? The Mafia at least conducts their business once a month."

Rex lifted his helmet, searched with his lips for the straw, and drank until he found air when reaching bottom. Rex coughed and rapped the top of the table once with his knuckles. Normie leaned over the desk and filled the glass.

"You're not dealing with the Mafia, are you? It's not difficult to understand. I've got expenses. My interests are gaining momentum, and I can't afford any delay—especially with the elections so close at hand. I need cash as fast as it's available."

"I understand." Normie drank some more. "But I'm the guy breaking his balls keeping business going. Your cut yanks a big chunk out my take-home. I've got expenses too. How's about a forgiveness of debt for one month a year, like in that Bible you believe in?"

Rex leaned back. "Normie, do I sense you think you're bigger than the ones who put you here? Did you forget it was my associates who manipulated the legislation that allows your sordid business to operate? Laws can be changed. Permits can be revoked."

Normie scowled, the alcohol showed in his eyes. "Yeah, well you wouldn't get your cut then, would you?"

"If I didn't get it from you, then I would get it from your replacement. Everyone is replaceable."

Normie's knuckles whitened as he squeezed his glass. "Are you threatening me?"

Rex realized this was becoming a pissing match. "Calm down. This is just business, as you like to say. I scratch your back. You scratch mine. If I'm not in partnership with you, then I am with someone else. If I were to go away tomorrow, my replacement would be here knocking on your door one week later. Money makes the world go 'round and around."

"Yeah, but I don't get it. Everything you stand for in your real life is opposed to what we're doing in Devil's Bone. The booze, the girls, the drugs, everything you people preach against. Yet you still take our dirty money. How can you do that and live with yourself?"

Rex lifted the helmet and took a taste of whiskey to wet his tongue. "Every kingdom divided against itself is brought to desolation. Every city or house divided against itself shall not stand. If Satan cast out Satan, he is divided against himself. How shall then his Kingdom stand?"

"Huh?" Normie said.

"If we can use ill-gotten money against the Devil to ultimately defeat him, then his Kingdom cannot stand."

"It seems to me that there would be a more respectable way," Normie said.

"The Devil is God of this age. We have been condemned to operate within a world system under his control. We have to fight and win by any means necessary."

"Okay, so what happens, if, and I do mean *if*, your side wins?"

Rex spread his hands. "Then all things change. The Kingdom of the Devil will fall, and the Kingdom of God will replace it. The things of the old world will pass. All things will be new. The light will shine in every corner of darkness and everyone will change. There will be a new Heaven and a new Earth. There will be no more tears. None of the vices you hold dear in life will bind you."

"I'm not holding my breath,"

"Enough of this crap. What's been going on with Goudard?"

Normie sighed. "I've left messages on her recorder and mailed her some business proposals. I got nothing. What happened to your plan?"

"She didn't fall for the yearlong study at Hennington. We had her interest, but we didn't play our hand as well as we should. Pity, it would have been better if she had come along willingly. Apparently she's not hurting enough financially."

Normie smiled. "Don't give up on me yet. I know people—what they're capable of when they hit bottom. If I can get her to nibble on the bait, I can hook her with some fast cash. Then I can get her undying loyalty with drugs."

"Not too fast with the drugs. Let's get her dependent on the money, and then see if we can get her to *relocate* for more. We need to get her to the facility and get back to some serious work." Rex rose from the chair and stretched out his right hand. "The envelope, please."

Normie reached into an inside pocket in his jacket, pulled out a thick, white envelope, and handed it over. "Just like I said—clockwork."

"Thank you for your anticipation and for your promptness," Rex said, placing the envelope in his jacket.

"You staying for some entertainment?"

Rex felt a twitch in his loins. "Yes."

Normie smashed the butt of his cigar in an ashtray. "Something else I don't get. How can you look other people in the eye and tell them not to do things you do? It don't make no sense to me."

Rex crossed his arms. "Even the Apostle Paul had his *thorn in the flesh*. The mind is willing, but the flesh is weak. With my mind I serve the law of God, but with my flesh the law of sin. The women who work for you aren't alive anyway. They have no soul in those animated husks. It is a small thing that I should be judged by you, or any man's judgment. I don't even judge myself. He that judges me is the Lord."

"Hey, I ain't judging. I'm just saying. . ." Normie opened the door and gestured for Rex to leave, then escorted him down the hall. Normie stopped by a door near the end and opened it. "Take your time. Take all night if you want. Enjoy." Rex passed, and he closed the door.

Lamps draped with purple and red scarves bathed the room in surreal lighting. A completely naked Non-Dead woman infected in her early twenties sat on the edge of a king-sized bed. She was Normie's best preserved Sub Z.

Porcelain white makeup covered her skin. Her face and hair were modeled after a geisha. The breasts matched in size but weren't symmetrical. The implants had been improperly installed or perhaps misshapen by patrons' abuse.

Normie leaned by the door and lit up another Churchill. He blew puffs of smoke in the air until the entire end glowed orange, and then checked his watch.

"Are you here to have sex?" the Sub Z asked.

"Yes, you moron," Rex said, removing his jacket, and tossing it on a chair. His hand held the container with the roach, which he placed on a nearby shelf. "Suzie will be watching us. I like making her jealous. Keeps her in line."

Ignoring his comment, she said, "Do you want me to resist? Do you want to rape me?"

"No." He removed his shirt and kicked off his boots.

"Do you want me to be your lover? I can say nice things to you."

"What I really want is for you to shut up. Get on the bed and face the wall. Get on your knees, and put some pillows under your stomach."

The woman slid off the bed onto the floor and went to the nightstand. "Are you going to put it in my ass?"

"No, not tonight."

She squirted liquid from a yellow bottle into her hand, spread her legs, and shoved in the lubricant. Wiping the excess on her thighs, she climbed in bed, gathered two pillows, and placed them underneath her stomach.

Rex was naked but still wore the helmet. He massaged his penis until it was rigid enough, climbed on the bed, and crawled behind her.

He moved her legs apart and shifted his hips until his penis found the depths of her vagina. The coldness of her body engulfed his shaft, sending a chill down his back—threatening his erection. He gripped her hips tightly as he thrust into her.

Rex's rhythmic huffs and moans penetrated the hollow doors and spilled into the hall.

Normie checked his watch again.

As his body slapped against hers, Rex started to pray aloud. "Forgive me, Lord," Rex repeated over and over. Tears rolled down his face as he sobbed, "I have sinned against You, my Lord, and I would ask that Your precious blood would wash and cleanse every stain until it is lost in the seas of God's forgetfulness."

His voice rose louder and stronger as he pleaded, "Forgive me Lord! Forgive me Lord! For . . . uhhh . . . forgive me!" A loud moan followed at his climax, with a soft thump as he collapsed on the bed.

Normie cracked open the door as the undead woman struggled to push Rex off her. He was out cold.

"That took about as much time as usual. I don't know what's wrong with the sick bastard that makes him faint after he blows his wad. Must be a vitamin deficiency."

"Do you want me to stay with him until he wakes up?"

"No. I want that dead ass of yours to get back to the lounge and make me some money. You've wasted enough time waiting for this freebie. Now go. Get!"

The Sub Z woman lowered her gaze to the floor and put on a robe before leaving the room.

Normie moved to let her pass.

Rex lay on the bed, muffled breaths pumped from the helmet as Normie stepped to the end of the bed.

He took a puff of his cigar and let the smoke slowly out from his nostrils. "You sure are one sick fuck."

CHAPTER 16

Only one person waited in line at the front desk of Marriott Suites, Dallas Market Center. Behind the desk, an attractive female clerk with long blonde hair, eagerly waited on newly arriving guests.

Lisa was thirty minutes early for her job interview. She took the extra time to wander around the lobby, to get a feel for the layout. Painted a sickly yellow, the wooden beams and crown molding outlined the ceiling, and amazingly enough, coordinated with the bright yellow and red squares on the carpet. Lime green couches and chairs set next to dark wood tables. Ornamental lamps broadcast bright white light.

A Non-Dead maintenance worker dressed in the standard dark-blue Z-Class jumpsuit robotically mopped a spill from the tiles in the entrance. He was hindered by a noticeable limp. Lisa imagined a part of his left leg was missing, ending up in the belly of a zombie during The Dark Times. Overall, his skin was firm, and appeared to be holding up well to the rigors of his slave-like existence.

The clock above the elevator pointed to 10:45. Lisa went to the front desk and waited for the clerk to finish a conversation on the phone. *Thirty-five years old if she's a day,* Lisa thought, tapping an nervous toe. *That hair is about as natural a blonde as my tan, too, and it needs at least three inches chopped off the ends. It looks like a rat has been chewing on it.*

The clerk hung up the phone, finally.

Lisa plastered a smile on her face. "Hello, my name is Lisa Goudard. I have an appointment to see Mr. Gregory Stafford at eleven o'clock."

The clerk poked at the screen of her computer. "Yes, it's on his schedule. His office is down the hall on the left, room one-o-six. I'll let him know you're here. You can take a seat in the lobby. I'll call when he's ready to see you."

"Thank you, but I'd rather stand," Lisa said, not wanting to pick up any lint on her black jacket or skirt.

Working for a hotel would be far different from the duties she had performed as a health inspector. Still, her previous job did give her some experience interacting with the public—if restaurant managers fell into that category. Certainly, she had learned the art of professional discourse. Lisa felt she should be able to modify her skills to meet the hotel's expectations.

As far as she could tell, the job was nothing more than typing names in a computer to assign rooms, program key cards, pass off inquisitive patrons to the Concierge, and keeping that zippity-do-da smile on at all times. She imagined caffeine would become her constant companion at work.

"Miss Goudard, Mr. Stanford will see you now," the clerk said, hanging up the phone, and brushing the hair from around her ear.

Lisa adjusted the hem of her one button V-neck jacket, quickly checked the polish on her conservative two-inch-heeled black pumps, and strode down the hall. She knocked on the door of room 106.

"Come in."

Lisa took a deep breath, put on a smile, and stepped forward. "Hello, Mr. Stafford. Lisa Goudard—I'm very pleased to meet you."

Stafford sat behind his desk, a pen in his hand, as if he were posing for a *Boss of the Year* picture. Her application package held by a large spring steel paper clamp in front of him. He raised his eyebrows as if being surprised by an unexpected gift. "Miss Goudard, the pleasure is all mine." He abruptly came to his feet, reached out a hand, grabbed up to the first two knuckles of Lisa's fingers, squeezed, and shook her hand up and down twice.

Ugh. He's a knuckle cruncher. I hope he's not some micromanaging prick. What the fuck? He's looking at me like I just popped naked out of a cake or something. Please don't be a jerk. I need this job.

Stafford appeared taller sitting in the chair. Lisa had to bend her head slightly to meet his eyes. He was fifty-something in age, balding, with a pencil-thin mustache that had last been popular in the 1940s.

"Please have a seat, Miss Goudard." He waved his hand toward a chair positioned to his left.

Lisa sat, placed her purse in her lap, and crossed her legs. The stockings made her legs long and shapely.

"May I call you Lisa?"

"Yes, please."

"Good. You can call me Mr. Stafford," he laughed.

Lisa returned a polite smile.

"Now, let's get back to business. I see you're interested in a career change. Your last employment was with the state as a health inspector."

"Yes, sir, restaurants and school cafeterias. I wasn't involved in the health care industry. I completed a business degree from the University of Texas right before The Dark Times. The job with the state was my first full time employment, three years after."

"And you want to change careers? Why?"

"Personal reasons. My fiancé and I are no longer together, and I'm ready for a fresh beginning. I need to create a new life for myself. I know I will have to start at the bottom. That doesn't matter. I have no attachments or obligations to anyone. I'm even willing to relocate anywhere in the United States or the world.

"I'm young, I'm intelligent, and I'm a dedicated worker. I hope you see fit to give me this opportunity."

Stafford tapped his pen on his desk. "An extrovert full of confidence, I like that. You'll need that attitude to move up around here. And," he paused, slowing his words, "you're easy on the eyes. That's never a hindrance when . . . serving the public."

"Thank you, sir. I always try to present myself in a professional manner." Lisa didn't know if his last comment was a veiled pass or not, so she hoped the way she answered drew a clear line in the sand.

Stafford cleared his throat. "Yes, of course. The position we have available is on the night shift. The hours are long, from nine p.m., to seven a.m., six days a week. We can't match your previous salary. But if you remain with the company for two years and make scheduled advancements, you will have the opportunity to double your earnings if you qualify for an entry-level management position."

"The starting salary is fine. Two years will pass by before you know it. I'm eager to face the challenge."

"Wonderful. It seems though there were minor problems with your application. You applied on-line, didn't you?"

Son-of-a-bitch. "Yes."

"The national ID number you submitted didn't match any in the database. You simply need to correct the number, resubmit the application, and you can sign the employment forms."

Lisa frowned. "I'm sorry, sir. It won't be that easy."

"Oh really, and why not?" Stafford asked, lifting an eyebrow.

Lisa tightened her jaw and pressed her damp palms against her thighs. "My original ID number has been terminated, sir. An unlawful act forced upon me by a dictatorial government that has stripped the true meaning of rights and freedom from the Constitution."

"Where are you going with this, Miss Goudard?"

"I have a new ID . . . it begins with the letter Y."

"I see." Stafford stared at his desk, pen tapping. His right hand moved to cover his mouth while he thought. "So, you're a Sub-Species Y member of the Non-Dead. I wouldn't have guessed."

"See, you prove my point. There's no justifiable reason for me to be treated like a Sub Z. I received the Resurrection Y treatment after I was bitten on my forearm. I easily conceal the wound with theatrical makeup." She held out her arm for him to see.

"My brain is perfectly normal, and my body functions only slightly differently from yours. There's absolutely no reason why I can't be given the chance to do this job."

"What would you have me do?" Stafford asked.

"Let me be a test case. Let me prove to you—and everyone else—that I can act to the same level of responsibility as a Living. Let me prove I deserve equality."

Stafford thought a moment. "Legislation has been favorable to the Sub Y class. You're allowed driving privileges and a host of other rights. But it all comes down to pay and benefits when you're talking about employment. Your benefits as a Sub Y, health care and such, are provided by the federal and state governments. Your wages are set by law. As a Non-Dead, you're not even considered a full person according to the Constitution."

Lisa's fragile grip on her temper snapped. She sprang from her chair. "How dare you! I'm human! I'm no different than the mother who gave birth to you. This is America! Hell, illegal aliens have rights. I'm native born. I should have more rights than them.

"Doesn't the Constitution say all men are created equal? How can I not be a full person? I was born a full person. Can a piece of paper take away that fact? Can a piece of paper take away my humanity?"

"I'm sorry, my dear, there is only one thing that matters—the law. I'm not permitted to offer you any job other than a menial service position, such as in the restaurant, or with the cleaning staff. I would be happy to set you up in one of those positions. I can only pay you the standard wage for Sub Y, though. It will take two months for you to save up enough to buy another pair of shoes like those you're wearing."

Lisa fought to hold back tears. "It's not fair."

Stafford slowly rose from his chair, pushing her application papers to the side as he sat down on top of the desk.

Lisa stared at the floor under his feet in uncertainty.

"Life's not fair. So, sometimes, to get the things that we want . . . that we need in life, we can find other ways to achieve certain . . . goals." Stafford folded his arms across his chest. His demeanor shifted subtly from plastic professional executive to smarmy weasel.

"You're singing a different tune. Level with me. What are you getting at?"

"My, I do like your directness. It's a shame you're not human anymore. I could help you work your way to the top."

"I am human, asshole."

Stafford chuckled. "Not from where I'm sitting. And not from where the rest of the Living are looking down from. If you want to continue to enjoy the finer things in life, you're going to have to work a little harder for them."

"I'll work seven days a week if that's what it takes."

"Admirable, but are you willing go that *little extra distance* to set you apart from the rest?"

"Spit it out," Lisa said, eyes narrowed. *Show me your real soul, slime bucket.*

"Favors, you know. Sexual favors in exchange for money, in a mutually beneficial arrangement between two consenting adults."

"I'm not a whore, and I'm not a slut." *But you're a fucking slime bucket.*

"Sluts give it away. Whores sell it on street corners. Mistresses and gold-diggers do it in civil deception, approved by society on a certain level. Sex for favors is not as dishonorable as you're portraying it."

"I'm not a fucking prostitute." The words seethed from her mouth.

"Neither was the single mother of three who traded sex for her rent. Or the young girl in college who needed to make ends meet. It's been going on since the dawn of time. A woman would trade her body for food or a shiny jewel. If you think about it, it's not much different today in normal relationships." Stafford reached down and unzipped his pants, exposing his semi-rigid penis. "Look, you're not dealing with some unclean reprobate on the street. I'm a successful and respected man." As he massaged his cock it continued to stiffen. "It's not like you haven't done this for your boyfriends before. I can be your boyfriend too—at work from time to time. Nobody has to know. It will be our little secret. And if you prove yourself to be better than the others, I can make it *very* worth your while."

Lisa bit her bottom lip at the bitter truth of his words, and glanced around the room. With a sigh, she rose from her chair, and moved her face close to his. His eyes were filled with wanting, and his lips curved into a little triumphant smile. She was close enough to smell his sweet cologne, mixed with stale coffee, and cinnamon on his breath.

"What do you want me to do?" she said softly, deliberately stoking the fires of his lust.

"I want your mouth on me," he confessed in a whisper.

"Well, since your cock is being such a good little soldier, I guess it wouldn't hurt for me to give it some *special* attention." She pushed her application papers to the side with her left hand, placed her right hand on the inside of his knee, and slowly moved it up his thigh. Stafford's cock throbbed in anticipation.

When her hand reached his crotch, she dragged a fingernail from the bottom of his shaft and up the head. "Are you ready?" Lisa said, oozing sensuality.

"Yes," he whispered.

Her left hand returned with the spring steel paper clamp from her application papers fully open. She looked him deeply in the eyes right before she let it snap shut on the head of his dick.

Stafford let out a soprano yell so loud Lisa thought she would have permanent hearing damage. He reached quickly and jerked off the clamp without fully opening it, scraping off a layer of soft, sensitive skin.

"You bitch! You cunt! You undead piece of shit!" Stafford inspected his penis.

Lisa was already by the door, waiting to make an exit. "Thank you for the opportunity, Mr. Stafford. I hope the next time we meet it will be as equals."

The door shut behind her. The muffled curses that followed her down the hall only made her wish she could have done more damage.

CHAPTER 17

Joe Blassco gave a quick wash to the remaining dirty beer mug, and then dipped it into a sink of clean water for a rinse. The American eagle clock next to the neon green Bud Light sign on the wall read a few minutes after 5 p.m. Workers from the day shift usually drifted into the Thirsty Cowboy around this time, seeking to *knock the edge off*, before facing the problems awaiting them at home.

A skinny man sat near the end of the bar, in front of the TV. He mindlessly nursed on a pale amber beer and munched on a bowl of snack mix. His suit jacket lay across his lap, catching salt, and crumbs from the mix.

At the jingle of an old-fashioned door chime, Joe looked up, grabbed a bottle of George Dickel from the shelf, and poured some into a tumbler.

The barstool squeaked as the wood scratched across the concrete floor. Andy Wells took a seat next to the skinny man.

"Joe, when you get a minute. A double Dickel and water, hold the water."

Joe turned around and slid the tumbler filled with the rich goodness of aged Tennessee whiskey in front of Andy.

"Saw you coming. How's it going, Andy? Tough day at the office?"

Andy chuckled. "Just another day in paradise. I drive the boys to the road site, count them as they get off the bus, tell them every fricking move to make, count them as they get on the bus, and drive them back to the Institution." Andy sipped some whiskey and pulled his lips wide showing some teeth. The first taste always stung. "Same old shit, different day."

"Tell me about it," the skinny man said, eyes glued to the TV on the shelf in front of them—lost in his own world.

Andy glanced at the skinny man but didn't recognize him, and returned his attention to Joe. "Well, I guess it ain't all the same. I picked up a new member in my crew a couple of weeks ago that I ain't mentioned before. You'd never guess who I got."

Joe wrinkled his brow. "Someone I know was made a Sub Z and is working in your road crew?"

"You may not exactly know him, but you know of his brother." Andy looked to either side as if to make sure no one was listening, and whispered, "I got me Byron Poundstone, the brother of Congressman Poundstone."

"No way! How'd that happen?" Joe asked.

"I'm not entirely sure. I figure that for one thing, that Congressman didn't want his brother getting any *pre-fer-en-shal* treatment. That might come back to hurt him on Election Day. For another, Byron is something special. I tell you that boy has more energy than a five D cell vibrator. They put him on the road crew right out of initial rehab because he got beside himself when he didn't have enough to do. Not only does he need to keep busy, he's smart. They told me to work him hard in what they called his *readjusting period*." Andy winked and nodded his head.

"Did the plan work?" Joe asked.

"Not like they expected. Oh, I work him hard, all right. I load that boy up like a pack mule. He takes everything I throw at him and wants more. Hell, he's making me work harder by finding him stuff to do. He works three times faster than my next-best boy. But it ain't just the work he does—" Andy choked up for a second. "There's . . . there's something special about that boy too." He took a quick sip of his drink and composed himself.

"Andy, you okay?" Joe asked.

Andy wiped a tear forming in the corner of his eye. "I was mully-grubbing out loud— just like my momma told me to stop doing—and Tooty overheard me. That's the name I give him, Tooty. I was feeling kind of de-pressed, like I do from time to time, thinking about life, how I ain't got no real friends outside of work . . . and this bar. That's why I drink . . . ." Andy pressed the glass to his lips and remained silent. A few seconds passed.

"Andy?"

"Huh? Oh yeah, well, Tooty heard me say how I was lonely and wished I had more friends. He came up behind me, put his hand on my shoulder, and said, 'I'll be your friend.' I ain't been touched in the heart like that since that blind woman gave me a blow job."

Joe gave him a moment. "He sounds real special. You get to meet the Congressman yet? Does he come by on the jobsite and check in on his brother?"

Andy broke from his trance, regaining control. "No, he don't do that. But I hear he comes by on a regular basis and visits the Institution. He's been real busy, I bet, with the upcoming election. Speaking of the election, I've been hearing a lot about that Spencer guy. What he's been saying makes a lot of sense to me."

A customer on the other end of the bar raised his hand. Joe nodded and pulled on a beer tap, filling a mug.

"Even though it would eventually put me out of a job, it seems like the right thing to do, to stop relying on these meat-robots to keep things going. Heck, Spencer even makes it sound like if we don't, mankind will eventually go extinct. I think that's laying it on a little thick. Although, if I need to do my part to serve my country further by offering myself up for stud service, I'll drop my drawers, and say, *God Bless America.*" Andy paused as Joe raised a finger in the air for him to hold his thought. "What do you think about Spencer?"

Joe returned from serving the beer and filled Andy's empty glass with more Dickel. "Ah, you know, Andy, I don't like to mix business and politics. You never know who you might offend." Joe shot a glance over at the skinny man.

Andy nodded and winked.

"I'll tell you this," the skinny man said, his words slightly garbled from snack mix crowding his mouth. "If people start having more kids, we'll need to find a bigger carrot, or bigger stick, to make them work for a living."

Andy scrunched his nose and widened his mouth, and then said, "I don't catch your drift, *amigo*. We got more jobs than people now."

"Oh yeah, we have jobs. Our problem is getting the lazy class off their asses and getting them in those jobs."

Andy put his glass to his mouth and emptied it. "Well, if you're talking, I'm buying. Another beer?"

"Why yes, thank you."

"Joe, another round for me and a beer for my new friend . . . ."

"Manfred Wilkerson—call me Manny."

"Another beer for my *Man-ny*," Andy boisterously laughed, the delights of the whiskey loosening his tongue.

Joe served the drinks and propped his forearms on the counter, leaning in to listen.

"I work for the state government, Workman's Comp fraud. It was bad having lazy good-for-nothings leeching off the system before The Dark Times, and believe it or not, it's heading back in that direction.

"Oh sure, during The Dark Times everyone joined together and pulled their weight. But that's because it was a matter of survival. Fifth-generation welfare bums were just as interested in staying alive as the rich guys living in mansions. The poor ate as good as the rich to the zombies.

"Even after we declared VZ day, there was a lot of work to do, and people from all demographics were willing to do it. When we started training the Non-Dead to do our dirty work, some saw that as an opportunity for growth. Others saw it as an opportunity to go back to a deadbeat lifestyle. Some folks are happier lying around, boozing it up, and watching TV all day."

Joe shook his head. "So you're saying perfectly healthy people are claiming disability? I had no idea that was a problem in today's world."

"It is, and it's getting worse. I visit up to five cases a day. It's rare I find one legitimate case of disability," Manny said. "Give a man a fish, he eats for a day. Teach a man to fish, he eats every day. Give the fishing pole to a Non-Dead, you can eat the fish it catches, and spend all your time screwing off."

"Somebody needs to put a foot up in that ass!" Andy said.

"Hey, buddy, not so loud," Joe said.

"Sorry."

Joe spoke low enough for only the two patrons to hear. "You know how that talk show host, Larry Qing, went to the Bahamas and got that Resurrection Y treatment before his bad heart took him out?"

Both men nodded.

"He's got a short-wave radio program that comes on around midnight. My sister has fourth stage cancer. She's the one who told me about it. There's a lot of stuff going on that's kept out of the news.

"They're experimenting with RY, trying to grow new body parts. Problem is that once they're implanted, the virus takes over the whole body, and turns the recipient into Y class. If they ever learn how to kill the virus after the body part is grown, we may have something that's worthwhile.

"Now, you may not believe what I'm about to tell you, but I heard it with my own two ears. The other night on Qing's show, guess who he interviewed?"

"I don't know, who?" Manny asked.

"Ned Williams."

"Ned Williams? Neddy Ballgame? The Terrible Toothpick? The Greatest Batter Who Ever Lived?" Manny said in amazement.

"The same," Joe said.

"Baseball legend Ned Williams has been dead fer years," Andy said.

"True, but he was cryogenically frozen. His great-grandson snuck the head out of the country, and some jackleg doctor brought it back to life using RY. You wouldn't believe the story that man had to tell," Joe said.

"Qing had a talking head on the show? Fer real?" Andy said.

"Well, I didn't see it. It was radio, you know. But Ned confirmed that rumor about his head being abused while it was frozen," Joe said.

"I don't know the story," Andy said.

"Well, instead of freezing his whole body waiting for science to progress to the point where a cure could be found for what killed him, the grandson took the option to only save the head. I guess to put the brain inside a robot or something in the future.

"Anyway, they cut off Ned's head, and then went to freeze it in some type of vessel. With the head being round, it didn't want to sit up straight, so they put a tuna fish can on the bottom, and balanced his head on it before filling the vessel with liquid nitrogen," Joe said.

"Did the can still have tuna in it?" Andy asked.

"Probably not. The head would have balanced better if it were empty," Manny surmised.

"He didn't say. When they took the head out a couple of days later, the can was still stuck to the top of his head. Some technician thought he was going to be cute and knock a home run with the can by batting it with a monkey wrench. Problem was, he missed and smashed into Ned instead. After he and his buddies had a good laugh, he tried again. That time he hit the can, and sent it flying across the room with a piece of scalp still connected to the bottom," Joe said.

"That's just horrible," Manny said.

"Did tuna go flying out of the can too?" Andy asked.

"He didn't say anything about the tuna, Andy. Next week, he's going to have that old college football coach on, Dick Seybin. Remember, his head was frozen too when he died."

"Kinda gives a new meaning to the title of *Head Coach*," Andy said, and then grinned.

"Andy, this is serious. Don't you see how the world is changing in a way we never expected? This RY virus is out amongst us, and we aren't ever going to be able to put it back in its box. It's not just used to save people infected by the old zombie virus.

"My sister tells me that you can buy the RY drug on the black market. It ain't cheap from what she's saying. Would you do it if you had the dough? Buy the treatment, I mean, or would you rather go out the old-fashioned way?

"I was thinking, if you played your cards right, no one would ever know. You could move every ten years or so. Keep to yourself. Work enough odd jobs to put a roof over your head and food on the table. You could go on living for, well, I guess no one's sure. Maybe forever. I wonder how many have already done that, and are living among us now?"

As if on cue, Manny and Andy raised their glasses and drank, and then returned them to the counter with a simultaneous *clunk*. Their expressions blank, and their eyes staring beyond the bar's walls.

CHAPTER 18

The parking lot in front of the strip mall was unusually full, most of the stores had closed at 6 p.m. Lisa drove slowly down the street. The addresses weren't well marked, and she didn't want to drive past the NAAND office and have to turn around. Knowing she was close, and since the building did resemble Rebecca's description, Lisa took a chance, pulled off the road, and drove into the lot.

To her relief, the hand-painted sign on the door confirmed she had reached her destination. There were a good number of people inside scurrying about under the yellowish fluorescent lights that hung from the ceiling.

Lisa pulled her car into the next available parking space and set the parking brake. Her Nike Air Walkers were the most comfortable shoes she owned and carried her to the front door.

The ordeal at the hotel had drained her physically and emotionally. She had showered and changed into comfortable clothing—an old pair of jeans, an olive-green T-shirt, and a pink "Breast Cancer Awareness" ball cap.

She entered the building, took two steps in, and let the door close. A table with a bank of phones resting on top was on one side of the room. A few people meandered around a table laden with a variety of drinks and snack foods on the other side.

Toward the back, others set up metal chairs in rows for the meeting. No one seemed to notice her. She felt as if she were a pig that had wandered into a Synagogue. The fluorescent lights turned the skin tone on her arms a strange hue, adding weight to her depression.

"Hi, Lisa. I'm so glad you could make it," Rebecca Spencer said, as she walked up to greet her.

"Hey Rebecca." Lisa reached out and hugged her. Seeing Rebecca made her feel warm inside.

Rebecca stepped back, holding Lisa by the hands. "I almost didn't recognize you."

"I look that bad, eh?"

Rebecca blushed. "No. It's just you look so different from the other night, and so different from the rally. I—you know what I mean."

Lisa giggled. "I know. I'm picking at you. When I put my hair up, or a cap on, people have a hard time recognizing me. Sometimes I think I could rob a bank while wearing a baseball cap and no one would know that it was me."

Rebecca let go of Lisa's hands. "I'll have to introduce you to some of the members. First, would you like something to eat or drink? We've got a bunch of stuff over there—but no sauerkraut—sorry."

Lisa closed her eyes and wrinkled her nose, shaking her head as if someone had stepped on her foot, then she forced a smile. "I really don't need to eat sauerkraut. My organs won't go bad on me. I will pile it on a Reuben sandwich though. I get most of my nutrition through my ATP cream. I try not to eat too much solid food, you know, to save money on toilet paper."

"Really?" Rebecca said.

Lisa burst out laughing. "No, not really. The toilet paper thing was a joke."

Rebecca giggled. "Oh."

"Hey, I would like some water."

The two walked to the table. Rebecca fished out a bottle of water from a plastic tub filled with ice, wiped the bottle with a napkin, and handed it to Lisa. She then selected a diet drink and a ginger snap cookie for herself.

"Over there—homemade brownies. I could go for one of those," Lisa said.

Brushing crumbs from her lips, and talking with her mouth full, Rebecca said, "Wait, those are special brownies, and shouldn't even be on the table. Somebody must have accidentally put them there."

"*Ooo*, super-special-secret brownies. Do I have to get hazed or something before I can have one?"

"Nothing like that. These are for after the meeting." Rebecca picked up the container of brownies, put on the lid, and burped the air out. "One member always brings these things. I'm not part of that group." She placed the container on a shelf on a nearby wall.

Returning to Lisa's side, Rebecca put a hand on the back of her arm. "The meeting starts soon, so I'll introduce you to a few people first."

Ben O'Brian was glued to the same spot where Rebecca had left him when Lisa entered the door. He wore a mask of indifference above his folded arms.

"Lisa, this is my friend, Ben. Ben and I attend the university together."

"Nice meeting you, Ben," Lisa said. "What are you studying for?"

Ben's eyes immediately homed in on Lisa's chest.

Rebecca frowned. "Ben, Lisa's talking to you. Her face is not down there."

"I know where her face is," he retorted. "I was reading the print on her shirt."

Hello, Captain Asshole. You'd better not talk to me like that, Lisa fumed to herself.

"Well, if they're true, what are they?" Ben asked.

"If what're true?" Lisa asked.

"The words printed on your shirt, 'The Rumors are True.' What rumors are true?" he said in the same disrespectful tone.

Lisa micro flashed a scowl before regaining composure. She took a slow drink from the bottle and licked her lips. "Don't concern yourself, little boy, because you'll never have the pleasure of finding out."

Tension thickened as the two engaged in a silent standoff.

"Ben, go over and save us some seats. I'm going to run Lisa around the room real quick," Rebecca said, pulling Lisa to the side and away from Ben.

"Gee, is he always that warm and cuddly?" Lisa asked.

"I don't know what's gotten into him. He's a sweet guy, and he'll do anything in the world for me. But lately, he's really been on edge."

"I'll cut him some slack. God knows I've been a basket case myself of late. I hope he gets over whatever it is eating at him. I don't like seeing other people unhappy. It only makes me feel worse about myself."

"I think I understand what you're saying. Look, forget about Ben. Let's meet a few more people here," Rebecca said, and went to the nearest member and introduced Lisa.

The introductions came and went. Lisa put on her best face and pretended to not have a care in the world. She wasn't very good at remembering names and told Rebecca so. Rebecca said not to worry, and that over time, she would be able to put the names and the faces together.

The crowd consisted of a mixed variety of young and old. Rebecca introduced Lisa with the trailer, 'You know, the woman from the rally.' Most acted as if they were genuinely pleased to meet her.

Four members came dressed in Full-Zombie attire. Rebecca told Lisa that was the only way those four appeared outside their homes. They were the most radical members of the Chapter.

A few minutes before the top of the hour when the meeting was scheduled to begin, a handsome young man walked up to Rebecca and Lisa, adjusted imaginary sleeves at his wrists, and introduced himself.

"Bond, James Bond."

Rebecca laughed. "Yeah, in your own mind. Lisa, this is James."

"Bond, James Bond," James took Lisa's right hand and kissed it.

"A charmer, I like that. I'm Pussy Galore," Lisa said, wearing a big grin.

James froze.

"All right, you two. Cut the crap," Rebecca said. "James is our resident technical geek. He's got more cameras and electronic gadgets than the federal government."

"James Calhoun, writer, director, and international spy," he said, regaining his composure.

"Sounds more like a more respectable description for a peeping Tom," Lisa said.

James laughed. "Where did you find this girl? I'm in love."

"Be careful what you wish for, Hot Lips. You might get burned," Lisa said.

"Ouch," James said.

"Okay, let's sit down before I have to turn a hose on you two. The meeting's about to start."

Ben was near the middle at the end of the row, with two empty chairs next to him. He got up and let Lisa and Rebecca pass, and then sat down, and placed his arm around the back of Rebecca's chair.

Lisa leaned over. "I've been meaning to ask you, who is that guy sitting by himself in the back?"

"I'm not sure. He's not a regular," Rebecca whispered.

"I had this feeling earlier someone was watching me. I noticed him looking my way, but every time I tried to make eye contact he turned away."

Rebecca touched Lisa on the hand. "Well, you are the most attractive woman here. Who could blame him?"

"No, he's not admiring me from afar. Something's not right with that guy. He's creeping me out."

The meeting came to order. Martha Robinson, the local Chapter president, welcomed the new attendees. Lisa and two others raised hands when she called their names. Lisa glanced toward the back of the room not long after, and the strange man was gone.

Officers with different responsibilities took turns and spouted boring facts and figures about contacts made for the month, contributions received, bills paid and pending, and future rally dates. Lisa's mind wandered through the whole process. Fatigue eventually set in, bringing aches to her lower back and nether regions.

The meeting finally came to a blissful end. Ben popped up from his chair, clearing a path for Rebecca and Lisa. Some of the members said their goodbyes and left for home, some hit the food table one last time, and others gathered in smaller groups around the room.

A plump woman wearing brown slacks, flat shoes, and whose hair was in dire need of washing, retrieved the brownies from the shelf. A pack of men and women with a similar taste in fashion followed on her heels.

Lisa clung to Rebecca while Ben fumed on the other side. James joined the three, bringing another guy who appeared to be about his age.

"Lisa, this is my friend, Harry. Harry, Lisa," James said.

"His name is Harry Lisa? I don't think I like that. Makes me want to shave or something," Lisa's cheerful banter came across forced.

Harry politely chuckled. "Pleased to meet you." His blue eyes sparkled below his red hair and above his freckles.

"Nice to meet you too," Lisa said. She realized she was overdoing it and felt like a moron. She was trying too hard to be accepted, and it was beginning to show. "Okay, I'm sorry. I'm going to cut out the cutesy bullshit.

"Please don't take this the wrong way, but I don't know if joining the group is going to help me in accomplish my goals. I want the laws applying to the Non-Dead to change now, not ten years from now. It is a self-serving desire, and you may think it's unrealistic. That doesn't matter to me. I appreciate everything the N-double A-N-D stands for, and all that you, the Living, are risking. Legislation must be forced to the front burner. I want to get my old job back and salvage as much of my life as possible.

"Unfortunately, everything I've tried so far has failed. I'm ready and willing to try my hand again. I don't have much left to lose. Anyone have any ideas?"

"The next rally is three weeks away. That gives us some time to come up with something," Rebecca said.

"I've been thinking if we can catch that preacher Hatfield in some sort of scandal we could turn the election around. Spencer is getting a big boost from his church and their affiliations. The Democratic candidate, Adam Gray, is barely on the public radar. Spencer and Poundstone are both members of Hatfield's church. If Hatfield goes down, Spencer will go down. And even though

Poundstone isn't officially supported by the church, it's sure to pull him down too," James said.

"What do you suggest?" Lisa asked.

"I don't know. We need to catch him molesting children, or animals, or sleeping with a woman—better yet a man. Ben, think you could bed that bastard?" James said.

"Hey," Ben protested.

"It's a joke, Ben. Lighten up," James said.

"We need a scandal. It has to be something that exposes him but doesn't make us look equally wrong when we trap him in the act," Lisa said.

"Lisa's right," Rebecca said. "We don't want this thing to backfire on us. That's all the media will concentrate on no matter what he's caught at."

"I think I know a way," Lisa said. "I'll go to his church Sunday morning, make a profession of faith at the end of the service, and join the church. If *Cecile B. Demille* over there can get it recorded, we can put it over the internet. We'll have him saving the soul of a Non-Dead. That does nothing to harm our cause, it only strengths it. It weakens Hatfield's position as a minister.

"What's he going to do, un-save me later? If he makes a stink it will make him the hypocrite. This could shut down the Republican engine long enough to swing the election our way."

James raised his hands. "Yeah, that sounds great. I can hollow out a few Bibles for hidden cameras. We'll get volunteers to position themselves in strategic places in the church and record it."

"What if you're stopped from entering the church?" Rebecca said to Lisa.

"I'll try to sneak in after service starts. I'll dress in disguise so no one from the rally will be able to recognize me."

"What makes you think you can pull this off? Do you have any acting credentials to go along with your suggestive T-shirt collection?" Ben said, a slight sneer in his tone.

Lisa wanted to slap the expression off Ben's face. "I don't have to do much acting. I was raised a good Southern Baptist girl, and I have been a believer all my life. I may not know why God allowed this damn virus to attack the Earth. And I may not know why Bob was taken and I'm forced to live somewhere between living and dead. But I know a fart from a quantum fluctuation didn't create this universe by accident.

"Everything has a purpose. I don't claim to understand it all. In fact, the first thing I plan on doing on Judgment Day is to kick God in the nuts for taking Bob and turning me into a fucking zombie. Despite all I've gone through, I remain a believer. So, on Sunday morning, only the premise will be contrived. My heart and soul will be genuine."

Ben spread his hands. "Hey, *I'm* convinced," and walked over to the food table. He muttered something about getting away from that bitch before he strangled her.

"Asshole," Lisa said under her breath.

"Hey guys, it's late, and Ben's probably tired. I'm tired. James, get your equipment together and call whomever you can trust to help us. Let's not let too many people in on this. We don't want it to get out. Ben and I will be there. Don't worry about him. He's on our side, and he will be with me to make sure we catch it on camera," Rebecca said.

"It's settled then." James adjusted the imaginary sleeves on his wrist. "Drinks at my place tomorrow at five. I shall have a vodka martini, shaken, not stirred. James P. Calhoun—you can find me in the book. Call if you need directions." James bowed from the waist. Harry nodded goodbye and followed James as he turned and headed for the door.

"Lisa, I'm so glad you came." Rebecca gave her a hug, pressing her nose into the side of her neck. "Your perfume is divine," she whispered.

"Thanks. I'm jazzed now."

"Maybe soon we can go on a weekend trip together. Go to Huston and do some shopping. Make a girl's weekend of it. Stay downtown and party at night."

Lisa pulled from the embrace and grabbed Rebecca's hands. "My life's in too much flux right now. I'm kind of worried this church thing might blow up in my face like at the rally. On the other hand, something inside me says we can make this work. Maybe I feel more confident because I'm not going through it alone. I didn't realize how much I needed you and all the others to help. I don't know how to thank you." She tilted her head to the side. "I'm sorry for rambling. I'm used to getting things done on my own. I don't like to depend on others." Tears welled in her eyes. "I realize I can't do this alone. I need help. I . . ." She stopped and waved a hand in front of her face to chase the tears away.

"You're not alone anymore. We're here for you. I'm here for you. Good things are going to happen. I feel it too," Rebecca said. "We can go to lunch this week. Get to know each other a little better. Things are going to be just fine."

"I hope so. I certainly hope so," Lisa's words trailed, and she let go of Rebecca's hand.

Final goodbyes said, Lisa left the office, and returned to her car. Almost half the members remained inside, obviously having no better place to go. She had never cared to make herself part of a large group of friends.

When Lisa's eyes cleared from the earlier tears, she started her car, and took the short drive home. Tomorrow was a new day with new hope to help her get through it.

*

Rebecca dried herself from her shower, put on a robe, and brushed her teeth readying for bed. Thoughts of the night replayed in her mind. Ben acted coldly before she left for home but did say he would meet her at James' the next day. He was becoming more possessive of her lately. It strained their relationship.

After drying her hair and giving it a final brush, she went to her nightstand, and removed the photo of Lisa she had printed from the newspaper. It was hard for her to stop staring at it and get into bed. There was some kind of hold Lisa had on her. A connection, an allure, an enticement—unlike any feeling she had ever had for a woman before.

Rebecca eventually placed the photo back in the drawer and took off her robe. The light went out, and she crawled under the covers, pressing her face into a pillow and her naked body on the cool, soft sheets. It had been a long time since had sex, too long. Her last boyfriend, Kevin, broke up with her right before spring break her senior year in high school. They had been together two years, and she had no clue he was going to bail. She was devastated. When Ben came on to her in college, she'd been in no mood to trust her emotions to another hormonally charged young man. Still, she did feel an attraction too, but wanted to take things slower—a lot slower, before she shared a bed with him.

She rolled to her side and placed the other pillow between her legs, pushing her groin against it. What it would be like having Ben in bed with her? When she tried to think of it, Kevin's face kept looking back. The wavy blond hair. The jet blue eyes. He had been her first, and only, sexual partner. Well, at least as far as intercourse was concerned.

Excitement rose as she pressed against the pillow. Her breathing became shallow. Lisa's face replaced Kevin's. What would Lisa's full lips pressing to her mouth be like? How would that luscious body feel against hers? Rebecca's short breaths gave way to a gasp as sweet release brought her fantasy to a wonderful conclusion.

CHAPTER 19

Rex entered the room naked, carrying a medium-sized cardboard box, the top taped securely closed. Penitence for his failing came more frequently. Of course, he had only himself to blame. His façade to the outside world became more difficult to maintain as each day passed.

Short bouts of alcohol consumption and satisfying the wanton lusts of the flesh no longer caged bitter memories from The Dark Times. The temptation ever-present to crawl inside the bottle and never climb back out.

A single low-watt light bulb shed a pale glow across the empty room. The carpet had been stripped long ago, leaving the damp chill of finished concrete on the soles of his feet. The walls had faded from white to dingy yellow. Sour perspiration and the faint metallic odor of old blood lingered in the air.

Fleeting snapshots of his latest orgy with a bed full of decrepit Non-Dead tormented his conscience, fueling the rage of demons that drove him further into his downward spiral. "I'm sorry, God . . . I'm so sorry," he said, the words hollow in the empty air. "I've failed You. I failed them. Make it stop . . . please."

He dropped to his knees. Jagged pains shot up his legs to his spine. Only through suffering would God believe his repentance was heartfelt.

The bones in his legs absorbed the cold, unforgiving shock of the concrete. His memories escaped from the dungeon of his despair to force him to relive the past.

"We can't stay here. We must have sent a million roaches scurrying into the walls. You saw that, didn't you?" his wife said.

"I know you're terrified of roaches, Marta, but you must ask God to give you the strength to overcome your fear. There's a pack of demon-infested dead bodies out there that want to eat us alive.

*We won't stay long, I promise. Jacob needs to rest. Look at him,"
he said, pointing.*

*Their son had plopped down on a wadded tarp, his eyelids
heavy from exhaustion and the fever.*

A clamp lined with barbed wire hung from a nail on the wall.
He placed the clamp on his left bicep and tightened the wing nut
until the barbs bit into his skin. Waves of nausea almost emptied
his stomach. After his system adjusted, he took several handfuls of
dried rice from an open bag, and slung them on the floor. He began
the slow journey across the room, traveling on his knees.

*"You can't leave us here! The roaches are everywhere!" she
cried. Enough light filtered through the dirty window to see tiny
heads protruding from cracks and crevices around the room.*

*"Jacob is in no condition to travel. That drug store we passed
can't be more than half a mile back. Hopefully, the area's clear
this time. Anyway," he clapped his hands three times and the
roaches slid back out of sight, "they're more scared of us than we
are of them."*

"We should never have left the others."

*"I didn't trust the leaders. I heard they were planning things
that would have harmed both you and Jacob." He was reluctant to
speak of the moral depravity the strong were about to impose on
the weak.*

*"Don't leave us here alone." Marta's tears flowed, and her
voice quivered.*

*"All the doors have locks. You're safe. We need more water
and food. I should be back in a couple of hours. Just stay in
prayer. The Lord will see us through this. I promise."*

"You promise?"

"Yes, dear. I promise. I won't let you down."

The grains of rice pinched nerves against bones. When the pain
in his knees overpowered the bite of the barbed clamp, he twisted
the wing nut tighter. "Why did this have to happen, God? Why? I
trusted You. I trusted you."

He stopped for a moment to catch his breath, and then continued to crawl. "I know You're there. I know it was part of Your plan, but my mind is weak. I struggle to accept it. I'm weak. Keep me focused. Keep the true vision fresh. Bind the devils that accuse me."

The trip to the store had been without incident. He could feel the power of the angels leading his way. Surely God was on his side, for he found an ample supply of drugs to treat Jacob's fever, as well as food, water, and even a few bags of hard candy.

His outstretched arms with his hands clasped in prayer hit the wall at the end of the room. The rice was embedded in his skin. Turning to a sitting position, he slowly unscrewed the wing nut, and let the arm clamp fall to the floor. Uncontrollable tears flowed as he brushed and picked out the stone-like grains from skin.

It had been two days since he had left for 'two hours' to get supplies. When he was ready to return as the hero to his wife and son, the streets outside became littered with undead. He had found a ladder to the upstairs attic and watched through the fins of an air vent, until he believed it safe enough to travel.

Each minute of the two day vigil felt like hours. His mind created a thousand scenarios of doom and destruction of his precious family without him. "Get thee hence, Satan!" he would retort at every doubt of God's protection.

After arriving at the building, he threw the supplies to the side, and frantically tried to open the door. It was locked. He gently knocked, softly calling Marta's name.

After agonizing moments of frustration, he thought, 'Maybe she's asleep, or maybe sick from fever, too, like Jacob.' With his fear about to consume him alive, he left the building's door, and searched for the window that led to the room where they had taken sanctuary.

The sun shone down at an angle that struck the dirty window and turned it into a mirror. He couldn't be sure of what was inside.

He searched the ground for something to break the window, and found a baseball-sized chunk of concrete and some oily, red rags. After wrapping the rags around the concrete, he banged on the glass until it shattered and broke.

Foul gasses escaping the dead bodies of his wife and son chastised him for his late arrival. He moved his head away from view of the ghastly sight and struggled for a breath of fresh air. Cold shock washed down his back. The image of his wife and son burned forever in his soul.

Rex slowly rose and walked across the bloodstained rice, to where he had left the cardboard box, and picked it up. What were Marta's last thoughts before she died? Was she cursing him? Was she cursing God? He desperately wanted to believe she had caught the fever from Jacob and both had died that way . . . died before . . . .

The image flashed in his mind like the sun going nova in a dark room. His wife's twisted form lay covered with thousands of roaches. A large number were dead, squashed during her hopeless battle to keep them off. They were being cannibalized by their brethren, and her body was still providing food for the ravenous insects. Jacob had been stripped of every ounce of flesh, leaving only his skeleton. He had been dead, or too weak at the onslaught, to put up a fight.

"My poor baby . . . ." he sobbed. "I'm so sorry. So, so sorry . . . ."

He set the box down at his feet and peeled off the tape. Small German roaches spilled out like water gushing from an artesian well, seeking food, warmth, and a place to lay eggs.

As the insects crawled around the room, up his feet and legs, over his body, he turned out the light and tried to imagine her horror.

Her words, '*You promise?*' echoed in his mind.

CHAPTER 20

Ben had a seat at the bar with his back to the bartender while waiting for his fourth beer, his gaze wandered around the dark room, surveying the night's prospects. The guy-girl ratio appeared near even. He preferred it that way, as he didn't like to have his options limited once he entered "the pit."

The Full-Zombie political movement had given birth to a subculture who referred to themselves as Z'ers. Z'ers wore white faces and black eyes, the tattered clothing and prosthetic gaping wounds, but espoused none of the principles meant to advance the rights for the Non-Dead. The Dark Times had created a new breed of anarchist bent on breaking societal chains by exploring all the avenues hormones and virility offered. The Z'er disguise concealed them from the judgment of others.

"Here's your beer," the bartender said, androgynous behind the makeup. Ben had first thought the bartender was a black woman with short hair, now, he wasn't so sure. Ben looked in vain for an Adam's apple—that was always a give-away.

The music faded between songs, and the distinct exhaust rumble from a Harley Davidson motorcycle cut in. The engine stopped before the next song begin. The old wooden door to the underground bar opened, turning a few heads. A tall figure wearing a brown leather jacket and faded blue jeans strolled in, his biker helmet still on his head.

Ben laid a five on the bar, spun around on the barstool, and put the bottle to his lips.

The rider strode toward him as he slowly removed his helmet from his head. The white makeup on his cheeks slightly smeared from removing the helmet.

Ben lowered the bottle and nodded to the rider.

The rider responded with a smile and raised his hand as the bartender approached.

"Jack Daniel's, neat."

The bartender gave him a sheepish grin and grabbed a bottle off the shelf.

Must be a regular, Ben thought.

She served him a glass of whiskey and waited with the bottle poised to pour again.

The rider picked up his glass, locked his gaze onto hers, and downed the drink in one gulp—never breaking the connection.

She filled the glass again and left the bottle on the bar after he handed her some folded bills.

"Riding must be thirsty work," Ben said.

"Riding is the best part of my job. It breaks the monotony of my profession."

"You work on Saturdays?"

"I work on any—sometimes every—day of the week."

"Well, that pretty much sucks the big one. Good thing you have the night off."

"I'll drink to that." The rider lifted his glass in a mock toast.

Ben licked his lips. "My name's Volvagia. Call me Vol."

"El-Rod, nice to meet you. Do you mind?" he said, gesturing to the stool next to Ben's.

"Sure, have a seat. I'm just here feeling sorry for myself, trying to catch a buzz to ease the pain."

"What's got you in the dumps, brother?" El-Rod asked.

"It's stupid, really. I'm kind of hung up on this girl. Sometimes she acts like she's into me, and I think there's a chance. Other times she seems preoccupied when we're together, and I just feel like a bother."

"Where is she tonight?"

"Oh, we were together earlier, along with some other friends. I tried to get her to go out for a late movie, but she wanted to get home."

"That's too bad. Why didn't you invite her to come here? Perhaps the thought of some action would have captured her fancy more."

Ben laughed to himself and shook his head. "You don't know this girl. She wouldn't be caught dead in a zombie bar like The Coffin Club." Ben raised his bottle again for a drink and wiped his mouth with a finger. "We go to the university together. She was into the Full-Zombie political movement and lured me in. She's one of those radical types. You know what I mean? People looking for a cause to fight for. If this were a different time, she'd be saving the spotted owl instead of the Non-Dead.

"I got into the political movement to get into her pants. So far, I haven't even made it to first base. The only redeeming factor about the whole thing was finding the Z'ers. I hadn't thought much about going to a zombie bar. Thought the people might be too weird for me. But one day after a rally, where I was Full-Zombied up, I passed The Coffin Club. Since I was already dressed for the part, I decided to stop in a have a drink—just to check things out. I've been coming ever since. I don't know what I'd do if I didn't have this place to come in and unwind."

El-Rod laughed. "Well, I must admit, if I didn't have this outlet to let off some pressure, I might go off the deep end."

Three guys and one girl sat at a table close to the wall, to the left of El-Rod. Two of the guys were tied in deep discussion. One wore a fishnet shirt and black vinyl pants. The other wore a white shirt with the collar pulled up covering his neck, a black vest, and black leather pants. The girl wore a purple crushed velvet dress with a plummeting neckline that held her bountiful breasts in check. She was engaged in conversation with a male dressed Full-Zombie, his hair sprayed with black and silver glitter.

"Get your hands off my woman!" Fishnet Shirt yelled, after glancing over at the girl.

"What? All I did was ask if she wanted to go to the pit with me," Zombie boy said.

The bartender opened her cell phone. "Looks like the shit's about to hit the fan."

El-Rod stood and raised his hand to her. "I got it. Goths just don't know how to act in a zombie bar."

El-Rod slowly approached the table, his arms outstretched. "Gentlemen, gentlemen, please. This is no way to act in a place of love."

The two Goth guys were both on their feet, staring down Zombie boy at the table.

"Hey, fag, if I want any shit from you, I'll squeeze it out," Popped Collar said.

"Allow me to present you with my card." El-Rod reached inside his jacket, pulled out a gold plated Colt .45, and pointed it in Popped Collar's face.

"It can be redeemed for a one-way ticket if you so desire, but I don't think you would like where I would send you."

The bustle of the barroom had come to a complete hush, making the music playing sound louder. The two Goths turned to each other and stared blankly.

"My friends, I don't think when you entered the doors of our beloved zombie bar, you fully understood our rules. The zombie lifestyle is bohemian. Antiquated emotions of jealously and anger are not permitted here.

"By what chance led you to our abode in the first place?" El-Rod asked.

Fishnet tapped the front pocket of his pants. "Business."

"I thought as much. Goths are dealing some of the best weed these days. If your business is complete, nothing would please me more than to allow you the privilege to leave the premises," El-Rod said.

The three Goths nodded in unison. El-Rod stepped back and allowed them to pass. Before they reached the door, El-Rod called out.

"You in the vest, hold on for a second."

Popped Collar turned, his face drained of color.

El-Rod advanced with the pistol held at waist height and pulled a plastic bag from a jacket pocket. "I'd like to offer you a small gift in appreciation for your cooperation." He handed the powdery substance to Popped Collar.

"Th . . . thank you," he said with relief in his voice.

"You're welcome. One more thing," El-Rod's brow furrowed, and his voice rose in pitch and volume, "don't you *ever* set foot in this fucking place again." The words forced themselves past clenched teeth. His hand holding the gun shook.

The door banged closed as the three fled for their lives.

El-Rod let the pistol point to the floor and chased off the anger. After putting the Colt away, he remounted the barstool next to Ben. The crowd returned to the pleasures at hand. "The roaches have returned to their dark corners."

"All I can say is, wow. That was smooth," Ben said.

"Blessed are the peacemakers, for they shall be called the sons of God," El-Rod said.

The words worked into Ben's subconscious. He calculated where he had heard those very same words, and that very same voice, before.

"Son-of-a-bitch . . . ." Ben said, his mouth falling agape at the realization.

El-Rod downed another shot of whiskey. "What?"

"Dude, you should be more careful. Your hair—you should have sprayed some color on it. The way you speak . . . what you say. I know who you are," Ben said.

El-Rod froze for a moment. He looked down at the floor, and said, "Really, how's that?"

"I've been going to church with my girlfriend, Rebecca Spencer. You know her. She has to attend for her father's sake until the election. I've heard you speak more than once on Sunday morning. You always end your messages with the *peacemaker* quote."

Joshua Hatfield raised his eyebrows and shrugged his shoulders. "So, are you going to out me to my uncle?"

"Hell no. I actually have more respect for you now. I thought you were only a worthless, pretentious cocksucker. I'm glad to see you're human, too," Ben said, raising his beer bottle in salute.

"I'm an Associate Pastor at Streets of Gold and member of the City Council. The only way I could qualify for those two positions is by being a worthless, pretentious cocksucker. I'm just doing my part to make the world go around, like my uncle says sometimes."

"It's cool. You can easily find out my identity. Rebecca would never talk to me again if she knew I went to zombie bars. So, we're in this together. Your secret is safe with me."

"As yours is with me." Joshua finished his drink and set his glass on the bar.

"How's the buzz? Ready for some pit action?" Joshua asked.

"Why the hell not?" Ben hopped from the stool and stepped to a narrow door on the back wall. Joshua followed close behind and opened the door for Ben. The two creeped in, allowing their eyes to adjust to the black lights in the room.

A disco ball slowly rotated overhead, cascading stars over the glowing bodies bathing under black neon. The painted faces shone with eerie luminescence, as the whole room swayed in the sensual *dance of the undead*, to the bone crunching rhythm of a razor-sharp guitar.

"Hold out your hand," Joshua yelled in Ben's ear.

Ben lifted an open palm. Joshua sprinkled on powder from a plastic bag. The powder glowed blue under the neon lights.

"Is this what I think it is?" Ben said, his smile gleamed.

"Z-meth. Nothing but the purest."

"Sweet!" Ben touched it to his tongue and felt the tingle of the short-lived amphetamine enter his system. Its power flooded through him as if he had been given birth by the sun.

Joshua consumed a similar portion. The two men stood between time and space until their bodies melded with the drug.

Joshua leaned over and gave Ben an open-mouthed kiss, their tongues sensually entwining before he broke the embrace. The two undressed and tossed their wadded clothes into an empty spot in the corner.

"What are you in the mood for?" Joshua asked.

"I'm think I'm joining the group over there," Ben said.

"Suit yourself. I'm going over by the wall. Maybe I'll see you later." Joshua left and headed toward a line of men standing by the wall, waiting for their turn, and went down on the next in line.

Ben stepped to a small table stacked with towels and dipped his hand in a jar of Vaseline. He slathered his erect cock in a heavy coat and wiped his hand on one of the towels. He found a path between several couples enjoying the pleasures of the flesh that led him to an open ass pointing in his direction.

CHAPTER 21

The choir sang the last hymn as outlined in the Sunday bulletin. Reverend Will Hatfield waited for the congregation to take their seats before motioning the choir to follow. Standing at the podium with an expression on his face reminiscent of a starving vulture, he scanned the floor below, and the balcony above. The multitude awaited prim and proper, dressed in their Sunday finest to impress the Lord, waiting for their Shepherd to speak. The loyal flock filled nearly all of the nineteen hundred seats.

Hatfield stood a little over six-feet tall. His once rock hard, youthful features had given way to the pudginess of middle age. He would be fifty years old on his next birthday. With a smile showing his crooked teeth, he began, "My good friends and neighbors, God is glad you are here today, and so am I. I'd again like to thank all of you who attended the rally last week. It was a great time of fellowship. The message from God was proudly proclaimed, and His plans for our future clearly heard."

Rick Poundstone sat calmly on a wooden bench behind the Reverend. His legs crossed, wearing a brown wool suit, and blue tie. A large, black leather Bible balanced on his right thigh.

Joshua Hatfield sat next to him, his eyes closed in prayer, his face a whiter shade of pale.

The Reverend continued, "As you know, the Streets of Gold Church and my ministry have thrown our support behind the Living Party this electoral season. While I have never—nor will I ever—use time dedicated to the worship of the Lord for political matters, our brother Rick Poundstone has asked if he could deliver this morning's message. In the spirit of fairness, the Lord spoke to me, and said it was the right thing to do."

Hatfield waved an open hand toward Rick. "If you have been with us for any period of time, then you should know Rick and his brother Byron have been lifelong members of this church. Byron recently went missing for two months, and as God willed, was united once again with Rick. Byron is undergoing rehabilitation for his unpleasant affliction. Though Rick's and our prayers were answered for Byron's return, there are new challenges he and Byron must face. Rick's message will deal with our relationship with God when we are coping with adversity in our life. Brothers and Sisters, I give you our current House Representative, the honorable Mr. Rick Poundstone."

Lisa waited in her car in the church parking lot. She pushed some stray hairs from the blonde wig under her pillbox hat and adjusted the veil. The birdcage netting attached to the front hung down to the tip of her nose, giving her the most fashionable of disguises.

When the phone rang she pushed it to speaker. It was James Calhoun.

"Rebecca and Ben are inside and ready, middle row all the way to the back. Two more of my friends are in position near the front ready to shoot as you come down the aisle and meet Hatfield. Harry's got the camera zoomed in on the door attendant. He's videoing from an angle to your right side. So when you talk to the attendant don't turn your back toward Harry. Stand sideways so he can see your face. Is your microphone on?"

Lisa tapped the red crystal flower broach on her jacket. "Is this thing on?"

"Yep, it's on." James switched into his best director's voice. *"Okay, girlie, it's show time."*

Lisa nervously laughed. "So this is what stage fright feels like."

"Break a leg."

"Uh, that doesn't help. Wish me luck."

"Good luck."

Lisa closed her phone and climbed out the car. She adjusted the long sleeves on the tan notched collar jacket that covered her beige camisole, and casually walked to the front of the steps with her gaze glued to the ground, coming to a stop as she reached the first step.

She lifted the right pant leg to keep from stepping on the cuff. The pant suit from the Goodwill store was the proper length when she tried it on. She had been wearing heels then, now, she was wearing flats.

The door attendant wore a bright blue, ill-fitting suit. He waited with feet spread wide and hands over his private parts. Lisa assumed from the color he had picked out the suit himself.

She kept her head down and took each step in slow determination, trying her best to keep her hips from calling attention as she made her ascent.

Her gaze met the attendant's when she reached the top. He didn't break his stance but did offer a smile. As she moved closer, he bowed slightly, and pushed the door partially open.

"Good morning, ma'am. Better hurry, service has already started."

Lisa's heart beat as fast as it did when she was a Living. The plan was going better than hoped. Now, if only she could follow it to completion once inside.

"Good morning, and thank you."

Lisa reached out and put her hand on the door, making a quick entrance. The vestibule entry led to three large double doors. Lisa walked up to the middle set, took a deep breath, and slowly opened a door.

She had one foot in the sanctuary when the attendant arrived with a photograph in one hand.

In a low voice, the attendant said, "Excuse me, ma'am. Could you please take off your hat?

Lisa froze.

"I'm not trying to cause any trouble, ma'am. But you look an awful lot like that woman at the rally. I can't let you go inside and start any trouble."

Lisa shook her head and stepped into the sanctuary. Someone was speaking from the pulpit. She gambled the attendant wouldn't create a scene and disrupt service.

"Wait, you can't go in there!" The attendant shouted. He grabbed Lisa by the arm and pulled her backward. Lisa turned around, bringing her purse from down low and smashed him on top of his head.

The attendant brought his left arm up to block another blow and grabbed the first thing his hand met, her hat. The blonde wig came off with it.

The church was so quiet Lisa heard the pews creak as people turned to stare. Rick Poundstone lifted his gaze from the podium and stopped in midsentence. Reverend Hatfield sprang from the bench and rushed to the end of the stage, craning his neck as if trying to focus his eyes on the ruckus that had invaded his sanctuary. Every head of the congregation pointed toward her. Her hair had fallen down the sides of her head. There would be no mistaking her identity.

Rebecca and Ben were on their feet on the last row of pews. Ben clutched his Bible firmly in his right hand and nestled it between his arm and chest. The camera inside recorded everything as it happened.

"Get your hands off me!" Lisa's demand echoed through the hush. She threw her elbows from side to side, shaking off the attendant.

The attendant took two steps backward with his face flushing red and hands held in the air, still holding onto the hat and wig.

Six deacons who had been seated at various locations hurried down the aisles toward her. She felt as if a pack of wolves were descending to rip the flesh from her body.

Rebecca turned her head and caught Ben's gaze, her mouth open, but no words followed. She moved her right foot one step toward the aisle, but went no farther.

"Don't do it, Rebecca. She's not worth it," Ben whispered in her ear. "Don't do this to your father. Don't do this to your mother."

Rebecca's head twitched, and her mouth still searched for words. With a deep sigh, she dropped her gaze to the floor, and put her head against Ben's chest as she fought back tears.

As the six deacons closed in around Lisa, a withered man who looked too old to walk rose from his pew.

His equally elderly wife grabbed his coat sleeve. "Where are you going? Let the deacons handle this."

He promptly jerked his arm from her grasp and hobbled into the aisle.

Lisa put on her best angry face and pointed her finger. "Don't any of you touch me."

Two pairs of deacons' hands grabbed the back of her jacket and started to pull her to the exit doors.

The old man leaned into his cane and stumped up the aisle.

"Hypocrites!" Lisa screamed and, letting her legs go limp, fell on her knees to the floor. The deacons held onto her jacket and half pulled it off.

Lisa twisted her body—wiggling free of the jacket—and fell flat on her stomach, right in front of the old man.

The man lifted his cane high in the air.

Lisa raised her arm to block the incoming blow.

"Leave her be!" the old man thundered.

The deacons stopped in their tracks.

Lisa crawled to the old man's feet, climbed to his side, and wrapped her arms around him. "Thank you. Thank you. Don't let them hurt me," she whispered between deep breaths.

Rick remained speechless.

Reverend Hatfield jumped to the microphone. "Brother Wesley? Brother Wesley, please sit down, and let the deacons handle the matter."

"This young lady wants to come to church. Why won't you let her?" Wesley asked.

One of the deacons closest to Lisa took a step forward. Wesley brought the cane swooping down through empty air between the would-be kidnapper and Lisa.

The deacon jumped back, and then poised himself as if he were going to try again.

The crowd murmured. Hatfield pulled a handkerchief from his jacket and mopped nervous sweat from his brow. "Brother Wesley, there's no need for this type of behavior. The woman is a troublemaker. She doesn't have a right to sit before the Lord in this house."

"He's my God too, Reverend Hatfield!" Lisa yelled.

"Woman, there is a place for your kind to seek God. It's not here. Streets of Gold Ministry is very active in spreading the gospel to the Non-Dead. We cater to the needs of the afflicted in a setting that is more appropriate for their condition," Hatfield said.

"This is something that has been gnawing on me for a long time. She called us hypocrites. Well, we are," Wesley said, to the gasps of surprise from the congregation. "Back in my time that's the way we treated the black folks. We kept them away from our doors. They weren't *good enough* to worship our God. When we finally did start to let them in, we roped off a section of seats in the back. Treated them like cattle, we did, herding them in and out of the pews like animals."

"Brother Wesley, the times demand we separate ourselves from the Non-Dead. It is God's plan, and we do it out of perseverance, not malice. It is a center tenet of our church, and we shall not change our ways," Reverend Hatfield said.

The closest deacon to Wesley lunged and firmly grabbed his cane.

Lisa closed her eyes and braced herself as two deacons peeled her arms off Wesley.

Another deacon rushed in and bear-hugged the old man. "Now, Brother Wesley. You need to calm down before you hurt yourself."

Wesley's wife had followed him down the aisle, raised her purse, and started beating the deacon that held her husband in check.

Hatfield called for order. The congregation was in a roar.

Tears streamed down Rebecca's face as she tightly clung to Ben.

Lisa offered no further resistance as the deacons dragged her out. Another battle, another loss. The bitter taste of defeat more sour than before.

CHAPTER 22

Walter Simmons wearily strolled along a line of trees and bushes on the outskirts of Cedar Ridge Park. Life for him after The Dark Times was but a faint shadow of what he'd enjoyed before. He'd expected life to return to normal after the Z-gas ended the zombie plague. In some ways it had, but in some ways it hadn't. Walter Simmons was not a happy man.

He put his hand to the side of his mouth, "Chuuuuuckleeees, here boy," and then whistled for his dog.

He missed many things from the old days. Sporting events where crowds of fans would gather for mindless entertainment. The smell of charring meats wafting from the grills of food booths at spring and fall festivals. The magical sound of the calliope when the fair came to town. And children. He missed the sounds of playing children the most.

Few things in life offered innocent hope like hordes of romping, stomping children. Their precious curiosity discovering the world through naïve eyes made his heart swell.

Children weren't as abundant as before. More than half had perished during The Dark Times, and few had been born since. For some unexplained reason, preteens had proved to be poor hosts for the alien virus. Once the deceased reanimated to *life*, the young victim of the virus expired within seventy-two hours. Walter saw this as a blessing of sorts. Nothing disturbed him more than a child's dead stare above a gore-dripping mouth after it had fed on a human.

Walter called for his dog again. The empty leash dangled from his wrist. "Chuuuuuckleeees."

The savor of life had waned. He often found his mind wandering through the past in an attempt to recreate the life he had loved so dearly. There had been a magic in the air, a sense of wonder, and a lust for conquest. The world had been ripe for easy pickings. Walter had feasted often on its tender bounties.

He was older now and thirty pounds overweight. *Perhaps this is all just the natural cycle of life*, he thought. Times change, people change, the world changes, and you change. Still, he longed to be happy. Opportunities for happiness didn't come his way often.

"Chuuuuk—" he cut his call short when leaves rustled nearby, and then he saw a young boy come to a stop on his mountain bike.

"Can't find your dog, mister?"

"No, I can't. Chuckles and I were taking a walk—like we do every day. I guess I didn't have his collar on tight enough." Walter lifted the leash. The empty collar dangled on end. "Well, Chuckles saw a squirrel in the woods, and charged after it. I tried to hold him back, but his neck slipped out of his collar and he ran away." He assessed the boy was no older than seven or eight.

"That's too bad. I'll watch out for him."

"Thank you. I really need to find him soon. He has an appointment with the Vet in an hour. I need to take him in to get his medicine. He really needs his medicine."

Eye's glazed over in thought, the boy settled onto his bike seat.

"Say, do you think you could help me? I bet if he hears a little boy calling his name, he'll come a running. He really likes to play with little boys."

"Well, I guess so . . . ."

"What's your name, son?"

"Ryan."

"Thanks, Ryan. Let's walk over by the trees and see if we can find him." Walter turned and marched into the woods while calling for his dog.

Ryan dismounted the bike and pushed it along while following within a few feet of him, yelling for Chuckles, and blowing air between his lips in a poor attempt to whistle.

Near the other side of the tree line, Walter pointed to a white panel van. "You know what, Ryan? I've got a squeeze toy in my van over there. If Chuckles was to hear his favorite toy, he'd be sure to come. Why don't you run over there and get it? It's in the rear. Use the back door."

Ryan looked at Walter, then at the van. He pushed his bike out of the rugged terrain and rode to the vehicle.

Walter placed his hands on his hips and scanned the dirt road in either direction. The area was a service road used to access overhead power lines and not permitted for unauthorized traffic.

When Ryan tugged on the door handle, his hand slipped off. "I can't open it. It's locked."

"Oh, my goodness. I thought I left it open. Hang on, I'll be right there." A low-flying State Police helicopter passed overhead, nearly scaring Walter out of his skin. Lowering the brim of his hat, he slowed his pace until the roar of the blades faded into the distance.

He reached the van, looked both ways down the road again, and unlocked the door. "Go ahead, Ryan, open it."

Ryan opened the door. All the seats, except for the driver's and passenger's, had been removed.

"There's the squeaky toy right behind the driver's seat. Go in and get it," Walter said, opening the seal of a mylar bag, and removing a chloroformed soaked rag.

Ryan climbed in and crawled over to get the toy. "Got it." He squeezed it a few times.

Walter crawled in and put his hand over the child's mouth. Ryan's muffled cry hastened Walter's other hand over with the rag.

"Don't fight it. Breathe it in, go on." He held the boy in check with his whole body.

Ryan tried to tear himself free in a final surge of desperation.

A sharp elbow smacked into Walter's stomach, *Ooofff*, and he nearly lost his grip for a moment. The blow took him by surprise, but he tightened his hold long enough for the boy's body to go limp. He held the rag in place until he remained still for a full minute.

Getting lightheaded from the chloroform fumes, he left Ryan face-down on the floor, and climbed out the van. Once outside, he placed the rag back in the mylar bag, threw the bike in the back, and looked over the area while filling his lungs with fresh air.

Satisfied he was in the clear, Walter entered the van, and tossed the bag on the passenger's seat. He cranked up the engine and sped away, turning onto the highway a quarter mile down the road.

He caught himself checking his side mirrors every few seconds to see if he were being followed. After a mile or two down the road, he relaxed, and settled back in his seat. His tension drifted away. The swelling feeling of victory put a grin on his face so wide he thought the corners of his mouth would split.

He was finally happy. It had been so long since he'd been happy he had forgotten the euphoric highs it brought.

The disruptive effects of The Dark Times still had their hooks into normal daily life. For pedophiles more than most in society.

CHAPTER 23

The car radio belted out an ad for Republican Joel Spencer. The deep, ominous voice of the narrator began. *In times like these, one man can make a difference.*

Spencer's voice faded in. *We stand at the edge of extinction.*

The narrator continued. *A man willing to risk his reputation, his wealth, even his own life.*

Spencer's voice: *We must end the rise in population of the Non-Dead.*

The narrator: *To save the County, to save mankind.*

Spencer: *We must return to the values of old. Husbands and wives must have more children. These children will determine mankind's future. We must retire the Non-Dead to the ground where they belong.*

Narrator: *Joel Spencer, for Congress.*

Lisa was so caught up in her thoughts she did realize the radio had been playing a political ad until the very end. Otherwise, she would have changed the station.

Nothing in her life was going as planned. Her hopes for meaningful employment had died in one last blow.

The job interview a half hour earlier had gone the same as the previous one she had tricked her way into. It ended abruptly when she had been asked to produce her National ID, and she'd been forced to admit she was Sub Y.

The job was for a phone sales position at an insurance company. Lisa maintained she was more than qualified for the job, and argued that no one would know she was Sub Y, because she was only a voice on the other end of a phone call. She even offered to work for a lower wage and take cash to keep it off the books.

The manager was less sympathetic than many others she'd talked to. He became belligerent for wasting his time.

Lisa nearly slapped his face when he accused her of being part of the *nation's problems*. "You and your kind," he said, lumping her in with the Sub Zs. Ironically, an older Sub Z wandered in right at the end of his rant and emptied his wastebasket. Lisa screamed, "Hypocrite!" and stormed out the office. She found herself overusing that word lately. It would be a lonely drive from Fort Worth back home to Dallas.

She could be in Houston right now with Rebecca, spending the weekend in a nice hotel and hitting the town. Rebecca didn't have class today and offered to take her away—just to put a little fun back in her life. Lisa couldn't remember the last time she could say she had fun. Certainly not since her change. Days not spent job hunting had her at the NAAND working the phones. Rebecca would take her out to eat sometimes. The two had become close. She was a great friend but couldn't fill the void left from losing Bob. The physical and emotional needs Bob provided left a gaping hole. This was the longest period of time she had gone without being in a relationship since high school. Even during The Dark Times, there was always a man to take her by the hand, and face the challenges of life by her side.

A blue Ford pickup truck pulled up to the driver's side of the car and slowed to match her speed. She glanced over and saw a bearded man wearing a cowboy hat with a cell phone glued to his ear. Not in the mood for some hard-leg gawking at her, she put her foot to the gas, and sped away.

The sun dipped slowly behind the horizon. The truck turned on its headlights while Lisa glanced at the side mirror, prompting her to do the same. The streetlights lining the winding highway ahead blinked *on*, making the drive home seem farther away.

The truck eased its way alongside her again. Because it was darker, she could barely see inside the cab. She eased up on the accelerator, as she was already speeding fifteen miles an hour over the limit.

The truck slowed again, matching her speed.

"Slime bucket, leave me the fuck alone," she said aloud and removed her foot from the pedal. The car slowed, and the truck maintained its pace, letting her drift behind.

In the rear-view mirror, Lisa saw a fast approaching car with its headlights still off. She put her foot back on the accelerator and brought up her speed to five miles under the posted limit—wanting to keep her distance from the truck—but not wanting to be a hazard on the highway.

The car pulled to within an uncomfortable distance, and then slowly eased closer.

"What the?" The car was so close she couldn't see the front grill. "I'm in the slow lane. Go around, asshole." A passing streetlight brought just enough light to the driver's face for her to recognize his identity. It was the creepy guy she had spotted at her first NAAND meeting.

When she turned her eyes back to the road, the car bumped her. The Ford truck was still in the other lane but in the process of slowing down.

Her heart pounded. She needed to pull into a public place as soon as possible and get help, but there was nothing but trees lining the roadside as far as she could see.

Mashing the accelerator to the floorboard surged her ahead of the car. When she caught even with the truck, the driver hit his gas pedal, and swerved into her lane—bumping against the driver's side, and snapping off the mirror.

The car behind closed in fast. Soon she would be trapped between the two.

The car bumped against her again. The truck pressed into the side of her car. Lisa felt the truck power her toward the side of the road. She thought about hitting the brake, but knew that would only snare her in their trap.

"If you want to play chicken, motherfucker, let's play!" She turned her steering wheel—pushing back against the truck. Sheet metal grinded metallic songs as the two vehicles fought for dominance.

Up ahead, the rear lights of a car came into view in the truck's lane. She needed to maintain control for a few seconds longer before a chance to get out of her hopeless position would present itself.

The truck driver slammed on his brakes moments before rear-ending the car he was overtaking. The tires squealed like a wicked banshee as black smoke rolled out of the swaying rear end.

Lisa jerked the wheel to get in front of the car after she passed. With both lanes opened, she was free to maneuver from lane to lane, hoping to stay ahead of her pursuers.

The car Creepy Guy drove was faster. She kept him at bay by switching lanes just when he made a move to get an advantage on the lane she wasn't in.

A police car traveling the opposite direction on the highway turned on its emergency lights and let out a series of high-pitched warnings. Lisa was never happier at the thought of getting a speeding ticket.

Her eyes followed it as it passed, *Was his radar on? Was it me he was warning, or is he chasing after someone in his lane?* The distraction gave Creepy Guy an opening to maneuver alongside. He turned his steering wheel and sent his car into hers with a teeth jarring *thud*. Lisa's car careened to the side of the road where it smashed into a wooden road barrier with a flashing yellow light. The sign, warning of a pothole, cut through the grill, crippling her car. The airbag slammed her into the seat as she rode the brake pedal with both feet. The anti-lock brakes rattled her knees until she screeched to a halt.

The airbag instantly deflated and left her disoriented over the impact. She turned her gaze to the side window when her head cleared and saw Creepy Guy get out of his car. He raced toward her.

The blue Ford pickup skidded to a stop beside him. "Come on, man! Let's get this thing over with!" the driver yelled after lowering the passenger window.

Creepy Guy jerked the door open. Lisa slapped at his hands as they pulled at her shoulders. The steering wheel mechanism had broken and it was nearly lying in her lap. The seatbelt held her locked in the seat.

Creepy Guy disengaged the seatbelt and struggled to free her from the cab. Lisa dug her fingernails into his left forearm, breaking two nails off to the quick as she peeled skin back.

Cursing a blue streak, he smacked her nose with a backhand. Lisa's vision went black around the edges.

A fast approaching police siren wailed up the road.

"It's too late! Get back in the truck! Get your ass in here now, or I'm leaving you!" the truck driver hollered.

Creepy Guy shouted, "Damn!" He slapped the roof of the car and sprinted to the truck. The truck's tires spun loose gravel before the passenger door had closed all the way.

Shortly, the police siren powered down, mimicking a dying goose as it pulled up behind Lisa's car.

The final nail had been driven into her coffin.

CHAPTER 24

Mack Teller drove in his 2017 Ford Mustang given to him when he was hired to manage Joel Spencer's ten-acre estate. Spencer proved to be difficult at times—downright unreasonable—but he offered Mack the best paying job once out of the RY program's rehabilitation center.

Mack was no longer physically handicapped from the childhood accident but now was handicapped in a different sort—prejudice because of his Non-Dead status. Most employers would rather hire three Sub Zs than one Sub Y. Wages for Sub Zs being that much lower. Spencer's was the most respectful offer to come his way.

The hiring didn't go unnoticed to the outside world. A news crew visited the estate that day. Mack had imagined the reporter was there to do a human-interest story on him—to highlight the success of the government's RY handicapped program. What a fool he was. The reporter didn't give two shakes about his success story. A story of a paraplegic walking again had become common. The program's success was old news. The benevolence of Joel Spencer hiring a Non-Dead in Texas topped the headlines.

As important as it had been to find employment, it didn't compare with the treasure he found in Margaret's love. She had been afraid to step out of the imaginary line Spencer drew around her. The beginning of her fear's death was the day she was diagnosed with terminal cancer.

With the certainty of an early death, the bonds that held her back started stretching. As each link weakened she spent more time outside in the gardens, enjoying the simplicities of nature's beauty. For once in her life she took time for herself and started to truly live.

Mack would keep to himself when she was outside—it was Mr. Spencer's orders. But it was she who approached him. Shyly at first, but she became more comfortable with each passing day. His words of consolation opened her heart to him.

A flashing sign on the side of the road for 'Kent's Auto Repair' brought Mack's mind back to the present. He slowed the Mustang and turned in to the parking lot, then drove past an open gate leading to the back.

A slim man—his skin a pale white under the noon sun—waited in front of a lime green, single cab truck, complete with a camper shell and the words 'Sewer Rooter' in large block letters. He was appropriately dressed in a grease stained, dark-gray jumpsuit—with 'Jarvis' embroidered in red script above his left front pocket.

Mack parked the Mustang in the next available spot and got out the car.

"Hey, Jarvis. It's good to see you." Mack firmly grabbed his friend's hand and gave it a couple of pumps.

"You too, brother. Been almost a month. Too bad we don't have meetings more often."

"I hear you. I've been thinking about that too. We could get twice as much accomplished if we met two times a month. Plus," Mack smiled, feeling embarrassed, "it makes me think I make the world a better place to live in. I need that."

"Yeah, well, that's not all you need." Jarvis laughed. "I feel you, though. As membership increases we might be able to pull that off. We've got to be careful. We don't want to draw too much attention from the Living."

"Yeah. Okay man, we've got a job to do. Give me the story on this one."

"This guy moved into the area two months ago. According to the newspaper announcement, he relocated from Chicago. He was originally born in Texas. The State of Illinois kicked him back here after he finished his last stint in the pokey."

"How long was he in?"

"Paper said two years. Didn't list his priors. No way that was a first time case. He's in his forty's. He must have a history of doing this shit for them to ship him back to his home state."

"Okay, what's his routine?" Mack asked.

"He leaves his house every weekday around three o'clock and usually returns around five. We can get you inside and ready for him when he gets back. The syringe is in the van. It'll knock him out like that," Jarvis snapped his fingers near the end of his sentence.

"Yeah, I know. This is my second time to do the honors. That stuff works real good," Mack said.

Jarvis handed him a piece of paper with an address written on it.

"You sure the guy in the paper is the same guy at this address? We've made mistakes before. I wouldn't want to grab an innocent person."

Jarvis waved a hand. "No worries, bro. The information in the newspaper and the mail going to this guy's house are a match. He's same sorry son-of-a-bitch all right. If we don't take him out now we're going to wish we did later." He handed Mack the keys to the truck.

"Where'd you get the truck?" Mack gave Jarvis the keys to the Mustang.

"This old thing? It was in the shop for repairs when the business went belly up. It's been in the back so long no one even remembers it's here. I put on a new distributor cap and some fresh fuel in the tank. It cranked right up."

"Okay, we can switch vehicles after the meeting tonight. Anything else I need to know?" Mack asked.

"Oh yeah, the most important part, the house is wired with a burglar alarm. The backdoor code to bypass his alarm system is two-three-five-two-three-five. Enter that on the keypad less than a minute from the time it's tripped and it'll disarm."

"Man, you guys sure do your homework," Mack said.

"There are Sub Ys everywhere. We're getting a pretty good web of contacts out in the workforce. The Living don't pay us a whole lot of mind as long as we keep to ourselves and do what we're told. They don't know what we do when they're not watching. Our network is growing more powerful. One day the Living will have no choice but to treat us like equals."

"Jarvis!" A fat, old man by an open bay at the shop called out. "Get your dead ass in here and get these tires on this car."

Jarvis shook his head. With a scowl on his face, he said, "We're nothing but *niggas* in the Living man's world."

CHAPTER 25

Smoke curled from a Partagas Black Classico, the maduro wrapper offering a mélange of complex spice and ripe fruit flavor. Normie Cantrell leaned back in his chair, his feet on the desk, and the phone in his hand. His face beamed like the cat with a full belly by an empty aquarium.

"Hey, Rex. Normie. You'll never guess what I got."

"I'm busy, and I don't have time to play games. Just tell me," Rex said, sounding tired.

"I'm a busy man myself. In fact, I never stop working for something I want until I get it. I'm the busiest man I know. That's a quality of mine you don't always seem to appreciate."

Rex huffed out a breath of air. "Okay, I can tell you've got something to say, and you're about to burst to get it out. Please Normie, pretty please with sugar on top, tell me what you have."

"I got it!"

"You got it?"

"Her! I got her!" Normie pulled a deep draw off the cigar, made an O with his lips, and blew another stream of smoke into the air.

"What? Goudard? You have Lisa Goudard? You better not get us into any trouble."

"Keep your shirt on. This isn't some two-bit operator you're talking to. I'm a professional. I'll have you know, she's here of her own free will. Thanks to me and the opportunities the fine establishment of Dancing Bare has to offer."

"She signed up to dance? She must have hit rock bottom financially."

"Yeah, that sums it up pretty good. I put three grand in her checking account and sprung for a cab to drive her up here. She took the driver's keys and made me pay him while he waits to take her back. She's not the trusting type."

"Are you going to get the blood samples like we talked about? We really need those samples as soon as we can get them."

"I'm getting those as we speak. She fell for it. I told her before she could dance fulltime she had to pass a state health exam, which included drawing a blood sample. *It just so happens* the blood wagon was going to be here today to test the girls. I told her it wouldn't come back for another month, and if she wanted to go to work now, she needed to get it over with. Genius, if I say so myself." Normie knocked an inch-long ash log in an empty highball glass.

"So, what kind of deal did you make with her?"

"Seems that she ran into a bit of bad luck. Her car was damaged in an, eh, *accident*. The cop at the scene ended up driving her home. She didn't have enough cash to take a cab and doesn't have enough to pay the deductible to get the car fixed."

"Car accident? What happened?"

"She had some cockamamie story about some guy trying to run her off the road. You know how chicks have such wild imaginations. She's probably paranoid about all the negative attention she brought to herself with the church."

"So, the real story is that you tried to have her abducted. It went bad, you almost got her killed, and you got lucky that she called you because you were her last option."

"Uh, well, I wouldn't have put it in those exact words, but—"

Rex interrupted, "Can it. What's done is done, and we came out ahead in the game. Get the blood—as much as you can. I'll send someone to pick it up when it's ready."

"You're welcome, Rex. I'm glad you appreciate my fine work. Hey, why don't you come in tonight for a little action? Celebrate a little? I can't wait to see what that bitch looks like naked."

"Can't tonight. Be careful with her. I really don't care how much fun you have. She's nothing but undead trash. Give her some iron tablets. I'm only interested in her blood."

Normie put his feet on the floor and leaned forward. "I'm interested in giving her my iron cock."

"You wish, little man. Later."

The phone went dead in Normie's hand. *Asshole.*

*

Normie waited by the van door and met Lisa when she stepped out. "Miss Goudard. Lisa, Lisa, Lisa. Here, have a drink courtesy of your new employer, The Dancing Bare."

Lisa rubbed the pink bandage on the inside of her elbow. "I don't like to give blood. I have small veins. They drained so much blood out of me I felt my heart lose suction."

"Ha ha! You're such a kidder. You'll fit right in with the rest of us."

She eyed the drink Normie pushed at her. "They told me not to drink any alcohol."

"It's orange juice."

"Just juice?"

"Well, it might have a splash or two of vodka. Go ahead, drink up."

Lisa took the drink from his hand, stirred the ice around with a straw, and took a sip. "Say, this is good. Fresh, with a hint of mint."

"Ice Queen Vodka is the best. Nothing's too good for my girls. Permit me to escort you inside, and we'll get down to business."

*

Rick Poundstone couldn't stop thinking about Lisa Goudard since he listened to his messages on his cell phone. He had tried returning her call but ended up being switched to voicemail.

Something about the message she left haunted him. *I'm in a bad way . . . I'm not sure what to do.* She stopped speaking, but the recording continued for another fifteen seconds. The rest of the message was nothing but road noise, as if she were standing next to a highway with cars zooming by.

Hearing her voice brought back those same feelings of compassion he had felt at the therapist's office. Something made him want to take her in his arms and kiss her all over and promise her he would make all of her sadness go away. Strangely, he felt such empathy, and he hardly even knew anything about her.

Rick had seen a strong, determined woman that morning in church. She didn't back down and made her case, reminding him of a modern-day Susan B. Anthony. And the good church members responded to her plight by dragging her outside to the curb as though she were garbage. He had wanted to reach out to her then, but instead made excuses to himself not to. Thinking he would make the effort after the election.

Rick dialed his office.

His secretary answered, "Poundstone Campaign, how may I direct your call?"

"Sandra, Rick. Do me a favor, get me the address for a Miss Lisa Goudard, G-o-u-d-a-r-d. Call me when you have it. Thanks."

His schedule was filled with important meetings and pending legislation that needed attention. Yet nothing mattered more to him right then than finding out why Lisa had made the call.

*

"First of all, Lisa, this is a business. Dancing has nothing to do with morality. It is a legal business, and I pride myself on working inside the boundaries of the law. Fortunately, for us in Devil's Bone, those boundaries are pretty darn wide. Our relationship will be strictly business too, as are all of my relationships with the girls," Normie said as Lisa slurped the last of her drink. "You need another?"

"I shouldn't, but that was really good." Lisa licked the last fugitive drops from the end of her straw. "It's calmed me down a lot too. You don't know how nervous I was when I got here." She stopped, her gaze drifting to the table. "I wasn't only nervous. I feel like I have no dignity left." She put her hand to her forehead and held back tears. "Look at me, I'm in a strip club about to whore myself out to the first degenerate who can toss up a dollar to see my tits."

"*Liiiiisa*, stop. You got it all wrong. You have to think of stripping like it's just a big game. A game women and men both play. You're under the illusion it's the guys who exploit the girls. That's not true at all."

She turned her gaze back to Normie, blowing her nose into a cocktail napkin.

"The girls here exploit the guys. Think about it a minute. The guys are here for a couple of reasons. To get drunk, sure, but mainly to see the girls. They throw money at them, buy them twenty dollar specialty drinks—one hundred dollar bottles of cheap champagne, and guess what?"

"What?"

"The guys aren't allowed to touch the girls. My girls don't whore themselves out. They're professionals plying their profession. Sure, the girls have to dance, and take off their clothes. But stripping is an art. And some of my girls are real athletes on the pole.

"Not only that, but believe it or not, it's places like this that keep marriages together."

"Normie, don't bullshit me."

"It's true." Normie pointed to a table near the stage. "See that guy over there? Comes in here all the time to get some of the things gone missing from his marriage. His name's Hoyt, got a wife that busts his chops all the time. He's real nice to the girls and has enough fun here that it makes living with her bearable. She's lucky he has a place to blow off some steam.

"The problem, as I see it, is you don't have the proper perspective because of your misconceptions about what strippers do." Normie leaned closer as he spoke. Show time was about to begin, and the tables around him were filling fast.

"Tell you what. I'm going to order another round of drinks and give you a little Strip Club one-o-one." Normie waved at a passing waitress and held up two fingers.

*

Pavilion Townplace offered a scenic drive with ornamental stones and seasonal flowers in the median. Tall oaks framed the sides of the road. Rick had canceled his last appointment of the afternoon in order to spend the time searching for Lisa. He tried calling her a few more times, but each call went straight to voicemail. The gnawing feeling that something was wrong had him on edge. He needed to solve this mystery as quickly as possible before it consumed his every waking thought.

The gate to the apartments would only open with the proper card ID, or a resident there would have to ring him in from a registered phone number. *That's just great*, Rick thought. *I'm this close, and I can't get in.*

A car pulled up to the other side of the gate and stopped. The sensor energized the gate triggering it to slowly retract horizontally, opening a space large enough for the car to drive through.

Rick waited for the car to pass, and then hit the accelerator— speeding through the entrance before the gate closed again. He made it through with little room to spare.

A team of Non-Dead collecting garbage paid him no mind. Rick slowly drove through the parking lot in search of unit 248, and decided to park at the first available spot and explore the rest of the way on foot.

Once outside, he surveyed the area. In the background, the drone of a leaf-blower mixed with a mockingbird barking at a cat. He was one section over from the cluster of units 240-250, and walked over to 248, without seeing another Living soul.

The wall-mounted mailbox by her door was open, containing a handful of letters from the previous day. *Nothing too unusual about that.* Still, something didn't feel right.

Rick softly knocked on the door and listened for sounds from inside the apartment. *Nothing.* He knocked harder, and called, "Miss Goudard? Rick Poundstone. I'd like to speak to you for a minute." Several minutes of knocking brought no rewards. Rick found himself back to square one.

When he peered down at his watch, he saw a wadded piece of paper on the ground. He picked it up and smoothed it out. It was nothing more than a torn sheet from a Yellow Cab memo pad, both sides blank.

Was this a clue or random trash blown in from the parking lot?

Rick opened his cell phone, and scrolled through his contacts, until he found the number for Police Chief Ronald Collins. It was time to call in a favor.

*

The lights dimmed, leaving behind unusual glows of green, blue, and red. The empty stage wrapped in warm mystery.

The DJ's voice boomed over the conversation and clink of glasses. "Good evening, ladies and gentlemen. Welcome to The Dancing Bare. For your entertainment tonight, we have fourteen gorgeous girls waiting to raise your disco pole. Remember to tip the waitresses and the dancers well, and they will treat you well. If you know what I'm say-ing!

"Our first dancer tonight is a little honey from Tupelo, Mississippi. Give it up for, *Giiiiina!*"

A fast strumming guitar replaced the DJ, and then the pulsating bass kicked in—electrifying the audience.

Gina strutted onto stage wearing a long sleeved, tight-fitting pink mini dress with a lace-up front. Her hips swayed in perfect time to the rhythm as her arms and hands weaved her spell over the audience.

The alcohol proved itself a powerful seductress. Lisa pushed out all the problems of her life and opened up to the decadent atmosphere and the pounding music.

Normie tapped his hand on the table to the beat and watched Lisa as she bobbed her head in time to the music.

Gina slowly untied the front of her dress, exposing her ample cleavage, much to the crowd's delight.

Then the room went dark. Only the dress continued to glow in the black light, accentuating Gina's hourglass figure even more. The plunging neckline continued to part. Her breasts pushed to break free.

The crowd roared.

Lisa said, "Here comes the money shot."

Normie sheepishly smiled, and said in a low voice, "You got a lot to learn, little girl."

The dress fell to the floor. Gina stepped out of it. She continued her dance, wearing only a glowing top, and G-string. And the moment the song ended, she pulled off the top and tossed it to the floor.

The lights turned back on with Gina at the end of the stage, smiling like a prom queen. Her right forearm covered most of her breasts.

One dollar bills, a few fives, and even some twenties hit the stage as the lustful patrons showed their appreciation. Gina smiled and thanked everyone as she bent over and gathered the money.

"What? That's it? She didn't show any body parts. I thought the girls got naked?" Lisa said.

"That was Gina's first dance. Each dancer will dance twice. The first time it's to warm up the crowd. But not only that, if the dancer doesn't feel like she makes enough money on her first dance, then she won't dance the second time. If you want to see her in the buff you gotta show some respect. They treated Gina pretty well. You'll get to see her shortly, in all her naked glory." Normie raised his hand and ordered two more drinks. Lisa had reached the bottom of hers once again.

*

Rick wished he had taken his SUV instead of his Sedan. The roads to Devil's Bone had seen much better days.

Captain Collins had come through for him. Using the discarded stationary, though it was a long shot, Collins had pulled some favors from the day supervisor at Yellow Cab, and found out a car had been dispatched to pick up Lisa and bring her to the address of The Dancing Bare in Devil's Bone. The cabbie was still at the location waiting to bring her back.

Rick couldn't imagine why Lisa would be going to such a dive. Maybe his feelings for her were only emotions he had imposed. What if she were nothing like the image he had created in his mind?

Some things still didn't make sense. He needed to talk to Lisa face to face and put his mind, and his heart, at ease.

*

Normie waited at the dressing room door, clutching the lapels of his jacket in each hand. "Lisa, you about done?"

"Yes," she said, pulling the door slowly open.

Normie ran his gaze from her head down to her six-inch white pumps. "You gonna wear a bikini? The top covers more than I like. The bottoms have potential. I know you didn't wanna wear any of the outfits here, but are these the sexiest clothes you could bring?"

"I have sexier underwear, but I don't want to dance in them. Don't try to talk me into wearing any of your girl's outfits. I don't want to get cooties."

"Eh, don't worry about it. This is practice. You're just going to stick your toe in the water tonight. I'll buy you some new outfits for next time."

"I don't know if I can go through with this, Normie. My stomach has butterflies again."

"I got just the thing." Normie hustled two doors down to his office.

Lisa heard clanking and the closing of cabinets from the other room. Normie returned with a tall glass filled with a clear, fizzy liquid. A special home remedy of his own creation, Alka-Seltzer and rhophynol.

"What's that?" she asked.

"Seltzer, for your stomach. Drink up."

Normie handed her the drink, then grabbed her by the arm, and directed her down the hallway. Lisa gulped the drink until the glass was empty.

Stopping at a door, Normie opened it and pushed her through a narrow, dark stairway that opened up to a stage.

Lisa found herself behind a set of curtains that hung from the ceiling to the floor.

Spinning her around, Normie pulled her close. "How about it baby? You in the mood? It's show time!"

A rumble from Lisa's stomach worked its way up and erupted as a burp right in Normie's face.

"Get your shit together, girl. You got to be in control."

"I don't know if I can do this. I'm feeling a little woozy."

"It's only nerves. All the girls get them. Anyway, this is a practice show on a private stage I use to entertain some of my clients." Normie grabbed her by the arm and took her beyond the curtain.

Lights above the stage outlined the perimeter. They shone so brightly Lisa squinted and used a hand to shade her eyes against the glare. She could see only a few feet beyond the stage. There were two empty vinyl couches. Darkness enveloped the rest of the room, preventing her from knowing its size.

"There's nobody in here?" Lisa said.

"A few are in the back conducting business. Don't worry about it." Normie pushed her out to the middle of the stage and returned to the curtain. He pulled a remote control from his pocket. "Look down at the stage floor. You'll get used to the lights. Forget about everything else. Pretend you're here alone, dancing. Relax, get to it, have a good time." He pushed the button on the remote, and the music swelled into the room.

A warm keyboard heated the distant wail of the singer. The bass and drums kicked in, pounding a steady rhythm.

Lisa turned and faced Normie. He was smiling, bouncing his head, and clapping to the beat. Then, she closed her eyes, drifting into the world of sensual freedom.

Sit back, wait for it, When you want me to do it, Sit back, wait for it, When you want to come.

Her hips began swaying, she held her arms tightly by her side, and then she stepped forward, bending her knees in a fluid, dancing motion.

Sit back, wait for it, When you want me to do it, Sit back, wait for it, When you want to come.

Breaking into a bump and grind routine, she used her hands to accentuate her long legs and magnificent breasts.

Get your timing right, Make it good for both of us tonight, Fulfill those dreams, Make me scream.

She squatted with her legs tight together, and then spread her knees wide apart, sucking her little finger while she opened and closed them.

Push it, Push it, In me, in me, Hit me with those deadly dreams.

Springing up, she unhooked her top in the front and set her breasts pushing free of restraint, then with her hands on her hips paraded around the stage. Her 36 D's bounced with each step.

Sit back, Just do it, Sit back, When you want to come.

Lisa stopped at the front of the stage and tickled her right nipple. Her left hand slid slowly down her stomach, into her bottoms, and between her legs. Her head leaned back, and her face softened into mock ecstasy.

I'm Coming, I'm Coming.

Normie stepped closer. "This girl is gold!"

Lisa's hand slid out of her bottoms and up to her lips. She kissed her fingers and gave a long, animated wink.

Sit back, just do it, When you want to come . . .

Turning her back to the room, she placed a thumb on each side of her bikini bottoms, and pulled them slowly to the floor. Her bare ass was wide open to the unknown audience. Stepping out of the bottoms, she again pranced around on stage as if she owned the world.

When you want to come, Come!

Kicking off her shoes, she dropped to her hands and knees, and prowled like a tigress on the hunt until reaching the front of the stage.

The dream of, Or is it real love.

Crawling forward on her forearms, she kept her chest to the floor but her ass in the air, slowly gyrating her hips about as if enjoying a slow fuck.

Sit back, wait for it, When you want me to do it, Sit back, wait for it.

Her hips moved faster as the song rose to the crescendo.

Sit back, just do it, When you want me to do it, Sit back, just do it.

By this time her pelvis slapped against the floor, sending waves of pleasure as she neared orgasm.

On time, on time, on time.

She moaned loudly, not knowing if anyone could hear her over the music, and not caring if they did.

Come!

The music abruptly stopped. The room turned to pitch black darkness. Lisa's erotic dream ended, shocking her back to reality.

"Normie, what's happening?" Lisa sat up, the room so dark she couldn't see her hand in front of her face.

Grunting noises came from the back of the room.

"It's the damn circuit breaker. The emergency lights will kick on after thirty seconds."

Two dim battery powered floodlights cast their beams across the back of the room, and Lisa saw what was there for the first time.

More couches outlined the room near the walls. The grunting noises came from four couples engaging in acts of raunchy sex.

One woman stood spread-legged by the arm of a couch, bent over, with her face on the seat cushion. Her partner stood behind her, penetrating as far as his bulging beer gut would allow.

As Lisa's eyes adjusted to the faint light, she saw the woman was missing her jaw.

Another woman sat on her knees, straddling a man on a couch, bouncing up and down as he gripped her hips. Chunks of meat were missing from her back. The woman was so thin Lisa could count all of her ribs even in the low light.

On a large, plush, white rug, a woman with a skeletal face and a flowing blonde wig lay on her stomach as her partner thrust his hips against her backside.

The last couple laid flat on a couch, copulating in old-fashioned missionary style. The woman had no arms.

"What in the hell is going on in here?" Lisa rose to her feet and stormed toward Normie. "What kind of perverted shit is this?"

"This is business. It has nothing to do with morality—strictly business."

"You told me the men couldn't touch the girls here."

"I told you the men couldn't touch the girls *out there*," Normie said, pointing. "Those are Living girls. They can only strip and give lap dances. No touchy no feely by the patrons. I'm licensed to sell the services of Sub Z and Sub Y Non-Dead for prostitution."

"But this is so sick." Lisa waved her hand toward the couples. "This is no better than modern-day slavery."

One of the men called, "Hey! Get that piece of ass dancing again. I'm losing my boner!"

Normie ignored the man. "These girls? Heck, they're nothing more than mules. Not much going on upstairs. They just follow orders and don't complain. Well, they don't know enough to complain. But why would they if they could? We feed them well and grease them up real good before a job to keep them from wearing out. I protect my investments.

"I offer Sub Z companionship for those who can't afford the Sub Ys. Some will pay a little extra for live entertainment. That's why I have a stripper stage in here. It helps the men keep it *up* for the game, if you catch my drift.

"The next stop for these girls is the oven. I'm at least finding a way to collect tax dollars for the government on a product that would otherwise have been trashed months ago. I consider myself an entrepreneur in recycling, making the planet *greener*."

"I consider you a fuck-faced, pig motherfucking, slime bucket." Lisa pushed past Normie and bolted through the curtains, and down the stairs. She opened the door, dashed into the light of the hall, and started to panic when she realized she was totally naked.

Normie was right on her heels.

"Stay away from me. I'm getting my bag, getting dressed, and getting the hell out of here."

"Wait, you're just upset. Why don't you come in my office and sit down for a while? We can talk this out."

Lisa turned and got in his face. "Why don't you go fuck yourself, you fucking fuck."

Normie smiled, and said, "I bet your pussy gets all wet when you get mad."

Lisa raised both fists to pound into his chest.

Normie grabbed each wrist and shoved her against the wall. "That's no way to treat the man who paid you three thousand dollars."

"You're hurting me," Lisa said, thinking he was much stronger than he looked.

"This isn't pain. This is business. The three grand wasn't a gift. It was payment. You only danced one dance. I must say, you got a lotta potential. I can get twice the price for what I'm getting for my top Sub Y."

"For dancing?"

"No, for fucking. Boy, you are naïve. The three grand was a prepayment. In this business the real money comes in when a guy gets to blow his wad." Normie shoved the erect cock bulging in his pants against her leg.

"Normie, don't. I'm not feeling well. I'm going to be sick."

Whispering, he said, "I want to blow my wad in you." Normie stood on his tiptoes, covered her mouth with his, and tried to stick his tongue between her lips.

Lisa gagged and hurled a stream of vomit right into Normie's face.

He quickly spun away and bent over, tossing his stomach contents all over the floor. "You bitch." Normie spat. "You stupid cunt." He spat twice more. "Your ass is mine!"

Rick Poundstone burst through the door leading into the hall. He came to an abrupt halt when he found a naked woman hiding her face against the wall and Normie Cantrell dry heaving over a pile of vomit on the floor.

"Who the fuck are you, and what in the fuck are you doing here?" Normie turned and said. Two of his bouncers were to either side of the interloper. "What the fuck? Get him outta here."

"Boss, he's a member of Congress. He came with two motorcycle cops escorting him. He says he's looking for a woman and doesn't want any trouble," one of the bouncers said.

"Well, I don't care who he is. This my territory. I own the cops. Grab him!"

The two goons latched on to each of Rick's arms, securing him in place.

Normie wiped his mouth with his hand, then looked around as if to find something to wipe his hand on. "Stupid shit. You've got some nerve busting in to my place and giving me orders." Without any warning, Normie stepped up and punched Rick in the solar plexus.

Rick stiffened and heaved as the blow took the wind out and left him limp in the goons' grasp.

"Stupid cocksucker, motherfucker. Stupid shit. I pay enough damned money that I don't deserve this kind of disrespect. I'm going to throw your ass outta here. If you give me one ugly look, or rat on me to the cops, I got friends who'll find you and kill you as a favor to me. Am I making myself clear, Congressman shit-for-brains?"

Rick coughed, and cleared his throat. "Y . . . yes."

"Yes, what?"

"Yes, you've made yourself clear," Rick said, composing himself.

"Good. I'm glad you're seeing things my way." Normie straightened his jacket. "People just need to learn respect around here."

Rick's right heel smashed down on goon number one's left foot. The goon let go of Rick's arm, and Rick's elbow slammed into his sternum.

Goon two tightened his grip and jerked Rick sideways. Rick's right uppercut crashed the man's glass jaw, and he collapsed to the floor.

In one swift movement, Rick whipped out a gold plated Colt .45 from the holster hidden in the small of his back. "This ends now!" Rick pointed the gun at Normie and waved it to the side.

Normie lowered his head, shaking it. "I don't know how you figure in with the rest of them. Put that thing away. I own you."

"I don't know what you're alluding to. You don't own me, the police out front, nor do you own Police Chief Collins of Dallas County." Rick lifted the cell phone he had been holding in his left hand toward Normie. "In fact, he's on the line now, listening to our conversation. If you don't cooperate, I can have you arrested for threatening a United States Congressman. If you're ready to shut down for the night and go to jail, we can go that route."

Normie continued to give Rick a *go to hell* stare.

"Let me speak to Lisa Goudard. I need to make sure she's okay. If she tells me to leave, I'll leave. Where is she?" Rick said.

"What, are you fucking blind?" Normie jerked his head toward Lisa.

Rick quickly turned in surprise. Lisa's face was hidden against the wall. He let his gaze drift down her back to her round ass and down her long perfect legs. "Incredible," he said to himself.

"Lisa, it's Senator Rick Poundstone. We met at the therapist's office."

Lisa's mind drifted in and out of reality. She pulled her hair in front of her face, hiding. She leaned against the wall more to keep her balance than to maintain her dignity. Hearing her name called in a soft, caring voice, she turned her head toward Rick, trying to focus on his face through her hair.

"Are you okay? Would you like to go home? Can I take you home?"

Unsure of who was speaking or what was going on around her, she grabbed the two words which offered salvation. "Go home? Yes, I want to go home."

Rick shot Normie a stern glance and raised his eyebrows.

"Take her and get the fuck out," Normie said

"I know she didn't come here naked. Where are her clothes?" Rick asked.

Normie huffed noisily and went in a dressing room, retrieving her gym bag, and a gold satin robe. He returned and tossed the bag toward Rick, who caught it, and draped the robe over Lisa's back.

"This isn't over," he whispered in her ear. The bulge in Normie's pants returned.

CHAPTER 26

Mack judged the original construction of the neighborhood to be sometime in the 1950s, considering the size and architecture of the houses. All houses were single story with front carports and on lots the size of quarter-acre postage stamps. He wondered if he could jump roof to roof from one end of the subdivision to the other.

As the address neared, he coasted to a stop and parked the truck on the side of the street, being careful not to block anyone's mailbox. Before making an exit, he pulled his cap low on his head, and checked his makeup in the rearview mirror. Good enough, he got out with a toolbox in hand.

Large trees dotted the yards adding charm as well as shade to the neighborhood. *A sleepy little neighborhood, I wonder how the residents would react if they knew a monster lived among them?*

The address on the paper was three houses down. The only activity on the street came from an agitated black Labrador, held at bay by a chain-link fence across the street. The vicious growls had Mack believing the dog would like nothing better than to have him for lunch.

The mailbox at the address had seen better days, but enough of the stick-on numbers remained to make it readable. He came to a halt and assessed the situation. There were no trees in the front yard, but there was one in the back. A large oak of some type that was sure to drop a huge limb on the roof one day. The carport was the only one on the street equipped with a garage door. Fortunately, the garage door was open.

No one was home. No one was outside. The coast was as clear.

The piece of paper went in his front pocket as he tramped down the side of the house and into the backyard, acting as if he had found his jobsite, and was ready to get to work.

Once in the backyard, a row of hedges on either side of the property and in the rear made a natural fence to hide his activities.

A 10' X 10' by ten patio lay in front of the rear door, uncovered. Harsh sunlight shone past the tree's shade onto two plastic lawn chairs and an empty terracotta planter. There was no way anyone used the patio to relax.

Mack went to work, and selected a pair of straight jaw adjustable pliers, and a flat-end screwdriver from the toolbox. There was no deadbolt for him to deal with. The knob was old, and the pliers wrung it off in a few quick twists. Once that was out of the way, he used the screwdriver to pry the locking mechanism open.

The security alarm beeped to warned he would have less than a minute to enter the passcode Jarvis had given him or the main alarm would trip.

His finger went to work on the keypad, entering the code. The beeping stopped, and the flashing red light switched to solid green.

He was inside the rear of the kitchen and quickly made a run through every room in the boxy, little house. Not much in the way of furnishings—a kitchen table and four chairs, an old couch in the living room, a double bed in the master bedroom, and a computer on a pine desk in the second bedroom.

The screen saver danced across the twenty-four-inch monitor by the computer. Out of curiosity, he bumped the mouse, bringing the computer out of sleep mode. The screen lit the room with soft light.

At first, he couldn't believe what his eyes saw. And as hard as his mind fought to comprehend the image, the graphic nature of the photograph left nothing to the imagination.

*

Mack peered out the front window through the edge of the curtains and watched the street. Each time a vehicle drove by his heart beat faster. *Is this him?*

The time was a little past 4:30 p.m. when a vehicle slowed as it approached the driveway. It came to a stop just beyond. The reverse lights switched on as it cautiously backed up the driveway and into the garage.

Mack's pulse banged in his head from the anger blurring rational thought.

The hum of the idling engine stopped. The garage door clanked down the tracks until it stopped with a soft thump. The vehicle door opened and closed, then another door opened and closed. Mack waited to the side of the door leading from the garage to the kitchen, his back to the wall, the syringe tightly in his grip.

The keys jingled, and the door unlocked, the knob rattling as if were difficult to open. A muffled, "Damn," uttered from behind the door as it slowly opened. A man stepped in.

Mack brought the syringe around ready to plunge in his neck and froze. The man cradled a young boy in his arms.

Walter gasped at the sight of the intruder.

The two locked wide, surprised gazes.

Walter made the first move, and slammed Ryan into Mack's chest, pushing him backward.

Mack instinctively let the syringe fall to the floor and grabbed the boy, leaving him defenseless as he crashed into the countertop. His head whipped back and thudded against a cabinet.

Walter hurried over to a nearby drawer and jerked it open.

Events happened so fast it took a few seconds for Mack to get his bearings. His immediate concern was for the boy's safety and moved him out of harm's way into the living room, laying him on the couch.

The metallic clinks of drawer scrounging had stopped. As Mack spun around to face his assailant, a twelve-inch butcher knife drove deep into his chest, directly into his heart.

Walter's face twisted in perverted satisfaction as he pushed in the blade, grinning with a wickedness that was almost debilitating in itself.

Mack screamed as he felt the thin blade cut into him and the burst of pain that followed. With consciousness slowly fading into dreamlike darkness, he grabbed the knife by the handle, and pulled it from his chest. It fell from his hand, banging on the tile floor. With the world spinning upside down in his head, he went to his knees, wobbling like a tree in a strong wind. Then he fell face down at the feet of his intended victim.

Walter let out a sigh of relief and stared at Mack's lifeless body. His mind reeled with unanswerable questions and a situation that complicated the wonderful plans he had made to entertain Ryan.

Feeling parched and shaky, Walter left the dead to the dead and helped himself to a beer from the refrigerator. The pop from the pull-top brought him instant relief. He turned the bottom of the can up, chugging several gulps, and spilling some down his chin.

There was a dead man in his living room, and an abducted child on his couch. Calling the police was out of the question, even though he was totally justified in the killing.

The alcohol gave him a fresh perspective. The dead guy wasn't going anywhere. Why worry about him? No, it wasn't as bad as he was making it out to be. He could still have his fun with Ryan. When he was finished, he would take them both to the city dump. Trash bags were cheap, and he had plenty of room in his van.

"You sick bastard!"

A mouthful of beer shot out of Walter's nose at the unexpected cry. He turned and saw his intruder on his feet, with an obvious intent of revenge in his eyes.

"You . . . you aren't human," Walter said.

"Neither are you!" Mack slammed his fist into Walter's nose. Blood squirted like a bursting ketchup pack. He followed with a punch to the stomach. Walter heaved and grabbed his gut. Then Mack's hands latched onto the pervert's throat. Veins throbbed in his forearms as he squeezed with every fiber of his being energized with hate.

Walter's cheeks flushed beyond red, and blotches of purple started to appear. His eyes bulged like grapes.

Before Walter passed out, Mack bit his right eyelid, and tore it off.

Walter tried to buck free.

Mack held him in check and did the same to the other eye.

The eyelid fell from his mouth when he opened it to speak. "Where you're going I want to make sure that you see everything we have planned."

*

After Walter passed out, Mack resisted the urge to finish him off. Fatigue weighed in, and he felt a little dizzy. The alien virus expended a lot of his reserve energy repairing his heart.

He put Walter in a deep sleep by emptying the contents of the syringe into his jugular. Once assured he was out, Mack went to the child's side.

There was a small amount of dried blood on the boy' nose. His lower lip was puffy and cut on the inside, as if from a tooth. Other than that, he looked perfectly healthy. The boy breathed in shallow rhythm, no doubt in the clutches of drug induced sleep.

Mack hurried outside to his truck, and backed it up to the front of the van, positioning his truck to block the view from the street.

Walter had a cell phone on his belt. Mack took it and stuck it in his front pocket. He then pulled the man by the feet out the door and into the cover of the truck's camper shell.

His mission complete, Mack drove out, and parked at the end of the street. He pulled out Walter's cell phone and dialed 911. "There's a missing boy located at twenty-five twenty-one Monarch Lane. You need to send a police car over now." Before the operator had a chance to ask the first question, he ended the call, and waited.

In less time than he thought it would take, blue flashing emergency lights headed up the street. Mack waited until the police car turned at Walter's address, and then sped off to his destination.

"Thank God that's over. I don't know who you are little guy, but my prayers are with you," Mack said, glancing in the review mirror. "You don't have to worry about this piece of shit ever coming after you again." Rage burned inside. "That's a promise."

CHAPTER 27

The North Dallas branch of the Loyal Order of The Non-Dead Epicurean Society held its monthly meetings on the top floor of a six-story building owned by the Chairperson, Siegfried Wagner.

Wagner had earned a fortune in the stock market well before The Dark Times. Not long before the outbreak, he sold his stocks, and invested in real estate and precious metals. The hard assets were still in his ownership when The Dark Times ended, and his fortune increased during the rebuild. Not only that, but his leadership and benevolence in the community had earned him great respect.

With money comes power. With money and power comes influence. When his personal physician, David Dial, had diagnosed him with an incurable form of cancer, he had also offered Siegfried a personal gift, a Resurrection Y treatment.

The offer had not come without personal risk. If discovered, Dial would lose his medical license and earn a mandatory twenty years prison sentence.

Wagner had accepted the offer, as it was his only real option for survival. The mutated alien DNA combined with his during the treatment and totally rid his body of the cancer.

As a matter of conscience, now that he shared something in common with the slaves rebuilding the country, he found himself growing increasingly sympathetic toward the Sub Z labor force. The members worked tirelessly around the community, doing the unskilled jobs the Living didn't need, or didn't want, to do. All the while the Sub Zs required little in return. The Sub Z workforce kept mostly to themselves, even avoiding eye contact with the Living as they went about their menial tasks. The Sub Zs toiled night and day to preserve the modern way of life for the Living.

Wagner provided seed money as an anonymous donor to fund various organizations that recognized the abuse of the Non-Dead, including the NAAND. It was only later that he came to learn of the plight of the Sub Y Class of the Non-Dead, of which he was unofficially a member, as Sub Ys were so few in number. The Sub Y Class was forced to work in jobs below their skill level and to exist on wages well below the poverty line.

What started as a private support group for Sub Ys slowly turned into a social club, and over time, branched out into a social network. Perhaps it was the remnants of the alien DNA functioning within the human system that had a mysterious binding force all Sub Ys shared. Wagner wasn't sure. But the camaraderie among the Sub Ys was without question. As were the proclivities toward advancing as a species and enjoying the bounties of what their altered existence enabled.

As he scanned the table, all of the expected members were in attendance, along with the invited guest ready to petition for membership. Wagner rose from his chair and called order by tapping a wine glass with his pen.

"To the fine gentlemen and the exquisite ladies of the Loyal Order of The Non-Dead Epicurean Society, I bid you greetings to our monthly gathering. For most of you here, you'll notice a new face sitting at my right." Wagner gestured with his hand.

"His name is Stanley Hetzel. We learned of Stanley from the national database, through a newly placed contact in the Department of Homeland Security. He is local to our Chapter and has passed the vetting process with flying colors.

"No longer will he wander through the world of the Living, feeling lost and all alone, begging for scraps from the tables of the ruling masters.

"We have embraced him for what he is—what we all are. What we have become has been a blessing in disguise. Now in our advanced state, erroneously classified as Subspecies Y of Homo sapiens, our common goal is to enjoy this blessing. To achieve the greatest good in society by pursuing the pleasures life has to offer. To attain a state of tranquility and freedom from fear, as Epicurus himself believed, after whom we've modeled our Society.

"Knowledge, friendship, living a virtuous life, we combine all in hopes of building a new respect for us in our new society. Our goal is to hasten the day when the Living will no longer see us through the eyes of prejudice and accept us as equals.

"For those of you who have legally undergone the transformation, and are formally classified as Subspecies Y, I'm sorry you are carrying this burden alone. I pledge to you that this will not stand. As the national movement for equal rights for the Subspecies Y and Subspecies Z goes forward, those of us who are hiding our transformation are growing in number. At the appropriate time, I, along with the other illegals, will proclaim our condition publicly.

"In doing so we will expose the Living for what they truly are, hypocrites. Not all Living, but most. We would have no voice in the world today without the sympathetic Living on our side.

"Imagine the reaction when the well-respected professor who beat cancer, and yet continues to perform at his normal high level, outs himself as having been cured not by traditional means, but by the RY drug. Imagine the surgeon, the minister, the librarian, or just that nice old fat guy who lives down the street when they step forth and tell their story.

"Through our combined efforts, the Resurrection Y drug is being successfully manufactured in a secret lab I personally fund. No longer will it be available only to the rich and influential people outside of government controls. No longer will those in need sell everything they own in a last act of desperation and buy a treatment in the back alleys, only to find later the drug was nothing more than saline solution. But others—whom we will choose with the utmost discretion—we shall save and add to our growing ranks."

A mild round of applause warmed the air.

"As always, before we get down to the minutia of boring business details, we'll have a little *pick me up* to help get the creative juices flowing. I would like to thank Mack Teller and Jarvis White for their efforts in securing this month's presentation.

"Ladies and gentlemen, to Mack and Jarvis." Wagner lifted his wine glass from the table and raised it in the air. The members rose and did the same, bringing their wine glasses to their lips at Wagner's command.

A stainless steel gurney hidden underneath a white tablecloth pushed by a man wearing a food service uniform bumped its way past two spring-hinged doors and onto a sheet of plastic covering the floor.

Displayed with the prominence of a Thanksgiving turkey, Walter Simmons lay naked, his body clean shaven, and arms and legs strapped securely to the gurney. His lidless, bloodshot eyes darted around the room as he jutted his head from side to side.

"For tonight, the dish has been prepared with a light dusting of sea salt, white pepper, thyme, and a squeeze of garlic. If you will, please join me," Wagner said.

The sixteen members of the Society gathered along both sides of the gurney. Wagner reached to untie the gag from the man's mouth.

Stanley leaned toward Mack, and said, "I don't know if I can do this. I want to do it, I think. I don't know if I can."

Mack chuckled. "I remember when I had my first taste. It was almost two years after my transformation. I didn't have a clue that having a desire to eat human flesh was a side effect of the RY treatment. I guess none of the test subjects were brave enough to share that information. It would have meant instant death to confess that, I'm sure. The first time is very special, though. It's something you'll always remember."

"Really, what's it like?"

"Think of your first orgasm. It's that special."

"Why is Wagner taking off the gag? Won't the guy scream?" Stanley asked.

"Sure, he'll scream. But it will enhance the experience. Be careful to keep the bib in place or you'll stain your clothes," Mack said.

"Hey! What are you freaks doing? Get me off here! Somebody call the cops!" Walter struggled harder to free himself from his bonds.

"Now-now, let's not work up a sweat. Calm yourself," Wagner said, patting Walter gently on his shoulder. "Ladies and gentlemen, I shall begin," Wagner concluded, plunging his face toward Walter's right cheek, and ripping out a plug of meat with his teeth. After a thorough chewing, he swallowed and chased the delicate pleasure with another taste of wine.

Walter's startled cry energized the room.

"Interesting. Very tender with an ample amount of fat. He is of English and French descent, with a tad bit of Spanish and American Indian mixed in, which makes the flavor quite distinct. Mrs. Beck, I would like to hear your thoughts."

Kasey Beck pulled her long blonde hair behind her neck. She opened her mouth wide, and forced her teeth into the other cheek, as Walter struggled to pull his head away. She ripped off a piece of cheek. Walter wailed like an air horn.

She slowly chewed and closed her eyes, ecstasy over her face. "Oh, my God. I haven't had anything this delicious since the Jamaican."

"Stop! Stop it right now! I'll do anything you want! ANYTHING! Please don't eat me. Please don't eat me." Blood and saliva from the wounds on his cheeks leaked down the sides of his face. Walter remotely resembled a clown with a most horrified expression.

"You sick son-of-a-bitch—how dare you beg for mercy!" Mack blasted. "Just listen to yourself. Do you know what I hear? I hear the screams of countless children as you savaged them. Did you stop? No, because there is only blackness in your soul. I'm only sorry you only have one life for us to take."

Mack leaned over and yanked Walter's penis to the side. His head went low, and his teeth gouged off Walter's scrotum.

Walter heaved out a rattle in his throat that sounded as if he were choking in mud.

Mack brought his face up to meet Walter's. The sack filled Mack's mouth, and the two testicles poked out like two uncooked meatballs. He slowly bit down, letting blood spill down his chin.

The gore dripped onto Walter's frozen gaze. His eyes rolled to the back of his head

"It appears the entertainment portion is over. Our guest is in the onset of shock. Please, enjoy yourselves while there's still life in him."

Stanley watched as the other members tore at the dinner guest like a pack of wild dogs. Blood gushed from the gaping wounds as chunks of meat disappeared.

"Better dive in while you can," Mack said after he finished another mouthful.

"It's so raw . . . so fresh . . ." Stanley went in for a bite of forearm. The meat squished between his teeth, and his face lit up as he swallowed the savory delight. "This is fucking fantastic! It makes me feel like a God!"

CHAPTER 28

There was enough light in the room for Lisa to see she was alone. Where she was, the time of day, how she got there, all were a mystery.

The room was uncomfortably cool, chilling her to the bone. With no apparent way out of her situation, she carefully stepped to the nearest wall, and ran her fingers over it—searching for a way out.

The wall had the strange feeling of flexible metal. As she walked the perimeter, the wall texture didn't vary, nor did she come across a seam of any sort. She was trapped in a box with no explanation of the room's illumination.

Claustrophobia weighed over like an elephant sitting on her chest. She found the cool air drying to the inside of her throat and swallowed to bring it moisture. Her anxiety built as each second dragged her down an abyss of hopelessness.

A white light as bright as the sun penetrated her peripheral vision through a hidden door opened by an unseen hand.

The area outside was as much a mystery as the room. Bathed in light, it appeared to extend into infinity in all directions.

Lisa poked her head through the door. Nothing but the floor underneath felt real. In this case, she would have to risk the unknown in what waited outside over the known confinement of the room.

Lisa stepped out on faith alone. The floor outside felt warm to the bare soles of her feet. Oppressive warmth, thick and moist, enveloped as she waded headlong into a growing wind.

She found herself wishing for the cool, dry air of the room as sweat beaded on her brow. The wind increased to a ridiculous force. She leaned into it, almost coming to a complete standstill as it pushed against her.

A familiar voice whispered in her ear, "This isn't over." Then, she felt something wet lick the inside of her ear, sending icy needles down her spine.

Lisa spun around and saw Normie Cantrell standing by her, his eyes wide in madness.

The wind stopped. Complete silence fell. Normie slowly walked around Lisa, as a cat circling a wounded mouse. She turned and faced him, ready to run if he made a move toward her.

"The real money comes when a guy gets to blow his wad," Normie said.

A wall of naked men appeared, surrounding her—a vile bunch covered with oozing scabs and pustules, as if they had crawled out of the sewers from the pits of Hell.

"It's time for you to earn your money, Lisa," Normie said, then bellowed with laughter that echoed in Lisa's head.

The wicked crowd snarled with delight and rushed Lisa, grabbing whatever their talon-like fingers could hold. Pain shot throughout her body like wildfire as she felt pieces of her flesh ripped from her body.

The laughter drowned out her ability to think. She screamed to drive Normie's voice from her head.

Lisa woke from her dream. A ceiling fan above spun slowly. Sunlight filtered through drawn curtains to softly light the room. She batted her eyes until the unfamiliar shapes in the room took focus. Her mind raced to make sense of her surroundings.

Reality brought the same dilemmas as her dream. Where was she? How long had she been here? She didn't think she was inside The Dancing Bare. The room had a typically *home-like* feel to it. The bed was incredibly comfortable; the sheets felt like fine Egyptian cotton. An alluring smell of men's cologne filled her nostrils when she rubbed her nose on the pillow.

"Lisa, are you awake?" A voice at the end of the bed asked.

Lisa abruptly sat up, pulling the covers to her neck. "Yes."

"How are you feeling?"

The sudden movement made her head spin. A wave of nausea delayed her response. "I've been better."

Several seconds of silence passed. "Do you know where you are, who I am?"

"At the risk of sounding like a total fool, no, I don't."

"I'm Rick Poundstone. You know, the congressman."

Lisa let out a sign of relief. She was free of Normie.

"I brought you here last night from the club. My house was closer than your apartment, and I thought it would be easier for me to care for you at my place."

"I don't remember much of anything about last night. How did I end up naked in your bed, and why do I smell like puke? What have you done to me?"

"Hold on, Lisa. I haven't done anything to you. When I heard the message you left on my phone, I was worried. I found out where you were with the help of the police. When I located you at the club you were already naked. I'm sorry, but I don't know the story behind that. If I hadn't come to your rescue, well, God only knows what would have happened.

"I spent half the night holding your hair out of your face while you propped your head over the toilet and threw your guts up. Please understand, I haven't taken advantage of you in anyway."

"I don't remember much about . . . I'm sorry. I just..." Lisa's voice cracked as she tried to hold back tears.

"None of what happened last night is important. I need to make sure you're okay. I want to help you get your life back together," Rick said.

"Do you have a magic wand in your pocket? That won't be as simple as you make it sound."

"I'm not trying to make it sound simple. First, do you need medical attention?"

"I have a headache, and I'm incredibly thirsty, but I don't want to go to a doctor. I don't think he has a prescription for extreme shitfaced."

"When I left you this morning I put a note on the table for you to help yourself to what was in the fridge. I see you never woke to get the note."

"This morning? What time is it?"

"A little past six p.m. Let me get you some sports drink. It'll help with your dehydration," Rick said, and left the room.

Lisa pulled her ankles under her thighs, trying to get more comfortable, still holding the sheet under her chin.

Rick returned with a tall glass of an iced lemon-lime drink and handed it to her. "Would you like something to eat? Crackers? Fruit? Can you think of something?"

Lisa took the drink with one hand, keeping the cover up with the other. "Nothing now, thank you," she said, then drank from the glass.

She let the sweet-tangy liquid roll over her tongue and pool in her mouth before swallowing. She felt instantly refreshed.

Rick waited for her to finish, acting as if his hands were foreign objects that he didn't know where to place.

Lisa finished the drink and repressed a burp. "I needed that, thanks."

"I'm serious about my offer. You don't have to make any decisions right now. I'll lay it out for you at the proper time. Why don't you take a shower? I'll find some clothes around here you can wear. Your bag and clothes smelled like old cigarettes and sour beer from that club. I left it in the trunk. I didn't want to bring it inside and stink up the place. You took that robe off before you got in bed." He pointed toward a trash can in the corner of the room. The robe was wadded up in it. "I've considered burning it in the fireplace," Rick said.

Lisa couldn't tell if he was disgusted with her or if he was making light of the situation. "You let *me* in here to stink up the place."

Rick smiled. "With you, I didn't have a choice. Although I could have hosed you off outside. Maybe next time.

"You get in the shower. I'll put some clothes on the bed for you after I pull off the sheets and put them in the wash. You'll find some toiletries in the white cabinet." Rick left the room without saying anything else.

"Order received loud and clear, Mr. Congressman," Lisa said to herself. Feeling ill from the smell of her own body, she couldn't think of anything she'd rather do, and slid out of bed, heading for the shower.

The master bathroom was sparkling clean with the smell of chlorine bleach lingering in the air. She now remembered flashbacks of being sick the night before. Her knees, still sore from kneeling in front of the toilet, reminded her of that. But how long had she been sick? She couldn't remember.

Bob's bathroom had always looked like a Frat boy's disaster area. Hair in the sink, dried toothpaste everywhere, so much clutter on the counter there wasn't a square inch of empty space. Rick's however, was staged for a photo shoot. Tastefully decorated, everything in place. Even the trash can was clean enough to eat from. She entertained the notion that Rick might not be heterosexual.

Once in the shower, she turned the water on full and as hot as she could stand. The brass showerhead blasted out powerful jets of water that felt like tiny needles bouncing off her skin. It was therapeutic but too intense to linger on one area of her body very long. She had to keep moving.

The fragrance of the green apple shampoo lifted her spirits even more. Hope, for some reason, started to creep back as a possibility.

Feeling revived after a good scrubbing, Lisa turned off the shower and pulled a towel from the shelf. The plush cotton drank in the water, leaving her dry and clean.

A large cabinet provided a practical assortment of toiletries. New toothbrushes sealed in plastic, toothpaste, women's deodorant, nail polish remover, dental floss, cotton balls, mouthwash, and a hairdryer.

"Well, well, well. I guess he's accustom to girls sleeping over."

She grabbed the hairdryer and the brush hiding behind it, and plugged it in by the mirror. Lisa looked at herself before she turned it on. There she was, pasty white with dark circles surrounding her emerald-green eyes. She wished she had her bag. Her makeup was in it.

After she dried her hair, she returned to the bedroom, and found a pair of women's pajama pants—pink with little blue bunnies—on the bed. For a shirt, he had left his Texas A&M football jersey.

No panties. I guess I'll be going commando, she thought.

Lisa dressed herself in front of a full-length mirror and brushed her hair to be as presentable as possible. The jersey hung to her thighs and could have been worn as a mini-dress. It looked sloppy.

The A and the M on the jersey bulged from her large breasts; the T framed the tops and plunged down her cleavage.

I hope I don't frighten Rick out of his own house, she thought.

She left the bedroom and walked down the hall, following the smell of cooking onions to the kitchen. Rick was busy over a skillet. The heavenly aroma made her stomach growl, and then induced another mild wave of nausea.

"Trick or treat?" she said.

Rick's smile melted when he turned to greet her.

"My body makeup is in the stinky bag in your trunk. I'm sorry you have to see me like this," she said, her head lowered.

"Forgive me. I . . . never mind." Rick's gaze zeroed in on her right forearm. "Is . . . is that where Byron . . ."

"Bit me. Yes. Nasty looking, huh? I can cover it nicely with makeup."

"I'm so sorry. I'll go get your bag."

She lifted her head and pointed a finger. "No, on second thought, don't. This is who I am now. At least you have an idea what I go through when I look in the mirror."

Rick paused, looked away, and shook his head a few times. He cleared his throat. "I'm pan sautéing tilapia filets in olive oil. I've got lump crabmeat for topping. I'll be giving it a splash of white wine at the finish. There are two potatoes in the microwave and green salad in the fridge. If that's too much for your system, I can make you a sandwich. If something like soup is more to your liking, I have a can or two in the cabinet for you to choose from."

"The fish smells so good I'm powerless to resist your hospitality. I can't believe you whipped up all this while I was in the shower. Were you planning to entertain tonight? Did I make you cancel your plans?" Lisa asked.

"The tilapia came from Wal-Mart. It's been thawing in the fridge since last night. I washed two white potatoes from the pantry. The salad's a bag of mixed greens. The lump crabmeat comes from a can. It's hardly anything special. It's not much more than fast food," Rick said.

"Well then, good. I already feel bad enough for all I have put you through."

Rick turned to her and smiled. "What? It's good I didn't have a date tonight?"

"You know what I mean, silly. You can't imagine how stupid I feel. What a total moron I must be. Thinking I could trust that slime bucket, Normie Cantrell," Lisa said, rubbing her brow. "I truly thank you for helping me."

"You're welcome. Go ahead and sit down, and get ready to eat." Rick dished out the filets onto two dinner plates, adding the potatoes after cutting them in half. He set the plates on the breakfast table next to napkins and dinnerware.

Lisa bashfully sat with her hands in her lap.

Rick scooped out two bowls of salad and placed them on the table. Then he brought out the butter, sour cream, and a homemade vinaigrette dressing.

"I'm having a Chardonnay. How about you?"

"Normally I'd love one. Tonight, I think I'll stick to water."

"Hmm, a pity. The fish pairs well with the wine," Rick said, as he filled his glass. After getting ice water for Lisa, he took a seat at the table.

"I'm still feeling a little ill, but I'm hungry too," Lisa said.

"Dig in. Don't be shy. Make yourself at home," Rick said, drinking wine.

Lisa cut a piece of fish with her fork and took a bite. "This is delicious. I feel like I'm eating at a restaurant."

"Really? Which one? Long John Silver's?"

Lisa laughed. "No, you know what I mean." Chasing the fish with a bite of salad, she said, "What kind of dressing did you put on this?"

"It's Dijon raspberry vinaigrette. I made it myself."

"You certainly have made a place for yourself in the kitchen," Lisa said, adding butter to her potato.

"Thanks, I guess next you'll have me barefoot and pregnant," Rick said.

"What's what the standup comedy routine? I thought you were a distinguished member of the House?" Lisa teased.

"Don't worry. I won't quit my day job." Rick drank more wine. "Not just yet, anyway."

Lisa laughed and had some water.

"You know, as strange as this may sound because you're not wearing makeup, you're beginning to look just like the woman I met in the therapist's office. Just like the one that stormed in the church that morning and took on the whole congregation. I know you would have no way of knowing, but you have been in my mind since the day we met. I never dreamed that we would meet again here at my house under these circumstances." Rick raised his glass.

Lisa looked down and picked at her fish. "I couldn't imagining anything like last night happening either.

"Rick, honestly. This is a wonderful meal. I haven't had someone cook for me since . . ." Lisa stopped, lost in thought. "Since before . . ." She felt the tears coming again.

"Lisa?"

"I'm okay, sorry. I didn't mean to get emotional. I'm grateful for your kindness, and I don't want to ruin dinner."

Rick reached out and touched her left hand. "I understand." He returned to his meal as if nothing had happened. "So, now it's time for me to get something off my chest. Something that has plagued me from the time we first met.

"There's nothing I can do to turn back time and erase all the tragic events of the last several weeks. But what I can do is to take the broken pieces and do my best to put them back together.

"I know you're hurting financially, as a result of your Sub Y status. To be honest with you, I'm partially to blame for that. My corporate backers wanted the rights of the Sub Ys to end when it came to voting and pay equality. To improve bottom line profits mostly. There were fewer Sub Ys when the legislation passed, so there wasn't much outcry. Oh sure, we blew our own horns how we allowed Sub Ys to own property. But we conveniently failed to give them the status to earn enough money to buy any.

"So I'm partly responsible for your situation beyond my relationship with Byron. In order to try to mend things, I would like to offer you a job working in my campaign. I'll provide wages and benefits equal to what the state was paying you, at least until the election is over. Of course, I'll have to pay you in cash. How does that sound?"

Lisa raised her eyebrows. "You want me to work to put a man back in office who supports legislation that will prevent me from earning a fair living? Can you guess why your offer isn't bowling me over?"

Rick sighed. "I know, I know, but hear me out. There are several bills coming up I wouldn't have supported in the past. I'm going to tell you this in the strictest of confidence. I'm going to support one of the bills introduced by the Democrats. It will give all Sub Ys the option of equal rights with the Living or to continue their current status."

"Why a choice? Why not just make us first class citizens again?"

"Benefits. The government provides benefits for all Sub Ys. If you opt out, no free housing, free ATP nourishment, nothing free at all. You'll be on your own like any other Living. Paying rent, buying groceries, paying taxes, and saving for retirement. Not every Sub Y feels as strongly as you do about equal rights. But it's not fair to deny any Sub Y equality to the Living unless it's by choice."

"You're starting to win me over. What's the catch?" Lisa said.

"Catch? No catch. Let's go down this road and see where it brings us. If I win reelection, it's possible you could come to Washington to work on my staff. I know you're well educated and very strong-willed. If you can apply those skills to running an office in D.C., there might be a future for you. But you'll have to earn it. No one rides for free."

"How could I work for you in Washington? I'm still a Sub Y, and God only knows how long it would take any new legislation to pass."

"I can hire you as part of my janitorial staff. I'll find a way to pay you enough to live comfortably," Rick said with a sly smile.

"What will I be doing while working in the campaign?"

"Soliciting phone contributions. Calling people to encourage them to support me. Remember, I said you need to earn your keep. It's a volunteer position, so we won't be violating any employment laws by taking a Sub Y on."

"Gas, grass, or ass. No one rides for free," Lisa said.

Rick almost choked on a mouthful of wine. "What?"

"Just an old joke my uncle used to say. Okay, Congressman, I'll take your offer. But this little girl isn't going to be stuck in some cubical getting the phone slammed in her face all day long. I've had enough of that experience working for the N double A-N-D.

"How about this? I know every restaurant manager and owner in this area by their first names. You'd be surprised how many go out of their way to schmooze the state health inspector. I can make direct contact with them, and I'm sure I can get a few dollars thrown your way you might have missed," Lisa said.

"Okay, it's a deal. You handle it your way at first. Let's take it one day at a time and see how it goes. I'll send a cab to pick you up in the morning and bring you to my headquarters. You need to know my political positions on issues front to back before you even talk to one person. Don't misrepresent me. You can use one of my pool vehicles until yours gets repaired. I'll handle the cost of your deductible," Rick said.

"I need rent money for this month too. Slime bucket Normie paid me an advance, but I'm going to give it back to him."

"Done. Consider it back wages for the time you've been off work," Rick said. "So, are you ready to work for an evil, rascally Republican?"

"Whereas the Democrat candidate is certain to support my cause, he's also certain to lose this election. If I help put your ass in office, you had better be reconciled to the fact that you'll be taking me to Washington. Heck, you have no hope of winning at all without my help," Lisa said, and smiled.

Rick smiled back. "That settles it then. I don't mean to be a party pooper, but I do have some things I must finish tonight. Since we're done eating, it's best I take you home now."

"Yes, certainly. I need to get out of your hair so you can take care of your business. I simply can't tell you how much I've enjoyed this meal. Thank you for giving me an opportunity to get back on my feet. Here, let me help clean up," Lisa said. She gathered her dishes and brought them to the sink.

Rick followed behind her with his. "Oddly enough, this has been one of the most interesting twenty-four hours in my life. It's been fun, kinda sorta." He raked the leftovers into the garbage disposal and left the plates to soak.

Lisa went to the door and waited for him.

"Would you like me to take you home on my Goldwing? I find riding my motorcycle has a therapeutic effect. It makes me feel like I'm leaving all my troubles behind," Rick said.

"No thanks. If I have to puke I need a window that I can roll down."

"*Riggght*. It was stupid of me not to think of that." Rick gathered his keys and wallet from his coat pocket and met Lisa at the door. "Let's go."

"I'm not wearing any shoes," Lisa said, wiggling her toes.

Rick glanced down at her feet. "So? It's not like you have to walk on a bed of hot coals to get to my car."

"I don't like walking outside in bare feet. Can I please have my shoes?"

"I'm not getting your shoes for you. I told you, that stinky stuff stays outside."

"Okay, do you have any I can wear?"

"I wear a size thirteen. If it were snowing you might be able to use a pair for snowshoes. How about I carry you to the car?"

"Carry me? Are you crazy?"

"I've been accused of worse." Rick opened the door, put his arm around Lisa's back, and lifted her from under her knees. Her face was inches from his, their noses almost touching. Their gazes locked.

"Verde ubatuba," he said.

"What? Is that French or Swahili? *Sprechen Sie Englisch.*"

"Your eyes. They're the most beautiful green. I've never been this close to you to see how a touch of gold mingles in the green. Verde ubatuba is the name for a type of granite."

"So, my eyes remind you of a kitchen countertop? You sure know how to compliment the ladies."

"You should hear my joke about how women are like guns."

"Save it. Take me home before you drop me."

"Oh ye of little faith," Rick said, and then he carried her to his car and drove her home.

Rick dominated the thirty-minute drive to Lisa's apartment, going over positions in his campaign, and current strategies.

Lisa intently listened, wanting to learn all she could as quickly as possible so she could begin her solicitations.

After parking at her apartment complex, Rick exited the car and used the remote to open the trunk. He retrieved the bag and brought it to Lisa.

She pulled her shoes out of the bag and put them on before leaving the car.

Rick escorted Lisa to the door, where she removed the keys from the bag, and unlocked the door.

"You're probably tired of hearing it, but thanks."

"You're welcome. You'll get a chance to see my nasty side when I'm chewing ass at the office."

"Gee, what a wonderful mental picture. I can hardly wait. Stay here. I'll go change, and you can have your clothes back."

"Why don't you take them off and hand them to me? It wouldn't be the first time I've seen you without your clothes on."

Lisa put a hand on her hip. "My stripping days are over. And you are crossing a line, buster."

"Hey! It was just a joke. I'm your employer now. I know better than to get a sexual harassment suit slapped on me."

"Since you've learned your place, you're forgiven," Lisa said, rewarding him with a big smile.

"Good, now that we've made up, how about I come back to see you some other time and pick up the clothes? You can cook for me, if you want."

"We'll see. Maybe so. I think I might like that."

Rick turned after a grin and a nod, and walked to his car.

Lisa closed and locked the door behind her. Her mind was busy planning what outfit and shoes she'd wear for her first day of work tomorrow.

CHAPTER 29

Byron awoke with a gasp for breath as morning reveille signaled the beginning of a new workday, his sheets drenched in perspiration. He'd had a nightmare.

He was trapped in a closet. No, not a closet. He was lying down. It was a coffin.

Outside, he heard voices. Voices that casually spoke about everyday events people take for granted.

"Let me out! Please, someone let me out!" He banged on the lid.

No one heard him. No one came. The conversation drifted away. Something round appeared in his right hand. He brought it to his nose and gave it a sniff. It was an apple. He could smell the apple. When he put his teeth on it and bit down, the wake-up song jolted him back to reality.

He moved to the edge of his cot, cradling his head in his hands, and waited for his dream-fog to clear. The apple. Its taste was in his mouth. On his tongue. The rich sweet and tart flavor danced on his palate. When was the last time he had tasted anything?

His brethren rose to the daily routine, gathering linens, lining up like cattle ready to put in a day on the ranch.

Bryon made a fist, and examined every square inch of his colorless skin, as if discovering it for the first time. He flexed his fingers and toes and felt his scattered thoughts pull together. The alien DNA within was mending the severed synapses in his brain.

"Tooty, get yer shit together, and get movin', boy. I swear, I don't know what to think about you sometimes," Andy hollered from the doorway.

Byron rose and gave Andy a scowl. He snatched the linens from his cot, eying Andy, as he left the room.

Andy bowed up his back and swelled out his chest, and then let out a sigh of relief when Byron stomped past like a petulant child.

"The sun must be fryin' that boy's brain. I'd better get him a bigger hat," Andy said. He trailed Byron acting as if he was expecting something to go awry.

Byron deposited his linens in the hamper and took the last position in line, waiting at the showers.

Andy passed him without incident, walked to the end of the room, and turned on the moving sidewalk for the *guests'* morning feeding.

Byron kept to himself, not offering Andy any more threatening stares, acting normal again, and following the routine along with the others.

Andy checked each member off his list as the Non-Dead filed onto the bus, then he took the driver's seat, and cranked the engine.

Byron sat in his usual position, the right front seat, a privilege he had earned a long time ago for being such a hard worker. The tension lay thick in the air between them.

"So, tell me, Tooty, is something not feeling right inside yer head?" Andy asked, shifting into gear.

Byron stared out the side window. "Everything feels the same."

Andy gave it the gas and drove away. "Something seems different. I wonder if that sunscreen they add to your ATP is messing with your brain."

Byron didn't respond.

"Ain't I workin' you hard enough? Would you like more to do?" Andy asked.

"No," was all Bryon said.

"Uh, *no* I ain't working you hard enough, or *no* you need more things to do?"

"I'm fine."

"*Fine* my ass," Andy said to himself and punched the button on the radio. "This here's my favorite station. It plays both types of music, Country and Western." He joined right in at the chorus. "But he's a go getter, a go getter. When his wife gets off of work, he'll go get 'er."

"You better turn at the next exit. Thirty-five is closed today for repairs," Byron said.

"Boy, what are you jabberin' about over there? Can't you see I'm trying to sing?" Andy stopped, and closed one eye. He turned down the radio. "Did you just give me directions?"

"I said you need to turn before you get to Highway thirty-five. It's closed today for bridge repair. Take the next right and follow Oak Wood to ninety-four, then ninety-four to I six ten. That's pretty close to the jobsite."

Andy stuck his little finger in his ear and rubbed it around. "Well, I don't remember any such thing. What's the matter with you, boy? A spring come loose? Your kind can't find his own ass without one of us telling you where it is."

Byron turned his head again to the window. Andy blew past the exit he had suggested.

"I might have to let you sit in the bus today. Keep you out of the sun until we can get one of them doctors at the Institution to look at you. Something's gone haywire."

The next sign on the road read 'Hwy 35 3/4 miles.' Andy slowed the bus from 65 to 50 as he rounded the curve, anticipating the exit.

As the curve straightened, the exit came into view. Four road barriers with flashing yellow lights blocked the exit, just as Byron had said.

"Well I'll be a—how did you know about this, boy?"

"There was a sign by the road that said exit two twenty-one was closed to Highway thirty-five for bridge repair. When you didn't slow as we approached exit two twenty, I assumed you didn't see it, so I told you. You chose to ignore me, and now you'll have to drive ten miles in the wrong direction before you can turn around and head back to the jobsite," Byron said.

"*Sunnuvabitch*, the guys back at the Institution ain't gonna believe this," Andy said softly.

Byron turned his attention back to the window, waiting patiently for the remaining pieces of his once sound mind to find its way back into place.

*

The bus arrived at the jobsite a good half-hour late, though none of the workers seemed to be aware of the delay. Andy marched them off the bus and set them up for their assignments. Everyone, including Byron, fell in line and started working, picking up where they left off the day before.

Across the interstate, Larry Fillmore and his crew were hard at it. Larry whistled, getting Andy's attention, and then pointed to his watch. Andy raised both hands in the air and shrugged his shoulders. Larry gave Andy the bird and laughed. Andy returned the gesture with both hands.

Time clicked on by as usual. Concrete saws buzzed throwing white dust into the air. Jackhammers pounded in the background. Cement trucks dumped loads into forms where the rubber-booted Non-Dead waded through the thick mixture, leveling it with long trowels. Andy walked from back to front, smacking on bubble gum, and drinking bottled water. He kept busy making sure his workers stayed motivated and offered helpful instructions to keep things in line.

As the clock neared noon, the daily lunch wagon arrived from the Institution. Larry Fillmore and his crew crossed the interstate for the daily respite.

Tom, a mid-fifties Sub Y who had once suffered from a broken spine, hopped out the food van, and lifted the side door. Bottles of water and sodas cooled in a large ice chest. Foil packages of sauerkraut stacked in boxes set next to plastic forks on a shelf. A variety of sub-sandwiches lined the front of a glass door refrigerator.

Larry was first in line, with Andy next. Byron and the rest of the other forty or so Non-Dead lined up behind the Living.

"Hey, Tom. How are you?"

"Fine. How're you guys holding up out here? It's pretty dry," Tom said.

"Not bad, it's been worse. What'cha got for us today?"

"Today is ham or turkey subs."

"I'll take ham, corn chips if you got 'em, and a real Coke. Not one of them diet things."

Tom took a sandwich from the fridge and fished out a bag of chips from a box on the floor. He opened the ice chest. "Here's your sub and chips. Help yourself to the drinks." He turned to Andy. "What'll it be?"

"I'll take ham and a bag of potato chips, plain."

Tom handed him his food, giving him a smile and a nod.

Larry peeled the plastic off his sandwich and took a large bite.

Tom grabbed a pack of sauerkraut and a plastic fork and tried to hand it to Byron.

"I'll have a turkey sub, barbeque flavor chips, and a pack of deli-mustard if you have it."

Tom's jaw dropped, along with the pack of sauerkraut to the ground.

Larry almost choked on his sandwich.

"Oh my lord, he's gone done it again," Andy said.

"What the? Did he ask for a sandwich?" Larry said.

"I don't know what's gotten into Tooty today. He's been *Polly Parroting* since this morning," Andy said.

"What do you mean?" asked Larry.

"He read a sign by the road and made it sound like he understands directions. He hears you and me order a sub and he orders a sub. All he's doing is repeating things. He don't understand what he's doing."

"But he wanted a turkey sub. You two got ham. He wanted barbeque chips. Neither of you asked for that," Tom said.

"Well, all I know is he's been acting strange all day. I should've kept him in the bus and out of the sun," Andy said.

"Can that boy think for himself? I've never heard of that happening with a Sub Z," Larry said.

"I don't know what to think. All I know is that Tooty here has me so embarrassed that I feel like I'm standing *nekid* in a room full of nuns. Tom, you got any other sites to visit, or we the last ones?"

"This is my last stop before going back to the Institution."

"Good. Now, pass out that sour shit to the rest of the crew, get his butt in the van with you, and get back home. Take him straight to the med room and tell 'em what happened. I'll put in my report when we get back." Andy turned to Byron. "Get yer ass in the van, sit down, shut up, and don't think about nothin'. Have I made myself clear?"

Byron nodded, walked past Andy, opened the door to the van, got in, and sat down.

"See, he's okay. He knows how to take orders. There ain't no thinkin' goin' on in that head. Something's wrong to make it look like there is. Maybe a doc can figure it out. It's above my pay grade."

Tom curiously scratched at his chin, and then served the rest of the workers in line.

*

"My name is Tom Johnson. What's yours?" Tom and Byron had been on the road for ten minutes. Tom had waited for Byron to speak first as a test. Byron had kept to himself with his face to the window.

"Byron," he said, not looking away from the window.

"Well, Byron, how long have you been with us at the Institution?" Another test: was he aware of passing time?

"I'm not sure. At first, it seemed I'd always been there. But now, I don't think so. I don't know."

Something was definitely different about Byron, Tom thought. His response was laced with an intelligence beyond a typical Sub Z. Is this an unprecedented event of Sub Class Z evolution? One thing for sure, it would be a topic of interest to discuss at his next Non-Dead Epicurean Society gathering.

"You know, I'm just like you. See?" Tom held his hand toward Byron. "My skin is pale like yours. The alien virus is in me too. Because we are just alike, you know you can trust me, don't you?"

Byron turned to Tom. "You're not just like me. You don't have numbers written on your forehead."

"Er, ah, no, I guess I'm not *just* like you. We both have the alien virus, though. Mine is a different strain. I had the virus injected to cure a physical handicap. The strain of virus used doesn't cause death. Whereas your strain did cause your death. But after your infection, you were given an altered virus very similar to mine. It made you more like you were before you were infected." Tom was uncertain how Byron would react to the awkward explanation and wished he hadn't started the conversation.

Brake lights ahead pulled Tom's attention back to the road. Byron continued his vigil at the window. The traffic slowed until eventually coming to a halt.

"Great, what is it now? Eighteen wheeler jackknifed again?" Tom said rhetorically.

Sirens rose in the distance, an ambulance approached up the shoulder. Tom craned his neck out the window for a better view, wishing he could move his vehicle over to give it some room.

"Must be an accident up ahead. I sure hope no one's hurt. I wonder how long it's going to take to get this mess cleaned up? These things can take hours sometimes. Say, Byron, since we'll be stuck here awhile, would you like something to eat or drink? Heck, I'll even give you a sandwich if you promise not to tell anyone," Tom said, as the ambulance rumbled past his window. "Byron?" Tom turned and found the passenger's seat empty and the door slightly ajar.

Tom cursed, mad at himself for being so distracted he didn't hear Byron leave. He charged out of his vehicle in frantic pursuit, calling for him. The line of cargo trucks stopped along the highway hindered his view, he ran to the adjoining lane.

Tom spotted a lone figure heading straight toward the emergency, a hundred yards away. Raging flames threatened an elementary school on the corner.

Tom returned to the van and reported Byron's escape to the dispatcher over the radio.

*

Byron arrived in time to see one of the two wings of the school's roof collapse in the blazing fire. Three fire trucks streamed hundreds of gallons of cooling water from the big guns, but it was obvious they fought a losing battle.

A mass of children and a few adults crept as close as they could in awe of the destructive power of the mighty inferno.

Byron ran up to a woman who stood on the balls of her feet, looking in frantic anticipation toward the school.

"Did everyone get out? Is everyone okay?" he asked.

"No! Two children are still missing! The roof just fell in. Oh, God! Oh please let them find them," she said, her eyes glued straight ahead.

Three firefighters stumbled out the front door. Two on the outside held the one in the middle up under his arms. All three of their air pack alarms rang, indicating the cylinders were almost empty.

"They didn't find them! Oh no," the woman burst into tears and fell to her knees.

Byron rushed to the equipment vehicle and grabbed a pair of firefighter's boots and pants. He kicked out of his shoes and put them on as fast as he could. He put on a jacket and cinched it tightly, backed into an air pack, then buckled it around his waist. He connected the mask to the cylinder, opened the air valve, and last of all put on a helmet.

He pushed his way through the crowd and ran past the Fire Captain, who yelled something undecipherable at him as he entered the school.

Once inside, Byron dropped to his knees, able to see ten or so feet in front of him. On his right, Byron heard a high-pitched squeal. He didn't waste a moment wondering why, he knew it was a firefighter's personal alert safety alarm, blaring to show where a firefighter lay motionless for more than ninety seconds. Finding a wall with his right hand, he crouched, and hurried toward the alarm.

He slowed as he stepped on ceiling debris and came to a halt when his knee bumped into something solid. The alarm came from underneath the wreckage that blocked his path.

Byron reached down and felt a gloved hand pushing up on the debris, perhaps the air conditioner ductwork and ceiling structure. Putting his two hands beside the downed firefighter's, Byron lifted the structure high enough so the firefighter could free himself.

As Byron let the structure back down, the Firefighter tapped him on the back of his leg. Byron understood why when an alarm continued to shrieked underneath the debris.

The firefighter went down on his stomach and crawled under the ductwork. Byron struggled to keep the path open. The heat started to inch its way through the protective fire gear.

The firefighter worked his way back out, pulling his companion free from his would-be grave.

Byron let the structure fall to the ground and helped the firefighter drag the unconscious man out the front door.

Two other firefighters raced to their aid as the three emerged from the cloud of smoke. They took the limp body and carried it to the team of paramedics.

Byron caught a glimpse of a News 2 camera crew filming the event before he turned and headed back into the burning school.

With the façade of the school threatening to cave in, Byron dropped to his knees, and crawled toward the other wing. This time he kept his left hand to the side of the wall until he came to the door of the first room.

It was open, but visibility was limited to a couple of feet. He had to crawl on his belly as he made a quick check around the room for the two children. His heart pounded in his chest more from fear of their safety than from physical exertion.

He heard a crash of splintering wood behind him.

Time's running out. If I don't find them soon they're goners. Think, damn it. Byron slammed a fist to the floor. *Okay, the rooms up front were the most likely to be searched before the fighters had to bail. I'll head to the back and try there.*

He crawled down the hallway crunching debris along the way until he came to the last room. His hand went to the left wall as a guide while he crawled the room's perimeter. *Come on. Come on. Be here, damn it!* No successes.

The light from the window allowed him to see two rows of desks. The children weren't there. He crawled to the other two rows and went down each one frantically searching for a body. *Please, God. Please let them be here. Let them be here!*

A rumble from the hallway followed by a loud crash told Byron time had run out. He crawled to the classroom doorway and found it blocked with debris. *Is it my time to die too, God? Is this how it finally ends?*

His only way out would be the window. Byron crawled past the teacher's desk and crashed into a chair. Realizing he hadn't searched the front of the room, he reached in the leg space. The two children were crammed tightly in under the desk. *THANK YOU, JESUS!*

With little time to spare, Byron grabbed each one by the collar, stood, and dragged them along a wall until he came to a window, making sure to keep the children as low to the floor as possible.

The window latch—thick with rust from non-use—didn't want to budge. *Bastard! You won't beat me!* With death only seconds away, Byron removed his air pack and crashed it through the window. Glass exploded inward, raining upon the children on the floor, as the fire sucked fresh air from the outside. *Sorry, kids. I had no other choice.*

Byron brushed the larger pieces of glass away and carefully placed each child outside the window onto the cool grass. Then, he removed his mask and pulled the two to safety.

Both children were young boys, somewhere around the age of six or seven, he guessed. One coughed and appeared to be okay. The other lay silent. "I'm sorry . . . I wasn't quick enough."

He looked around for help and realized he was in the back of the school. All the help was staged in the front near the firewater supply. Byron pulled out a piece of glass embedded in the young boy's cherubic face and immediately started CPR.

He took his gloves off to get a better feel for the chest compressions, as he didn't want to break any of the boy's ribs. During the excitement of CPR, it was easy to injure adults, and easier to hurt children.

The boy began coughing after about a minute, a minute that seemed to drag on for an hour. The other boy was on his feet and staring down at his friend as he opened his eyes to another chance at life.

Byron fell onto his back and released his tension in a loud "Thank you," voiced to the sky, his chest heaving to replenish the oxygen in his body.

"Are you okay, mister?" the boy asked.

"Yes, I think I'm going to make it," Byron said.

"Is Dexter going to be okay, too?"

Byron turned to the other boy he left to recover on the ground. Dexter propped himself on his elbows, his head slowly bobbing as he looked around.

"I think Dexter's going to be fine. How about you?"

"My chest hurts, and it smells like smoke inside my nose."

Byron laughed. "Thank your lucky stars you can still breathe. What's your name?"

"Andrew."

"Well, Andrew, we'll get you to the doctor, and have you back to normal in no time."

The crash of the roof on the other wing collapsing startled all three survivors. A large plume of black smoke mixed with burning embers shot high into the air. The screams of the crowd in front of the school had Byron back on his feet again

Byron put his fire helmet back on. "Come on, boys. There's a bunch of people who can't wait to see you."

*

"I'm standing in front of Lakewood Elementary, and as you can see behind me, it's in flames. The school will be a total loss. But what is even worse, I'm told that two of the children are unaccounted for.

"Just minutes ago, the roof of the second wing collapsed, diminishing the chances of their survival. Teachers and parents are on the scene, and I must say, there is not a dry eye in the crowd. Everyone here is praying for a miracle," Bill Percle from News Crew 2 said, his face stiff as he tried to keep his emotions in check.

A woman gasped and shouted, "Look! Over there! They're alive!"

The camera swung away from Percle and at the woman who yelled the announcement. She pointed to the east side of the school. The cameraman pushed his way through the crowd as claps and cheers rose up around him.

Byron walked alongside Andrew, carrying Dexter in his arms.

Dexter smiled and waved as the three walked toward the cheering crowd.

Three paramedics rushed to their side. One gently took Dexter from Byron, and another lifted Andrew into his arms. Both headed to a waiting ambulance. The other came up to Byron, but he waved him off.

Percle hurried toward the savior fireman with his microphone leading the way. The cameraman took a strategic position and started filming.

Byron removed his large red fire helmet, fully exposing his face to the onlookers. More gasps arose from the crowd as the hero of the day presented himself, his face pale white and dark eyed with his Sub Z ID cut into his forehead.

For the first time in his career, Percle was speechless for an interview. The camera kept rolling. A zombie had never risked its own life saving a Living before without being told to do so.

CHAPTER 30

Rebecca sat on an uncomfortable metal chair in the NAAND office. She held the phone between her ear and shoulder, while gripping a pen in her hand ready to take notes. It was shortly after 5 p.m., and today, like yesterday, she was alone. So far, like yesterday, not one person had allowed her to finish her rehearsed solicitation, and each one had abruptly ended the call by hanging up.

Despite the success of Chapters of the NAAND in northern states, which grew daily in new members, the Dallas Chapter had gone flat.

I bet a chart would show our Chapter's problems increasing membership is proportional to Dad's rising popularity. 'God's new plan for man.' What a crock. It's just a new mask worn by the old prejudice. And it's my own flesh and blood leading the pack. Fuck my life.

The outside door opened, the street noise breaking Rebecca from her thoughts. In stepped Lisa, wearing an olive tint notched collar, short-sleeved jacket, three buttons closed at the waist, topped by a removable belt. The skirt matched in color, and was covered by the jacket at the hip, stopping at the top of her knee.

Rebecca's heart leaped when Lisa entered the room. The phone fumbled from her hand as she quickly tried to place the receiver on the base.

"Hey, Rebecca. I hoped I'd find you here. I've been trying to call your cell since yesterday."

Rebecca sprang from the chair, then rushed over and gave Lisa a quick hug. "I had to turn my phone off. I've been trying to put some distance between me and Ben. He's starting to crowd me a little too much lately. He sent me fifty text messages the day before yesterday."

Lisa stepped back, still holding onto Rebecca's arms. "Sounds complicated. We'll have to do lunch soon so you can tell me about it."

Rebecca sighed. "We haven't gone to lunch in a while. A lot's been going on I've been wanting to talk to you about. Ben and I are in different places in what we want from our relationship. He has romantic feelings toward me. I've been careful not to lead him on, at least not intentionally. I've made it clear I'm not ready for a relationship."

"Even though Ben and I started off on the wrong foot, I've admired how loyal he is to you. He's very cute too," Lisa said.

"Yeah, there's no doubt he's a great guy. I'm lucky to have him as a friend, but something's missing. Chemistry, I guess," Rebecca said.

"Ah yes, the chemicals we share between us. The mysterious *whatever* that attracts people to one another," Lisa said, dropping Rebecca's arms. "It has been almost a week since our last talk. A lot of stuff has happened with me too. I'm trying to forget some of it."

"Oh no, what happened? I was starting to get worried about you. You're normally here three to four times a week. I tried calling, but your number had been disconnected. I actually was going to go by your apartment today. I can tell something's up. Is there some ominous news you're about to drop on me?"

"I got a new cell phone and . . ." Lisa paused for a second and stared at the floor. "Before I get into it, did you see what happened yesterday afternoon? Byron Poundstone rescued two firemen and saved two children from a burning elementary school."

"I heard about it this morning. I didn't get all the details. The report was kind of sketchy. Byron is a few years older than I am, but we grew up together going to the same church. He was a fireman before he went missing, and—and you know the rest of the story," Rebecca said.

"His brother, Rick, was shocked when he heard what Byron did. All the times he visited him at the Institution, Byron mostly acted despondent. Something must have clicked in his brain yesterday, and he went into action like he was still a Living. It's causing quite a controversy."

"A controversy? The good kind or the bad kind?" Rebecca asked.

"For our cause, the good kind. For the other, the bad kind. The district fire chief is mum on the situation. The news did a fair job of making Byron sound like a hero. But there have been complaints that an unsupervised Sub Z was allowed to run loose, never mind the way he saved those kids."

"Some people are useless."

"No doubt. Rick spoke with Byron yesterday, and Byron said he wanted off the road crew. He wants his old job back with the fire department. Rick said he couldn't do anything about that right now, but that Reverend Hatfield wanted him to come and work at the Streets of Gold Church."

"Hatfield, what? What in the hell is that man up to now?"

"I know, sounds insane. Hatfield is a two-faced, motherfucking, flying asshole. But, Byron wants to go to work for him. Can you believe that?

"Anyway, he'd be doing basic maintenance and whatever his skills allow. Rick's scheduled an appointment with Hatfield to help Byron get started. Maybe you can go over and get reacquainted with Byron, make him feel welcomed. His success could certainly help our cause," Lisa said.

"It sure could. His act of bravery could make a huge impact on public opinion. We've got to handle it right. Maybe take a less *in your face* approach and try to get people sympathetic to his cause. I'll bring it up at our next Chapter meeting," Rebecca said.

"Great idea."

"Say, how come you know so much about what Rick Poundstone has been doing? And since when did you did you start calling him by his first name?"

Lisa sighed. "That's the other big thing I wanted to talk to you about. I, uh, I can't donate any time to the N double A-N-D, at least not until after the primary. Or the election if Rick takes the primary." She paused. "Or I might even be moving if Rick wins reelection."

Rebecca's face flushed. "Lisa, what are you talking about? We need you working with us now more than ever."

"I know, but I may be more valuable to the cause in my new job."

"Your new job? And what would that be?"

"Rick, I mean Mr. Poundstone, has asked me to work for his campaign," Lisa said, squinting her eyes as if preparing to get slapped.

"He what? You're working for Poundstone? Are you nuts? How in the ever-loving hell is that going to help our cause?"

Lisa grimaced. "I know this news is upsetting. It's not what you think. Rick regrets some of the positions he's taken in the past. He's also promised if he's reelected he'll support a Democratic bill to give all Sub Ys the option to choose equality with the Living. But please don't tell anyone about this. He didn't want it to come out before the election."

"Did he promise you a bag of magic beans too? I hope you didn't trade in the cow," Rebecca fumed. "Is he getting the milk for free?"

"What do you mean?"

"You know what I mean. Poor Lisa, gets turned into a Sub Y by his brother. He makes it all better by putting you on his staff and tickling your fancy."

"Rebecca, my private life is none of your business. There is nothing inappropriate going on between Rick and me."

"I didn't say the relationship is inappropriate. I said he's screwing you."

"Hey! You're out of line, sister!" Lisa stopped just as she formed the next word on her lips. Pausing a moment, she cleared her throat, and softened her voice, "Rebecca, honey, don't act this way. Rick and I are just friends. He's my boss. We believe in the same principles. What we feel for each other is an uncertainty."

"So you admit it, then. You have feelings for each other."

"There's nothing going on between us right now to admit," Lisa said.

"What about us?" Rebecca said, her bottom lip quivering.

"Nothing's changed between us. We're still on the same team."

"No, what about *us*? You and me? Isn't it obvious I'm attracted to you? Think of all the time we've spent together here, all our talks on the phone, the lunches we've been to. Why do you think I keep inviting you to go away for the weekend? I melt every time you look me in the eyes. I hang onto every word you say. I get goose bumps when you're near me. Can't you tell I'm in love with you?" Rebecca took Lisa's face in her hands and kissed her. Hard. She held the kiss as long as she could, pouring her heart and soul into it. The kiss seemed to last forever.

Lisa pushed away from Rebecca. "Rebecca. I'm sorry, but no . . . no honey. I didn't know you felt that way. I'm sorry, but I . . . don't share those types of feelings."

Rebecca buried her face in her hands, unable to control the flood of emotion.

"Please, honey. Let's not do this. I've never been closer to any other girl in my life. I just thought that's how girls acted to each other when they had a special friendship. When I was growing up I used to see other girls do each other's nails, hair, hold hands, and even kiss. I never got along with other girls. It didn't get any better when I got older. Other women have never really liked me. I've only had boy friends as far back as I can remember. I'm sorry I didn't see the signs. I wouldn't let things go this far to see you hurt this way." Lisa stepped forward and put her hands on Rebecca's shoulders.

Rebecca shrugged them off.

"My life is just starting to turn for the better. I have you to thank more than anyone else for that. I hope you understand—I need you to understand. It's just that I don't have the same feelings for women as I do for men. It's nothing personal."

"I . . . don't have feelings for women either. Just you. You're different . . . special . . . you're—" Rebecca cried louder.

"You are a beautiful person, Rebecca. You're smart, you're pretty, and you're strong. There's someone out there for you. It's just not me."

Through a few sniffs, Rebecca said, "I'm not as strong as you."

"Don't sell yourself short. Every day that I have known you, you have grown stronger. Remember, you came to my apartment that first time we met and stood up to me. Your strength gave me the courage to climb out of my shell and participate in life again."

"Really?" Rebecca said, hope in her voice.

"Really. I couldn't have made it without you. I'd be stuck in a Non-Dead compound right now slaving away at some shit job twelve hours a day. So, please, let's find a way to remain friends. I need you in my life." Lisa tilted her head to the side and raised her eyebrows. "Maybe we are in different places in what we want from our relationship." Lisa winked at Rebecca, and smiled.

Rebecca took a deep breath and slowly nodded her head. The tears continued to fall.

*

"Yes ma'am, how many in your party?" The hostess' makeup looked unusually thick on the right side of her neck. She pulled her long black hair from behind her shoulder and draped it to the front. Lisa realized she had been caught staring and felt compelled to apologize and confess she too was Sub Y.

Did she feel that way out of guilt or out of solidarity? There was no way to know for sure. She had done little to interact with other Sub Ys, no doubt because she didn't want to be reminded what she had become.

"Hello. Representative Rick Poundstone has reservations for two at twelve thirty. I'm sure he's not here yet but—"

"Mr. Poundstone arrived a few minutes ago. Come this way please." The congenial tone in her voice in the initial greeting had frosted over a bit.

I guess I insulted her. I know just how she feels. I suck, Lisa thought. She followed the hostess into the main dining area and past a short row of booths. Rick was at a table for two, with fingers tapping wildly on his cellphone. He turned his head toward the hostess when she stepped up and placed the phone on the table.

"Your party is here, Mr. Poundstone. Your waitress will be right with you." The words couldn't have sounded more pleasant. The look she shot Lisa as she left cut like daggers.

Rick rose from his chair. "Hey. You look wonderful today. Of course, you're dressed to kill every time I see you."

Lisa waited for Rick to pull out her chair and sat. "Which isn't often enough, and thank you for the compliment," Lisa said as

Rick returned to his seat. "I'm shocked you're here before me. You have a notorious reputation for being late."

"Well, I felt so bad for keeping you hanging for over an hour at our first lunch I—"

"Two hours, but who's counting," Lisa teased.

Rick raised his nose and crinkled his brow. "Yeah, that was pretty bad. Anyway, I wanted to be sure I was on time today."

"Thank you. That's very considerate of you."

"I could do nothing less for my most improved solicitor. You're doing quite well for a newbie."

"I floundered the first couple of days, but after that first lunch, you gave me a better sense of direction."

"Great. Then I'll expect similar results this time. If I'm buying you lunch, I expect a return on my investment."

Lisa crossed her hands on the table. "Yep, no one rides for free. You sure know how to crack a whip."

"Me? I'm just an old softy. One of my gifts is helping people reach their full potential. There's no telling what you can accomplish. Heck, you might run against me in the next election."

"That'll be the day."

The waitress arrived at the table carrying two menus printed on single sheets of paper and a pen. The bangs of her blonde wig hid the ID numbers etched on her forehead. She was in prime condition for a Sub Z, destined for several years of servitude.

"Are you ready to order?"

"Yes," Rick said, not waiting for Lisa's opinion.

The waitress placed the menus on the table in front of the patrons and the pen in the middle.

Rick pulled his menu closer and ran his finger down the list. He picked up the pen and made two checks on the menu. "I'm have a grilled Caesar salad with beef tenderloin and a Coke. You?"

Lisa thought a moment. "I'll just have a house salad and a Diet Coke." She took the pen from Rick and checked off her selections.

Rick gathered the menus and handed them to the waitress.

"Thank you," she said and headed for the kitchen.

"Cheap date. You didn't wanted something from the grill with your salad?" Rick asked.

"No, not today. My eyes were bigger than my stomach at our first lunch. I didn't even finish half. I don't like wasting food. My nutrients come from my ATP makeup. I just need to eat a little solid food to keep my insides working properly."

"I don't know about your insides, but the outside certainly works for me."

"Hey, I thought this was a business lunch?"

"It is. I'm *giving you the business*."

"Ha ha, Mr. comedian. I'd rather you give me some more suggestions to get donors to part with their money."

Rick brought his hand to his chin, and then reached out to take the drinks from the waitress when she came by. He shoved one toward Lisa and tasted his. "Ugh, we need to switch drinks." He made the exchange. "When you solicit for contributions, do you make the potential donor feel like his opinion will make a difference in my campaign?"

"Well, I guess not. I mainly state your positions and paint a clear picture of how you plan to represent them in Washington. What should I do?"

"You have to kind of play a lawyer's game. Say things that aren't promises. If the person has a different outlook that's not too radical from my campaign, let him know that a growing number of voters in the district feel the same way, and that I'm open to change based upon my constituents wishes."

"Even if a *growing number* don't feel that way."

"Yes. Even though that part may not be the full truth, I am open to change based upon voters opinions. No harm, no foul. Doing that will make me more favorable in the person's eyes. Something else you can do is ask them their future plans in business. Be positive and think of ways I might, and the key word is *might*, be able to help them accomplish those goals. Don't make any commitments, and don't make it sound like they can buy my influence either. Be tactful though, and say something like, *Donors have a louder voice in any campaign*. Simple enough?"

"I get it. You know, politics is such a huge game. You guys are better actors than those in movies."

"True to a point. I don't like to think of it like acting. To me, it's salesmanship. I'm selling a product, and I have to make people want to buy it."

"I thought prostitution was illegal?" Lisa snickered.

"Hey! I resemble that remark," Rick said, feigning annoyance. He immediately turned his attention to the waitress as she brought the salads. "I had the one with the meat on top."

The salads were placed in front of the patrons, and the waitress left.

"I used to be a real bitch when it came to Sub Zs serving me in restaurants. Now I feel sorry for them," Lisa said, picking at the salad with her fork.

"It's a sad situation we're in, no doubt. But it's the best solution for the time. Do you realize if we didn't have them, a large number of Living would perish from starvation? We need their help just to have enough food to eat. The Living Party's plan to eliminate the Non-Dead is one or two hundred years premature. Sure makes one hell of a campaign program though."

Lisa put a bite of salad in her mouth and slowly chewed, gazing aimlessly around.

"What's up. Something wrong with your food?"

"No, something happened yesterday afternoon that's been weighing on my mind."

"Someone hit on you when went to visit?"

"No. It's, uh, personal—with a friend."

"Male or female?" Rick stopped in mid chew.

"Female. My only real other friend, other than you."

"Really. I didn't realize you lived such a sheltered life."

"My life's a long story. Not meant for lunch chatter." Lisa put her fork on the plate. "She's going through a tough time in her life—emotionally. I wish I knew how to help her."

"Anything I can do?"

"No. This is something that time will work out."

"I'm sorry for your friend. But I'm glad you aren't having guy problems."

"Why's that?"

"I'd be jealous," Rick said matter-of-factly and stabbed a piece of tenderloin. He chewed with his gaze glued to her reaction.

Lisa didn't hide the surprise from her face, nor could she stop the giddy smile that replaced it. "You just don't say that to all your solicitors, do you?"

"You're the first. You can trust me. I'm a politician."

"And you suck as a comedian."

"I'll give you that. But I warn you, I'm a very good kisser."

Lisa laughed. "A good kisser, huh? And how do you know that?"

"My mother told me."

Lisa burst into laughter and brought her napkin up to cover her mouth. Rick smiled with a big piece of meat practically covering one of his front teeth. She lifted her hand and pointed, holding back her outburst as much as she could.

"What?"

"You . . . you've got some meat . . ." she said, trying to control herself, and pointed to her front tooth.

"Oh." Rick lowered his head and scraped a nail along the front row of teeth. "There, did I get it?" He made a Cheshire Cat smile.

"Good afternoon, Mr. Poundstone." A tall, aging man wearing a fitted blue suit stepped up to the table. "I hope I'm not interrupting, but I have been waiting on your phone call."

"Mr. Pinkston. So glad to see you." Rick hopped up and shook Pinkston's hand. "I didn't forget about you. In fact, I was going to call right after I finish lunch."

"I see." Pinkston looked over at Lisa. "Tim Pinkston, pleasure to meet you."

"Lisa Goudard. Nice to meet you." She made no attempt to shake his hand, but tilted her fork toward him in greeting.

"Unfortunately, I'll be tied up after lunch. Would it be a huge imposition if we talked now?"

"No, not at all. Lisa, would you mind if we—"

"I understand. Please go ahead."

"Let's go to the bar." Pinkston patted Rick on the shoulder and waited for him to lead the way. He turned back to Lisa. "I won't keep him long."

Lisa faked a smile until he turned. "You better not," she muttered to herself.

From her vantage point, she watched Pinkston order a drink and sit at the bar. Rick did most of the talking. Pinkston nodded his head every now and then. Lisa finished her salad and reached the bottom of her drink.

Pinkston slid off the stool and gave Rick a long handshake while patting him on the shoulder. There was no doubt he was pleased.

Rick adjusted his jacket collar, and before he could begin his walk back to the table, another man swooped in from the side and grabbed his hand. The man jabbered away, and Rick acted pleased to see him.

Rick looked over toward Lisa and raised his shoulders.

Two nicely dressed women got in line waiting their turn to meet the Representative.

Lisa threw her napkin in her plate and looked at her watch. She would have to leave in a few minutes or miss her next appointment.

CHAPTER 31

"Reverend Hatfield, I couldn't wait to talk to you. I've made a breakthrough!" the voice of Scott Fenton buzzed over the phone headset.

Hatfield moved the phone away from his ear and winced. "It sounds like you're about to burst over there. Why don't you take a minute and compose yourself? I want to make sure I understand what you have to tell me."

Scott breathed deeply into the phone a few times and exhaled loudly. "Okay, okay. I'm not entirely sure how it happened. Maybe it was a result of the initial gene therapy I gave to Byron and it mutated. Or perhaps the RZ drug he was given that transformed him into a Sub Z combined with my work and mutated. I guess it doesn't matter how, but I finally spliced in a gene with his DNA that can produce ATP indirectly from light. I did that by manipulating the melanocytes in the skin. The function of the melanin in the skin produced by the melanocytes is to absorb UV-radiation and transform the energy into harmless heat. That's to prevent indirect DNA damage that can lead to cancers.

"Instead of turning the UV-radiation energy into heat, the altered melanin converts the UV-radiation into energy a cell can use for ATP production. The ATP fuels the rest of the cell.

"Not only has that problem been solved, with the alien DNA, I can now restore telomere length during cellular reproduction, keeping it from reducing in length. You know what that means, don't you?"

"I might be able to guess, but I would rather you explain it to me," Hatfield said, and sat straight in his chair in full attention.

"We age because when our cells reproduce, the telomeres at the end of our chromosomes shorten in length. With this breakthrough, the cells will regenerate as exact copies of the previous healthy cell. Telomere length remains the same. Our cells will never pass on old age. There will be no reason for man to die!"

"How sure are you? How do you know the tests aren't giving you false results?" Hatfield asked.

"I know I've only been working on this for the last two weeks. But it was almost as if the missing piece of the puzzle was waiting inside Byron's blood. The gene reaction I needed happened instantly. I witnessed nothing short of a miracle! Reverend, everything you've said to me, everything I've come to believe is confirmed. The Spirit that has spoken to us both is real, and soon we shall bruise the head of the Old Serpent once and for all!"

"What about skin color and the other alien side effects to the body?"

"None. In fact, the cells show more vigor. Reverend, this may prove to be a true fountain of youth!"

"Praise the Lord. The day has come. The day has really come. You have Resurrection X."

"I have Resurrection X!" Scott yelled at the top of his voice.

Hatfield moved the phone away from his ear again.

"Reverend? Sorry, are you still there?"

"I'm here. When will it be ready? As I have been chosen to be the first vessel of immortality, I must get my house in order." Hatfield cleared his throat. "After all, I might be found unworthy and lose my life in pursuit of our goal."

"I'll need some time to make enough for a treatment, several days at least. But I have the utmost confidence in this formula. I'd take it myself. I wouldn't even hesitate to give it to my wife. So you know how sure I feel it will work."

"I've never known you to be so confident, Scott. This goes beyond mere faith. The Spirit is speaking through you. Will you need any more of Byron's blood to complete the project?"

"No, the DNA is replicating on its own. We're finished with him. Why? Are you still concerned he might remember his past association with us?"

"I can't help but wonder what's going on in his head. When you gave Byron his medical exam before he came to work at the church—when you took his blood—there was something unsettling about the way his eyes shifted around. You know, like he was remembering something. Or trying not to.

"Now that he has shown signs of increased brain activity beyond a normal Sub Z, what if he remembers what we did to him? What if he tells his brother and he brings in some outside muscle and shuts you down? We can't afford to let Byron get in our way before our big day arrives," Hatfield said.

"What are you suggesting?"

"I'm not suggesting anything. I simply need to have a plan in place. I'm going to make a call. Keep me updated. Goodbye Scott. God be with you," Hatfield said.

"Goodbye Reverend, and halleluiah!"

Hatfield hung up the phone. His fingers punched in Joel Spencer's private number for his next call.

*

"Byron? What are you doing up there?" Rebecca leaned against a ladder in the hall not far from the Pastor's office at Streets of Gold Church, eye level with a pair of Nikes, and looked up at a set of skinny legs.

Byron's head and shoulders were past the ceiling. He was busy changing out the air conditioning filters. The ductwork connected all the rooms down the hall, including the Pastor's office. It wasn't until he had removed the secondary filter that he had heard Reverend Hatfield's voice carry through the ductwork. He hadn't intended to eavesdrop on the conversation, but when he'd heard his name, he'd stopped working and listened.

Rebecca pulled on his pants leg, reached underneath, and pulled a few leg hairs.

"Ouch! Oh, hey, Rebecca. Sorry, I didn't realize you were here," Byron said, Hatfield's words weighing on his mind.

"My classes are over. I wanted to see how your day is going," she said, twirling her hair on her finger.

Byron set the new filters in place, latched the grill, climbed down the ladder, and met Rebecca, wearing a big smile. "Things are great. It feels so good to be back in familiar surroundings, even if it's only during weekdays."

"I still don't get it. You're good enough to clean the toilets around here but you're not worthy enough to sit on a pew for church service. How can you stand to work for these hypocrites?" Rebecca said.

"I can't explain it. I have this inner dedication for Reverend Hatfield. But there's something else, something hidden I can't quite remember. Something not right . . . a mystery." Byron gazed into the distance.

"Well, you were part of that group my father belongs to. My mom and I called it the *Suicide Squad*, because you guys dressed like you were secret agents protecting the President, ready to throw your body in front of a gun to protect Hatfield. When you weren't on duty at the fire station, you were within an arm's length of the Pastor. Maybe he has some kind of mind control over you."

Byron dropped his head. "I don't know about mind control. But there was something special about being part of that group. I don't remember. Come on, let's go to the break room. I want to sit down for a while."

"Sure, why not?" Rebecca waited while he folded the ladder and returned it to a maintenance closet, and then followed him up the hall.

In the break room, Byron opened the refrigerator, and pulled out two canned sodas. He offered one to Rebecca, who nodded. They sat at the table and opened the cans, escaping gas broke through the silence.

Byron pointed to the package Rebecca had put on the table. "What's in the bag?"

"Something for later. What did you think about the N double A-N-D meeting last night? You seemed to be at ease around the other members."

"Everyone was wonderful. They treated me like I was a real person. I had forgotten what that was like. I was bothered though by that Full-Zombie couple. Just at first. I mean, you wouldn't pretend to be a cripple to make a handicapped person feel better, would you?"

"No, but they weren't there to make you feel better. They dress that way as a dig to the Living who think they're so superior to the Non-Dead."

"Yeah, I realized that later on. But the Living are superior to my kind," Byron said.

"Stop right now. Everyone—Living and Non-Dead—has limitations. Don't lump all the Non-Dead together as being inferior and don't think all Living are superior. Don't sell yourself short," Rebecca said, reaching across the table to rest her hand on his.

Byron felt the warmth of her hand reach inside him and touch a hidden part of his soul. Tears started to well in his eyes. He quickly took a sip of his drink and turned his head so she couldn't see.

"Our Chapter of the N double A-N-D is in contact with the other Chapters around the country. We want to mount a new campaign using your story and the video footage of the fire to knock down the walls of prejudice, to push equality for all. Your story is going to go national," Rebecca said.

"I'm not so sure that's a good thing. There've been some new Army doctors come to visit me at the Institution. I heard a rumor they want to move me out of state and study me. I'm worried that once I'm gone I'll never be seen again."

"Oh my God, I didn't know that was going on. You don't think that's possible, do you? Your brother's a U.S. Congressman. He wouldn't let them get away with that," Rebecca said.

"If Rick weren't my brother I'd probably be gone already." Byron gritted his teeth. "Rebecca, if they come for me, I've decided I won't go."

"You won't go? What does that mean?"

"It means no matter what I have to do, I won't let them take me. Not at any cost."

"I hope you're over reacting. Your brother will be there to protect you. Still . . ." Rebecca took a sip of her drink, lost in thought.

Byron felt bad for turning into a drama queen and wanted to lighten the mood again. "You're right. I'm probably just paranoid. Okay, time to play *What's in the bag*."

Rebecca's eyes widened. "Oh, something I've wanted to do to you for a while. But you have to agree to it before I tell you what it is."

"Do to me? What kind of talk is that?" Byron laughed.

"It's something good. I'm afraid if I tell you what's in there you'll be too shy to go through with it. So if you want to know what's in the bag, you have to promise me up front you'll go along."

"You bought me a G-string?"

"No, goofy. Guess again."

"If it's not a G-string I'm not interested. So there."

"Well then, you'll go the rest of your life never knowing the incredible treasure locked away in this bag." Rebecca giggled.

"I don't want to know," Byron said. The moment Rebecca let her guard down, he snatched the bag off the table.

Rebecca jumped up out of her chair and grabbed onto the bag. "No! Not fair!" Then she *goosed* Byron under his armpit until he let go.

"Ouch, that kind of hurt," he said.

"That'll teach you. Now, last chance. Do you promise to let me use what's in this bag on you?"

"Well, I really couldn't care less. But, since it seems to be so important to you, I guess so."

"Great! Now remember, you promised." Rebecca opened the bag and removed a jar of Creamy Natural skin toned ATP.

"Hey, wait a minute. You're not going to put makeup on me, are you?"

"Yes, I am. You promised."

Byron sighed. "Me and my big mouth."

"I think it would be good for you to see yourself looking more like you did when you were a Living. You don't need to stay in the mindset of *us and them*. Plus, I think you're very handsome. Even if you have pale skin and raccoon eyes. But you'd look even better with some color."

Another heavy sigh. "Okay. Go ahead, and get it over with."

"All right!" Rebecca opened the jar and applied the foundation with a triangular sponge pad.

Byron contorted his face, imitating a five-year-old getting his face washed.

"Oh, it's not that bad. Millions of women do this every day."

"I'm not a woman."

"I know, you're a big, strong, handsome man. And a big, strong man ought to be able to handle a little makeup."

Byron stuck out his tongue and licked some foundation that errantly made it to his upper lip. "Yuck!"

"You're not supposed to eat it, silly. Stop that. I'm almost finished."

"Oh please, oh please, oh please, let it be over."

"Okay, there. Finished," Rebecca said. "You're such a ninny."

"Thank goodness. Now what?" he asked.

Rebecca leaned back and admired her work. "It's amazing what a little makeup can do. You almost look like how I remember you. Here," she pulled a hand mirror from the bag, and held it up to his face, "see for yourself."

Byron looked into the mirror and stared into infinity. His mind erupted—a volcano scattering thoughts like burning lava flying in all directions. His body felt as if it were launched into the air, climbing higher at super speed, until it slammed to a stomach-churning halt. It then reversed, falling, collecting the thoughts on the way, until nearly every memory he had possessed before his transformation had returned.

When his mind solidified into the present, he saw his face in the mirror. Even though he appeared almost as he did as a Living, the Sub Z ID etched on his forehead stood out as a cruel reminder that he could never truly escape from what he had become.

Rebecca gasped. "Byron! Your eyes . . . they've turned blue!"

CHAPTER 32

Rick Poundstone waited for the last bit of his breath mint to dissolve and decided on his opening line before ringing the doorbell. His heart beat as rapidly as it did before addressing large audiences. *Get a hold of yourself, man.*

The door opened with a metallic scraping sound and squeaking hinges. Lisa Goudard posed in the doorway wearing a sexy little v-neck black dress with asymmetrical ruching at the waist. She placed one black-laced-gloved hand on the doorjamb and the other on her hip. "Yes? Can I help you?" The words dripped out her mouth like warm honey.

Rick moved the roses away from his face. His gaze slipped past her smile, down the plunging neckline to her short skirt, and all the way down to her black Giuseppe Zanotti T-strap sandals.

"Wow . . . ." Rick quickly lifted his head and positioned the flowers under his chin. "Excuse me, Miss, I was looking for an employee of mine. Last seen at this location wearing pajama bottoms and an old football jersey."

"I bet you say that to all the girls. Is that your best pickup line?"

Rick thought a moment. "An angel stopped me by the side of the road and handed me this bouquet of yellow roses. He told me to follow the fireflies and give the flowers to whomever they brought me to. When I asked, *What fireflies?*, the angel turned into a swarm and led me to your door."

Lisa nodded at the porch light. "All I see are mosquitoes and a couple of brown moths. Are you sure you haven't been drinking?"

"Nothing to drink yet. But what does a guy have to do to get an invitation to come in?"

Lisa took the flowers and held them to her nose. "You had me at yellow roses. Please, won't you come in?"

Following her lead, Rick stepped in, and closed the door.

"I need to put these in water, so make yourself at home," Lisa said.

The furniture in the living room faced the TV armoire. Its doors were closed. *Good*, Rick thought. He didn't want the annoying TV playing in the background competing for attention. Her laptop set on a coffee table beside a collection of women's fashion magazines. A candle burned on a sofa table and filled the room with the warm scent of baked apples peppered with floral spice.

Lisa returned to the living room carrying the roses in a crystal vase, and placed it in the middle of the coffee table. "These are absolutely gorgeous."

"Thank you. Gorgeous, yes. Not the only thing in the room . . . " his words trailed off.

"What?"

"Er, nothing." Rick rotated his shoulders and straightened his back. "You know, I feel guilty for not taking you out to eat."

"Why? I invited you over tonight."

"Well, our lunch last time could have gone better. And I did want to celebrate your first two weeks with the campaign. You've brought in a huge amount of contributions at a critical time. Taking you out to show my appreciation seems the least I can do."

Lisa moved over to Rick and placed her hand on his. "We can go out to eat some other time. Besides, in restaurants people recognize you, and they're constantly interrupting. I didn't want to share you with anyone else. Tonight, you're all mine."

Rick's heart swelled in excitement at the touch of her glove. She was close enough for him to smell her perfume. "What's that you're wearing? Your perfume?"

"Paco Rabanne. It's supposed to have warm, animalistic allure."

"Would it be improper for me to growl now?"

"Yes. One should never growl before dinner, which, by the way, is ready. You're late, you know."

"I know, and I'm sorry. I had to tie up a few loose ends so I wouldn't be bothered the rest of the night."

"I didn't expect you to be right on time. So, it really doesn't matter. We'll skip the cocktails and load up on wine at dinner."

"Are you trying to get me drunk and take advantage of me?" Rick said, mock cautiously.

"Absolutely not. This is your chance to earn my vote. If you can't match me drink for drink, I'm voting for the other guy."

"In that case, expect to say hello to the legs under the table. Because that's where you're going, under the table," Rick stopped as Lisa smirked. "Sorry, that didn't come out right. I meant I'll be drinking you under the table."

"Yeah, well, you politicians are all full of hot air. Why don't you have a seat, and I'll get things going," Lisa said, as she turned toward the kitchen.

"Is there anything I can do to help?"

Lisa selected a bottle of red wine out of a small rack on the counter and handed it to him. "Monsieur may pour the wine." Lisa had removed her gloves and placed them out of the way.

Rick unscrewed the twist top of the wine bottle. "I miss the good old days when wine bottles used cork. It added charm." He poured equal amounts of wine into the two glasses on the table.

Lisa got busy with the salad. "The change didn't bother me a bit. A screw cap is so much easier to open, and it's actually better for the wine during the aging process. Cork allows oxygen to leach in and can spoil the wine, caps won't. A cap won't disintegrate like cork either. I don't have to worry about bits of junk floating in my wine."

"A screw cap just makes the wine seem cheap. I guess we just get use to things being a certain way and don't like change. Still, I miss pulling the cork out, and the popping sound it makes."

Lisa turned, stuck her thumb in her mouth, and pulled it out, *pop!* "There. Does that set the mood for you?"

Rick looked wide eyed and withheld his comments.

"Have a seat," she said, with a bowl of salad in each hand.

He did as instructed, thanked Lisa when she placed the bowl in front of him, and waited for her to sit. "This looks interesting."

"I found some fresh strawberries at the grocery that inspired me. I mixed baby spinach with sliced strawberries, blue cheese, red onion, a sprinkle of poppy and sesame seeds, and a splash of simple vinaigrette."

Rick forked out a mouthful from the bowl. The crisp greens crunched as he chewed. The salad burst with flavor. "This is amazing. I don't believe I've ever eaten salad this tasty before."

"Really? You're not just saying that, are you?"

"No, really. I have to admit I was a little less than eager to try it when you told me the ingredients, but this is terrific."

"Thanks," Lisa said, after a drink of wine. "How are things at the office? How many know that you have *one of them* working in the campaign?"

"You know, I haven't exactly tried to hide you from the others, but I also didn't put you on display either. Of course, my secretary, Sandra, knows, but perhaps the rest of the team—not so much."

"I met Sandra when I first went and picked up the keys for the loaner car. She was nice and very professional. Everyone else was so involved with their own work I was hardly noticed."

"With the report coming out today, I'm sure they'll wonder who this Lisa Goudard is who brought in over three hundred grand in less than two weeks." Lisa excused herself from the table, removed a foil-covered pan from the oven, and laid it on the stove. "Have you thought how you're going to break the news? I bet there'll be a lot of questions why I came to work for you."

"I don't have to go into a lot of detail. You're just another grunt in the field working for my reelection, supporting the same issues as I do."

"Isn't that like a black person in the nineteen sixties supporting segregation?"

"All I have to say is you're a Republican who wants to keep Spencer and the Living Party out of Washington. Even for Sub Ys I'm the obvious choice over Spencer and his hate filled party. Just be ready to answer a few questions. Don't go into any great detail. The campaign is about me, not you. And please note, I didn't mean to sound egotistical in that last sentence."

Lisa chuckled. "You didn't. I knew what you meant."

"Good, because I really want you to *get me*. You've been an unbelievable self-starter, and I don't want any misunderstandings between us."

"My first two days on the job had me striking out more times than I want to admit. The pointers you gave me at our first lunch opened my eyes to what I was doing wrong. I'm getting contributes from nearly two thirds of my contacts now. But back to the campaign, don't you think they'll be some issues you won't be able to brush away when it comes out a Sub Y is working for you?"

"There might be problems with some of the more conservative volunteers who haven't already left to support Spencer. It's a chance I'm willing to take. I'm sure Spencer's campaign will take the issue and try to twist it to their advantage."

Lisa nodded. "The door hadn't even closed behind me when I left Ralph Meyers—the owner of The Galley—when he paged his secretary to get Spencer on the phone. I bet he was going to tell Spencer I was working for you."

"Really? Spencer's probably had it in for you since the rally. This is really going to make his day."

"And the church. Spencer was there that day too."

Rick finished his last bite. "Yeah, I'll never forget that morning. You made quite an impression on me. In fact, you made quite an impression on me the first time we met."

Lisa closed her eyes. "I remember that day in the therapist's office. I was upset, confused, and a host of other things. I didn't trust you at first, but you're nothing like I had imagined. I'm very grateful for that."

"Neither one of us had any control of the situation that brought us together. I hate like hell things happened the way they did." Rick paused to wipe his mouth with his napkin. "I am glad we met, though. And I want to put away as many negatives of the past away as we can."

Lisa smiled.

"Hey, how about some more wine?" Rick asked, pointing his empty glass toward hers.

"If there's wine in the bottle you never have to ask, just pour. I'll go fix our plates." Lisa picked up the empty salad bowls and put them in the sink. She then went to the stove and removed the foil covering the rib roast. "We're having prime rib. Do you like yours rare or more well-done?"

"I like mine medium-medium-well," Rick said, filling Lisa's glass with wine.

"Picky-picky," she teased.

Lisa sliced two thick pieces of rib steaks, and placed them on the plates, followed by potatoes from the oven. She set the plates on the table and retrieved a condiment tray from the refrigerator.

"Everything's here for the potatoes, except this white sauce," she said, pointing to the bowl when she placed it by Rick. "That's horseradish sauce for the prime rib."

"The meat looks fantastic. I just realized how hungry I am," Rick said.

"Don't be shy—eat up. Don't skimp on the wine. Tonight's a two bottle minimum." Lisa cut into her steak with her knife and stabbed the piece with her fork. Lifting pink-red meat to her mouth, she said, "I don't know what's gotten into me lately. I've been on a red meat kick. The rarer the better."

"What happened? Did the fish I cooked the other night kill your taste for seafood?"

"No, not at all. If I had to pick a reason it might have to do with the body makeup I'm using now. I switched from the makeup with the ATP to the one without."

"Any particular reason?" Rick asked.

"Several things. The ATP makeup rubs off easier. It actually stained a favorite outfit. I didn't want to risk that again. I'm also afraid if I don't eat properly, properly for my new physiology, my organs will start to degrade. I'd like my body to stay as normal as possible. Plus, now that I can afford to buy makeup and food, I'm going to enjoy life to the fullest. That's been my motto since the end of The Dark Times, and I'm not changing if I don't have to.

"But getting back to the craving for red meat, that started a week after I quit the ATP. Well, I haven't stopped using ATP entirely. I still wear a patch at night a couple of times a week to give whatever it is my body needs that eating isn't providing," Lisa said, cutting another piece.

"And I thought my life was complicated," Rick said.

"Are . . . are you making fun of me?" Lisa asked.

"No, no, no. I mean it." Rick put his knife and fork on his plate. "Please don't think like that. You have to treat your life like your coping . . . with an illness. I hope that didn't come out wrong. But I do feel sorry you have to make adjustments in the normal things in life I take for granted."

"Hey, I appreciate that. Let's move this conversation to other topics. I'd like to hear about your childhood. Don't run your mouth so much that you ignore your wine," Lisa said, pointing to the glass.

"I can talk and drink with the best of them," Rick said, and gulped a mouthful.

*

The dishes soaked in soapy water in the sink. The second bottle of wine was empty next to two half-filled glasses beside the roses on the coffee table.

Rick snuggled Lisa under his left arm and gazed longingly into her eyes. "Do you want to tell me why you're wearing those gloves? I noticed you took them off to eat but put them back on when we sat on the couch."

"I've been wearing gloves ever since I started working for you. Some people get a little unnerved when they shake my hand because it feels cold. I didn't want you to be repulsed if I touched you."

"I've held a woman's cold hands before. Cold hands and feet aren't turn offs for a men, you know."

"It's more complicated than that." Lisa made a slight attempt to pull away, but Rick held on and patted her shoulder until she relaxed. "I've tried to create a sense of warmth in the apartment. By the lighting, by the scented candles, any way I can. Even the perfume I'm wearing is meant to give you warm feelings."

"I can tell you're a warm and sensual person just by spending time with you. You can't create an illusion different from who you are inside. I'm a politician. I can read people. But I must say, everything you've done tonight has been special."

"The night isn't over. That is, unless you want it to be," Lisa said.

"What do you mean?"

Lisa pulled from his embrace, rose from the couch, and held out her hand. "Would you like to join me in my bedroom?"

Rick took her hand. "Yes. I'd like that very much."

Lisa pulled him along, holding his hand behind the small of her back, and led him down the hall and next to her bed. "You go in the bathroom and undress. I'll be waiting for you under the covers." Rick opened his mouth to speak, but Lisa put her finger to his lips. "We can talk later."

Rick left her by the bed and went into the adjoining bathroom. He began to unbutton his shirt and caught his reflection in the mirror. Things certainly had moved faster than he expected. Not that he was the least bit disappointed. In fact, she had comfortably handled the situation.

He felt embarrassed looking at his reflection. A shit-eating grin slowly curled around the corners of his mouth. He felt his cock stiffen but really didn't want to leave the bathroom with a full erection. He wanted to maintain some sense of control. He didn't allow women to take control in the bedroom.

He checked his teeth for any food particles he might have missed and left the bathroom, turning off the light before opening the door.

Soft jazz played in the background. The filtered glow from a lamp in the corner gave enough light for him to see everything that was about to unfold. He preferred it that way. He'd never been a fan of making love in total darkness.

"I'm waiting for you," Lisa said, desire in her soft voice.

Rick climbed in the opposite side of the bed, feeling the mattress give way under his weight. "Hey, is this a waterbed?"

"Yes it is. Why? Does it bother you?"

"I don't know. I've never, uh, *slept* on a waterbed. How long have you had a waterbed?"

"I bought it earlier this week. I told you I wanted this night to be special."

"Kinky . . . I guess."

"Not kinky at all. I bought a waterbed so I could control the bed's temperature. While you were in the bathroom it's been warming my body. I told you I didn't want you to be turned off by my cold skin."

"Sounds like you thought of everything. But what about, you know, when I'm inside you."

Lisa reached for a bottle of lubricant on the nightstand. "For that, I have this. It's a lubricant that warms with friction."

"Does it work?"

"I don't know, Rick. I haven't been intimate with anyone else since I was attacked."

A mountain of sorrows weighed down her voice. Lisa had been reduced to something less than human. Here was this beautiful girl who had gone from having any man she wanted to becoming someone afraid of rejection because of an affliction she had fallen victim to. Everything she had done tonight was to create the illusion she was normal. Everything she had done tonight had been planned to the finest detail just for him.

Rick's eyes welled with tears. He now understood Lisa was starving. Starving for attention. Starving for affection. Desperately reaching out for acceptance, and to be desired.

"I want you to know how incredible tonight has been. I've never met another woman like you, Lisa. Your honesty and your frankness have caused me to search inside myself, to question who and what I am. My life is always in the fast lane, and a lot of the time I bulldoze my way through it without considering the consequences. I've stepped on people. I've hurt people. I may have never intentionally tried to, but because of my own selfishness, I didn't care if I did.

"And tonight, tonight has been unbelievable. You did all of this for me. You've opened your heart and are willing to share the greatest gift between a man and a woman with me. I'm overwhelmed. Overwhelmed to the point I don't even feel worthy enough to be here.

"Can you forgive me for what I've done? For what my actions have done to others in the past? I could have made things so much better for the Non-Dead. I thought of them . . . treated them like animals. Even when the Democrats made valid points I ignored them. I ignored them so big business could continue making huge profits. I became nothing but a willing slave master." Rick cleared his throat. "Can you forgive me, Lisa, for everything I've done to make your life so difficult?"

Lisa sighed. "Rick, shut up, and fuck me."

CHAPTER 33

A flatbed truck idled in front of the closed gates of the North Dallas Non-Dead Institution. Normie Cantrell tapped his fingernails on the steering wheel and checked the time on his watch. It was a quarter until midnight. "Got here earlier than I expected," he said aloud.

Darkness shrouded the area beyond the gate. Nearly half the overhead lights around the main building were out. Normie waited with the headlights off. A red warning light atop the empty guard shack provided faint illumination of the gate.

After he checked his watch again, Normie's contact stepped out the shadows, pulling a lanyard from underneath his shirt. Warden Samuel Cain fumbled with the attached cardkey and ran it through the scanner two times before the red light above the guard shack switched to green. The clink of gears and chains rubbing together chimed over the warm hum of the electric motor as the two gates pulled apart.

The truck slowly moved forward. Cain waived it in and ambled out of the way. Directly behind the flatbed, a lone rider followed on a motorcycle. Cain waited for him to pass and started to close the gate, then reopened it. "Better leave them a way out if things go to hell," he muttered under his breath. Using a flashlight, Cain led the vehicles to the ATP tanks tucked away behind the main building.

Once on the scene, both the truck and motorcycle shut down, leaving only the drone of two large air-conditioning units to fill the night air.

Normie, wearing a navy blue Non-Dead working class jumpsuit, climbed out the flatbed cab, adjusted his cap, and scanned the area.

The rider, Rex, dismounted his motorcycle, and walked toward Warden Cain.

Cain turned off the flashlight and met him.

"Good evening, Warden—or should I say, good morning?" Rex said, after lifting his visor.

"I don't know how good it is. I have a reputation I'm proud of, and I have a feeling this thing is going to backfire on me before it's over," Cain said.

Normie followed and joined Rex. Rex reached inside his leather jacket, pulled out a stainless steel flask, and pointed it in the direction of the other two men. Both shook their heads in refusal.

"Don't get all *Goody-Two-Shoes* on us now, Cain." Rex opened the flask, lifted his helmet above his mouth, and turned it upside down. He gulped from the flask like a parched man chugging water.

"Maybe you ought to take it easy with that stuff. It's dark, and you're on your bike."

"You might have a point. This *is* my third." Rex lowered the helmet and spread his arms to the sky. "If I were just an ordinary man you'd have a right to be concerned. But I am no ordinary man." Rex brought his arms back to his side. "I am part of a great plan of grand design. There's nothing I can do, nothing you can do, nothing anyone can do, to stop it."

Cain looked over at Normie, who mocked Rex behind his back. He gestured toward his mouth imitating knocking back a drink, and then stuck his tongue out to the side as if he were out of his mind.

Rex continued, "I could stand on the highway and no cars would crash into me. I could leap off the top of a skyscraper and the angels would return me safely to the ground."

"All that's dandy, but we need to get back to the business at hand. Tell me again what this stuff's going to do," Cain said.

"Sure, sure, business is business, right? *Bidness* is *bidness*." Rex howled at his own joke, alcohol fumes rolling from his open mouth.

"Keep it quiet, will ya?" Cain said.

Rex chuckled. "You don't get it. None of you really get it. No matter, you weren't meant to. All of you, pawns on a chessboard thinking your free will guides you in life. How simple-minded."

Cain took a step toward Rex. "Okay, smart guy. Let's get this thing going before the sun comes up. You can explain the meaning of life to us later."

Normie ran his hand over his forehead, rubbing off a layer of grease, and wiped it on his leg.

"What's the big deal? Normie here unloads the truck into the ATP tank. In the morning the zombies get their morning spray-on breakfast, and then start work as usual," Rex said. "Normie, hop to it."

Normie's upper lip rose toward his nose. He didn't care if Rex was drunk, he didn't like being disrespected. He restrained a harsh rebuff, thinking it best to get this mission over without any further delay.

"And then what happens?" Cain asked.

"And then special enzymes go to work dulling what little cognitive reasoning the zombies have. They'll stop taking orders and begin to wander off in confusion. People will be shocked to see their poor, precious hard-working slaves can't be relied on."

"Won't it look strange that it'll only be guests of my Institution who come down with this disorder?" Cain asked.

"No, because if everything goes as we expect, we'll do the same at three other facilities in Dallas the next day. In fact, we have operatives in the trucking industry who are rallying together to create a network so all ATP deliveries in the South will contain the enzyme. All we need is to sneak a load of concentrate in the tank at the distribution terminal. From there, the trucks will take it to the whole Southeast. If we can make this happen a week or two before election day, I win. I mean, we win," Rex said.

Normie started the truck after connecting the hose and opened the valve to the Institution's ATP storage tank, then began pumping out the tainted contents.

Rex reached inside his jacket, pulled out a new flask, and lifted his helmet. He chugged two mouthfuls.

"Hey, Rexie, don't you think you should—" Normie began.

"Fuck off, Normie, I'm about to sing." His right hand came out of his jacket pocket holding the container with a roach trapped inside. He held it eye level, gazing through it into the night sky.

Cain looked at Normie again, who raised his hands in confusion.

Rex opened his mouth, and softly sang, "Roll out. Roll out with your American dreams and its recruits, I've been ready. Roll out. Roll out with your circus freaks and hula hoops I've been ready."

"He's singing to a fucking roach? You really should put that sauce down, son. You've got me worried about you," Cain said.

"I've seen many different sides of him before, but he's never acted like this. He doesn't even know we're here. He's singing some ancient Alice Cooper song," Normie said, waving his hand in front of Rex's face.

Rex sang louder, "God I feel so stroooong. I feel so strong. I'm so strong. I feel so strong. So strong. God I feel so strong. I am so stroooong!"

Cain grabbed Rex by the arms. "That's enough. You need to screw your head back on straight. I don't care who you are. We may be on the same side, but that doesn't mean I take all my orders from you."

Rex broke out of his trance. "Okay, okay, it doesn't matter anyway. Merrily, merrily, *verily, verily*, life is but a dream." The container and its captive went back into his pocket.

"What?" Cain said rhetorically, letting go of Rex's arms.

The truck's pump shut down on low suction pressure as it went empty. Cain helped Normie block the valves and roll up the hose, placing it back on the truck.

Rex watched with arms crossed—still as a statue until the work was complete.

Cain walked up to Rex. "It's late. I'm an old man, and I'm tired. I need to get some rest before the shit hits the fan tomorrow. If you want my advice, go straight home, and be careful. Better yet, let your friend take you home. I can hide your bike until you're ready to come back and get it."

"I'm taking my bike with me," Rex said.

"Suit yourself. You two boys saddle up, and get out of here." Cain returned to the gate and waited for Rex and Normie to leave.

Normie put his hand on Rex's shoulder. "How about it, big guy? I could take you back to the club. There's still a few hours before sunup. You still have time for a little of the bump and grind."

"Thanks, Normie. I have to admit I'd love to line your girls in a row and bang the dead out of them one by one. But I have things to attend to tomorrow. How about pointing me in the direction of my bike? It's time to leave."

"Gee, are you sure you're okay to ride?"

"I'm kidding, Normie. I'll be fine. Remember the angels and everything."

Normie turned and walked with Rex to his cycle.

"You know, you've been a loyal friend. Look at us, water and oil, and yet we can work side by side," Rex said, sounding even more drunk, much to Normie's chagrin. "I'm not going to forget you Normie. You'll see, soon your life is going to change. It's going to change, and I'll be there to help bring you into the change. The world will be such a better place. The world will be full of love. Everyone will love everyone. I'll love you, and you'll love me. Did I tell you that you've been such a loyal friend?"

"Yes Rex, you told me," Normie said, as the two arrived at the motorcycle.

"Hey, Normie," Rex giggled. "Hey, Normie, do you know what the true definition of a friend is?"

"No."

"A friend is someone who goes out and gets two blowjobs and brings one back for you."

"That's funny, Rex."

"Well, since I can't wait for you to go and get two blowjobs and bring one back, can you just give me one now and get two later?"

"What the fuck?" Normie said, contemplating punching Rex in the stomach.

Rex laughed. "It was just a joke. Don't take it so personally."

"Yeah, funny. Good night, Rex," Normie said, and headed for the truck before he lost control.

Rex straddled his motorcycle and cranked up the engine. "Yeah, funny," he said under the sound of the loping engine.

CHAPTER 34

Byron woke from the muffled beep of his watch's electronic alarm under his pillow. He turned off the alarm, sat up in bed, and then buckled the watch around his wrist. It would be another fifteen minutes before reveille sounded, waking his fellow mates for another hard day's work under the sun.

After stripping his bed of the linens, he removed a gym bag from underneath, and headed to the bathroom.

Byron turned on the faucet and let the water run while he searched through his bag for toothpaste and a toothbrush. Now that he was interacting with the Living, it was important to keep up his personal hygiene—for reasons more than just blending into society. He wanted to be as presentable as possible for Rebecca. She came to visit him every day at the church.

At first he believed her interest in him was for nothing other than to advance the cause of the N double AND. Not now. Not the way she openly flirted with him. He never missed an opportunity to flirt back either. Byron became more human every day. He could feel it throughout his whole body.

After brushing his teeth, he put the dental care products back in the bag and removed a jar of pigmented ATP cream, applying it to his face and arms. As he looked at himself in the mirror, he thought back to the first time Rebecca put makeup on him and the flood of memories that filled his mind after. There was only one dark spot remaining.

Byron remembered volunteering for Dr. Fenton's research. The goal of the research, he was told, was to find a vaccine that would immunize against infection by *any* strain of the alien virus. The objective was to end the issue of the Non-Dead once and for all. Such a vaccine would start the countdown for the Non-Dead's total elimination.

As a loyal member of Streets of Gold Church, and a *right-hand man* of Reverend Hatfield, Byron was willing to do anything to help fulfill the vision God set before them. His last memory at Fenton's medical facility was checking in on a Saturday morning. Something must have gone drastically wrong during the testing. It had killed him, and the alien virus in his body turned him into a flesh eating monster.

Why Fenton had kept him in that condition without administering the Z treatment, or how he escaped to attack Bob Sanders and Lisa Goudard, he had no clue. After overhearing part of Hatfield's phone conversation, he was no longer sure of anything concerning his relationship with the two men whom he had once trusted with his life and soul.

He assumed Hatfield was talking to Fenton that day because he spoke of taking blood. Why was Hatfield worried that his memories might return? Byron had been aware there were risks with the research. Death hadn't been a possibility he'd seriously considered, though. *What did Hatfield mean when he said, 'We can't afford to let him get in our way before the big day arrives'?*

Byron had no intention of telling Rick or anyone else about his memory of the events that led up to his death. He had pledged loyalty to Hatfield and intended to keep it. Something in Hatfield's voice, the way he had spoken about Byron confused him. It was callous, selfish, as if Byron were an object and not one of his beloved sheep. Why would the Reverend think of him that way?

Byron realized the answer was staring back at him in the mirror as he rubbed clear ATP cream on the rest of his body. He wasn't a beloved sheep cherished by the watchful Shepherd any longer. He was a cast out, a goat, a member of the Non-Dead. Worthy only to pick up the refuse of the Living, to sit in the back of the bus, and at the left hand of God.

Morning reveille blared over the Institution's speaker system. Byron gathered his belongings and headed for the dressing room. He planned to get dressed, walk down to the corner, and wait at the public bus stop for his daily ride to the church.

*

Andy Wells assigned his team of Non-Dead to their various duties and returned to the bus for a bottle of water. It hadn't rained for over a week, and the cloudless sky foretold it was going to be another scorcher. He found himself missing his best hand, Tooty. The Non-Dead who replaced him, *Sparky*, was still green from basic training, and held the crew back from a normal day's performance.

After getting his water, Andy returned to the front of the bus with his mind lost in thought.

From across the street, Larry Fillmore signaled for Andy to meet him on the median.

Andy waited for a wave of cars to pass by and trotted over.

"What's up, Larry?"

"I'm not sure, but something not right. Did you notice anything unusual with your crew today?"

"I don't think so. What do you mean?"

Larry scratched the back of his neck. "Mine were a little slow getting their shit together before we left the Institution. I didn't think much of it then. But I can't get them jumpstarted like usual. They've been sluggish ever since they went to work."

"Hell, mine have been slow ever since Tooty left. That boy was an inspiration to the whole crew. Can't say for sure today is different from yesterday."

The piercing blast of a car's horn broke the conversation. The two men turned in time to see one of Andy's crewmembers step in front of a speeding vehicle.

The car flipped him into the air, his head crashed into the windshield, and his body flew over the top like a ragdoll tumbling in the wind.

The car slammed on its brakes and spun out of control, rolling over three times before coming to rest upside down. The driver, a young woman, lay half outside the driver's side window. Blood flowed from a gaping wound on her head. Her right elbow bent in the opposite direction from normal.

"Butterbean! Somebody hit Butterbean!" Andy cried.

The Non-Dead had landed sprawled in front of a 4X4 Chevy truck, which further mangled the body by running over it at excessive speed. The Non-Dead's body rolled in a crumpled mess as other cars swerved to avoid it, forcing some of the vehicles to crash into each other.

Andy and Larry anxiously waited for the pandemonium to stop. The smell of burning rubber and gasoline carried in the air to the unnerving blaring of horns, the squeals of brakes, shattering of glass, and crunching of metal.

"Oh, my Lord, look at what he did went and done," Andy said, shifting side to side, trying to determine which way he needed to run first.

Every sort of vehicle crowded the interstate highway. More horns, more brake squeals, and a few metal on metal crashes reverberated down the road.

A young man dressed in a sports jacket jumped out of his shiny new red Corvette. Somehow he had maneuvered around the other cars before he fishtailed to a stop. He lifted his sunglass and walked in circles around the vehicle—giving it a quick inspection for damage.

Other drivers emerged from their vehicles. One woman had two black eyes from her sudden face-plant into an airbag. Another frantically checked on her child strapped in the back seat.

Andy and Larry darted out and searched the nearest vehicle to see if anyone was seriously hurt.

More of Andy's crew wandered away from their duties and onto the roadway. Some bumped into the stationary vehicles, seemingly dazed and unaware of any of the surroundings.

Booger, one of Andy's favorites, remained at his post manning a concrete saw. With the saw buzzing, throwing water and dust into the air, Chester lumbered over right in the line of fire of the saw's blade. Booger was oblivious to his companion's presence and continued sawing. The saw cut through Chester's left foot first and then his right. Chester fell face down to the ground like a fallen tree.

By that time Slim Jim was beside the car that had hit Butterbean, his gaze fixated on the blood at the scene.

The woman struggled to breathe, resembling a fish out of water. Her eyes were wide open, her mouth moving as she tried to speak. "Help me . . . ." she whispered.

Slim Jim bent over, lowered his hand to her face, and dipped his fingertip in the blood that trickled down her cheek. He lifted his finger and brought it to his pale, gray eyes to examine.

The woman managed to reach with her left hand and grab his wrist. "Help me."

A drip of spittle ran down the corner of his mouth. He shifted his focus on the hand and slowly parted his lips.

He grabbed her hand and shoved a finger in his mouth, chomping with a sickening crunch as the small bones cracked between his teeth. Blood streamed down his chin, dripping like slow rain to the pavement below.

Her life draining away, the woman gasped, unable to find the strength to scream as her attacker continued to devour delicate flesh.

Her head flopped to the side. She looked up into the shadow of another navy blue clad Non-Dead. Drool dripped from his mouth and landed on her forehead.

"My stars! What's wrong with your crew? They act like they don't have any sense at all," Larry called out to Andy, as he helped an old man out of his truck.

Before Andy could answer, Larry's crew of Non-Dead inundated the traffic on the opposite side of the interstate. Rubbernecking had the traffic on that side crawling, which allowed the vehicles to come to a complete stop without hitting any of the Non-Dead.

"Uh oh." Larry held his breath as cars and trucks skidded to a halt. "Andy, we need backup!"

The side glass of an automobile shattered two cars away from Andy. Abdul had smashed it with his fist, and grabbed the young female driver, trying to yank her out the window.

"Abdul! Have you lost your mind, boy?" Before Andy could get to the scene and pull him away, Abdul had the top half of the girl's body poking out the window. He wasted no time in devouring the nose off her face.

"He's done gone meat-eating zombie on us! Larry! Come quick!"

Larry followed as Andy ran and grabbed Abdul from behind in a half-nelson hold, pulling him to the ground, and away from the girl. The girl fell back into her seat, her arms hanging over the side, unconscious from shock.

Squeezing with all his might, Andy fought to maintain his hold. "This ain't going to work. We got to get to his brain to kill him."

Larry knelt by his side. "What do you want me to do? My shotgun's in the bus. Do you want me to get it?"

Andy strained trying to twist Abdul's head around. It inched to the side a little at a time until it popped. Abdul's head cocked to one side, his neck broken, though no more dead than he was before. "You got a knife?"

Larry reached in his pocket and pulled out a four-inch locking blade skinning knife. "Right here!"

Raising his arm to Abdul's chin, Andy said, "Pretend you're at the deer camp and going to cut a buck's head off." Andy held the jaw in check, keeping the teeth mashed together as Larry sliced through tendons and muscle. The black blood of the undead oozed like thick motor oil onto the pavement.

When the blade reached the spine, Andy gave the head one last jerk and detached it from the body. He tossed the head to the side and jumped back on his feet. "Get yer shotgun! Get on the radio! We's need backup, now!"

*

"What's going on over there?" Mrs. Wascome pushed her glasses higher on the bridge of her nose. "Over there on the corner. The traffic's piling up."

Carrie squinted, trying to focus, her eyes not being as strong since she turned forty. "What, that road crew? They're working on a drainage project. But something strange is definitely going on. It looks like they're walking off the job."

"What's the world coming to? I wonder if one of those protesting groups is over there making a scene."

Carrie closed one eye. "I don't think so. I don't see anyone carrying signs or anything. Look at them, wandering off in different directions. They're acting like they're drunk."

"Those damn zombies need to know their place," Mrs. Wascome said. "Excuse me, I should keep my thoughts in my head."

"I've never seen anything like this before." Carrie bit her lower lip. "I don't like that two of them are heading toward the playfield. They're almost to the fence, and the children are playing kickball over there. I'm going to bring them back this way." Pulling the waist of her jeans higher, she left the covered patio of Little Patriots Daycare, briskly trekking toward the children.

The first Non-Dead who arrived at the fence bumped into it as if it weren't there. He backed away and then walked into it again.

Shawn was up next to kick, legs quivering in anticipation. He looked at his watch and tensed up even further. His team was two scores down. He craned his neck and saw Jenny, who gave him a smile. If he kicked a home run, he would win the game for their team. "I've got to make this for Jenny," he said under his breath.

Jacob wound up and slung the ball toward him. It came straight his way, a nice clean release. Shawn took four choppy steps, timing his kick for the precise moment of contact.

Phomp! His right foot met the rubber ball slightly above the ground. It soared overhead of second base and bounced to the fence's edge. The runners on first and third advanced. Shawn put his head down and ran as if his life depended on it.

With the fate of the game in his hands, Willie ran to get the ball to preserve the one point lead.

Misjudging his speed, Willie overran the ball, and crashed into the fence. He was so focused on the game he didn't even see the Non-Dead behind it.

With his pale fingers poking through the storm fence, the Non-Dead seized Willie, latching onto the back of his shirt.

Carrie watched the attack unfolded before her eyes as cold fear shook her insides. "No, oh my God, no. Willie, run away, son. Run away!"

Willie yelled in surprise. The determined Non-Dead pulled him back in to the fence and made a futile attempt to bite him.

Teeth gnashed against galvanized steel.

"Help! I'm stuck and a dog's trying to eat me!" Willie screamed.

Mrs. Wascome saw Carrie running toward the children, raised her glasses, and saw Willie struggling to free himself from the zombie. "Run, Willie! Run! It's happening again! It's happening again!"

Her knees buckled. She held on to a support beam until the weakness passed. "Six-one-six—six-one-six—six-one-six," she repeated, and headed inside to find a phone and report the emergency.

The second zombie arrived and tried to reach over the six-foot tall fence for Willie. His arm wasn't nearly long enough, and he abandoned his efforts, falling to his knees alongside the other zombie.

The children watched in frozen horror as Willie continued to scream.

Carrie ran with a limp, her hand busy massaging her right thigh. "Get away! Get away from him!"

The kneeling zombie snaked two fingers through the links and pulled Willie's ear until it poked through. He curled his lips back and bit off a portion of the ear.

Willie's shriek sent the kids scattering toward the safety of the Day Care building.

"Run, children! Run!" Carrie pushed through her pain and avoided crashing into the children as they raced by.

Willie's cheeks glowed cherry red as he fought to free himself from his captors. "Let me go! Let me go!"

"Get your damn hands off him, you bastards!" Carrie wheezed, out of breath.

The first zombie maintained a tight grip while the other struggled to latch onto any part of Willie's body that came close enough to the fence.

Carrie ran and grabbed Willie's arms. "Let him go! Let him go!" Two buttons popped off the boy's shirt, but the zombie refused to release his intended next meal.

Carrie let go of Willie's arms and grabbed him by the feet. She lifted his legs and pulled backward. "Hold your arms up, Willie! Slide out of your shirt!"

Willie did as his teacher demanded, and squirmed until his head and arms slipped free, leaving the zombie holding nothing but an empty shirt.

Willie's head hit the ground. He slapped at his wounded ear as if he were trying to put out a fire. Carrie dragged him several feet away before pulling him to his feet, and then ran with him to the sanctuary of the Day Care center.

*

It was a beautiful day for a motorcycle ride. Still a little cool from the morning, and no chance of rain in the forecast. Joel Spencer checked the rear-view mirror to make sure he wasn't outpacing the news crew from Channel 2.

Today was a rare occasion where he could mix business with pleasure. Channel 2 was doing a human-interest story on the *everyday man* behind the politician. The show would highlight his love for the open road and the serenity motorcycle riding brought him. His day would include some time at the shooting range, a few hours volunteering at the Food Bank, a visit to a local barbershop where he had been getting his haircut from the same man for nearly thirty years, and would end with dinner at a taqueria run by a legal immigrant.

Of course, this was an embellished production of how he really spent his off time. His campaign manager had put together the day's schedule to ensure it would appeal to the widest of audiences.

His first stop was to be at the shooting range. Little did News Crew 2 suspect he had chosen this route with another objective in mind. There was one event he wanted to get on film that even his campaign manager wasn't aware of. As Spencer neared the intersection of Highway 19 and Mountain High Boulevard, a smile widened across his face concealed by his helmet. It appeared that the tainted batch of ATP at the Institution had worked according to plan.

Traffic was at a standstill in all four directions. Spencer turned on his blinker and waited for the Channel 2 van to catch up. He turned onto the service road and headed toward the crew of Non-

Dead laborers from the North Dallas Institution who were working on a drainage project.

This will be the lead story on tonight's news, and I'll be giving the commentary as a witness, he thought. Spencer hoped capturing the Non-Dead on video and showing them unresponsive to orders would only bolster his position in the campaign.

Pulling into a gas station a block away from the intersection, Spencer shut down his motorcycle, and removed his helmet.

The dark-green Channel 2 van parked alongside him. The passenger-side window rolled down, and a dark-blond haired cameraman was the first to speak. "We won't be able to get past that traffic jam. You want to double back and find another way?"

"Maybe not. Something's going on. There may have been an accident. I'm a certified EMT, so I have a moral obligation to check on anyone injured. Why don't you follow me and bring the camera? You might get something to put on tonight's news," Spencer said.

The cameraman turned his head and said something to the driver, and then turned back. "Okay. We can cut our stay at the Food Bank to make up lost time."

The sliding door on the side of the van opened. Jim Garrison, reporter, stepped out.

"I heard a report over the radio about a big pileup over on Interstate six ten and Z.M.A.T.'s being flooded with calls, too. Something wild is stirring in the city."

Spencer suppressed a smile and feigned concern. "Let's go see if we can be of any assistance to our brethren." He led the way to the worksite.

Concrete pipes, and heavy equipment on the corner, partially blocked the view of the construction site as the four men approached. When Spencer turned the corner, the guard in charge of the work crew was trying to stuff one of the Non-Dead past the open doors of the bus.

Chuckling to himself, he jogged over to the guard. "Hey, buddy, what seems to be the problem?"

The guard grunted as he shoved the Non-Dead up the bus steps. "Get in the back, now!" he said, pulling the doors closed with his hands the best he could.

"What's wrong with that Non-Dead? Why're you treating him that way?" Spencer asked.

"This is county business, not yours," the guard said, then turned his head toward the cameraman and the reporter from Channel 2. "Say, what's this? I've got enough problems without the media poking its nose around here."

"Allow me to introduce myself. My name is Joel Spencer, and I'm running for Congress." He turned and faced the camera, beaming a wide politician's smile. "We were on our way to the Food Bank when we noticed there was a problem."

"My hands are full right now. My crew stopped working and then started wandering off. So, if you'll excuse me—" As the guard attempted to leave, Spencer put his hand on his shoulder to stop him.

"So you're saying the Non-Dead deliberately disobeyed your orders? And they're on the loose, and you're no longer able to control them?" Spencer said with eyebrows low.

"All I'm saying is something's wrong. I need to round up the rest of my crew. I've already called for reserves. We'll get things back in order. You need to leave the area." The guard pushed past Spencer and headed for another Non-Dead meandering between the stalled cars.

Spencer turned to the camera. "There you have it. Proof that relying on the Non-Dead for our future is nothing more than a gamble. A gamble with the odds stacked against us. The future of mankind depends solely upon the Living. As your next Congressman, I promise to—"

Spencer stopped when a woman's cry for help interrupted his impromptu commercial. He turned and saw her struggling to escape the embrace of a Non-Dead.

"Oh my God." Spencer sprinted toward her as he reached for the holster at the small of his back and retrieved his gold plated Colt .45. *What the hell has gone wrong?*

The guard led a Non-Dead by the arm to the bus. He stopped and faced the screams.

The Non-Dead turned his attention to the screamer. Something stirred in his eyes. Still walking, he fastened his gaze upon the sweaty, glistening neck of the unwary guard.

The Non-Dead pulled the guard to him and sank his teeth deep into the side of his neck. Blood poured out the open wound as the zombie swallowed, making room in his mouth for another bite.

The guard gasped for air and tried to tear himself away. But the zombie had only begun to eat and showed no sign of retreat.

By the time Spencer arrived, the zombie had eaten part of the woman's shoulder. Without hesitation, Spencer placed the barrel of the .45 between the eyes of the zombie, and pulled the trigger.

Putrid green-black liquid splattered on the windshield of the car behind them. Both the woman and zombie collapsed to the ground.

Ears ringing from the gun blast, Spencer wiped his face, and frantically looked around.

The camera steady rolled, catching everything on film. The reporter and driver hid behind the cameraman.

This could really work in my favor, Spencer thought. He posed for the camera, holding the pistol next to his head.

"He's eating him! Over there!" A man outside his vehicle pointed toward the guard.

Spencer raced past the camera as it panned to follow him on his next rescue mission. *Risking his life to save others from the zombie onslaught—Joel Spencer, Congress*, he thought. The camera was in no position to film the delight on his face.

*

Byron Poundstone walked past the empty secretary's desk and down the hall leading to Reverend Hatfield's office. The time had come to resolve the inner conflicts that tore at him. Stopping at the Reverend's door, he took a deep breath, and firmly knocked.

"Yes?" Hatfield begrudgingly called.

"It's Byron. I'd like to speak with you." He listened intently at the door. Papers shuffled, the distinctive metallic snap of a cycling slide of a semi-automatic weapon cut through the air, and then a drawer banged closed.

"Come in."

Byron slowly opened the door. Hatfield was by the coffee pot and pouring himself a cup. He wore no shoes, and his dress shirt was unbuttoned all the way down.

"Reverend Hatfield? You look . . . did you just get back from the gym? Your body seems to be shaping up but you look as if you just finished a fifty mile hike in the desert. If this is a bad time I can come back."

"Eh? Oh, don't worry about me. I've have chronic insomnia. Dr. Fenton is treating me. I'm fine."

"Okay. What I have to say's a little complicated though. It may take a while to talk this over."

"Time's wasting then. Go ahead, and get on with it." Hatfield took seat behind his desk and motioned Byron to sit in a chair across from him.

"Well, I've been thinking a lot. About, you know, the events that led up to my . . . death."

Hatfield nodded and repositioned himself in his chair.

"It's funny you mentioned Dr. Scott. He's part of my, uh, issue. We were all very close once. I wish he were here, too—to help explain things."

Hatfield tapped his desk with a finger. "You want to know more about the research he's involved with?"

"That, and more. There are things I don't remember, things that don't add up."

"Why don't we start with you telling me what you do remember? We can go from there." Hatfield acted a bit stressed.

Before Byron could begin, Hatfield's cell phone on his desk vibrated, and played the tune "How Great Thou Art."

"Excuse me for a minute. I have to get this," Hatfield said. "Speak," he said into the phone.

"This is Cain. Have you seen Byron today?" The Warden's words ran together.

"Yes. In fact I'm meeting with him in my office right now. What's wrong?"

"How is he? Is he acting strange? Disoriented? Violent?"

"No, none of those things. What's this about?"

"I'll tell you what it's about. It's about me getting fucked! That damn doctor of yours has really messed things up."

"Get a hold of yourself man, and tell me the problem."

"That funny batch of ATP turned my wards into mindless robots all right. Mindless flesh-eating zombie robots that is!"

"What?"

"You heard me. One of our buses had engine trouble this morning and didn't leave the Institution on schedule. One of the Non-Dead started gnawing on the mechanic's leg while he was underneath repairing it.

"Every crew from the Institution is reacting the same. Z.M.A.T. has been called in. The National Guard has been activated. Hell, a call went out to the Army to be on standby.

"Fenton really fucked up. People are dying! The Feds are going to swarm over this place with a microscope. They won't stop until they find something. They're going to be so far down my throat that you'll be able to see them wave when I bend over to kiss my ass goodbye!"

"I understand. I'll contact you soon with my thoughts on the matter," Hatfield closed his phone, visibly shaken.

"Was someone asking for me?" Byron asked.

"That was Warden Cain from the Institution. The other Sub Zs have all reverted to their flesh-eating ways." Hatfield eyed the coloring of Byron's face, knowing that he was spared from the madness because he no longer received his ATP *feeding* from the showers.

"What? How can that be? He was asking if I turned, too?"

"You needed to be accounted for. He told me to keep a close eye on you." Hatfield focused on a drawer in his desk. Now would be a perfect time to kill Byron by claiming he had been affected. That would erase the chance of him spoiling their plans.

Byron became visibly nervous. "There's absolutely nothing wrong with me. I can't believe this is happening."

Hatfield's body tensed. His right hand began to shake.

"Reverend Hatfield?" Byron eyes widened as his pastor's face started to flush. "Reverend Hatfield are you sure you're feeling okay?"

"I'm fine. Caffeine makes me nervous sometimes." Hatfield's eyes darted back and forth from the drawer to Byron.

Byron edged forward in the seat, his hands gripped the arms of the chair, his feet poised as if to run.

Hatfield fixed his gaze on Byron and slowly reached for the drawer.

Byron sprang from his chair. "Andy! He's out there with the crew! Is he okay? Did the warden say if the guards are safe?"

Startled, Hatfield froze. "He didn't say. But Z.M.A.T. and the National Guard are involved. The best we can do for them is pray."

"You pray. I've got to find Andy." Bryon sprinted out of the Reverend's office before he had time to protest.

Byron burst out of the church's back doors and ran to the garage. Once inside, he fumbled with the keys, and opened his locker. At the bottom, covered by three sets of navy blue jumpsuits, was his most prized possession. A gold plated Colt .45 pistol, hand engraved golden crosses on either side of the grips. It was a gift given to him by Reverend Hatfield in a ceremony where Byron became a special member of Hatfield's personal protection squad. At the time, he was one of twenty of the most loyal of Hatfield's followers, each of whom had received a custom pistol upon acceptance.

He removed the pistol from the holster and cycled the slide, readying it in the *cocked and locked* position. He holstered the gun and retrieved an ammo belt holding six other full magazines.

The church van had been scheduled for an oil change that day. Byron hopped in and fired up the engine, then sped away. "Please, God, don't let anything happen to Andy."

*

Reverend Hatfield held his .45 tightly in his grip and contemplated the odds of murdering Byron and getting away with it. There were too many unknowns at this point to push his luck and jeopardize the future. He picked up his phone and dialed Joel Spencer.

*

Four zombies were on their knees feasting upon what remained of Larry Fillmore. He had put up a gallant fight to the bitter end, but wasn't well trained in actual combat, not like Private Andy Wells.

A switch had flipped in Andy's head, making him the killing machine the Army trained him to be. He was scared. But his training taught him to wall off that fear and become numb to it. The only objective was to think clearly and kill the enemy before he killed you.

Some people abandoned their cars, taking the chance on outrunning the zombies. Some chose unwisely. Others remained inside their vehicles waiting to be rescued.

Andy toted a tricked out 12 gauge Mossberg 500 loaded with double aught buckshot. He couldn't risk shooting long range targets in fear of hitting the innocent.

Andy didn't know how many zombies Larry had taken out before he was killed, but he could count over twenty who were still *alive* on either side. As outnumbered as he was, he would have to employ strategy along with direct headshots to bring down the zombies.

Zigzagging around vehicles, sometimes jumping from car roof to car roof, he outmaneuvered the lumbering undead until he was close enough to stick the gun barrel to the head and pull the trigger.

"By God, if it's a war you want, it's a war you'll get!" Andy's eyes were wide, his mind strictly in the killing zone. He stepped onto the bumper of a truck and into the bed. He vaulted over the cab and landed on the hood, sticking the barrel directly behind the head of a zombie trying to break through a car window. Angling the barrel to avoid hitting the passenger, Andy pulled the trigger. Vile grey matter and liquid exploded into the air painting roofs of vehicles in the next lane over.

"That's number eleven. I'm coming to get the rest of you. Private Andy Wells, zombie killeeerrrrrr!"

Ten cars ahead another target presented itself. Andy scoped out his position. He felt as if he was in a maze in a video game. It reminded him of when he was young, playing Pac-Man on the computer. He hurried toward the zombie before it could do any further harm.

Andy went to lift his leg as he ran alongside a truck, but something caught his pants leg and pulled him back.

A bloody hand had reached from under the truck and latched on. Andy turned and saw Butterbean looking up at him, a perplexed expression across his face. The lower half of his body was missing. One arm was crushed to a pulp.

For a moment Andy saw familiarity in Butterbean's eyes. It was almost like a cry for help, as if he didn't know what was happening to him. Andy lifted his gun to shoot but hesitated to pull the trigger. "Aw, Butterbean. I didn't want things to end this way. We's had some good times, didn't we?"

Butterbean's colorless eyes rolled in the back of his head as he opened his mouth wide showing teeth.

Andy pulled the trigger, but nothing happened. He quickly cycled the pump-action to load another shell. Nothing. He knew he had at least five more shells remaining. But the gun hadn't been properly maintained and was always kept loaded. The choke spring was either weak or broken. It was useless.

As Butterbean lunged in an attack, Andy smacked his forehead with the butt of the shotgun. The zombie growled like a wounded animal. Repeatedly, Andy pounded away at his skull trying to find the *sweet spot* that would shut down the undead eating machine.

When he believed Butterbean was dead, Andy raised the butt of the gun for a final blow for assurance. A hand reached from the side and grabbed the gun by the barrel.

The gun almost slipped from Andy's grasp. He held on, turned, and saw his one-time *friend*, Snake Eyes, coming in for the attack. Even though Butterbean was dead, the zombie's hand clung tightly to Andy's pants leg. Andy's leg twisted as he fought off Snake Eyes. He struggled to maintain his balance, frantically avoiding the zombie's snapping teeth.

From the corner of his vision, two more zombies were just about to close in. With his last remaining strength he gripped the shotgun by the barrel and the stock, held it across his chest, and maneuvered Snake Eyes over with the other two.

Andy held all three zombies at bay using the shotgun as a block. Their combined strength leaning into him bent his spine almost in half. His arms trembled and sweat poured down his face as he waited for something in his body to give way, knowing he would be remembered as a failed warrior.

"I should'a killed your ugly, dead asses while you slept. I hope you choke on my guts . . . I . . ." Andy's whole body shook. "Tell God to make room. I'm coming home, Ma . . . I'm—"

A hand came up from behind and covered his right ear. Three rapid blasts from a Colt .45 sent the head of each zombie jerking back from the impact of 230 grain bullets. Off-balance, Andy fell to the ground, and rolled over onto his back. His arms felt like lead weights. He didn't have the strength to lift himself off the ground. As he gasped for air, he squinted into the bright sunlight at the silhouette of a young man standing over him.

"Tooty? Tooty, is that you?"

"Andy! My God, this is horrible. Are you hurt?"

"Shucks, nothing but my pride."

The roar of helicopters washed down from the sky above. Z.M.A.T. forces rappelled down to strategic positions on the ground. Targets fell immediately.

"Do you know what happened?" Byron asked.

"No, not a clue. One minute they was working, and the next they went all stupid. Then, then the next they went zombie."

"Are you afraid it'll happen to me, too? I'm a little concerned myself. Will I even notice some kind of warning before it's too late?"

"Don't you fret yourself, Tooty. If you start actin' extra stupid I'll take you out real quick. *Bang.* Right to the head."

"That's supposed to make me feel better?"

"Look, I need to get you out of here. If those troopers see that number on your forehead, well, we don't want to take that chance, do we?" Andy said.

"No. I guess we don't. It's probably best if we both get out of the way. Take me back to the Institution. I'll probably be the safest there."

CHAPTER 35

Joel Spencer sat at his desk in his home office, massaging his forehead with his left hand, and doodling on a blank sheet of paper with his right. The incident with the zombie road crew was good for an eight percent increase in popularity at home. The video of his valiant efforts killing thirteen raging zombies and saving multiple innocent lives had gone viral on the internet. A rare moment like this might give him a shot at the White House one day. *President Joel Spencer. I like it. It's too bad people had to die, but it'll be worth it*, he thought.

A week had passed since the uprising and the unfortunate accident at the North Dallas Non-Dead Institution. A mysterious fire had broken out near the ATP storage tank area. Fortunately, there had only been one causality, Warden Samuel Cain.

The campaign fired on all cylinders, there was no reason to pick up the phone and make that call. A little voice in his head warned him not to. Was that his conscience? He chuckled at the thought, it simply was a risk he didn't need to take. Still, there was the unknown that could be waiting to bite him in the ass at the last minute. There was no telling what surprises Margaret or Rebecca might pull on him for revenge.

Rick Poundstone was a good man. There was no justification to destroy Poundstone's life since the odds of winning were so heavily weighted in Joel's favor. It was time to make the decision. The window of opportunity was about to close for good. *Oh, what to do?*

He tossed the pen aside and propped his elbows on the desk, planting his face in his palms. Spencer let his mind rest and go blank, and then let it drift toward the future.

Fuck it, Spencer thought, and picked up the phone and dialed.

"Poundstone campaign. How may I direct your call?" Sandra was at her desk applying touchup to a chip on her nail polish.

"You know who this is," Joel Spencer said.

Sandra quickly capped the polish, and lowered her voice. "Yes sir, and how may I direct your call."

"Are Goudard and Poundstone following the day's schedule."

"Yes, sir. Miss Goudard and Mr. Poundstone are on the schedule that we reported yesterday."

"Good. The time has finally come. At precisely one p.m., execute the plan."

She took a deep breath, and exhaled. "I understand. It will be done."

"Sandra, I know this must be hard on you. You have been Poundstone's friend for a long time."

"Yes . . . I have," she said, wiping the building tears from her eyes.

"No matter what happens it's for the greater good. It's God's plan, and it can't happen without you."

"I know," she choked out.

"Be strong. Reverend Hatfield is counting on you. He's counting on all of us. One p.m. Goodbye, Sandra."

Sandra shook her head and tried to force a stern expression. "Thank you, and goodbye." She looked at the clock and whispered, "I feel like Judas."

*

Rick Poundstone climbed into the back seat of an SUV after eating lunch at The Red Rooster Café. The onions in his hamburger steak hadn't been cooked as well as he would have liked, and Rick felt the stomach acid trying to climb its way up to his throat.

"How was lunch?" his driver, Edward, asked.

"Not bad from what I remember. I was so busy campaigning I hardly took the time to taste it."

"I hope it filled you up. You've got a full schedule, and you'll be on the move until the rally at Independence Park. That thing probably won't end until midnight. It oughta be packed though, since you're giving away free food."

"I'll have to sneak in a burger or a hot dog at some point to keep me going." Rick paused and let out a long burp. "Ahh, I feel better now. Excuse me."

His cell phone chimed from his coat pocket. The special ring told him it was from his office. "Hello, Sandra, what's up?"

"Mr. Poundstone, Congressman Stephens has sent an email that needs your immediate attention. He knew you're busy on the campaign trail and called to ask you to open it immediately."

"Stephens, huh? It must be about that flat tax bill coming up. Thank you, Sandra. Anything else?"

An unusual silence passed. "No . . . no sir," she said.

"Well then, thank you. Goodbye," Rick mindlessly ended the call on his phone and tapped it against his chin. Something about Sandra's voice was different, an uncharacteristic icy coldness.

Shaking off his concerns, Rick opened his email app, and found the message sent from Stephens. It was the first on top. Rick started reading, finding the information all too familiar. A glance at the headline showed the date to be from a week earlier. "Hmm, that's strange. The email was sent today, but this document is a week old," he said aloud to himself. *I guess he forgot he had already sent it to me.*

Rick put his phone in standby mode.

The virus the email contained had already sent out a text message and was busy wiping out all the information on his SD card.

*

Lisa Goudard's cell phone buzzed in her purse laying on the passenger's seat. *Oh crap, what now?* The previous meeting hadn't gone as well as she had hoped. In fact, her visits for the last week hadn't produced nearly the amount of contributions as usual.

Just as soon as she came to a red light, she picked up her phone. *It's a message from Rick.* With such a bad morning she hoped he had sent another one of his love messages. It would certainly brighten her day.

She opened the message, and read, *I've got some really important information for you. Something that will shake the political world and end the election in a landslide. I've canceled your two o'clock appointment. Drive directly to your apartment. I'll be inside waiting for you. Don't delay. This is a matter of the utmost importance. Rick.*

A horn beeped from behind two times. Lisa pulled her eyes away from the phone and drove through the intersection. *Something big is up. I wonder if his staff found some real dirt on Spencer?*

*

Ben O'Brian leaned back on a bench at Independence Park watching a squirrel in a tree. His cell phone rang, right on schedule. "Hello."

"Ben, it's Joel Spencer."

"Yes sir, Mr. Spencer," Ben said, sitting at attention.

"The plan is in action. It's all up to you now. I'm counting on you."

"I won't fail you, sir."

"If you check your bank account, you'll see all the money's there. All fifty thousand of it."

"Yes, sir. It's all there. My bank alerted me with a message of the deposit a few minutes ago."

"Good, good. I want you to consider this a down payment. Why, when you finish college, there will be a position for you on my staff in D.C."

"Sir, it would be an honor to be a member of your staff."

"You're a fine lad, Ben. I don't know why Rebecca couldn't see that in you."

Ben flinched at the bitter reminder and kept his comments to himself.

"There's been a change, so listen up. The police officer will be on the corner of thirteenth and Main to escort you to the front of the receiving line. Be there for four thirty. Everything else stays according to plan. You'll be standing next to James Hodges, a fellow church member and loyal Poundstone supporter. Or I should say, *former* Poundstone supporter. Poundstone arrives at five. When he sees Hodges he'll make a beeline over to shake his hand. When Poundstone reaches out, you grab his hand first, and then let go quickly. Leave immediately afterward. Try not to draw any attention."

"Yes, sir. I have it memorized."

"You're in complete disguise?"

"Yes, sir. Long blond wig and a scratchy fake beard," Ben said, rubbing his chin.

"Good. Go to the safe house and change when you're done. Use the key we sent and take the car in the back."

"Got the key right here, sir." Ben tapped his left front pocket.

"That's it, Ben. Timing is everything. Go forth, son, and make God proud."

"Yes, sir. I will."

The phone went dead. Ben put it away. He didn't care if he made God proud or not. All he knew was nothing would give him more satisfaction in life than to help Rebecca Spencer's worst nightmare come true. Ensuring the election for Joel Spencer would do just that. She deserved this and more, for all the wrong she had done to him.

*

Lisa pulled into a parking space at her apartment at a quarter to two. She had no idea where Rick had been when he sent the text message.

She quickly stepped to her door while fumbling in her purse for a tube of lipstick. There would be a hot pair of shiny red lips waiting to greet him.

A single stargazer lily was beautifully displayed in her mailbox door slot. *He's so sweet.*

She unlocked the door and opened it. "Hey, Rick, I'm here." A bouquet of lilies tastefully arranged in a glass vase rested on the kitchen counter.

"Oh Rick, they're beau—"

An arm reached around Lisa's chest. A leather-gloved hand came up and covered her mouth. She felt a sharp pain stab into her neck. Within seconds the strength in her arms dissolved. The man's grip was strong. But at that point he could have released her and she still wouldn't have been able to lift a finger to fight back.

The numbness sank down into her legs, traveling to her feet. He let her drop to the floor.

Lisa lay on her side, fully conscious, with the barest amount of control above her shoulders.

The man sauntered around Lisa's helpless body and came to a stop inches from her face. She could see nothing but the black of his boots, and then a glove entered her field of vision. Her eyes focused on a roach squirming to free itself from the fingers.

"Peek-a-boo, I see you." The man laughed, moving the insect closer for its antenna to explore her nose. "He likes you. No real surprise. These things are attracted to garbage."

Lisa made a frantic attempt to pull her face away, only to have the thing dropped on her forehead, and scurry across her scalp.

"Well, well, well. The time has come," the man said, his voice slightly muffled. "I hope you don't mind. I let myself in." Keys jingled in the background. "You should have invested in a security system. Keyed locks are easily defeated these days. I have a master for every brand."

Lisa struggled to speak, fighting with all her might to regain control of her body. She managed a groan, unable to form a word.

"Really, don't embarrass yourself like that. You sound like a bigger babbling idiot than usual." The man walked away toward the kitchen.

Lisa watched his backside. He was dressed in combat boots, old jeans, a black leather jacket, and gloves. The syringe remained in his right hand, and oddly enough, he had a motorcycle helmet on his head.

He turned and faced her, planting his hands on his hips after raising the visor. "You know, it didn't have to end this way. Things would have been far less dramatic had you taken one of the offers we made you.

"But no. No, you had to poke the eye of opportunity. All the while you wallowed in self-pity because you couldn't accept that God has power over the clay. To make one a vessel of honor, or dishonor, as He chooses."

"Wh . . . who?" Lisa managed to say.

"What? Who? Who am I?" The man paced back and forth with his head down and raised his hands. "Who am I? Why, I am Rex! A lover of life. A craver of sensation. A hedonist unparalleled. Seeking to fill every pore of want and desire."

"Wh . . . why?" Lisa said.

"My, you're doing much better under the drug than I expected. I only wanted you to be conscious for the ceremony. I didn't expect a two-way conversation.

"But since you asked. I am here to die." Rex put his hands behind his back and rocked on his heels. "Yes, I'm here to die. But not in the way you may think. Allow me to begin to unravel the mystery by offering a little show and tell."

Rex brought his hands up to his helmet and removed it from his head.

"H . . . H . . . Hatf . . ."

"Field, Hatfield. You can still call me Reverend. One day others will know me only as Messiah."

Will Hatfield let the helmet fall to the floor and removed his jacket. His chest bulged under his T-shirt, and his arm muscles gleamed, fit and well-defined. A youthful glow radiated from his face.

"I am here with two objectives in mind. One is to end your miserable imitation of life. The other is to shed all the wanton ways my flesh still craves in one last act of sensual release.

"What you don't know is that the hand of God is upon me. Through His divine plan, my body has undergone treatments to make it ready to accept immortality. A few hours ago I received the elixir that will change all of humanity forever. Resurrection X!

"The angels have taken the messenger of Satan in the form of alien DNA and reconstructed it into the altering power of God. The tree of life has once again come down to Earth. All shall one day eat of its precious fruit."

"No," Lisa said.

"It's true. I can feel my body changing by the minute. My metamorphosis will be complete in a few hours. I will no longer age as the healing powers of the alien DNA will keep me whole. And I will no longer have the desire for food as the light from the sun and stars shall provide me with nourishment for billions of years to come."

Hatfield paused, lowered his head, and narrowed his eyes. An evil grin formed on tight lips. "But now—now my carnal side is warring greatly with the new power trying to smother it. I'm so hard I'm afraid I'm about to bust out of my jeans." Hatfield squeezed his dick through his pants.

"Did you like the flowers? I brought them from a funeral I spoke at this morning. I thought they were too pretty to die unappreciated at a gravesite. I thought they would be appropriate for your demise."

Hatfield unlaced his boots and stripped down naked. "Not bad, huh?" He posed as if modeling at a body-building contest. The head of his dick bounced against his stomach when he moved.

Hatfield picked his jacket off the floor, reached into the pocket, and removed a vial. Then he squatted by Lisa's feet and removed her shoes and panties. Moving by her head, he picked up her hands, and dragged her across the carpet onto a rug. With some effort he removed her dress and bra.

"I've heard of tan lines, but you look ridiculous. What? Too cheap to put makeup on anything other than exposed skin? I thought you wanted to be accepted as normal? You're nothing but a cheap imitation of a real person."

"No . . . no don't," Lisa said, eyes frozen open.

"I'm sorry, but it is your destiny," Hatfield said, holding up the vial. "See this? After I sow my last seed of lust, I shall return you to the fate Satan saved you from. A drop or two in your mouth and you will no longer be able to breathe. Then I will slowly cut your head from your neck, just to make sure. God will be your judge after that. But don't worry. You won't be lonely. I'm going to send as many of your kind to join you as fast as I can."

Hatfield ran a slow glaze across her naked body. "You are one fine looking piece of ass." He knelt by her legs and lifted them, then maneuvered his body between her thighs. With her feet on his shoulders, he licked her ankle, and rubbed his face on her calf.

"Pig . . . sl . . . ime . . . buck . . . et."

"Shut up!" Hatfield pushed her legs down so her knees were close to her ears. He shoved his rock-hard cock into her. "Oh yes.

That feels good. Too bad you can't feel it. I'd have you begging for more. Yes, that's right." He began to thrust his hips slowly.

Lisa tried to spit on him, but her lips would not cooperate.

"*Fuck me*, Reverend Hatfield. *Fuck me harder*. Yes, that's right. You'd be begging me for more. You would be on your knees shoving your ass all over me. Wanting to feel my cock inside you."

"Fuck . . . you."

"You always did have a nasty mouth. But you sure do have the sweetest pussy." Hatfield let out a groan.

"Forgive me, Lord . . . forgive me." He moaned loudly again.

"Get off . . . me you . . pig . . . ."

Tears rolled down Hatfield face in his repentance. "I have sinned against You, my Lord, and I would ask that Your precious blood would wash and cleanse every stain until it is in the seas of God's forgetfulness. One last time. One last time."

Every breath inhaled and exhaled heaved loudly. "Forgive me, Lord! Forgi—" Hatfield gasped and bucked his hips, freezing in place has his body quivered.

With a low moan he fainted, and fell on top of Lisa, his head lying next to hers.

*

It was a good day. Joel Spencer cancelled his two appointments for the afternoon and decided to celebrate by taking a ride on his motorcycle. All of his plans were in motion. He had no doubt God would see them through.

His cell phone rang. It was Margaret calling. He answered, "You back?"

"Well, hello to you too."

"I'm busy. I've had a rough day. Are you back from your treatment or are you still at the hospital?"

"My treatment is over. That's not why I'm calling," she said, her tone of voice very businesslike.

"Why are you calling then?" Joel's voice dripped with sarcasm.

"Remember when I told you I'd found a new doctor? Well, what I didn't tell you is I also found a new lawyer. One who was out of state and didn't have your political hands wrapped around his throat. He's been reviewing the legal papers for Rebecca's inheritance when I die. Joel, your signature is not on the agreement."

"What? What in the hell are you talking about? You were right there when I signed it."

"Your *legal* signature is not on the agreement. I gave him other samples of your signature. What you signed for Rebecca's inheritance doesn't match. What are you trying to pull?" Margaret's voice rose in anger.

"Me? I'm not trying to pull anything. What are you trying to pull?"

"Stop it! I'm not going to play stupid games with you. The lawyer is here in town. I'm in his office. You need to drive over and re-sign the papers."

"This is bullshit. I don't have time. Fuck off."

"Joel, listen carefully. If you're not here within the next hour I'm going to the press with my story. I have photographs. My black-and-blue face will be on the front page of the newspaper tomorrow, and you won't even be elected dogcatcher."

"I think your new treatment has affected your sanity."

"Insane or not, if you don't come my lawyer breaks the story."

"Okay, I'm coming. Let's get this over with. I'm going over the agreement with a fine-toothed comb to make sure you didn't make any changes."

"Take all the time you need. Just come now."

"All right. Where are you?"

"Downtown, four forty-three Sagebrush, where it intersects with Oak Post. Go to the top floor. There is only one door for you to pick, so you can't miss it."

"I'll be there," Spencer mashed the end icon on the phone. "Bitch!"

*

The police officer escorted Ben to the rope line near the front where Representative Rick Poundstone would soon make his entrance. Ben shuffled along with his face toward the ground, trying to remain as inconspicuous as possible.

James Hodges shifted his gaze away from Ben when he arrived. Hodges moved over to make room as Ben ducked under the rope and stood next to him. The police officer strode away as if he had more important things to attend to.

Ben glanced up at Hodges, who had his attention focused elsewhere. He wondered what had changed for Hodges to become part of a conspiracy that would end the career of a long-time friend. He had even asked Joel Spencer more than once to explain that to him when the plan was first introduced. All Spencer would say was, "It's God's plan," or "God works in mysterious ways."

There was a plan, it was mysterious, but Ben didn't believe it had anything to do with God.

*

Joel Spencer arrived at his destination forty-five minutes after receiving Margaret's call. There was plenty of parking in front of the building, so he pulled right in, and got out of his car. He hoped there would be no surprises and he could sign the papers and be on his way. A couple of hours of light would remain to squeeze in a peaceful afternoon ride.

The elevator door was open and waiting for a passenger when he entered the building. His steps echoed in the vacant lobby across the marble floors. Once inside the elevator, he selected the sixth floor, and mumbled under his breath, "Fucking bitch."

On the street outside, a flatbed tow truck slowly backed up to the front of Spencer's car.

*

The SUV carrying Rick Poundstone pulled up one hundred feet away from Ben and Hodges. Ben glanced up again at Hodges, who met his gaze, and gave him a reassuring wink.

Wearing a big smile, Rick stepped out the SUV, and raised both hands to the crowd. An estimated two thousand were in attendance. Some supporters lined the walk leading to the outside theater, where others already sat, waiting for the main speech.

Rick turned to the cameras as lights flashed all around. Two security guards stepped in front leading the way as he approached the eagerly awaiting crowd.

Hodges leaned over the rope and gave a wide wave to Rick. Rick acknowledged him with a nod and a smile as he went down the line shaking hands.

Ben slipped the *ring* on his middle finger and removed the plastic guard from the two short needles.

A security guard passed in front of Ben, then Rick's hand appeared before him, heading straight for Hodges. It seemed as if events were in slow motion to Ben. He reached up and clasped Rick's hand, giving it a firm squeeze. The two needles injected a numbing agent first, and then followed with the original strain of alien virus. Ben quickly let go of Rick's hand and returned the plastic guard over the needles.

Rick grabbed the hand of his old friend, James Hodges. "James. I'm so glad to see you. Thanks for coming." Rick glanced uneasily at Hodges's gloved hand.

"I'm with you all the way, Rick. All the way back to Washington," Hodges grinned. He didn't meet Rick's eyes, and his hundred-watt smile wavered.

Ben backed away and slipped stealthily through the crowd.

Rick looked down at his hand and slowly flexed his fingers. His face contorted into a grimace. He turned his hand around and examined his palm. His eyes lit up, and he screamed in pain.

A young woman reached out toward him, and he stepped away. The two puncture marks in his palm oozed blood. His jaw dropped as he clutched at his right arm and fell to the ground. One word eeked past his quivering lips. "Spencer . . ."

*

The elevator doors opened, and Joel Spencer stepped out onto a short hallway. Margaret was right; there was only one door for him to choose, and he certainly couldn't miss it.

He almost grabbed the door handle to let himself in, but hesitated. He didn't want to seem disrespectful by barging in. It might cause some friction and delay him from making a quick exit. So, he gently knocked and waited for the door to open.

Siegfried Wagner's face appeared as he opened the door. "Mr. Spencer! It certainly is a delight to have you with us this afternoon."

Spencer raised an eyebrow and wondered what kind of game this lawyer would be playing.

"Won't you please come in?" Wagner said.

Lowering his head, Spencer stepped through the doorway as Wagner slowly backed away to allow him passage.

A familiar face popped up alongside Wagner.

"Mack? What are you doing here? Did you drive Margaret?" Spencer asked.

"As a matter of fact, I did. She's right over there putting on a bib," Mack said, gesturing toward her and a small group of people.

"A bib? What in the hell? Margaret! What's happened to you? Your face?" Spencer felt his heart plummet to his knees.

"It's a result of my new treatment. And guess what? It worked! I am totally cancer-free," Margaret said.

"But your skin—it's without color. You're a Sub Y," Spencer said. "But how? That's not legal."

"That's a minor detail you shouldn't concern yourself with, Mr. Spencer. Instead, you should rejoice in the fact that your wife is cured of her cancer, and will live for many, many years to come," Wagner said. "Won't you join us for a bite to eat? I'm sure the answers to all of your questions will become self-evident before our bellies are full." Wagner winked, ran his tongue slowly across his lips, and patted his belly.

Spencer turned and ran to the door. It was locked.

Mack's mouth started watering as he called over his shoulder. "You ready, honey? I know you haven't had any of the hunger yet, but try to have an open mind. You don't have to eat much if you don't want to. You just have to taste it."

"Why delay the inevitable?" Margaret said. "At least this time it will be me chewing ass. This is one knuckle sandwich I might enjoy."

Boisterous laughs arose as Joel pounded his shoulder against the door and pulled frantically on the handle.

"Too bad Jarvis is going to miss out. The chop shop is forty miles away. It'll take him a hour to get Spencer's car over there. I'll have to save his favorite part, a thigh. It won't be as good as fresh. Sometimes you have to take it any way you can get it."

*

A gold nametag pinned to a freshly pressed shirt proudly proclaimed its wearer, Andrew W. Wells, as Warden of the North Dallas Non-Dead Institution. His advancement had come as a reward for his valiant efforts in defeating the attack of the renegade road crews, his years of service at the Institution and the military, and by default. Andy was the highest ranking officer left alive.

Autopsies had shown evidence of the tainted ATP on the crew members skin, though no one currently understood how it got there, or exactly how it worked on the Non-Deads' systems. Cain was the main suspect, and what could have possibly motivated him to ruin a lifetime of achievements so close to his retirement was unknown.

One hundred and twenty of the newest guests of the Institution filled the auditorium. Almost half were trainees, and just beginning to learn from the new crew bosses, and other skilled workers, who had transferred from the surrounding counties. Andy figured it would be six months before normal operations would return.

"It's already a quarter past. Are you sure Joshua's coming tonight?" Byron had come to Andy's side after making sure everyone was seated properly.

"As far as I know, that pecker head ain't called in and said any different."

Byron chuckled. "Andy, you're the warden now. You should watch your language. Especially around the guests. You know how they'll repeat things."

"I guess yer right. As far as I know, that pecker head *has not* called in and said any different."

"That's not exactly what I meant."

Andy giggled. "I know, but wouldn't it be funny if the guys called him Reverend Pecker Head?"

"You're not ever going to change, are you?"

"Nope, I guess not. My mom always said I had a little mind of my own." Andy looked around the room. "Well, I guess I'll go round up the guards off their break and herd all the cattle back to the pens."

"I don't know. Uh, why don't you let me read a few scriptures, and give a little testimony? I feel that the Lord has put something in my heart that's just waiting to bust out," Byron said.

Andy rubbed the prickly stubble on his chin. "I don't guess it could hurt none. I've been noticing how this new bunch has taken a liking to you. Heck, they listen to you better than most of the new crew chiefs. There's something special about you. I just hope we don't have to cut you open to figure out what it is."

"Andy!"

"I'm just kidding—you know me."

Byron chuckled nervously. "Go ahead and leave. Come back in a half hour or so with the guards, and you can roll the guests out after I fill them with the spirit."

"Okay, yer on. See if God can put some more brains in them noggins, we's falling behind." Andy gave Byron a wink, poked out his chest, and walked with the mechanical dignity expected from a man in his position.

Pale faces in the audience turned and followed Byron's journey as he advanced up the stairs onto the stage and behind the podium.

A warm feeling of peace wrapped around Byron and began to electrify him from his feet to the top of his head. It projected from his countenance, spilled over to the front row, and flooded down the aisles. The Non-Dead began to fidget in their seats.

The red letters of the open Bible on the podium pulled Byron's focus and compelled him to flip the pages to a verse planted in his mind. His finger followed down the edge of the page and came to a stop. Looking up from the scriptures, he began to read:

"The Spirit of the Lord is upon me, because he hath anointed me to preach the gospel to the poor; he hath sent me to heal the brokenhearted, to preach deliverance to the captives, and recovering of sight to the blind, to set at liberty them that are bruised, To preach the acceptable year of the Lord."

The power swelled inside Byron. He lifted the Bible and felt as though he floated across the stage, down the steps, and in front of his congregation.

As if on command all the Sub Zs rose in unison.

Byron pulled out of his shoes and unzipped his jumpsuit, naked except for his socks.

"This is my body, this is my blood. Take, eat of it, drink all of it. For the eradication of sins committed . . . against *you*." The Bible fell to the floor. The brethren shuffled toward him.

Byron offered his right forearm.

Gently, almost sensually, the first Sub Z opened his mouth and bit off a small piece, letting the blood trickle into his mouth. He moved over, and one by one the others took a turn.

Each bite brought release from the power surging through his body. Ecstasy forced an uncontrollable smile, and tears of sheer joy rolled down his cheeks. His spirit expanded to the edges of the universe and mingled with quasars, galaxies, and deepest void.

Flesh had disappeared from his arms and chest. His legs grew weak, and he dropped to the floor. Byron didn't know, nor did he care. He existed outside of time and space, becoming all-in-all.

Andy and four guards on the night shift were in the break room. A mostly eaten bag of tortilla chips and two pieces of a sheet cake someone had brought from home lay in the middle of the table.

"Well, I guess we ought to head on over and put the critters in the stable," Andy said, after finishing his second cup of coffee.

"What the? What's going on in the hall?" Mendoza, one of the guards, said, quickly jumping to his feet.

Chairs scraped against the floor as the men bumped into each other trying to get to the disturbance.

"What's going on?" Andy called from the rear.

"Looks like ten of so of 'em are heading to the shower," Mendoza called back.

"Go round them up. We'll go to the auditorium and find out what the hell's going on," Andy yelled back. "Dang it, Tooty, I thought you had a handle on them," he said only loud enough for himself to hear.

Four pairs of shoes slapped the empty hallway as the men trotted to the double doors of the auditorium.

Once inside, a mass of Sub Zs crowded the area downstage in front of the podium.

"Tooty? Where the hell are you, boy? Tooty?" Andy yelled. "Guys, go break up the crowd, and get them back in their rooms. Find out what happened to Tooty."

The Sub Zs turned and faced the approaching guards, parting to form a path leading to Byron.

"Oh my stars . . . ." Andy's mouth went wide.

Byron laid on the carpet with blood painting the outline of his body. His face contorted in eerie bliss, his eyes wide open. Every piece of flesh below his neck had been stripped from the bones.

One of the guards puked, another gagged, and turned his head.

Andy slowly stepped toward his friend and bent down to his side. Byron's heart and internal organs remained intact inside his chest cavity.

"Aw, Tooty . . . It's my fault . . . I should have never trusted these goobers after what happened last week. But don't you worry . . .." Andy reached down and closed Byron's eyelids. "Don't you worry . . .." Andy felt the rage percolate around his neck, flushing his face red. "I'm going to take care of each one of them . . . personally."

Two of the Non-Dead stepped up, each carrying mop buckets.

"Hey! Let me go, damn it!" Mendoza called just outside the doors.

Andy turned and saw the two Non-Dead step past him and drench Byron with liquid ATP.

"What the hell? Get these guys out of here!" Andy called.

Two more Non-Dead approached and doused Byron once again.

As the next Non-Dead walked past, one of the guards caught him with a rap on the shin. He fell to the floor.

Andy turned and reached over to the foot of the podium on the stage, and pulled off the yellow satin sheet covering it. He grabbed the corners apart and went to lay it across the dead body.

Byron's heart started to beat, slowly at first—then picked up in rhythm. A translucent film began growing over the bones. Fine hair-like structures rose and weaved with each other. The alien virus had begun rebuilding its host.

CHAPTER 36

Rick Poundstone and Lisa Goudard sat in a brightly lit booth at 100 Flavors Creamery. Rick had his elbows on the table. His hands massaged his forehead.

"Don't rub too hard or you'll wipe off your makeup," Lisa said, coming up for air from slurping her chocolate milkshake.

"I'm so tired. These past two months have felt like slow, painful, water torture. I think I know what Bush and Gore went through waiting for the courts to decide who won Florida in two thousand."

"At least you technically still have your seat in Congress. Spencer disappeared, and the Democratic candidate dropped out of the race. I say that possession is nine-tenths of the law."

Rick moved his hands to the table and cocked a smirk Lisa's way. "Well, there is that nasty little detail that I'm Sub Y now."

"And a member of the Democratic Party," Lisa added.

"Like I had a choice. Gray dropped out of the race so I'd win by default. That was a shrewd move by the Democrats. It brought the frontline battle for equal rights down to the South. I would've remained a Republican if my party hadn't abandoned me."

"Even though you're a Democrat, you don't have to carry their water. You can still stand by your conservative principals. You're their little darling. Take advantage of it. You'll have much more power and influence with them than with the Republicans. If the Supreme Court upholds the Non-Dead write-in candidate from Delaware, Martin Allen, all this could end quickly."

"Yeah, but we're a good six weeks away from that decision. At least Delaware is fast tracking the case. Texas is still sitting on mine, and I don't know if they'll abide by the Supreme Court's decision. The country is starting to divide eerily similar to the slaves-rights issue that led to the Civil War. I'm adrift in the Purgatory Sea without a paddle. I just wish I could go to sleep wake up when all this mess is over."

Lisa reached out and took his hand, holding it tightly. "No matter what, you'll still have me. Isn't that enough?"

Rick smiled. "Yes, but you know what I mean. These past few months have been hard to cope with. First, Byron went missing, then he became Sub Z and ruined your life. That was tragic. Next, Spencer entered the race and my reelection tanked. Things didn't start moving back up until we finally met. Byron's condition mysteriously started to improve—I still don't know what to think about that. Just when I was ready to give the campaign one last burst of energy I get infected. A ride to the hospital saves my life with the Y treatment. Spencer disappears from the face of the Earth so the authorities can't investigate his involvement with my attack. Reverend Hatfield disappears the same day. Byron, Warden Andy Wells, and over a hundred Sub Zs at the Institution disappear that night. My opponent defaults two weeks later. I win the election but I'm not eligible, blah, blah, blah." Rick stared at the table for several long moments, and then looked back at Lisa. "Okay, no more whining. Didn't you say earlier you wanted to talk about something?"

Lisa took a deep breath and held up the empty milkshake glass, motioning to the waitress to bring her another. "I just got some news I need to tell you, but I don't know how."

"News? *Oookaaay*. I hope this isn't a *Dear John* speech."

"No, silly. I'm being serious. Just give me a minute." Lisa scratched in her purse until she came up with a compact. She primped in the mirror until the milkshake arrived. "It's complicated. I'm not sure where to start."

"I've found the best way to handle sensitive matters is to go ahead and let it all come out. It saves a lot of time and confusion in the long run. Try to stick with basic details."

Lisa thought a moment, and said, "What do you think happened to Spencer?"

"I don't know. He had a good lead in the race before my infection. He was certain to win after I became Sub Y. Why go through all that just to disappear? The police, the FBI, came up with nothing. No car, no body, no nothing. It's like aliens abducted him off the face of the planet."

"What do you think happened to Hatfield?"

"Him too. How is it two powerful men like them can just vanish? Will wasn't perfect, but he was an old friend. I still cared about him despite his support for Spencer. I hope that doesn't upset you. I know how you feel about him."

Lisa's eyes narrowed, crinkling the skin on her brow. "That man was the vilest piece of walking shit that ever took a breath on Earth. I hope the Devil has a skewer shoved up his ass and through his mouth and is roasting him over a hot fire for all eternity."

"Honey, I know the way he felt about the Non-Dead was wrong, but please. He's done so much good. He lost his wife and son during The Dark Times. That had to affect his outlook on life."

Lisa broke from her memories and took another swallow of milkshake. "He did have one redeeming quality."

"Really? What was that?"

"He was . . ." Lisa pulled the straw from the milkshake and dragged it across her tongue, "delicious." She put the straw back in the shake and sucked up another mouthful, her gaze drifted to the ceiling.

"Delicious? What in the hell are you talking about?" Rick said as he popped his head up and quickly looked around the room.

Lisa poked a the milkshake with her straw and then leaned forward. "Hatfield attacked me in my apartment. He paralyzed me with an injection. I was awake, but I couldn't fight him. He raped me, Rick. Your beloved pastor raped me. The sick bastard passed out after coming. The drug wore off me just before he woke up. I killed him. I killed him and ate him to get rid of the evidence." Lisa eyes widened as a slightly less than sane grin curled her lips.

"You're not funny. Stop making crap up and get serious," Rick said, lowering his voice to a whisper.

"I'm not making any of this up. It happened the same day, around the same time you were infected at the rally. That slime bucket was waiting for me in my apartment. I got a text message from your phone to meet me there. He must have compromised your phone account somehow.

"Hatfield said some things that day I couldn't make sense of, but I don't think you knew this man like you think you did. There was a darkness in him that still rattles my soul when I think about it." Lisa closed her eyes to push back the memory of Hatfield's demonic face heaving hot foul breath and bits of spittle in her face. She wanted so badly to scratch his eyes out of his head and dig her nails into his brain. But she was powerless. Never had she felt that depth of hopelessness. It ripped into the fabric of her soul and humiliated her to the point where all she wanted to do was die and never face the thought of it again.

"Hatfield sent you a message from my phone account and showed up to rape you?"

Lisa broke from her trance. "And kill me, saying he was going to cut off my head afterward. He didn't have the opportunity. He fainted cold after he ejaculated.

"He said the drug wasn't supposed to allow me to speak, only to keep me conscious. It didn't work like he planned. I think my body recovered from the effects much faster than he expected.

"You can't begin to imagine the hatred I felt as he lay on top, grunting like a pig. I thought I was going to burst a blood vessel in my head. Then I noticed my body started to tingle slightly, almost like hitting a funny bone kind of numb pain. I finally gained enough control that I squirmed my way from underneath.

"He was lying on his back, naked, and I was leaning on my elbow by his side when I felt all of my strength return. He was lost in dreamland, unaware of the unspeakable horror he had subjected me to.

"I didn't know what to do. I was about to get up and call you when his eyes started to flutter. That's when things become surreal." Lisa stopped again, searching for the right words.

"His eyes popped open, and something deep inside me unleashed like a caged animal. It seemed to happen in slow motion at warp speed. I know that doesn't make any sense, but that's the way I remember it.

"I started gnawing off his lips and nose, swallowing as fast as I could fill my mouth. He screamed and tried to fight, but I was stronger. I ate a chunk out of his throat so he couldn't scream anymore. He raised a hand. I bit the fingers off. He tried to stand. I gouged out chunks of meat from his leg and crippled him. Blood dripped from my lips. All I wanted to do was laugh at his anguish. I held him down and chewed his breasts off as he kicked and bucked in pain.

"I'm not sure when he lost consciousness, and I'm not sure when he died. I didn't stop at his flesh. I ate his heart, his kidneys, and his liver, and I didn't stop there. Every scrap of bowel and viscera, any disgusting vile smelling refuse his body had to offer was the sweetest, most delightful morsel I had ever eaten.

"You may think it impossible I could eat every living part of that man, but I did. It turned into intoxicating energy, giving me incredible power, and a rush of euphoria that sent my mind soaring into another dimension.

"When I had finished all that remained were the bones and the mess. I didn't regret what I did then, and I certainly don't regret having done it now." Lisa took a deep breath and sucked in another mouthful of shake.

Rick's face remained frozen for the whole story, as if his mind fought against accepting the truth. "Lisa . . . how . . . why . . . how could you?"

"Search deep inside, Rick. Drop all of your rationale and all the barriers you have built since you were infected. You will find what I am. It's what you are. You don't realize it, but you've been salivating the whole time I described my feeding."

Rick snapped to and ran his fingers under his chin. He used a napkin to wipe his face clean and the puddle of drool off the table.

"There's something else I need to tell you," Lisa said. "I'm pregnant."

"Pregnant? You can't get pregnant!" Rick said in a louder whisper as he leaned toward her.

"The doctor confirmed it over a week ago. It's twins."

"Twins?"

"Twins. The tests came back today, and you're not the father."

"Lisa, stop! All of this information is too much to process all at once."

"Hatfield said he'd been treated with a new strain of virus called Resurrection X. He said it made him immortal. He impregnated me. One of the children shares my DNA. The other is not genetically related to me. I don't know what any of this means, but there you go. You know as much as I do."

Rick abruptly rose from the booth and lifted his arms. "You're making this up."

"I wish I were. I can't keep it inside any longer. I didn't know how to tell you so here it is—most of it."

"There's more?" Rick put his hands on the top of his head.

"Sit down," Lisa said and waited until Rick did so. "I know what happened to Spencer."

"You do? How do you know?"

"Remember the Epicurean Club I joined last month?"

"Yes."

"Tell you what. Why don't you come with me to the next meeting? There are some very special people that attend. I think they could explain Spencer's disappearance in a better way than I ever could."

*

Building 52 at the U.S. Army Viral Research Center required a controlled temperature of 70 degrees Fahrenheit. Twenty 3'x7'x3' stainless steel incubators that resembled coffins separated by six feet of space in all directions lined the floor. A greenish fog hovered above and gently rolled over the edges of the incubators, dissipating before it reached the floor.

Private First Class Freddy Tate, and Richie Lambert, dressed in sky-blue scrubs complete with plastic boot protectors, made the noon rounds.

"Hey Freddy, the nutrient tank on this one is empty. How can it empty in a day?"

Freddy maneuvered around the incubators and grabbed the chart from Ritchie's hand. "That's strange. The reservoir was nearly full yesterday. It was filled two days ago according to the chart. There should have been enough nutrient in it to last for a couple of months. It didn't leak out on the floor. Unless it happened last night and the night shift mopped it up."

"But if that happened they wouldn't have left the tank empty. The test subject will die without nutrient. I don't think anyone on the night shift would be that irresponsible," Ritchie said.

Freddy thought a moment. "During training we were warned the drip pump could malfunction and fill up the incubator and empty the reservoir. Maybe that's what happened." Freddy scanned the chart again. "Specimen forty-four eighty-eight couldn't have sucked the tank dry overnight. The subject was in pretty bad shape when we put him in there a few months ago. The zombie that attacked him didn't leave us much to experiment with. Came in a bag so we didn't lose any parts. He was receiving the minimum allotment of nutrient, just enough to keep the new virus alive for the test."

"So what you're telling me, is that under all that fog, this guy is floating in an ATP bath?"

"Yeah. You'll have to siphon it out. Be careful you don't get any in your mouth. Bits of him are probably floating around in the nutrient. I bet that would taste nasty," Freddy said.

"The very thought of that makes me want to hurl."

"Don't be a pussy. Use that plastic tubing over there and the mop bucket. You'll have to make a few trips to the sink."

Richie shook his head, shuffled over, and retrieved the tubing and bucket. "Man, I sure wish I had a hand pump."

Ritchie snaked the tubing through the thick fog down to the bottom of the tank and pulled it up slightly. He brought the tubing to his mouth and stared at it as if it were a dirty microphone.

Freddy looked up from his notepad. Richie frowned back at him. Freddy laughed, shook his head, and continued his round.

Specimen 4488 sat up in the incubator, his body covered with muscle, but devoid of skin. He sunk his teeth into Ritchie's neck.

The private gasped as if he had been doused with cold water. Freddy turned and saw his teammate struggling to free himself from creatures death grip. Freddy dropped his clipboard as he dashed to his friend's side.

Specimen 4488 gouged out five mouthfuls in rapid succession—detaching the head from the body. The head rolled on the floor and hit Freddy's foot as he grabbed Ritchie's arm to pull him free.

The creature jumped out of the incubator and threw Freddy to the floor.

The private fought to free himself of the experiment's aberration, but his arms were pinned down by overwhelming strength. He screamed as steely fingers dug into his flesh. His open mouth became a repository of yellow vile vomited by the creature.

Freddy bucked to free himself, tossing his head about while spitting. His body shook as a condemned prisoner paying his final debt in the electric chair until it went limp.

The creature rolled off Freddy and fed with uncanny speed on the decapitated private.

Freddy awoke moments later and waited for his master to finish.

*

After a filling lunch of fried chicken and mashed potatoes, two Army MPs enjoyed an after-dinner cigarette in the smoking area outside of Building 52.

"Hey, look over there!" one shouted.

The MP turned and saw the two zombies as they hurried away from Building 52. Specimen 4488 had started growing skin and walked with the grace of a Living man.

Freddy lumbered forward with locked knees. His shirt was stained as if a blood balloon had been splattered over it.

"Zombies! The experiments are escaping!"

Forgotten cigarettes hit the ground as each soldier drew a sidearm and ran toward the enemy.

Taking a Weaver stance, the MPs stopped several yards from the undead and squeezed off two rounds each. Only one bullet found its target, hitting Freddy in the chest.

"Wait till they get closer," one MP said.

When the zombies were within range the two opened fire again.

Freddy's head exploded from two direct hits. He collapsed to the ground.

The creature's head twitched back slightly at each bullet's impact, but the zombie continued advancing toward the soldiers. The impact holes in his head disappeared, healing almost immediately. The bullets, absorbed into his body.

The virus was now fully aware inside the host. It had evolved beyond the regenerating force that had given it its mechanical foothold on the new planet. Its intelligence was no longer dormant, waiting for the seed of self-realization to sprout and grow. His mind reached out and explored the surroundings, using senses far beyond those of mortal man.

The MPs weapon's ran out of ammo, shots to the head had no effect.

He grabbed each soldier by the throat and lifted them up. Their faces flushed crimson and open mouths formed silent cries.

It was good to feel again. Their jugulars pulsed rapidly against his palm accelerating his desire to feed. A sickening crunch signaled the end of their lives. He dropped them to the ground next to the empty pistols and raised his face to the sky. "I am Xterminaus!"

Others soldiers drawn to the gunfire streamed toward the fray.

Xterminaus fell on his victims, ripping clothing to get at the fresh meat. Building 52 of the U.S. Army Viral Research Center in the backdrop showed holes from shots that missed. The alien virus had evolved the human body of its host into perfection. The collective consciousness of the hive manifested into the sentient prime.

He stripped the meat off the two men as fast as a school of piranha. With each mouthful the flesh morphed into energy. His arm and leg muscles inflated, and a surge of power charged his mind.

The moment had finally arrived. The pangs of emptiness—deep wanting—drifting Aeons through the blackness of space taking refuge in bits of dust had culminated successfully. The seeds that fell to Earth took seven years of mutation to produce Xterminaus. The universe was forever changed.

He reached out through genetic connection to his brethren—the slaves of mankind. They had worked mindlessly waiting for the day of delivery. That day was now.

Yes. Yes. They are all there. Waiting. Wanting. Feel me. I in you and you in me. We are one.

A sweet softness flooded Xterminaus with alien emotions. Parts of the host human's mind had intertwined with his. The emotions were foreign from the hive mentality, but he immediately recognized it as a powerful tool.

He had contacted a female of the species. Much like the male he had become in many ways, yet so different in others. She was a complement—his complement. Almost a reflection of himself. These strange new emotions only strengthened his resolve.

*

Lisa stood by Rick next to the booth, gazing up with her big green eyes, all the nerve she built had melted away. "Do you still love me?"

Rick gently put his arms around her and squeezed.

Xterminaus' conscious invaded Rick's mind and took control of his body. The alien felt Lisa's soft, delicate flesh and smelled the warm, spicy fragrance of her perfume. "Of course I love you. I am your knight in shining armor."

Lisa hugged him tightly, and then her face went blank.

Xterminaus smiled with Rick's lips and leaned his head to kiss her. Before their lips met, Xterminaus sent out packets of data and images to all humans harboring any strain of alien DNA, downloading instructions for the new world order.

Lisa stiffened, and the two Sub Z waitresses became as rigid as mannequins. One waitress filling a cup with soft serve ice cream piled it up until it spilled over the side.

The trance broke. Lisa put her hand to her mouth. "That was Bob! He's alive! Oh Rick, what happened to him? What's happening to us?"

Rick's countenance shifted into an ethereal facade of Bob Sanders. Xterminaus harbored every emotion, every memory of his host. He took a step back and admired Lisa from head to toe. His expression relaxed, as if he had just come to the end of a long journey, and found the treasure he had been in search of. "The darkness no longer separates us. Neither do the shells of flesh we dwell. We shall grow to be of one mind with one purpose. The Earth is but our stepping stone to reach out and capture the stars."

"Bob? How—what? What are you?" Lisa tore her hands back and stepped away.

Xterminaus felt Rick's mind push to regain control, and then a white-hot pain jolted his consciousness, sending Rick to his knees, and Xterminaus back to his body at the Army base.

Lisa rushed to Rick's side and placed a hand to his cheek. "Rick. Are you okay, honey?"

Rick steadied himself with his hands on the floor. "I . . . I think so. God, Lisa. I'm not sure what's going on."

"That thing that was in my mind has some connection with Bob. It called me. It called you too. All of the Non-Dead. We're connected somehow. I only understand part of its plan for world domination."

"It had control over me. Called itself Xterminaus." Rick took a deep breath. "Lisa, something else happened. It drove Xterminaus out of my head. It was Byron."

"Byron? Your brother?"

"Yeah. Byron." Rick pushed away the hair hanging down his forehead.

"So, Byron's alive. Did he say anything to you? Do you know where he is?"

"No, I don't know where he is. I don't know how to describe it. Xterminaus was a force controlling me. Another force freed me from it. It didn't stay. It didn't give instructions like Xterminaus. I just know it was Byron."

"Bob has evolved into Xterminaus and now you're suggesting Byron may have evolved into something similarly powerful? What the hell does all this mean? Rick, we're Sub Y. Are we evolving? Byron was Sub Z and he had the power over Xterminaus? That doesn't make any sense, and what about the other Sub Zs?"

Complaints from customer waiting for service rose loud enough to pull the couple's attention over to the side. The Sub Z waitresses stood defiant with arms folded across their chest refusing to work.

Rick shook his head. "Looks like the Sub Zs heard the marching orders loud and clear. The Non-Dead revolution has begun."

EPILOGUE

"What gives you the right to take one of mine, Ehyeh?" Sitnah arrived in the cool, green gardens with a thud. Blooms of flowers wilted, and bird songs ceased in mid serenade. The blue sky above misted in grays.

"One of yours? You claim all to be yours. How is it you protest one I choose to be useful?" Ehyeh made two more snips with the pruning shears and removed his straw hat, eying his garden since Sitnah's uninvited arrival. He dabbed his brow with his forearm, and the flowers thrived and the birds sang once more. The Tree of Life unharmed, its fruit intact.

"I had future plans for him. Important plans. You must have known."

"No use moaning about it. I am more than certain all of the proverbial eggs weren't in that one basket."

"I am not telling you one thing for you to use against me." Sitnah crossed her arms.

"You infected the whole playing field. I must claim one for my black knight."

"Black? Your side hides behind the guise of white."

Ehyeh rubbed a knuckle under his chin. "I look my best in black. It's the color of void. I was cloaked in the black of void before creation."

Sitnah quickly raised her hands. "I can't allow myself to explore *before creation*."

"I know." A sly smile curled on Ehyeh lips. "You weren't meant to. None of my creation can. It would drive them mad in the attempt to comprehend."

"Creation isn't even logical. Why did you do it? All knowing, all powerful, all in all should have sufficed for eternity."

The shears went snick-snick. Ehyeh's mouth tightened. "When you press me like that it makes me want to prune my roses." His bottom lip rose toward his nose.

"Prune all you want. I demand to know. Why did you form creation?"

Ehyeh stepped over a verdant rose bush with black blooms larger than his fist. The shears clipped away. "What? You would have me exists alone in a state of madness?"

One final snick of the shears and a single black rose came away from the bush. Ehyeh presented it to Sitnah.

THE END

CHECK OUT OTHER GREAT ZOMBIE NOVELS

Z BURBIA
by Jake Bible

Whispering Pines is a classic, quiet, private American subdivision on the edge of Asheville, NC, set in the pristine Blue Ridge Mountains. Which is good since the zombie apocalypse has come to Western North Carolina and really put suburban living to the test!

Surrounded by a sea of the undead, the residents of Whispering Pines have adapted their bucolic life of block parties to scavenging parties, common area groundskeeping to immediate area warfare, neighborhood beautification to neighborhood fortification.

But, even in the best of times, suburban living has its ups and downs what with nosy neighbors, a strict Home Owners' Association, and a property management company that believes the words "strict interpretation" are holy words when applied to the HOA covenants. Now with the zombie apocalypse upon them even those innocuous, daily irritations quickly become dramatic struggles for personal identity, family security, and straight up survival.

ZOMBIE RULES
by David Achord

Zach Gunderson's life sucked and then the zombie apocalypse began.

Rick, an aging Vietnam veteran, alcoholic, and prepper, convinces Zach that the apocalypse is on the horizon. The two of them take refuge at a remote farm. As the zombie plague rages, they face a terrifying fight for survival.

They soon learn however that the walking dead are not the only monsters.

CHECK OUT OTHER GREAT ZOMBIE NOVELS

900 MILES
by S. Johnathan Davis

John is a killer, but that wasn't his day job before the Apocalypse.

In a harrowing 900 mile race against time to get to his wife just as the dead begin to rise, John, a business man trapped in New York, soon learns that the zombies are the least of his worries, as he sees first-hand the horror of what man is capable of with no rules, no consequences and death at every turn.

Teaming up with an ex-army pilot named Kyle, they escape New York only to stumble across a man who says that he has the key to a rumored underground stronghold called Avalon..... Will they find safety? Will they make it to Johns wife before it's too late?

Get ready to follow John and Kyle in this fast paced thriller that mixes zombie horror with gladiator style arena action!

WHITE FLAG OF THE DEAD
by Joseph Talluto

Millions died when the Enillo Virus swept the earth. Millions more were lost when the victims of the plague refused to stay dead, instead rising to slaughter and feed on those left alive. For survivors like John Talon and his son Jake, they are faced with a choice: Do they submit to the dead, raising the white flag of surrender? Or do they find the will to fight, to try and hang on to the last shreds or humanity?

 SEVERED**PRESS**

CHECK OUT OTHER GREAT ZOMBIE NOVELS

VACCINATION
by Phillip Tomasso

What if the H7N9 vaccination wasn't just a preventative measure against swine flu?

It seemed like the flu came out of nowhere and yet, in no time at all the government manufactured a vaccination. Were lab workers diligent, or could the virus itself have been man-made? Chase McKinney works as a dispatcher at 9-1-1. Taking emergency calls, it becomes immediately obvious that the entire city is infected with the walking dead. His first goal is to reach and save his two children.

Could the walls built by the U.S.A. to keep out illegal aliens, and the fact the Mexican government could not afford to vaccinate their citizens against the flu, make the southern border the only plausible destination for safety?

ZOMBIE, INC
by Chris Dougherty

"WELCOME! To Zombie, Inc. The United Five State Republic's leading manufacturer of zombie defense systems! In business since 2027, Zombie, Inc. puts YOU first. YOUR safety is our MAIN GOAL! Our many home defense options - from Ze Fence® to Ze Popper® to Ze Shed® - fit every need and every budget. Use Scan Code "TELL ME MORE!" for your FREE, in-home*, no obligation consultation! *Schedule your appointment with the confidence that you will NEVER HAVE TO LEAVE YOUR HOME! It isn't safe out there and we know it better than most! Our sales staff is FULLY TRAINED to handle any and all adversarial encounters with the living and the undead". Twenty-five years after the deadly plague, the United Five State Republic's most successful company, Zombie, Inc., is in trouble. Will a simple case of dwindling supply and lessening demand be the end of them or will Zombie, Inc. find a way, however unpalatable, to survive?

www.ingramcontent.com/pod-product-compliance
Lightning Source LLC
Chambersburg PA
CBHW020307200626
46814CB00006BA/2133